I0834138

HULDA

OR

THE DELIVERER

A ROMANCE

AFTER THE GERMAN

F. LEWALD

BY MRS. A. L. WISTER

TRANSLATOR OF "THE OLD MAM'SELLE'S SECRET" "ONLY A GIRL" ETC

PHILADELPHIA
J. B. LIPPINCOTT & CO.
1875

HULDA.

PART I.

CHAPTER I.

WHAT has become of solitude, now that locomotives and steamers, careering around the globe, unite its most distant countries, while the electric spark flashes intelligence north, south, east, and west, confusing all ideas of time and space, bewildering the minds of the aged, to whom the world in which they find themselves is a strange land, unlike the home of their youth?

But in the earlier decades of this century there was still deep solitude to be found in many parts of Germany, and especially in the most northern parts of East Prussia: there, where the billows of the Baltic Sea break upon the shore, it was lonely, very lonely, in a village upon the coast, and in the quiet parsonage of that village.

The house, or rather cottage, was small and low, and the life led within it by the pastor and his family was as confined. The father and the grandfather of the present occupant had both dwelt there, and there was nothing in or around the place in any wise changed. The pastor was as thoroughly attached to his home as were the counts, his and his forefathers' patrons, to their old castle, half a league from the village and the sea, standing upon the only eminence in all the country round, in the midst of a wooded plain, whence there was a view both of the eastern sea and of the Courland Bay, with the isthmus, called the Courland Flats, that separated the two waters.

The village, too, was small, and the church was small, although large enough for the thinly-peopled neighbourhood; and ugly though it was, built of the roughest stone from the fields, it was accounted one of the wonders of the land and held in high honour. Had not the holy Adalbert, converter of heathen Prussia, built and consecrated it? There were, to be sure, no documents extant in proof of this; but the church was certainly very old. And what harm was there in the poor and lonely pastor's belief, whereby he was cheered and inspired, that it had been granted to him to declare the word of God in a spot especially sanctified and hallowed?

The country about the village was sparsely inhabited, the poverty of the soil not inviting cultivation, and the French and Russian armies had successively ravaged and laid waste the little fishing-villages along the coast.

You might have driven far without seeing a single hamlet,—even the post-stations were many miles apart. Only twice a week did the mail, as it was called,—it consisted of a man driving a one-horse cart,—traverse the Courland isthmus to establish communication between the capital and this distant border; and there never passed either a spring or an autumn without bringing tidings of another postilion, with his horse and wagon, drowned in crossing those treacherous quicksands.

Under these circumstances, intercourse with the capital and with the surrounding country was often rare enough for months during the winter. Even the post scarcely visited the village then, but crossed the bay upon runners; and life in the parsonage was so monotonous that it was counted an event if the sledge of a Courland peasant or of a Polish Jew was seen passing in the distance from the frosty window-panes of the cottage. And if an extra post passed through the village, which was some distance from the parsonage, or travellers chanced to stop for rest at the little post-station, the old lame postmaster, a retired captain, was sure to make his appearance a few days afterwards at the parsonage to relate the occurrence and to tell the news. Those were delightful evenings. The pastor and the captain would light their pipes, and, after the late event had been well discussed, would pass on to talk over earlier times. The captain would tell of his campaigns,—of Paris, whither he had gone with the allied armies and had been detained by a wound,—and of his relatives on the Rhine; and the pastor, who was now well on in years, would speak of his youthful university days, and of his life as tutor in the castle; while his wife and only daughter always listened to these stories as if they had not heard them again and again before. Each evening brought fresh enjoyment to them, transporting them, as it did, to a world so different from their own.

CHAPTER II.

EVERYTHING in the parsonage was old, and had been old during the memory of man. Each day was like its predecessor. The pastor, his father, and his grandfather, a forester's son, had all studied in Königsberg,—at the expense of their patrons, the counts of the castle. After our pastor had finished his university course, he had been attached to the family as tutor to the eldest son, and thus the present head of the family in whose gift was his living had been his pupil. He held it matter for daily gratitude to Heaven, that in his connection with his patron's family and in his life in the capital consequent upon his position as tutor, he had enjoyed many advantages of culture from which most of those in his circumstances were excluded.

In those times the tutor to the young scion of a noble house accompanied him on the grand tour that was considered necessary before his education could be thought complete; and our pastor was just about to set out upon his travels with his noble pupil, when, as he was wont to say, Heaven ordained it otherwise. His father was taken ill, and a curate became necessary for him. The count, that there might be no diminution of the good man's income, appointed the son to the curacy; and, although the young man had anticipated with no little delight his foreign tour, he retired cheerfully to the solitude of his native village. Faith in the divine ordering of every event of life was his to a remarkable degree, and was a perpetual well-spring of cheerful content in all the trials through which he passed.

In spite, however, of the incurable disease to which his father was a victim, he lived many years, and only after his death did the son feel able to marry, so small was the income of the little living. He was then thirty-six years old, and his eyes and heart had been set upon pretty Simonena ever since he had heard her her catechism before her confirmation, although she was many years younger than he. She had been born of very poor parents, on the count's estates in Lithuania, and in her early orphanage her great beauty had attracted the notice of some of the ladies of the family, and they had consigned her to the care of their bailiff, who, with his sister, lived in a comfortable house connected with the castle.

Pretty Simonena had never dreamed that the Herr Pastor, her teacher, could so far honour her as to wish to marry her; and even after she had become his wife she always regarded him as a being of a superior order, in spite of the fact that his loving counsels and teaching soon fitted her to be a true companion to him. Two children, born in the early years of their married life, died; and when all hope was gone of ever again hearing childish voices at the parsonage, ten years later, Simonena gave birth to a daughter. In the mother's lonely life, and with the great difference in age between her husband and herself, this child was especially a blessing to her; and the pastor, in his grateful delight, insisted that the little one's name should be Hulda.

The peaceful existence of the parsonage was now happy indeed, and the only child of the house grew in beauty like a flower in perpetual spring. Whatever of joy her parents' tenderness could procure for her in their straitened circumstances was hers without stint. The days were all alike,—she had her study-hours with her father, and early learned to be useful to her mother in household tasks. In summer she helped both father and mother in the cultivation of their little garden, and in winter, while her father studied and she sat with her mother by the great green porcelain stove in which their soup was cooking for supper, she would read in some of the books which her father had collected in those early days of his tutorship when such luxuries were not forbidden him.

It was Hulda's office to keep this modest library, now and then increased by a kind remembrance from some one of the count's family, free from dust; and to lose herself in these books, which even her mother opened with great veneration, was her chief delight,—just to hold one in her hands was a pleasure; and when the storm outside beat against the window-panes in such thick white flakes that the noonday light with difficulty struggled through them, and the sea beat in hollow thunder on the frozen coast, she would often sit silent, with a volume open upon her knee, not reading, only gazing upon its pages, and seeing there far other visions than the printed words. There seemed a magic hidden in those letters. Could she but find the key, what a glorious world would be hers!

There was an unconscious worship of culture and beauty among the inmates of the parsonage that is known in its entire purity only among the poor and solitary. If, after such times of musing, the old postmaster chanced to pay one of his visits, and to dwell, as was his wont, upon the incidents of his past life, the young girl's fancy became filled with vague, alluring pictures of a world as distant and strange as the stars at night, and regarded by her as were the stars, with a longing curiosity that despaired of gratification.

And when winter was gone, and summer was near at hand, when the icy fetters were torn asunder by soft spring gales, when ships floated by on the horizon like giant swans, and the swallows and wild geese sailed through the blue air, the storks came again upon the sacristy roof, and the village woke to new life. Then the boats could put to sea again, and the pastor's wife and daughter would walk down to the shore, when they came in, to hear what luck the fishermen had had. Then those who were wealthy enough to own a horse would drive to the capital through the clear night, to carry thither fresh and smoked fish, and on their return would bring many a thing needed at the parsonage; for the parson's modest income allowed of no horse, and there was nothing to be had in the village which the sterile flats did not produce. Save the commonest vegetables and some blackberries and sour cherries, there was little to be procured there.

The four Scotch firs in the parsonage garden, the elder-bush that shadowed the bench before the door, sunflowers, pansies, and lavender, were all of greenery and bloom in which the pastor and his family could rejoice. The two rose-bushes that Ma'amselle Ulrika, the bailiff's sister, had brought to her foster-child from the garden of their house, did not bloom every year, because the pastor's garden was too much exposed to the wind from the sea, so that Hulda could not enjoy the triumph every summer of wearing to church a bunch of rosebuds in her bosom, and thereby being wafted into a dream of delight, which was recalled to her in winter by the perfume of the dried rose-leaves whenever she opened the drawer where they were laid.

CHAPTER III.

THE spring in which Hulda was confirmed seemed in its gentle breath to herald a fruitful year, and Easter was to bring the great event of every spring,—the day upon which the bailiff and his sister, called in all the country round Ma'amselle Ulrika, or simply Ma'amselle, dined at the parsonage. To be sure, the bailiff and Ma'amselle sometimes stopped at the pastor's after church on Sundays, for Ma'amselle had brought up the pastor's wife, and Hulda was her godchild, but then it was only for a few minutes. The bailiff's sister did not pay many visits in the village, although she was greatly respected there and in her brother's house kept a generous table and a ready welcome for all guests.

The reserve thus maintained by the bailiff and his sister was called pride in the village, and certainly they did conduct themselves as if they were at the head of affairs. But it was all natural enough. The count had been absent for many years, ambassador at some foreign court, and Ma'amselle Ulrika was quite right in saying that she did not know why she should pay visits,—people might come to her when she wanted them. Besides, it vexed her to be obliged to neglect her own household, and she never found anything anywhere else half so comfortable as at home.

She certainly had her eccentricities; and there was always a great deal of gossip in the village concerning her, because none of the small misfortunes that are so usual in a household ever seemed to befall her. Whatever she took in hand succeeded; man and beast prospered beneath her care, in illness she was better than a doctor, and she knew more about the weather than any one else in the world. The bailiff, her brother, said it was because she knew how to keep her eyes open, but the villagers maintained that she slept with her eyes open too, and saw some sights that she never spoke of, and that it was best never to speak of. Every one who stood in need of advice consulted her, but nevertheless she was not beloved, and she knew it, and did not care.

For all these reasons the little household at the parsonage was made to bring forth its best on Easter Sunday. The Easter feast was the result of much economy, and the pastor's wife used to reckon time in the year to and from Easter Sunday. This year it came very late, and the weather was beautiful. The whole week had been spent in sweeping and freshening the house; and Hulda's white gown, which was to be put on for the first time this season on the great day, because Aunt Ulrika liked white dresses, was fluttering, perceptibly lengthened, and well washed, on the clothes-line in the fresh spring breeze. It was towards evening on Friday, the pastor was busy with his sermon, his wife was cutting paper decorations for the two candlesticks that always stood upon her table before the mirror, the candles in which were never lighted, and Hulda, seated at her work-table, was plaiting the muslin border of her mother's Sunday cap, when, looking up from her work, she saw a vehicle swiftly approaching the village. The girl's quick sight recognized it in an instant. "The bailiff's wagon!" she cried, putting down her work. Her mother could hardly believe her, but, as it approached, she also recognized the bailiff's little Lithuanian pony, and Ma'amselle Ulrika sitting in the wagon.

"Something must have happened," she exclaimed, "to bring Ma'amselle away from home just before the holidays. What can it mean?"

They did not have much time to wonder. The carriage noiselessly approached the house through the soft sand, and the pastor, roused by the artistic crack of Christian's whip, came from his study, and went to the door with his wife and daughter to see what was the matter. A glance at Ma'amselle Ulrika confirmed the pastor's wife in her suspicion that some misfortune must have occurred. Ma'amselle—she was small and spare, and, in spite of her years, as active as the youngest —was out of the wagon before a hand could be extended to help her, and the pastor's wife saw with amazement that she was dressed in her morning gown of striped linen, and had not even taken time to put on the high cap without which she never left the house, since "people must always pay a decent respect to the bailiff's sister."

"Don't be frightened, Herr Pastor!" she cried, as soon as she saw him; "and, Simonena, don't wonder at my driving over just as I was. You'll be as much shocked as my brother and I——"

"I trust no misfortune has befallen the bailiff," the pastor interrupted her, his gentle dignity of manner always compelling Ma'amselle Ulrika to a certain corresponding repose.

"No, thank God! no, Herr Pastor; my brother is quite well. But you must be told,—and it will be a double shock to you, because he was your pupil, and ten years younger than yourself."

"The count is not dead?" asked the pastor, turning pale.

"Indeed, indeed he is, my dearest Herr Pastor! You have guessed it! The count is dead. Yesterday morning the express arrived in Königsberg for the countess's brother, the Baron Emanuel, and to-day he sent a courier here to us. He wrote us all about it,—all about it. The count was only ill in bed a few days; they could hardly tell how it happened. And they have embalmed him, for of course he must be buried here in the family vault. The leaden coffin is already on the road, and the family are coming, too. The Herr Baron went to meet them yesterday. They are every one coming,—the countess, and the young Countess Clarissa, and the Herr Baron Emanuel, who is, you know, the countess's youngest brother. He hasn't been here since he was a little boy. And all the servants are coming, too,—even the cook, and the old English miss who has always been with the family, and always will be with them until she dies. Only, the young countess's lover is coming a little later, and the young count cannot get leave of absence even to come to his father's funeral."

She might have talked on much longer, for her hearers stood speechless with sorrow at the sudden news. Not until Ma'amselle Ulrika stopped for breath did the pastor's wife exclaim, with a sigh, "The poor Gräfin! Poor Countess Clarissa!"

"Yes, indeed!" Ma'amselle Ulrika went on, "it is too terrible! but then they can sit still in their carriages and cry as much as they like. While I?—Everything must be arranged and ready in the castle and the vault. In four weeks, at the latest, they will be here. No use to say a word about Easter, or day after to-morrow. I cannot leave home. To-morrow I shall have the house full of work-people."

She spoke so quickly that her thin cheeks burned and her eyes sparkled. They begged her to come into the house and sit down, but she would not even listen to the request; without heeding her friends' surprise or the pastor's sorrow, she went on immediately to tell how many people she had already engaged to work in the castle and grounds, how the under-bailiff had been sent everywhere to buy all the poultry he could find, and how much provision there was stored in the bailiff's house, in spite of the unfavourable time of year. All this she recounted to her former foster-child, and had mounted into the carriage and driven off before any one had time to reply to her.

The pastor turned and went silently into the house. When his wife and daughter followed him, they found him in his study, standing at the window, gazing out upon the sea, whose waves were tipped with the gold of the setting sun. He put his arm around his wife's waist, and held out his other hand to his daughter. His face was calm, but sad. "I laid his father down in his last rest," he said, as if to himself, "and my father, his two eldest sons, and my two, and now he has gone!" He passed his hand across his eyes, and, slowly shaking his head, went on,—"Our life passes like a vapour and a dream! So it stands written, and we know it, and yet it is always a shock and a mystery, this death. It is always a grief, like the vanishing of that sun in the sea, sure though we are of a brilliant sunrise and a joyful resurrection."

He sank into a long reverie, from which he roused himself with a sigh. "I should have liked to see him here once more. I had left you to him, to his care. But it was not to be. God's will be done!" And then he went quietly back to his study-table.

His wife leaned her forehead against the window-pane, and looked out into the gathering twilight; the tears rushed to Hulda's eyes,—she had never before seen her father so moved, never before had distinctly felt that he was an old man, and that the time must come when there would be an end to her home, when she and her mother would have to wander forth poor and alone to seek some other abiding-place. She threw her arms around her mother, who must have guessed and shared her thoughts, for she kissed her daughter and clasped her tightly to her breast. But she said nothing, as if fearing that the spoken word might have power to bring down upon their heads the grief still veiled for them in a near or distant future.

CHAPTER IV.

NOTHING was talked of in the parsonage from this time but the family at the castle, the counts, and the barons, brothers of the countess, whose ancestors, like those of the count, had come to Prussia centuries before, as German knights, and were of the most ancient nobility.

The pastor often spoke of the beautiful house and charming grounds which belonged to the count in the city; of the splendid carriage in which the deceased count's father used to drive, with two heydukes behind, and two outriders; how he had been a learned man, well versed in Latinity, and had been above all things anxious that his son should be thoroughly educated; and how the late count had answered all his hopes, and had, moreover, been so gentle and courteous in manner that the future diplomat was very evident in him even when he was quite young. His countess, too, of the ancient and richly-dowered house of the lords of Falkenhorst, had been just the wife that such a man should have.

And then they talked of the Falkenhorst family, upon whose estates the pastor's wife had been born. The race had been splendid and numerous, but now of the countess's five brothers only two were alive,—the childless heir, and the youngest, Baron Emanuel, who spent most of the time in Italy or the South of Germany on account of his health, and in whom were centred all the hopes for the future of the noble line. They lived and moved at the parsonage only in thoughts of the family at the castle, and of course nothing else occupied the bailiff and his sister, whose hands were full indeed, with the preparations all conducted beneath Ma'amselle Ulrika's eye. She never even appeared at church, and it was three weeks after Easter, when one day the pastor's wife determined to go with her daughter to her foster-parents', to see how the preparations at the castle had fared. A visit to the bailiff's house was an extraordinary event, and usually took place only on Sundays. It was full half a league from the parsonage to the castle, and, truth to tell, Ma'amselle and her former foster-child were not the best of friends. The bailiff's sister was not fond of children, and the charge of little Simonena had been a task undertaken only at the bidding of the countess. The child's life in her new home had not been a happy one, and her marriage with the pastor had not made her more dear to Ma'amselle Ulrika. It was whispered among the villagers that Ma'amselle had had views of her own with regard to the young pastor, and she made no secret of her surprise that he should burden himself with a wife so young and poor, when he might have done so much better. What that better was she did not say, but people availed themselves of their usual privilege of drawing their own conclusions.

To-day, however, Ma'amselle Ulrika was evidently glad to see her visitors. She had worked so hard and accomplished so much in such a limited time that it was a real satisfaction to show the result of her labours to the pastor's wife, who could understand and appreciate it all, while the countess, after the manner of such great ladies, would only find it extremely natural and fitting that everything should be in perfect order and ready for her at any time that she might choose to appoint, without giving a thought to the labour and pains it had cost.

Hulda had never seen the inside of the castle but once, when she was a very little child, for in all the years since her birth it had never been opened, except to be aired and swept, which naturally never happened upon Sunday. In her memory of it there was nothing save a vision of suites of long, dark apartments, feebly illuminated by the daylight that entered through one or two half-closed windows. Now, indeed, everything looked very different.

The windows were all open, and the bright sunshine and the warm summer air penetrated everywhere. Hulda had never seen any dwelling grander than the parsonages of one or two of her father's brothers in office, or the houses of the wealthiest men in her father's parish, where all were poor, and to her this castle, which was in reality quite imposing in its way, was like a gorgeous royal palace, and the fleeting remarks made by Ma'amselle, as she hurried her visitors from room to room and along the lofty corridors, completed the charm that the castle had woven around the girl's fancy. Everything here seemed a wonder to her, and, indeed, there was much that possessed historical associations. The oval table in the saloon looking out upon the garden was the very one at which the queen and her children had breakfasted when, in her flight from the victorious French, she sought refuge in the remotest borders of her kingdom. She had rested upon the little sofa in the adjoining boudoir, and had sat before the dressing-glass there while her maid knotted up her fair hair. In the spacious apartment above, where the great state bed looked like a throne with its gorgeous crimson silk hangings, the French marshal, a man of very low extraction, had slept for three nights on his way to Russia, and, hard as Ma'amselle had found it to make all ready for such a man and to provide refreshment for the enemy, his occupation of the castle had been a piece of good fortune, since it had preserved it from pillage.

There was some story, some event, connected with every room and every boudoir, and although she had heard it all often enough before, it seemed fresh and novel to Hulda, told as it was in the midst of the very scenes where it had been enacted. She could hardly walk on, and at last in the long hall where the family portraits hung she stood still; there was too much to see here.

When Ma'amselle Ulrika carried her mother off to the servants' rooms, that she might show her how well all were accommodated, the girl, unperceived, remained behind in this hall; and yet in a few moments she wished herself away, for the grave and stately knights in armour, the gallant counts in flowing wigs, and the haughty dames in stiff collarets, with little crowns in their towering structures of hair, and looking down upon her as if in cold surprise at her presence there, made her shiver. Even the pictures of the children seemed to regard her with amazement, and when, looking away from them, she saw her own figure reflected on all sides from the mirrors hanging between the portraits, such terror took possession of her that she would have fled from the place if her attention had not been enchained by the picture of a youth on the wall near the door.

In contrast to all the other family portraits, which were the size of life, this was only a small head in an oval frame. But this head was so beautiful, the flowing black hair waved so naturally on either side of the pale cheeks, and the large, dark-blue eyes had such a fathomless depth of expression, while the mouth was so kindly, that Hulda at first did not notice the melancholy that sat upon the broad, low brow.

"How beautiful!" she exclaimed, involuntarily, and, as the sound of her own voice struck upon her ear, she blushed scarlet and looked round to see if her mother and Ma'amselle Ulrika had not returned and heard her. She was ashamed at having spoken aloud, but her longing desire to know who was the original of this picture entirely conquered all her dread of the grave dignitaries on the walls and her own reflection on every side of her. A name was written just above the head in the picture, but it hung rather high, and the letters were illegible on the dark background. She went to the right and left, but in vain, the gloss of the varnish prevented her from deciphering it. Still, she could not leave it unread, the mysterious eyes haunted her. With the sensations of a guilty child afraid of detection, she mounted one of the antiquated, high-backed chairs, and then she read it easily and knew who it was,—Baron Emanuel, the countess's youngest brother.

The name and the date of the year in which the picture had been taken, with the age of the original at the time, were written above the head. As she stood thus so near to the handsome head, the eyes had a still more powerful effect upon her, and she could not tell whether it was delight in the beauty of the picture or dread lest her mother and Ma'amselle Ulrika should return and find her there that made her heart beat so loud and fast.

She jumped down out of the chair, and, that she might not be found near the picture, walked to an open window at the farther end of the hall and gazed out where the road led far inland away from the castle. Her mother asked her what she was looking at, but Hulda made no reply. How could she say, "That way he will come"? Fortunately, her silence was unnoticed, and Ma'amselle Ulrika advanced to close the windows, that the rising mist might not tarnish the gilt frames of the mirrors and pictures. Hulda and her mother assisted her, and the beautiful portrait soon vanished in the darkness. But not for Hulda; she still gazed into the depths of those wondrous eyes, and they shone before her as she walked home by her mother's side through the dewy twilight, they hovered through her dreams in the night, and the next day she listened eagerly in hopes that her father and mother would speak of the baron. But, although they mentioned every other member of the family, not one word was said of Baron Emanuel. Three or four times she made up her mind to ask some question concerning him, and as often did the words die on her lips; for what should she ask? His age? She had already reckoned that in the night, and according to her ideas he was no longer young; he had entered upon his thirtieth year. How he looked? She knew that too,—just as she thought Tasso and the Marquis of Posa must have looked,—different from the rest of mankind, and so handsome. Yes, she had once heard her father say that he had a noble heart, full of true impulses, and those large, dark eyes could not deceive.

CHAPTER V.

THE pastor had requested the bailiff to send him word as soon as the family arrived, and the messenger was daily expected at the parsonage; but day after day passed without bringing him. Never before had Hulda looked forward to anything so eagerly; and although each day brought its accustomed round of studies and occupations, the hours dragged slowly for the first time in her life. One evening, as the sun was again setting, bringing no message from the castle, her impatience drove her from the house; she was sure tidings must come before night.

She went into the garden, but no one was to be seen. She opened the garden-gate and ran around to the road, thinking that thence she should surely see one of the bailiff's servants approaching. And it was far more delightful in the open air than sitting expectant within the house. The evening was so lovely!

The fresh breeze blowing from the sea stirred her dress

and tossed her curls. Her long shadow hurried on before her so merrily that she ran after it as after some companion whose presence prevented loneliness, and in a few moments she found herself on the borders of the nearest field of rye. The ears were forming, and the field was sprinkled over with cornflowers. As if these had been the object of her walk, she began to pluck the lovely blue blossoms and to weave a wreath of them. Her father loved these flowers, with their soft fragrance suggestive of the ripening grain, and at this season of the year his study was never without a wreath or bunch of them. She seated herself beneath a blooming hawthorn in the hedge and finished her wreath, and then, putting it on her head that her hands might be free, she went on plucking the flowers. With her hands full of them and some branches of wild roses just pulled from the hedge, she was turning to go home, when she heard a loud neigh, and a rider on a brown horse rapidly approached the spot where she was standing.

She knew the horse,—it was the same that she had seen exercised by a groom upon her late visit to the castle; and she ran towards it to ask if there was any news from thence. But, to her astonishment, as she drew near she did not recognize the rider. It was no servant from the castle, but a gentleman in a blue cloth riding-coat and horseman's boots, with black crape around his hat. He was tall and spare, his face, marked by the smallpox, was set in a frame of dark, waving hair, and in spite of the pélerine that he wore, in compliance with a fashion borrowed from England, it was evident that one shoulder was a little higher than the other,—he was slightly deformed.

Hulda, startled, stopped short at sight of the stranger, who, reining in his horse, lifted his hat courteously and asked whether the village close at hand were not N——. The girl assented. "Do you not live there, mademoiselle?" he asked further.

"Yes, at the parsonage," she replied, and would have turned away, for intolerable confusion suddenly possessed her; but the words had scarcely left her lips when the rider sprang from his horse. "Then I will walk with you," he said; "it is to the parsonage that I am going. Shall I find the pastor at home?"

Again she replied shyly in the affirmative, and the stranger, who could not but see that she was wellnigh unable to speak from embarrassment, seemed desirous to put her at her ease. "I arrived at the castle at noon," he said, "having hurried on before the countess; it is so dreary to reach home and find no one belonging to you to welcome you. If my sister and my niece arrive to-morrow——"

"Are you, then, the countess's brother?" Hulda involuntarily exclaimed, looking him full in the face in her surprise. But, ashamed of her sudden question, she became still more painfully embarrassed, and could not tell what to say or which way to look.

The baron saw how she was suffering, and, stepping closer to her side, said, with a kindly glance, "For whom did you take me?" That glance from those fine eyes, the eyes of the picture, completed Hulda's confusion; she could not speak; shame and distress so overcame her that she had much ado to keep from crying. She walked on by his side, her eyes riveted on the ground.

He had hung his horse's bridle upon his arm, and although Hulda could not look up at him she felt that he was watching her narrowly. Suddenly he spoke again: "I wish I could divine your thoughts, my child. How gay you were when I saw you first! With your wreath, and your hands full of roses, you were like none other than Ceres's lovely daughter. You came towards me so confidingly that I accepted it as a good omen, here where I am a stranger; and now that you know who I am, you turn away from me." He took her hand, and, bending over her, said, "Do you know anything of me to make you afraid?"

The clear, melodious tones of his voice increased instead of soothing her agitation. "Oh, no, nothing!" she cried, and her eyes filled with tears. She would have withdrawn her hand from his clasp, but he held it firmly in his own, which, with a sense of guilt towards him for which she was unable to ask forgiveness in words, she suddenly raised to her lips.

The baron would have prevented her. "My dear child, what are you doing?" he cried. "What is the matter? I am tempted to believe in magic, and that some malicious sprite has been at work here. What can have happened to agitate you thus? Come, tell me all about it."

But every word that he spoke made matters worse, and losing all power of reflection, she said, hastily, "It is nothing, nothing, only I had seen your picture at the castle." Scarcely had she uttered the words when she longed to recall them; so melancholy was the smile that passed over his grave face that she felt it as a punishment for her thoughtlessness.

"Ah, that indeed," he said, releasing her hand. "I quite understand it. It was the same with myself. I was just as much shocked when I looked into a mirror for the first time after that horrible illness. I perfectly understand your surprise, my poor child!"

He was silent, and she could say nothing, she did not even know what she wanted to say, and they quietly walked on towards the village. Before they reached the parsonage, however, the baron had entirely recovered himself, and, with a friendly glance at Hulda, he said, "We have already had an adventure together, and I do not even know your name, my child."

She told him what it was.

"A charming name, well suited to its owner, in whose eyes tears should never stand," he said. "At all events, I trust I may never cause them to rise there; and if you will only remember that I am no longer seventeen years old either in person, mind, or heart, I dare say we may still be excellent friends. I pray you now, tell me where I shall find some one in whose charge to leave my horse, and then say to your father that I am here and hope to have the pleasure of seeing him."

CHAPTER VI.

The count's body had been consigned to the ancestral vault with all due solemnities, and the family at the castle were pursuing the even tenor of their way, the countess declaring that the quiet and retirement of her home were most beneficial in their effects upon her.

But she must have had peculiar views as to quiet and retirement, for as soon as the numerous relatives who had assembled at the castle to attend the funeral had taken their departure, others arrived to express their sympathy, and, as the season was now at its height for watering-places and the sea-side, there were many family friends desirous of enjoying sea-air, to whom the countess would have thought it discourteous not to extend an invitation to visit her.

Thus the castle was constantly filled to overflowing, and Ma'amselle Ulrika complained bitterly of the pains her old head was put to to contrive that everything should be satisfactory, while the new servants brought by the visitors turned all upside down, and there was as great a bustle as if the French had come again. But it was easy to see, in spite of these complaints, that the bustle, the coming and going, the ordering and arranging, were an immense satisfaction to Ma'amselle. Most especially did she enjoy the private gossips with the various lady's-maids, and the praise that was bestowed upon her clever management. With all that there was to do, she came much oftener than formerly to the parsonage, where she delighted to recount to the pastor's wife the wonderful events that took place and the stories she heard. At these times it seemed to Hulda that the old parsonage was transported bodily into the midst of the gay world. She was never tired of listening and admiring. The girl's vivid fancy was filled with the images of the stately, beautiful countess, and the fair, slender daughter, still wearing gloomy mourning robes in spite of the warmth of the season, the servants in black livery, and the old English governess, her gray curls slightly tremulous with age, who had educated both the mother and the daughter, and was still, so said Ma'amselle, their valued friend and counsellor. Not a day passed without bringing to her fresh matter for interest and reverie.

Sometimes the handsome Clarissa would ride past the parsonage in the cool of the evening, her veil and black plume fluttering in the wind, in company with a party of noble ladies and gentlemen, or an officer in brilliant uniform would dash through the village. Then again, the whole party at the castle would be brought down in their light droschkés to the sea for a sail, and the servants would prepare lunch on the shore for their return. In short, the week would pass before she knew it. Sunday seemed to come far oftener than ever before, and on Sundays the countess never omitted coming to church with her guests.

From her earliest childhood Hulda had looked forward with delight all through the week to Sunday, and in summer it had always been a double holiday. How her heart swelled with pleasure as she sat in her place opposite the chancel beside her mother, the bright sunshine streaming through the low windows into the church, lighting up the golden dome above her father's head, which caught from it a reflected glow, while the soft plash of the sea seemed to keep time with his words, and the sea-breeze stirred the curtain before the church-door, and every now and then swept through the building, filling it with fresh, damp odours of the ocean! All was just as it had always been, but the cheerful content that had filled Hulda's heart was no longer there. She thought no longer of her father's words, or whether she should meet this or that young girl of her acquaintance, as she had been used to hope when she thought of Sunday. Her thought now was, Will he be at church? and she did not know whether she desired or feared his presence there.

She had seen him but once—at the count's funeral—since that first meeting, and, greatly impressed as she might have been at another time by the imposing ceremonial, it had scarcely interested her, so entirely had her attention and sympathy been absorbed by the baron. Would he speak to her? would he recognize her? She longed for one word from him. She wanted to read in his eyes whether he was angry with her. She reproached herself repeatedly for her silly exclamation. It lay heavy upon her heart that she, who had never wittingly harmed a living creature, should have wounded this man who was already so far from happy.

But the funeral was over, and her hope was unfulfilled. The castle family had exchanged a few words with the pastor after they left the vault, and had then got into their carriages and driven home, the countess only bowing kindly to the pastor's wife as she passed her. And after this the countess had sent for the pastor several times to discuss parish matters with him, the schools and the poor. She had asked him to dinner, and had inquired for his wife and daughter, promising to come soon to the parsonage to see them.

The presence of the family at the castle brought new life to the pastor. The days of his youth spent in daily intercourse with them recurred so vividly to his mind that he seemed years younger, and his enjoyment reacted upon his wife. The quiet home seemed a different place: there was animation in all its old rooms. The countess's visit was the theme of daily expectation, and Hulda asked herself in secret the question she dared not utter aloud, Would the baron accompany his sister when she did come?

Her father had made special mention of the love of the countess for this brother, and of the pleasure she took in the improvement in his health, now so much better than formerly that he considered himself quite robust. The pastor had had several long talks with him in his own rooms at the castle, and together they had gone over the collection of national songs that the baron was at present occupied in making. There had been some talk, too, of his coming to the parsonage to hear, in the original, the Lithuanian melodies that Hulda and her mother knew so well. But the visit had never yet been paid: he had not even appeared at church with the other inmates of the castle.

It was the fourth Sunday after the funeral, and the count's pew, with its glass windows that screened it from the rest of the church, was filled as usual; but as soon as the singing after the sermon was finished, the countess and her people rose and departed. As she passed the seats where Hulda and her mother were sitting, she made a sign to the latter to follow her. She obeyed, taking her daughter with her, although the pastor was about to perform a baptismal rite. Outside the church-door the countess said, as the pastor's wife stooped to kiss her hand, "I want to spend a short time with you. My young people are going for a sail, and I will await at your house the return of the carriage. They must stop for my brother."

"Then the Herr Baron is not ill?" the pastor's wife casually remarked.

"What should make you suppose him ill?" curtly rejoined the countess, who, like all others of her class, was not fond of interrogations from inferiors, among whom she reckoned the pastor's wife, who, embarrassed by her manner, said, by way of excuse, "I thought, as the Herr Baron has never been to church——"

"Oh, he has entirely lost the habit of church-going," replied the countess, walking through the parsonage garden into the house, and then into the sitting-room, where the pastor's wife hastily drew aside the table before the sofa, to make room for her guest. The great lady put up her eyeglass, and, looking around the cosy little room, said, "How very nice you keep everything! your house really looks quite pretty. And you yourself are very well preserved, and are perfectly content, I hear. I am very glad of it. Your daughter, too, looks very well," she added, directing her glass towards Hulda. "How old is she, and what is her name?"

She spoke kindly enough, but not in a way to place either mother or daughter at her ease. When the pastor's wife had answered her questions, the countess continued, "The girl is so well grown that I thought she was older. Is there any prospect of settling her in the neighbourhood?"

"Hulda is so young!" her mother exclaimed, betraying by her manner how foreign to her thoughts as yet was any idea of Hulda's future settlement in life. But either the countess did not perceive this, or she did not think it worth while to notice it, for she replied, "Of course she is young, but your husband is growing old, and it is your duty to think very seriously of your own and your daughter's future. That is the reason why I ask if there is no prospect of settling her near you. Is there no young clergyman in the neighbourhood to whom you could marry her? He might be your husband's assistant, since you have no sons. My husband once spoke to me of some such arrangement, and mentioned distinctly that he would provide the young man's salary in such a case, and increase the income of the living. He had a great regard for your husband, and I should like to act in strict accordance with his wishes. So pray have no hesitation in speaking."

This was all very just and prudent, and showed more kindness perhaps than the pastor's wife, in her moments of anxiety, had ever pictured to herself; but the idea of making the future marriage of her daughter, who was little more than a child, a subject for speculation, was contrary to every feeling of her heart and to all her religious convictions. The countess's curt, imperious manner terrified her, and in hopes of avoiding further discussion of such a topic, she said, gently, "The future lies in God's hand."

The countess smiled. Resolute and decided by nature, and accustomed to succeed in all that she undertook, in her means to gain an end she had once proposed to herself she ruthlessly disregarded any hesitation on the part of those whose wishes and actions are influenced by their sensibilities.

"Of course it lies in God's hand," she said, "and so does the result of the harvest or the yearly crop; nevertheless, the seed must be sown at the right season, and the earth tilled. You know we should like to keep this living in your family. Hulda is quite good-looking, and when her father's salary is increased she will be a very good match for a young clergyman. So, if you have no other views for your daughter, look about for some one in the circle of your acquaintances; for however firm our faith may be in the wise designs of Providence, the marriages that are not made in the heaven of love, but built upon a firm basis of good sense and ripe judgment, are sure to turn out the best in the end. Meanwhile, something might be done to improve the girl's education. What do you know, child?" she asked, beckoning to Hulda to approach.

It was fortunate that the pastor, his duties in the church completed, entered just at this moment, having learned that the countess was visiting his wife. It relieved poor Hulda from all necessity of replying, for the lady immediately repeated her offer to the father, and asked him the question she had previously put to Hulda. His answer was satisfactory, for he understood the significance of all that his patroness said much better than did his wife or his daughter, and knew how to testify that gratitude for kindness which is expected by the great ones of this world when they confer unsolicited favour. The countess arose and approached Hulda.

"Why, you have made an excellent beginning," she said. "Knowledge is a capital sure to bring in a due amount of interest, and as it is entirely uncertain how soon we can find a suitable settlement for you, we must try to add something to your accomplishments in the mean while. We must see." Again she put up her eyeglass, and, scanning the girl from head to foot, she asked, "Is she as healthy as she looks?" Her parents eagerly assented with a "thank God!" "Is she patient? not irritable?" the countess asked further. The pastor replied that she had always been treated justly and reasonably, and her conduct had never given cause for complaint.

The countess laid her hand upon his shoulder, and, with a slow shake of her haughty and still beautiful head, said, "My dear pastor, I am afraid she has much to learn. For justice and reason have so little share in the world we live in.' Just at this moment the carriage, with the baron riding by its side, came along the road before the parsonage, and the countess went out to take her place in it. In the doorway she turned and held out her hand to the young girl. Hulda stooped to kiss it, and the lady kindly stroked her cheek. "Take heart, child," she said, "I shall not forget you, and you shall soon know what I have decided to do."

Countess Clarissa and the other occupants of the carriage waved their hands towards the house in token of friendly greeting, and the baron rode up to the garden-gate. He exchanged a few pleasant words with the pastor, asking him to come and see him, and offering to send a carriage for him at any time he might appoint. Then, turning to Hulda, he said, "Where is your wreath to-day? You ought always to wear a wreath."

And he was gone; and before Hulda could collect herself, the whole party—the countesses, their guests, and the baron—had vanished. But she knew now that the baron was at least not angry with her.

CHAPTER VII.

One afternoon soon after this, a heavy storm came on; but, although it lasted a long while, it failed to cool the atmosphere. The rain was still falling, the windows in the countess's boudoir were open, but no fresh breeze penetrated into the room, and already, an hour before sunset, it was almost dark. The plashing of the rain drowned the noise of the sea.

The countess was occupied with her netting; her brother sat reading in one of the window-recesses. From Clarissa's room came the sound of music. The baron threw aside his book.

"'Tis odd," he said, "but the rhythm of Clarissa's song is so entirely opposed to the rhythm of these verses, that I cannot endure the discord it makes."

"And it really is too dark for your book or my work," the countess rejoined, laying down her netting. Then, turning to the window, she added, "The wind comes from the southwest, and is sultry as a sirocco. It is just the day to make one long for our lofty, cool apartments in Italy."

"But how is it in those wretched, over-crowded Italian huts on such a day? Ugh! how oppressive it must be!" said the baron.

"It is all a matter of habit; they become, as it were, acclimatized," said his sister. "Their sensibilities are not so keen as ours. I really believe, too, that the straitened circumstances in which those people live contract their views and deprive them of the power of freedom of thought. I was very much struck with this the other day at the parsonage. Those women are child-like, not to say childish, in their want of all forethought. They call it trust in Heaven; and yet they must see how short-lived their families are, while ours flourish for centuries."

"With exceptions. And we have more chance, too, than the masses," the baron remarked, not knowing to what special instances the countess alluded.

"Of course, melancholy exceptions there will be, if all chances are relinquished," she rejoined, eagerly.

The baron, who had hitherto borne his part in the conversation with but indolent interest, suddenly raised his head, and, with a smile that well became him, asked, "Are these remarks of yours only an introduction to a new variation of the theme so often discussed between us?"

"No, indeed!" cried the countess. "What put that into your head?"

"You have made me suspicious," he replied.

"Because you do yourself such injustice," said the countess; "because you always distrust yourself. And why should you regard a sister's care for a brother as an assault upon his freedom?"

"Not as an assault upon his freedom, but as a want of confidence in his penetration; especially since the craving for happiness, innate in every man, naturally urges him to embrace every opportunity that offers of attaining it."

The countess felt the rebuke without resenting it; for she had, as we have already said, almost more tenderness, and far more anxiety, for her youngest brother than for her own children; and, avoiding the pursuit of what seemed to be to him an unwelcome topic, she explained that her remark really had borne no reference to him, or to the arrangement of his future, but that she had been thinking of the pastor's family, and in particular of his daughter. Then she told him, in a few words, of her conversation with the father and mother of the girl, and said that she had since formed a new plan with regard to her. The girl was, to be sure, very young, and if her mother was to look to her for future support, it would be well to do something for her further education and culture, that she might secure an independence for herself, in case of necessity.

Emanuel asked how his sister proposed to carry out this plan.

"I should like to have her here in the castle for awhile," she replied.

Her brother remarked that she would thus certainly add to his pleasure.

"To your pleasure?" she cried. "How so?"

"The girl is very beautiful!"

"A fair specimen of the beauty of her class. The mother was very pretty, too," said the countess.

"The daughter's beauty really startled me," said the baron. "The first time I rode over to the parsonage she suddenly started up before me on the borders of a field of grain,—a brilliant vision of the goddess of the fields. It was a charming picture; and then I had a little adventure with the child that quite touched me."

The countess asked what it was; her brother refused to tell her, whereupon she insisted, and at last he said that he had destroyed an illusion in the mind of the pastor's daughter,—the first that had been dispelled in her young life. She had shown so much tenderness of disposition in the matter that he should be very glad to have any kindness shown her.

The countess pursued the subject no further, but arose from her seat and placed herself by her brother's side, on the broad window-seat.

His behavior towards women had frequently been matter of remonstrance on her part. A great admirer of feminine beauty, and keenly susceptible as he was to beauty in every shape, he thought himself so much more disfigured by the smallpox than was really the case, he so clearly felt the contrast between his youthful and his present self, that he had resigned all hope of ever winning a woman's affection for his own sake. His convictions on this point had induced him to keep aloof from women's society, and to oppose the wishes of his family, who were anxious that through his marriage the ancient family of Falkenhorst, now threatened with extinction, might flourish anew.

It struck the countess as very odd that her brother had never before mentioned to her an adventure that seemed to have produced so pleasant an impression upon him, since he usually liked to speak of such things, and she wondered still more that, as he daily rode for a couple of hours, he had not ridden again to the parsonage to see the girl who had so charmed him. Did this betoken reserve consequent upon a decided impression, or did it proceed from indifference? and had the circumstance been recalled to his mind for the first time by her words? She must understand this,—his state of mind in this direction was very important to her.

"I sent for the bailiff's sister yesterday," she said, "and told her I wanted her to take the daughter in charge, as she had taken the mother years ago, and that my good Kenney should do what she could for the young person. Her mother did very well with Ulrika's teaching, and, as the daughter has been well taught by her father, and, besides, comes of a better stock upon his side of the house, I trust something more may be made of her."

"More? what do you call more in this case?" asked her brother.

The countess hesitated a moment, for she did not like to explain her plans, even in small matters, lest she should not afterwards feel free to change them; but she departed from her usual course on this occasion.

"I think Kenney is failing," she said: "this last journey seemed to cause her more fatigue than her age would warrant, and after Clarissa's marriage I may have to lead more of a travelling life than I have led hitherto. Kenney has been with me from my earliest childhood; she can hardly imagine life without us, and yet I cannot answer it to my conscience to expose her to the constant fatigue of travel. That, and our residence in the south, have not agreed with her health lately, for, like all Englishwomen, she needs sea-air——"

"You do not wish to take her with you in future, but to give her a quiet home here in the castle," her brother interrupted her.

"Don't say I do not wish to take her with me," said his

sister. "I am afraid that, for her sake, I must sooner or later leave her here behind me. I shall miss her greatly, for I have never been without her, and she will think it hard at first to stay here without me, unless I can find some occupation for her. I have said nothing to her as yet upon the subject, for there is plenty of time, and I learned, years ago, to wait for the day and the hour; I acknowledge them my masters."

She leaned her head upon her hand, and seemed sunk in melancholy reverie. The baron regarded her with a smile,—she was so unlike herself.

"These reflections lead you astray from your plans for the pastor's daughter," he said.

"Not at all," she replied, very well content to resume the thread of the conversation; "my plans concerning Kenney are closely connected with those for the pastor's family, but I can decide upon nothing positively until I know the girl. Of course it will be best that she should have a thorough knowledge of household matters; if she is capable of loftier acquirements, Kenney may be of use to her. She enjoys teaching as we all enjoy doing what we can do well. If Hulda pleases her, I would arrange that she should stay here with her, and at some future time a well-educated person, devoted to our family from her birth, might prove a great acquisition to Clarissa, for such a one really is a blessing to a woman much in society. If, on the other hand, any advantageous marriage among the pastor's friends should offer itself for the girl, it will be a satisfaction to have contributed somewhat to her education."

The baron asked if Hulda's parents, or the girl herself, approved of these views.

The countess replied that people who, like the pastor's family, were seldom in a position to carve out their future, should be approached on such matters more in the way of command than of consultation. She had lately noticed this especially. Every proposition startled such people, and made them thoughtful and shy, and they delayed, to weigh and ponder, until opportunity had passed and they had accomplished nothing, while, used as they were to subordination, if they were placed in a certain position, without regard to their own views in the case, they soon accommodated themselves to circumstances and learned to appreciate their advantages.

As her brother received these remarks in silence the countess grew impatient. "You do not entirely approve of my plan," she said, "and yet you have just told me that the girl's presence in the castle would give you pleasure."

"It was a very innocent remark, and the pleasure that the constant sight of so beautiful a girl would give me would certainly be as innocent a pleasure," was his reply. "But those people have only this one child; the pastor is an old man, and, as he himself told me, she is the sole delight of their seclusion. It seems to me a bold proceeding to attempt thus to decide the fate of a girl,—of an entire family, rather,—and especially hard to deliver over the poor child to such adverse teachings as Miss Kenney's and the bailiff's sister's will certainly prove."

"If that is all, I am quite content," cried the countess, "for the right of free choice signifies very little to people born in dependent circumstances; and although you may paint a future for mankind in ideal colours, you must admit that obedience of the lower to the higher is a fundamental law of nature."

"Certainly! only I cannot consider myself one of those 'higher,' simply because I enjoy accidental advantages of rank and wealth, since nature has——"

The countess would not let him finish his sentence. "I should like to see," she said, interrupting him, "how you would act if the desire for self-gratification should ever come into collision with your theories."

"Be sure I would do my best to be just to the latter," the baron maintained.

"Doubtless," rejoined the countess, "you would try, and then console yourself, as we all do, with the thought that you really had tried."

"Remind me of this if you ever have occasion," said Emanuel, with quiet self-confidence.

"I shall not forget to do so," his sister assured him; "for, with my views, I should regard it as a matter for praise if you would emerge from your ideal world, and perceive that there would be an end to our ancient and noble families if we were all to determine philanthropically to lose ourselves in universal humanity. My dear brother, your lonely life makes you unpractical. If you were married, if you had children, you would know how dear the preservation of one's name and race naturally is to all of us."

The baron gave her an odd, good-humoured glance. She asked what he was thinking of. "Oh," answered he, "I was only pleased to see how diplomacy has really become your second nature, and how well you know that all roads lead to Rome."

She took his reply in the spirit in which it was given, and they joined the others in the best possible humour.

CHAPTER VIII.

THE countess had judged the pastor's family correctly in one respect. Her visit and her remarks had disturbed the calm of the parsonage, and to a certain extent troubled the harmony hitherto subsisting among its inmates.

The pastor reproached his wife for want of gratitude to the countess for her thought of them, and to Heaven for providing them with so kind a benefactress; and she, while passing in mental review all the young clergymen of her husband's acquaintance, to select from them, if possible, a fitting assistant for her husband and a fitting husband for her daughter, rebelled in her heart against the idea of thus making her idolized child a means of securing her own future comfort. Her sentiments and her prudence were in a state of constant warfare; and Hulda was more agitated than her mother, not to say frightened, by all that the countess had said.

The presence of the family at the castle had lent actual shape to all the vague dreams and wishes of her youthful mind, and converted her old desire to see something of the life that lay beyond the limits of her father's parish into a restless longing which, like some evil spell, robbed of its interests and charm all that had hitherto sufficed her. The thought that, with every capacity for enjoyment, her days were to be forever passed within the four walls that for nearly a century had seen the cradles and the coffins of her forefathers, oppressed her like a bad dream. The little garden, with its firs, where she had passed such happy hours, was no longer dear to her. She had no peace in her home; her thoughts were always at the castle. She was ever on the watch for some of the family there who might chance to visit the village; but they were all absent with relatives residing much farther inland, and for a week no one had appeared, even from the bailiff's. At last, one evening the bailiff himself rode up to the gate of the parsonage garden, tied his horse there, and, dismounting, walked sturdily into the house. Scarcely had he replied to the greetings of the pastor's wife and daughter when he asked to be shown into the study where the pastor was writing. There, in answer to the good old man's hope that he brought some good news, he said that news, it was true, he had brought, and that he hoped it would prove good.

"I ought to have come a week ago," he said, "and not upon my own account either. Hulda is to come to the castle."

"To the castle?" three voices asked, in a breath, and the daughter's eyes danced with delight.

"Yes, to the castle, or rather to my house," replied the bailiff. "She was to be sent for the day after the family left upon this visit. But you know my sister of old,—nothing pleases her that she does not propose first herself, and so in the beginning she was unwilling to have Hulda."

The pastor looked first at the bailiff and then at his wife in undisguised surprise, and remarked, not without a certain degree of displeasure, that there seemed to be a plan proposed here of which he knew nothing. At least, he was not aware that he had ever requested the bailiff's sister to undertake such a charge.

"Of course not, of course not," cried the bailiff; "you have nothing to do with it. It is the countess."

This amazed the pastor. "The countess lately alluded to other views for our daughter," said he.

The bailiff knew nothing of that. The countess had sent for him, and told him that she wished Hulda to be instructed in household matters by Ulrika, as her mother had been before her, and that she desired upon her return to find the girl established in his house.

All this neither lessened the pastor's surprise nor soothed his dislike of the proposal. He knew Ma'amselle Ulrika well, and remembered the many bitter hours she had caused his wife; moreover, he was perfectly aware of her superstitious tendencies, and that he had much ado to contend with and suppress foolish gossip of this kind concerning herself among his parishioners. He therefore joined in his wife's exclamation, "But what induces the countess to take such an interest in Hulda?"

The bailiff, whose face was almost always a mirror of good-humoured self-satisfaction, laughed at this. "What induces her? That you must ask herself. They are all alike! Good heavens! she is used to have something new to interest her every day, something new to do every day. Here in the country she has nothing, and so she busies herself with one thing or another, with building, with the school, with compelling others to be happy as she pleases. But she has a clear head, and really means well. We must not take it ill of her."

This speech of the worthy man soothed the pastor, who had a high opinion of the countess, and had not been able to understand her apparent change of mind. Far other thoughts occupied the mother. She could not forget what she had suffered in her youth from the frivolity of the young noblemen, guests at the castle, and yet her case had been different from her daughter's. She, a poor daughter of a serf, could never have dreamed of a marriage with a nobleman. But what surety could she have that Hulda might not give ear to what would awaken within her wishes and hopes perhaps now dormant in her heart, and for which there was no possibility of gratification? What good could it do the child to be at the castle or with Ma'amselle Ulrika, if the countess intended to establish her in future in the parsonage? Not daring to give utterance to these fears, she tried to advance other objections to the project; but the bailiff answered them all, and, in the habit of proceeding quickly to action, he turned to Hulda, who had been listening to the conversation with intense interest, and said, "Come, my child, what have you to say? Will you come with me?" Hulda blushed for joy. She looked from her father to her mother, and found no encouragement in the face of either; but her longing to see somewhat of that new life was stronger for the moment than her filial devotion, and, carried away by a youthful love of pleasure, she said, with a beaming countenance, "Oh, how I should like it!"

"Well, then, Herr Pastor," said the bailiff, "we are all agreed. To-morrow I will send for her; and every Sunday, of course, she shall come to church. It will be just as if she were still at home; and no one ever starved at my house,—you may be sure of that." Then he arose, declaring that he could not keep his horse standing any longer; but the pastor's wife begged him to take some refreshment, and sent Hulda to prepare the modest luncheon. During her absence, the time of her departure the next day was arranged, and when the bailiff had drunk his glass of wine, he turned to her, and said, "Come, I think you will be happy with us, for now that Ma'amselle is used to the idea she is very glad that she is to have you with her; she often needs help now-a-days, and she thinks more of you than of any one else." And then he mounted his horse and was gone, while parents and daughter stood at the garden-gate looking after him.

"Then to-morrow you will go forth among strangers to begin life upon your own responsibility," the pastor said, solemnly, looking gravely into Hulda's eyes. But even this admonition could not banish the delight from her face. She kissed her father's hand and threw her arms around her mother's neck, assuring them that she would take pains to please Aunt Ulrika; and while her parents' hearts were full of the grief of this first separation from their daughter, she could only repeat to herself, in a dream of expectation, "To the castle!"

It was what she had thirsted for since the visit paid in early spring, when she had first seen those wondrous halls, and she could hardly wait until the conveyance sent for her should arrive. Dread lest something might intervene to prevent her departure, and impatience, scarcely allowed her to sleep. The hours of the following day dragged slowly along, and when at last she was seated in the light one-horse wagon from the bailiff's, her joy was greater than any she had ever known before. She kneeled upon the seat, and, looking back at her parents, tossed them kisses and farewells with both hands, and then seating herself again and leaning back, as she had seen the castle ladies do, she resigned herself to the hopes and visions that seemed to hover before her upon the background of golden shimmering sunset clouds in the west.

How could she, in her youthful exultation, give a thought to her father and mother sitting alone on the bench in the little garden? How could she know of the depth of fervour with which her mother in her prayers that night invoked Heaven's choicest blessings and tenderest care for her darling child?

CHAPTER IX.

THE weather on the sea-coast is always variable even in the driest season, and a rainy day often follows a clear evening. When Hulda went to her little room after supper at the bailiff's, the stars were shining brightly; but the next morning the rain fell in torrents, and a week of cold, damp weather ensued. All the windows were closed, and the bailiff, who was vexed at the sudden change, since the grain was still in sheaves in the meadows, went from room to room in a state of discontent. His labourers came in dripping from stable and barn to speak with him in his office, the shepherd stood at the open door of his fold gazing right and left at the clouds; and Aunt Ulrika, as she had specially requested her new inmate to call her, was much crosser than her brother, for the rain had sadly interfered with her household arrangements. Every one was reduced to a state of inaction, and "What is death," said Ma'amselle, "but inaction?"

Every now and then the bailiff and his sister went to the window and tapped the barometer in hopes of seeing it rise, and Hulda secretly followed their example, for the castle family had sent word home that they should not return until the rainy weather was over. This was another interruption to Ma'amselle's plans; but it was also a reason for more hard work, and to the girl, accustomed to the monotonous quiet of the parsonage, the restless life at the bailiff's, the loud orders, and the running to and fro of the many servants in house and court-yard, had the charm of novelty at least. True, she soon discovered that there was much more than the long corridor to separate from the main building the wing of the castle appropriated to the use of the bailiff and his sister; but from her little back-room she had an extensive view of the park behind the castle, the windows of which she could also see, and when the family returned there would certainly be constant change and excitement.

Not only did Hulda, with the supple facility of youth, quickly accommodate herself to her new surroundings, but Ulrika herself, after the first few days, was well pleased with the addition to her household. The evident pleasure that it had been to the girl to come to her had gratified her, for Ma'amselle was perfectly aware that, in spite of the hospitality which was a part of her brother's scheme of life, no one felt at all intimate with her, and as her housekeeping had always occupied the first place in her mind she had troubled herself very little with the people about her, except as they came beneath her jurisdiction, when she appointed their duties to each and saw that these duties were well and rigidly performed. If this were the case, they might say and think of her what they chose. She was perfectly convinced that she understood everything better than any one else. It was but natural that people should give her credit for greater wisdom than falls to the common lot of mortals, and should even suppose her possessed of hidden knowledge which she did not, could not, communicate. She was content to be feared and sometimes avoided; it had been so with all about her, even with Simonena, who had always had a shy terror of her. She was, therefore, greatly surprised to find, as she did in a few days, that Hulda was not one whit afraid of her, or in the least abashed in her presence, but received a scolding with the greatest good humour, and evidently liked to be with Aunt Ulrika, following her about and listening with wide-eyed, eager interest to her tales and legends, all of which related mostly to the ancient family whom she served.

Instead of nodding over her knitting, as had lately been her wont, when her brother retired to his office after supper to have interviews with his work-people, she now enjoyed a talk with Hulda; "for," said she, "you are far better company than your mother ever was. Not that I have anything to say against your mother,—Heaven forbid! I wouldn't have you think that; but your mother did want spirit, and, whatever the men may say, no woman can get along well in this world without spirit. Spirit is everything! Just look at the countess,—there's spirit for you! She is just like me; knows every morning what she means to do, and when evening comes it is done. That is why she succeeds in everything."

Hulda listened gravely. "If you have never failed in anything, you must be very, very happy," she said, aftei awhile.

Ulrika gave her a searching glance out of her dark eyes, and then replied, speaking more slowly and in more measured tones than was her wont, "To be sure! to be sure! only——" She paused a moment, and then, as if she must disburden herself, went on: "Only once I did not succeed, and it would have been better in every way and for all parties if I had succeeded; it was all because I had not the proper spirit to speak and act at the right moment. But it was only once, and there's no help for it now. At all events, you shall not suffer for it, —rely upon that."

She seemed to suppose that the girl would understand her, but Hulda only looked up at her in amazement and asked, "Was it my fault, then, that you had not a proper spirit that time?"

Ma'amselle grew impatient. "Just like her mother!" she exclaimed, and fell silent.

Hulda was afraid that she was angry. "What was it you failed in, and why did you not show a proper spirit?" she asked, in hopes of soothing Ma'amselle and prolonging the conversation.

"Because"—she paused—"because I have a weakness."

But even this did not explain the matter to the girl, and Ma'amselle, aware of it, and desiring nothing better than to talk of herself, went on: "Has not the countess a weakness just as I have? Does not she always show it with regard to her brother, Baron Emanuel? Can she carry out her plans with him as she does with other people? To be sure, he is not like other people. Miss Kenney is right when she declares that the baron is really holy."

Hulda was all ear. At last that name gleamed in the midst of Aunt Ulrika's confused talk, like a star among wreaths of mist, although the allusion to the baron was mysterious enough. Why was he, who, of all the inmates of the castle, never entered the church, holy? She could not help expressing her wonder.

"Oh," cried Ma'amselle, "when I said holy, I did not mean

what your father does when he talks of 'holy' in his pulpit,—but holy like the family vault or some old heir-loom!" She reflected for a moment, as if vainly searching for words in which to explain herself, and then said, mysteriously, in a low voice, "Did you never hear of it? Did you not see it? The curse is on him!"

Hulda started in terror. "Aunt!" she cried. "Not upon Baron Emanuel! It cannot be! What wrong has he done?"

"He?" Ma'amselle's look grew graver, and her tone more solemn. "He has done no wrong,—none in the world. You saw him in the picture-gallery. He was beautiful as an angel, and all life and joy, when he was here as a boy with his mother. There was nothing of it then to be seen; but it all came, nevertheless, afterwards. It always is so with one of his race. The little folk are neither to be defied nor laughed at; Baron Emanuel knows that well enough, and that is the reason that no persuasions of the countess can induce him ever to take a wife. The family will die out with him."

Ma'amselle's voice sounded strange and afar in Hulda's ears. A cold shudder ran through her. Aunt Ulrika, the room, the castle, and the baron suddenly seemed weird and uncanny to her. She had the greatest desire to know what it all meant, and yet she did not like to ask, for now she understood her father's meaning when he had expressly warned her, on the eve of her departure from home, to pay no heed to Ma'amselle's superstitious tales and fancies.

But, as if Aunt Ulrika could read what was passing in the girl's mind, she pushed her old arm-chair nearer to the footstool where Hulda was sitting, and, laying her long, skinny hand upon her shoulder, bent over her and almost whispered in her ear, "You must have heard of them, although stupid people hereabouts say they have disappeared and crossed the sea since the churches were built, and that there are no longer any little people here. Nonsense! they are not afraid of churches,—they believe in God, and have their own religion. They never cross the seas, nor do they stir from the place that they have made their home so long as they are unmolested. They have been here from the beginning, although they appear only to their favourites. They are sure to be true to those who trust them. But they must not be angered or injured, for they never forget or forgive."

"But, aunt," cried Hulda, incredulously, and yet so impressed, in spite of herself, by the solemnity of Ma'amselle's words and manner, that she did not dare to laugh,—"but, aunt, these are nursery-tales! This is superstition!"

"Do you think so?" Ma'amselle rejoined, and her gaze became fixed as she looked towards the dim corner where from time immemorial the great green stove had stood, with the broad bench built into the wall behind it. "Do you think so? Yes; many believe these are nursery-tales, because they put their faith in the stupid proverb that was born of crowded cities—'The night is no man's friend.' But those who live here in the country, in old castles, beneath which are still more ancient cellars and subterranean passages, which, if they do their duty, they often visit at night, when others are sleeping, to see if all is as it should be, well know how diligent and watchful the little people still are, and how they never weary of assisting in the house in which they have taken up their abode, provided always that the drop of milk and the morsel of fruit or grain that they require is not begrudged them."

Hulda became more and more absorbed in the words of the speaker. Involuntarily her eyes followed Aunt Ulrika's, which were still riveted upon the dim corner, although she could discover nothing but the two huge yellow cats, who usually took their evening nap there. To throw off the spell that threatened to take her reason captive, she asked, "But what has all this to do with Baron Emanuel?"

"Your mother could answer that question better than any one else, if she chose, for she was born upon the estates of Falkenhorst; and every child there knows that the little people had made the Preussenburg their home before the Falkenhorsts came with the Germans into the country, and that they continued to dwell in the new castle that the Counts Falkenhorst built upon the ruins of the old one. They kept upon the best of terms with the little people for more than a hundred years, and everything prospered with them. There were always goodly sons and daughters of their house,—a fair race they were, renowned for strength and beauty. And the little people were very quiet, never appearing except in the bounty and blessing that they brought to the family. Suddenly, in the time of the great-great-grandfather of our countess, there were strange noises heard in the castle, both by day and by night. Some said that the bats had grown too numerous; others that the martens had fled to the shelter of the cellars from the cold of a hard winter. But no harm was done; and the baron, who had, of course, his own opinions upon the subject, wisely said nothing. And thus all went on until the day before midsummer, when the baron was sitting, at noon, in his garden, beneath a huge linden, the oldest tree in all the country round. There was no living soul in the garden beside himself, for every one had gone to dinner, and nothing was to be heard but the humming of bees and the chirp of the grasshoppers. Suddenly he seemed to hear something like the ringing of a tiny bell, and the earth among the gnarled roots of the old tree bunched up as if a huge mole were working his way to the surface. The baron watched the spot, and in a few minutes there issued from the ground, just as if he had grown like a blade of grass, a little man. Small as he was, the baron could easily see that he was a king. He had a royal crown upon his head, a golden robe about his shoulders, and a sceptre in his hand; and his whole little person so shone and sparkled, that the baron rubbed his eyes in surprise. The little man, however, gave him a friendly nod, telling him to have no fear, since the little folk were no strangers in Falkenhorst, and had always been good friends with the barons there. He had come to ask a certain friendly office of him. His pretty young queen was dead, and it was time for him to choose another. He had selected to share his throne a little scullery-maid at the castle, only fifteen years old. 'I pray you, then,' he concluded, 'have the girl to-morrow, midsummer-day, when the sun is highest in the heavens, in the grand hall of the castle, where I wish to celebrate my marriage, and see that no one comes near the spot, that no human eye may see what takes place there. Do this, and you shall not repent it; but woe be to you if you betray me! for we are no less implacable as foes than constant as friends.' With these words he vanished as he had appeared, and so quickly, that the baron was half inclined to think the noonday sun had made him sleepy, and that he had dreamed the whole thing. Nevertheless, as he was a prudent man, he determined to use every precaution to guard against misfortune. He took care that all his servants should be absent from the castle, upon some pretext or other, the next day at the approach of noon.

His labourers were all at dinner in their cottages, and he told the baroness, his wife, to shut herself up with her children in the nursery until the sun began to set; for he had a foreboding that noon would not pass on this midsummer-day without bringing some terrible misfortune. When he had arranged all this, he sent the little scullery-maid up to the grand hall, locked her in there, and put the key of the door in his pocket; after which he retired to his own apartments. The sun stood high in the heavens, when the baroness, who was sitting with her children, noticing the deathlike stillness that reigned throughout the castle, grew first a little terrified, and then suspicious of her husband, who had hitherto never had a secret thought that she had not shared. So she locked up her children—there were three of them, a boy and two girls; it was just before the birth of the fourth—in the nursery, and stole noiselessly to her husband's room, where she peeped through the key-hole, and saw him sitting quietly alone. Nothing had happened or was likely to happen; and so, utterly neglecting his commands, she went on from room to room, until she came to the door of the great hall. This she found locked; and, as she stooped to peep through the key-hole, she received a sudden shock, and fell so violently to the ground that her husband heard the noise of her fall, and came running upstairs to see what was the matter. What he then saw and heard his lips never revealed; but there is an old parchment still existing, whereon the whole story stands written by his own hand. The doors of the hall were wide open; in the middle of the large apartment the little scullery-maid, dressed like a queen, lay cold and dead at the foot of a scarlet throne. Upon this throne sat the king; and small as he was, he was fearful to behold. With fiercest anger in his looks, he threatened the baron with his flaming sceptre, saying, in a loud, distinct voice, 'Since you are not master in your own house, we will no longer dwell beneath your roof. Since you do not know how to rule your wife's eyes, my eyes shall never more watch over your interests; and since your false wife has fatally disturbed my marriage with my young queen, your race shall never thrive as it has done hitherto, until the love of some fair young creature, born of the people, shall free it from my curse. The son about to be born to you shall go stooping all his life, as your wife stooped to spy upon us. Never more shall there be, as at present, seven men of your name; and among those that do exist there shall, so long as that name lasts, always be found one whose crooked back shall keep alive the memory of the treachery practised upon us this midsummer noon! And that you may remember my words, take this ring! He whom my curse deforms shall always wear it; and woe to you all if he lay it aside!' With these words the little man, the throne, and the scullery-maid all vanished, a sudden flash of lightning set fire to the hall, and it was with the greatest difficulty that the flames were extinguished. The baron and his wife, as you may suppose, told no one the truth of the matter. It was believed in the country around that the little scullery-maid had been smothered and burned up in the fire. When shortly afterwards the baroness gave birth to a boy, upon the very day upon which two brothers of the baron were killed, and when, in addition to this, it was found that the newly-born son was slightly deformed, the baron wrote down the whole history, all about the ring, and everything, in a huge parchment book devoted to the family records. And all of the little man's prophecy came true. Never, since then, have there been seven men of thé House of Falkenhorst alive at the same time, and among them there has always been one wearing the ring, and slightly deformed. And the race has dwindled with each succeeding generation, until now there are only two living, the childless heir and Baron Emanuel, upon whose little finger any one who chooses may see the ring. He wears it on his left hand; and his servant says that he never takes it off even at night. It is small, and seems grown into its place on the little finger."

Her story finished, Ma'amselle arose and began to make all ready for the night in the pantry and sitting-room, and then proceeded to make the rounds of her domain, as was her custom every evening before going to bed. Hulda accompanied her as usual, but Ma'amselle never noticed the girl's unwonted silence, nor how closely she kept by her side, avoiding being left for one instant behind in the dim vaults of the cellars or in the long corridors.

Hulda was ashamed of herself; but she would have given much not to stay at the bailiff's that night, but to go quietly to bed in the cosy parsonage, in her little room adjoining the one where her father and mother slept. She was nervous and timid when she found herself alone in her bedroom. In vain she said to herself that her terrors were idle; that Aunt Ulrika's story was really nothing more than any silly tale of her childhood, that she had heard time and again. Everything sounded different to-day, far more probable than ever before. It seemed all to have happened so close at hand—hark! was that a wing that swept across the leaded panes of her casement, so that they rattled again? What was it? And that rustle over the floor,—what was that? She drew the pins from her thick fair hair, as she stood before the mirror, and it rippled down almost to her knee. What if something upon the floor should seize it? or if, raising her eyes, she should see in the mirror the face of the little king, or the pale cheeks of the poor dead girl? She cowered in terror, and looked shyly around her. All was quiet in the dimly-lit room; and hurrying to bed, she hid her face beneath the bedclothes. But sleep, usually a faithful companion to healthy youth, for the first time in her life refused its aid. She lay listening hour after hour, although she said to herself that, even according to Aunt Ulrika's story, it was not this castle, but the countess's ancestral home, many miles distant, that the little folk had haunted. For whom, then, did Ma'amselle, usually so frugal, duly set the little bowl of cream in the room below? For whom did she, who hated to see even a straw upon her cleanly-swept floors, scatter grains of wheat upon the cellar-stairs every night, if not for the little folk? And who could tell that they did not pursue through life those whom they had cursed, watching over the ring that was the token of the spell they had woven?

She shuddered at the idea, and tried to banish it from her mind; but the question would recur to her, "What will become of him if he loses the ring?" She could not even pray; she had no control over her thoughts. Strange, incoherent images floated across her brain. She thought she was awake, starting in terror from one confused dream to sink into another as vague; and through it all she saw the baron and his ring, until broad daylight looked in at her window, putting to flight the ghostly visions of the night.

And yet, even in the daytime, she thought of it all, and could not forget that an evil spell rested upon him, which he had been innocent of bringing upon his head.

CHAPTER X.

THE hunting-season in that part of Germany begins upon St. Bartholomew's day, and three days before then the family returned to the castle, bringing various guests with them. Countess Clarissa's betrothed, the young prince, was expected on the following evening. The marriage had been postponed on account of the death of the bride's father, and was to be celebrated at the castle at New Year. Although their mourning prohibited the family from indulging in any great gayeties, the countess was desirous that the prince, who had never visited the castle by the sea before, should be agreeably impressed with the ancestral seat of his future wife's family, and also that the last days of girlhood spent there by her daughter should leave only pleasant memories in her mind.

The afternoon was clear, the sun shone brightly, and the berries of the mountain-ash, at the entrance of the park, gleamed fiery red through the dark leaves as the countess and her daughter waved their kerchiefs to the prince as he drove through the huge gates, accompanied by the baron, who had gone to meet him. Hulda was standing in the doorway of the bailiff's house, eagerly watching the arrival. She saw how the prince hastily sprang from the carriage and Clarissa received him on the castle terrace, how he put his arm about her waist and conducted her into the castle, how the servants unstrapped the luggage from the carriage, while Baron Emanuel looked around for his groom, who was not at hand. Without thinking, she hurried across the court-yard to call him; but in an instant the rider was by her side, and leaning towards her, as he reined in his horse to wait for the servant, he said, "Are you always to present yourself thus suddenly and charmingly in my path?" He dismounted, drew off his glove, and holding out his hand to the blushing girl, walked with her across the court-yard to the bailiff's. He asked her how long she had been at the castle, and how she liked the change, but her answers were vague and confused, for her eyes were looking for the ring upon his hand. She had not long to look: the narrow circlet of gold, with its single blood-red stone, was the only ring there. The sight of it affected her strangely. She started, and looked up in time to meet a kindly glance from the baron's fine eyes.

"How you have grown in these last months!" he said. "When I met you first, you had to look up to me much more than now. You will soon attain my niece's stately stature; and you look even stronger and more blooming. Well, I hope life here in the castle will do you no harm. But if," he added, with so charming a smile that he looked almost as young as herself, and quite like an old friend, "any one or anything here should ever cause you annoyance, only give me a hint of it—the smallest—and I shall understand and know how to advise and arrange so that it shall cease. I must at least requite you for the service you would have rendered me to-day." He shook her kindly by the hand, and was gone before she had even gathered courage to thank him. She listened so intently to what he said, and paid such heed to his manner of saying it, that she always forgot to answer him.

But while she was busy assisting Aunt Ulrika in the labour of the day, now greatly increased by the new arrivals, she pondered incessantly upon the baron and all that he had said. How could he requite her? and what could happen to her that she was not fully competent to encounter and endure alone? She felt equal to all that the future had in store for her, and, looking at herself in her mirror, she, too, thought that she had grown strong and tall.

This pleased her. She was so merry and light of heart that she could not think of sleeping yet; the night, too, was so warm. She opened her window wider to admit more air. From the castle came the sound of music. It was the wild, melancholy Polonaise that the Polish Count Oginski had dedicated to the beautiful queen of Prussia. They said he had loved her with a silent devotion that hurried him to the grave soon after her death. Hulda had always liked to hear and to play this Polonaise. Her father had studied it with her, and she knew every note of it; but never had she so understood it as now. It went to her heart, and for the first time she felt a melancholy emotion at the thought of the composer. The lights vanished; all was dark in the bay-windows of the castle. But the side-windows began to glimmer, and candles were lit in the baron's rooms, until at last they too were extinguished, and the waning moon rose slowly above the trees, and began her nightly wandering through the fleecy clouds that threw faint shadows upon the shaven lawn. Night-birds hovered abroad from the group of giant hemlocks; a screech-owl hooted from the tower; frogs shrilled from the pond, and now and then, as on the previous evening, a bat flitted close to the casement. But there was no terror for her now in these sounds of nature; no dread came near her to disturb her happiness, not even a longing thought of her old home.

For she was not alone. Her protector was close at hand; and asking herself if the morrow would bring him again, she closed her window just as the moon was beginning to descend behind the castle.

CHAPTER XI.

THE next morning, before the sun had entirely dispersed the mists which in that country rise from the sea during the night, Clarissa, with her betrothed and the baron, rode across the court-yard and through the gateway. They wanted to show the prince the country along the shore before the sun grew too hot. Every one who was not absent at work went into the court-yard to see the bridegroom; and indeed he was a sight worth seeing, sitting his horse so firmly and gracefully, and casting joyous glances all about him from his large dark eyes. It was a pleasure to look at the party with the countess waving a farewell to them as she stood at the window, her old English governess by her side. As she was gazing with pride after her daughter, her eye chanced to light upon Hulda, and, turning to Miss Kenney, she said, "There is the pastor's daughter; have you seen her yet?"

Miss Kenney replied in the negative, alleging as an excuse that really she had been miserable in health during the family's absence.

"You were perfectly right; you are not so strong as you

used to be," said the countess; "but since you feel better now, pray see her as soon as possible, that we may advise together with regard to her." And the lady withdrew to her private room, where she was busied with matters connected with the settlement of her husband's estate.

Miss Kenney prepared to obey her behest. As she was very fond of being in the open air, two rooms on the ground-floor towards the garden had been assigned to her. The windows, looking out upon beds of flowers, reached to the ground, and were provided with awnings, beneath which she could enjoy the air even at high noon. Hither Hulda was bidden to come.

Supposing that she was wanted to minister to Miss Kenney's personal comfort in some way, the girl eagerly hastened to the garden wing, and, with her prettiest curtsy, presented herself before her, asking for her commands.

"I have none for you, my child; I only wished to see you. I must always feel an interest in any protégée of the countess." She spoke in the softest of tones, and her whole presence was wonderfully in harmony with her voice, pleasing and gentle. Neither tall nor short in stature, she was still so slender and upright that at a slight distance her age could hardly have been guessed. Her features were delicate, and her color was so fresh that one scarcely noticed the many little wrinkles that time and the experience of life had graven on her countenance, while the profusion of little gray curls that encircled her brow and cheeks almost concealed the want of the roundness of youth in their outline. Her white morning wrapper, her cap with pale-blue ribbons, and the pale-blue India shawl that was lightly thrown about her figure, became her well, while the modest grace that had been hers from girlhood completed the impression which she made upon Hulda's warm heart.

Without the girl's being aware of it, the wise, experienced governess easily formed from the artless replies and conversation of her guest a correct estimate of her knowledge and acquirements; and when Hulda remarked that under her father's tuition she had devoted much time to music, and that she sadly missed her piano at the bailiff's, since the guitar which she had brought with her was but a poor substitute for it, Miss Kenney declared that she had a special delight in the instrument, and told her that she must bring her guitar and play for her in the evenings when Ma'amselle Ulrika could spare her. Then, rising, she conducted Hulda to the piano, and seeing that the girl, after preluding a few moments, struck the notes of a Lithuanian song that she loved, she asked her to sing it to her.

Hulda scarcely waited to be asked. In her simplicity she knew no shyness with one who seemed so kind, and after a slight prelude she sang,—

"Yes, I, poor lonely maiden,
  When bright are spring's fresh bowers,
And all the air is laden
  With fragrant breath of flowers,
Would these fair lilies blooming,
  In pledge of true affection,
Send where my love is roaming,
  Wak'ning fond recollection.
But here afar they wither,
  No messenger is mine,—
Strong wind, ah, waft them thither,
  The power not mine is thine."

The air was composed of soft minor tones, which the girl's clear contralto rendered with wonderful feeling; in the entreaty of the last few lines her voice grew hopeful and confident, and when, after the national fashion, she ended by repeating the last verse two or three times, with slight variations, there ensued a loud clapping of hands, and several voices cried, "Brava!" from outside the open window.

She started from her seat in confusion, for there stood the Countess Clarissa, with Prince Severin and the baron, and Clarissa declared that to be the loveliest Lithuanian melody she had ever heard—Hulda must send her the notes immediately. Prince Severin, too, praised the melody, which he said was sweeter than the music of his home; but still more did he admire the charming voice of the singer. They asked her if she had ever had any instruction. Clarissa wanted to know how long she had been at the castle, and how her parents were. The baron alone asked no questions, and said nothing.

They were all three in their riding-dresses, and Clarissa said they had dismounted in haste, and were come, hungry and thirsty, directly to Miss Kenney, "for ever since I can remember," she said, turning to the prince, "I have been in the habit of taking lunch with my dear Kenney, and I am convinced there is something particularly good ready for me to-day."

But this time she was disappointed. Miss Kenney had not supposed that Clarissa would cling to her old habits after her lover's arrival, and really had nothing to offer to her guests; but Hulda instantly volunteered to bring from the pantry at the bailiff's, which was much nearer at hand than the castle kitchen, all that was wanted, and was gone before her offer could be accepted. Shortly returning, followed by a maid-servant, she quickly and invitingly arranged a cold luncheon on the little table in the garden beneath the awning outside the window, and then quietly took her departure.

Clarissa and her companions were really hungry from their ride, and declared that the lunch was the best they had ever tasted. The young countess begged her bridegroom to have just such a modest little dwelling as Miss Kenney's present quarters arranged in the home where they were to pass most of their time in future, and to install her old friend there,—it was so delightful to go out to lunch so near home; and no one ever had things so nice as her dear Kenney.

The prince promised to do everything that Clarissa desired. Miss Kenney, full of grateful affection for her pupil's devotion, and modestly wishing to divert the conversation from her own excellencies, said, "But your highness must take care to have a girl like the pastor's daughter to arrange the repast, since she certainly has contributed to-day to your enjoyment."

The prince took up the idea. "You are quite right," he replied: "it is not and should not be a matter of indifference to us who arranges our tables and serves our wine. The princes and magnates of earlier times were far beyond their successors of to-day, in that they insisted upon employing handsome pages for such service. There is nothing more tiresome than the usual servants of the present time,—rough fellows, who imitate our vices without attaining our culture; they are too often anything but our well-wishers, while they are, from their position, spies upon our actions. I am never more struck with all that we suffer in this respect than when, traveling in Switzerland, I am waited upon by the host's pretty, well-educated daughters. The contrast is most striking. Can we not, perhaps, secure this girl for our future household?"

"Oh," cried Clarissa, "the pastor's daughter? Impossible! Besides, what good would this one girl do us?"

"We might employ her only in our own personal service, and thus, at least, often avoid the presence of a liveried spy."

The idea pleased Clarissa, and Miss Kenney, who could imagine no greater good fortune than to be taken into her favourite's service, also found it a happy one. The girl, she thought, was already possessed of culture rarely met with even in the higher classes. Her father, an accomplished scholar, had richly endowed her with all that he had to give; she was well read in German literature, had a very fair knowledge of French, was a good musician, and her beautiful voice, so soft and full in speaking, was a great additional gift.

The young countess laughed. "Our dear, good Kenney!" she cried, "she is ready to fall in love again with her pupil. She is just like Jean Paul!"

The baron, who had hitherto taken no part in this talk about the pastor's daughter, asked what she meant.

"Jean Paul says somewhere," she replied, "'Give me one day and night, and I will fall in love with anybody!' Our Kenney says, 'Give me any one for a pupil, and I will love her with my whole heart.' My mother asked her to test the girl's ability and acquirements, and the good creature, after the first hour of trial, is ready to adore her pupil. Do you know, dear, that you will make me jealous? You are far more in a hurry than Pygmalion,—you don't wait until your work is finished; you begin to adore instantly."

"Have you never seen a genuine artist regard his shapeless block of marble or his blank canvas most lovingly?" asked the baron, gayly. "With the eyes of the spirit he sees the beauty that is to be, where we poor children of clay see only raw material. But this does not apply to Hulda, who impressed me favourably the first time I saw her. I cannot approve of your mother's delivering over so lovely a creature to the charge of that whimsical, irritable Ma'amselle Ulrika."

Miss Kenney, who could see no wrong in any arrangement made by the countess, began to defend Ulrika; but Clarissa, who was in the gayest of humours, painted Ma'amselle's character to her bridegroom in the blackest colours, and finally declared that it was impossible that Hulda should stay with her. Conscious that all around her were ready to indulge her every whim, she turned to her former governess, and, in a pretty tone of entreaty, said, "Let her come here to you; she can get lunch ready for us every day, sing us Lithuanian songs, and become used to us generally; indeed, I think the plan of attaching her to our household admirable,—it will be so charming to take away to my new home some one from my old one."

In spite of her wonted amiability, Miss Kenney did not immediately agree to her favourite's request; she pleaded limited space in her apartments, saying that there really was no space in her dressing-room where Hulda's bed could be placed. But Clarissa was her mother's own child, in that she could not understand opposition to her wishes; she laughingly invited the prince into the "Temple of Vesta," as she called Miss Kenney's modest boudoir. There her lover began to pace off the distance from wall to wall, gayly singing, with an excellent voice and method, the opening bars of the first duet in "Figaro"—"Ten, twenty, thirty; yes, 'twill do." Clarissa instantly took up the part of Susanna, and the pair, together, moved the furniture and rearranged the little room, in spite of Miss Kenney's gentle but only half-sincere remonstrances. The more she reproached, the more they laughed, the gayer grew their humour, until Clarissa finished by throwing her arms around her "darling old Kenney" and assuring her that no one would enjoy the new arrangement of the rooms more than their occupant; after which the young people departed to dress for dinner.

CHAPTER XII.

THE countess was very well pleased that Clarissa had inaugurated an arrangement that she, too, had contemplated with regard to Hulda, and good Miss Kenney was not the person to offer serious opposition to any desire of her two countesses. It is true she suggested several mild objections to the new plan; but these were quickly overruled, and Clarissa's zeal for the new favourite, who had made for her so pleasant a day, was content with nothing less than an order dispatched on the same evening to Ma'amselle Ulrika to have Hulda's modest belongings removed to Miss Kenney's apartments.

But Ma'amselle Ulrika took her own view of the matter. Was it for this that she had overcome her objections to a new inmate of her household and received Hulda beneath her roof? Besides, in the last few weeks she had, as it were, got "used to the girl;" in short, she really liked her, after her fashion. Therefore she regarded it as an infringement of her rights, an offence that could not be condoned, when she was told to yield all title to her new charge and send her directly to Miss Kenney. Accordingly, she presented herself before the countess, to declare that this was quite impossible. The pastor had intrusted his daughter to her care, to learn the various branches of housekeeping, and to be an assistance to her now when she so sorely needed help, with the castle so full of guests as it was. And she could not answer it to her conscience to allow Hulda to leave her without consulting the pastor, any more than she could give away articles in the castle in her keeping, of which she always kept a strict inventory. But she would drive to the parsonage that very evening, and, if the pastor saw fit, Hulda should go to the Englishwoman as soon as she chose; although, in her humble opinion, it was much better for a girl who had not a penny to bless herself with to stay with her own country-people and be well instructed in household matters, than to waste her time learning fine manners, and a foreign tongue that no one thereabouts understood, with a person who was to stay only a limited time at the castle.

The countess quietly waited until she had said everything that she had to say and was quite out of breath, and then, without any irritation, remarked, coldly, "I had expected nothing less of you, and fully appreciate your conscientiousness. There is no cause for alarm, however; I will speak with the pastor myself. If your duties are too heavy for you, you can retire as soon as some one else is found to take your place. It is still undecided whether Miss Kenney will not remain here longer than I shall; therefore dismiss all anxiety with regard to the girl, and see that she goes, as I have ordered, to Miss Kenney, to whom I have given my directions concerning her." She added a few gentle words in acknowledgment of Ulrika's faithful service, to which the astounded Ma'amselle felt constrained to reply gratefully; though the hint that her place could be supplied, and the prospect of Miss Kenney's long stay in the castle, fairly enraged her. And whose fault was it but Hulda's that my lady countess had shown her the door, as it were, just put her aside as if she and she alone had not kept everything in order for so long, year out and year in?

With tightly-compressed lips, and avoiding an encounter with any of the servants, she reached her own dwelling, and, throwing herself into a chair, began to cry aloud and bitterly.

Hulda and the bailiff hastened to her to know what was the matter. The bailiff was well aware that no emotion save anger could wring tears from her eyes; but it was long before she could be prevailed upon to tell what had vexed her.

She roughly pushed Hulda away when the girl came up to her, declaring that she was her mother's own child. She maintained that never in her whole life had she known anything but deceit and treachery from Lithuanian blood, and she bitterly reproached her brother for prevailing upon her to do the countess's pleasure and receive beneath her honest roof that treacherous, hypocritical Simonena and this frivolous, ungrateful girl. All her brother's soothing speeches and Hulda's silent distress were of no avail to console her. At last the bailiff sent Hulda away, and then, as if some spell had been broken, Ulrika crossed her arms before her upon the table, and laying her head upon them as if to shut out forever from her sight a world so unworthy of a glance, repeated angrily from time to time, "To tell me that some one could be found to take my place! It will be my death-blow!"

The brother had never before seen her thus. No reasoning had any effect upon her, and the worst of the matter was that all the wrath the countess had provoked was poured out upon the poor pastor and his family. She declared by all that was sacred that never again would she set foot inside the church, even although her refusal to do so put in peril her immortal soul, and that neither the pastor nor Simonena nor their daughter should ever cross her threshold again. Then, as her active habits made her present state of angry idleness irksome in the extreme to her, she suddenly started up, saying that since Hulda was to go she should go immediately,—yes, this very evening, she and all belonging to her should be sent to the Englishwoman's, where the girl thought everything was so much better and pleasanter.

In vain did the bailiff and Hulda remind her that it was not the desire of the latter, but the will of the countess, that the change should be made. It did no good for her brother to warn her that by sending the girl to Miss Kenney before she was expected she might embroil herself still further with the countess. Nothing availed to bring her to reason. She went to Hulda's room and commanded the trembling girl instantly to pack up everything belonging to her, and there was nothing for the poor child to do but, after a hasty consultation with the bailiff, to tell Miss Kenney the true state of affairs and beg her to grant her for this night also the shelter that was to be hers in future.

It was with an anxious heart that Hulda left the bailiff's. This was the first time in her life that she had been treated with harsh injustice, and the first bitter experience is hard to bear. The short distance that she had to walk seemed interminable, so long that she asked herself whether it would not be better to turn in the other direction and go back to her own home, where she was sure that eager affection and the truest welcome were to be had without the asking. Was this life in the castle? Was this the world she had been so desirous to enter? Now she understood what her father meant when he told her that there was need of a true heart and humble mind in the new world she was about to see. She could hardly walk, so faltering were her steps. It was terrible to be thus thrust out-of-doors; in spite of her air of girlish dignity she was still but a child, and she sat down and cried as if her heart would break. She pitied herself so, it seemed to her that she was pursued by an evil destiny, and with a sigh she suddenly exclaimed, "Ah, he knew how it would be! He told me if it was more than I could bear to let him know and he would help me."

Scarcely had her thoughts taken this direction when she felt cheered and encouraged, ready, as she said to herself, to endure everything in the lot that Heaven had assigned her. She had no conception of the fact that she had suddenly transformed her own personality into a heroine of romance, whom she was quite ready to admire, and no idea of the motive power newborn within her beginning to control her actions.

When she knocked at Miss Kenney's door,—when Miss Kenney, good soul, who could not endure the sight of tears in any eyes, noticed that her eyes were red, and asked her what had happened and why she had come to her at so late an hour, the idea of herself as a lonely outcast grew more vivid than ever in Hulda's mind, and, throwing herself into the old lady's arms, she hid her lovely face upon her bosom and sobbed forth an entreaty for shelter and protection with as much fervour as if there had not been a loving, paternal home always open to her near at hand.

Miss Kenney, too, seemed quite to forget the parsonage. The girl's looks and entreaty went to her heart. She desired nothing better than to lose herself in loving care of some one else. All her weak opposition to the countess's plan, her fear of annoyance, vanished on the instant; she folded Hulda fondly in her arms and called her her child, her daughter, and the girl, as she pressed her lips to the delicate, withered hand and looked up at the kindly smile beaming in the old lady's eyes, thought that she had never before felt such loving trust in any one, not even in her own mother.

Thus unexpectedly the countess's plan was carried out in a few hours. The gay humour of the lovers, and Ma'amselle Ulrika's jealous rage, had brought Miss Kenney and Hulda together, while the fact that the old governess, long used to dependence upon the will of others, had at the last moment received the girl of her own free choice, rendered her charge doubly dear.

CHAPTER XIII.

A GOOD star must have presided over Hulda's installation in Miss Kenney's rooms, for it was followed by a series of gay, happy days, each pleasanter than the preceding. As the countess and the betrothed pair each had a different plan for the girl's future, and as Miss Kenney regarded her as her peculiar charge, all took special interest in her. Every one was ready to praise her and bring her forward, and as her cleverness and sweet temper made her a desirable companion for the ladies, while her beauty was much admired by the gentlemen, her services were in constant requisition.

To-day she would be sent for to the castle, that she might arrange the young countess's hair as she wore her own, in wreaths of braids about her head, after the Lithuanian fashion; to-morrow she must teach Clarissa the art of embroidering mottoes and initials upon knots of ribbon, used as love-tokens in Lithuania; and as, since that first morning of the prince's visit, the lovers had adhered to the custom of lunching with Miss Kenney, Hulda grew thoroughly accustomed to the noble society at the castle, and they, on their part, admitted her to an unusual degree of intimacy and friendship.

Thus several weeks passed, and wrought a great change in Hulda. During her stay at the bailiff's she had gone to church regularly every Sunday, and her mother had always accompanied her for the greater part of the way upon her return to her new home, so that she had still kept up an intimate intercourse with her parents; but now this was no longer so. The prince was as little addicted to church-going as were many others of the guests, and as there was no hunting on Sundays, various means of passing the time were devised; and in preparations for these amusements, Hulda was often obliged to omit altogether going to church or to the village. Dancing was out of the question, as the family were in mourning, and resort was had to dramatic readings and representations, in which the girl's assistance was most valuable; and no one of the castle family, accustomed as they all were to be obeyed by those around them, hesitated to make any demand upon the time of those who were considered in their employment.

When, after some weeks of absence, she occasionally visited her home, she seemed like a stranger to her parents. Her dress, which had been plain almost to poverty, had greatly changed its character since Clarissa's lavish generosity to her favorite had so enlarged and beautified her wardrobe. She wore her dress with a new grace; and as she was quick to observe and imitate, she gradually adopted the manner, and even the mode of speech, of her new associates. Her views of life, her opinions, were of course changed; and, although she altered not one whit in her love and submissive reverence for her parents, her mother sadly reflected that her misgivings had not been causeless. And the pastor acknowledged to himself that the effect of intercourse with the castle family had been different upon his daughter from that produced in like circumstances upon himself. For his self-consciousness had always kept present in his mind a sense of dependence. He had never been able to forget the world-wide difference between his own social position and that of his patron. But this was not the case with Hulda. She had no special dignity to maintain, no position to vindicate, that could cause her to be self-occupied. She innocently accepted all the delight that the friendliness of those around her caused her to feel; she knew that the young men who were the countess's guests admired and sought her for the sake of her beauty; and as the especial protection that Clarissa extended to her precluded all thought of any impertinent advances on their part, it was quite natural that her mind and heart should be refreshed and enlarged by what had served only to cramp her father's powers.

Her evident satisfaction, the cheerful gayety that won her so many friends in the castle, disquieted her parents. Hulda seemed entirely to forget that the countess and her family would not always remain there, and that the delights of her present life would soon come to an end. Even the ease with which she endured Ma'amselle Ulrika's ill will, now that she was no longer in daily intercourse with her, distressed her parents, who were obliged to feel the weight of Ma'amselle's displeasure. Still, they were too entirely accustomed to submission to the will of the countess to venture to recall their daughter to themselves. They had to remain content with constantly exhorting her not to forget her father's straitened circumstances and her own humble prospects. But what effect could such exhortations have upon the girl, filled as she was with an exulting sense of happiness and freedom, save to create in her a distaste for her home, and stronger attachment to the castle and its inmates?

For if she sought the parsonage full of love and pleasure, she was sure to leave it dispirited and anxious. If she had not been able to go to church on Sunday, the thought that her parents might be displeased, and think she was to blame, pursued her through the week; and since she could not endure the idea of their displeasure, she would sometimes, when she was not specially needed at the castle, ask and obtain leave to visit the parsonage upon a weekday.

She was returning one afternoon from one of these visits. Both her parents had accompanied her a part of the way, and before they left her had spoken to her in a tone of warning, almost of reproach, which she felt was undeserved. She had preserved a respectful silence, but she had rebelled against their words in her heart; and yet, when they had turned away, she had looked after the dear receding figures again and again; and, overcome with remorse for even her mute rebellion, she could scarcely refrain from hurrying after them, to throw herself into their arms and entreat their forgiveness. But she had stayed quite late at the parsonage; daylight was beginning to fade, and the last part of her way lay through the most thickly-wooded portion of the castle park, where it soon grew dark. The gray clouds hung low in the quiet air; and late as was the time of year, it was still sultry. Hulda felt oppressed and uneasy.

As she reached the boundary of the park it began to rain. She threw her wrap over her head and hastened her steps. But it grew darker and darker, and she could see no opening in the wood before her. The rain dripped from the boughs of the old hemlocks, while the leaves that had already fallen from the other trees rustled with an uncanny sound beneath her tread. Every moment she feared that some one would come, that something would happen. She glanced timidly around her as she hurried along, but she could see nothing but the gloomy shadows of the coming night, and on she went, not daring to take another look. Suddenly she started aside. Just in her path, as if sprung from the earth at her feet, stood the prince's valet. He had asked for leave to hunt on this afternoon, for he was an excellent shot, and a favourite with the prince, whose foster-brother he was. His master placed great confidence in him, and he occupied the first position among the servants of his household. He had been well educated, his manners were good, and he was so excellent a penman that his master often employed him as his secretary, by which title he was politely addressed by the other servants in his presence, however they might speak of him when he was not by.

Hulda started with terror at sight of this man so near her. He laughed. "What! timid? And yet out alone so late, Mademoiselle Hulda? Where have you been?" It struck her unpleasantly that he did not address her by her last name, as he had been used to do in the castle when sent by the ladies to her with messages. She replied that she had been to the parsonage, and had unfortunately delayed returning until late.

"Not unfortunately; you need have no fear," he said. "You must not spoil great people by too much punctuality, or they come to regard you as a mere machine, wound up to do their bidding regularly, without any will of your own. You will soon learn that when you are really established in our household."

Hulda did not understand what he meant; but his familiar manner annoyed her, and she made no reply, but hurried on, that she might be rid of his society as soon as possible. He was no whit abashed.

"I see," he said, "you do not share my views. Service in a noble family is very different from life in one's own home. So long as one cannot be master, with a perfect right to live up to one's convictions and follow one's inclinations, one must learn how to maintain, as a servant, some scrap, at least, of liberty of action. I, too, was most dutiful and faithful so long as I was only foster-brother and playfellow; but since I have had the honour to be my noble foster-brother's valet I have grown rather lax, I confess. There is no need to be so much better than one's position. I do my duty as a servant and take good care of myself, and because you are in the same position, and seem just as full of innocent confidence as I once was, Ma'amselle Hulda, I am really sorry for you. Upon my honour I mean you nothing but kindness, for, for my own part, I should like exceedingly to have you with us; but you are the child of honest people, and I advise you to consider well before you decide."

Hulda hardly knew what to do. The idea of having any conversation regarding her future with this stranger, a servant, too, alone and in the gathering darkness, was entirely repugnant to her. But then he must have some foundation for his seeming knowledge of the intentions of the castle family concerning her, and she at last decided to tell him that there had been no talk of her leaving her parents or entering any noble household.

"If you know nothing of it, then," the secretary rejoined, "you are the only one in the castle ignorant of the fact that the prince is perfectly enamoured of your beauty, and has encouraged Countess Clarissa to take you into their personal service. Do you really not know that it is for this that you are to learn all that you can with the Englishwoman, that you are so often sent for to the castle to learn all that is necessary to fit you for your future position about the young countess? Whether or not other service may be required of you the future will show. But I know, and you know too, well enough, that ladies' maids or companions—it's all the same thing—pretty girls, in short—who are greatly admired by the husband do not long stand very high in favour with the wife; and if you have no good friend at hand to trust to, Ma'amselle Hulda, your lot will not be very enviable. I tell you this beforehand, and I advise you to believe me."

Every word that he spoke stabbed Hulda like a dagger. All that she could understand of the secretary's malicious hints terrified and outraged her. Such ideas, such thoughts, had never occurred to her, had never been alluded to in her presence. It was therefore impossible for her to reply to him, or even to tell him how insulted she felt. She was silent, and reproached herself for being so. She could find no words in which to express herself; she could not but listen involuntarily to her companion's words, which fell thick and fast upon her, like the rain that steadily increased. All she could do was to hasten forward in the direction of that wing of the castle where were Miss Kenney's apartments. At last, with an indescribable sense of relief, she reached the door of the gardener's house; but just as her foot was upon the threshold and her hand upon the latch, the secretary came close to her side, seized her hand, and said, "I see by your terror that my friendly warning has fallen upon fruitful soil. 'Tis strange at first, and the light is hard to bear, even for the strongest of us, when we have been sitting long in the dark. But consider the matter well, Ma'amselle Hulda, and if you want advice I am ready to give it. Everything can be arranged. If you want to come with us, just tell me. For my part, I should be delighted. It would be easy to find ways and means to make some arrangement, if you come, that would be for the advantage of both of us, if your sentiments for me correspond with mine for you, charming Hulda."

She tried to escape from him; he held her tightly by both hands, and she did not dare to call, for not for worlds would she have been found with him. But when he followed up his words with an attempt to press her hand to his lips, while he passed his arm around her waist, she thrust him away from her, and, with a slight scream, pushed open the door, and hurried into the house.

In the quiet evening, in spite of the falling rain, the gardener's wife heard the low cry and the opening of the door, and came running with a candle in her hand to see what was the matter. In answer to her inquiries, Hulda said she had been running to get out of the rain, and had slipped and almost fallen at the threshold of the door. The good woman was shocked to see how pale she was when she took off her wrap, and would have had her take off her wet clothes then and there and have them dried, but Hulda rejected her kindly proffers. She was ashamed, and imagined that all who looked in her face could see that she had told an untruth, and what had happened to her. She wanted nothing but to find herself once more in the quiet parsonage, where, in solitude and prayer, she might cleanse her soul from the memory of the last half-hour.

CHAPTER XIV.

MISS KENNEY was not yet in her apartments. It was her custom, when the countess was not engaged, to go to the castle at dusk, and to spend the evening there, if her presence was desired by the ladies. The gardener's wife, however, had kindled a fire in the sitting-room, on account of the dampness that was apt to invade the rooms on the ground-floor, and, after placing lights on the table, she left Hulda to herself. As soon as she had taken off her wet clothes and knew herself alone, she was overcome by a sensation of terror. She took up a candle and examined both the little rooms. She looked into the closets and, although she reproached herself for childishness, behind the window-curtains. She closed the back window-shutters, and would gladly have done the same with those looking towards the castle, if it had not been the custom to leave them open until Miss Kenney's return. All sense of comfort, and even of security, had deserted her,—she was a prey to an agitation that left her no repose.

To compose her mind, she took up a piece of embroidery that Miss Kenney had designed as a wedding-present for Clarissa. Hulda had assisted her with it before, but now she could not sew: she could neither count the stitches nor make a correct choice of colours; there was but one thought in her mind: to whom should she go to declare that she could no longer remain in the castle? She longed to tell her parents frankly all that had occurred; but they had warned her so repeatedly, and her mother especially had so often represented to her that she, a girl of good family, and a pastor's daughter, could be subjected to no insult that she did not invite by her own conduct, that, blameless though she felt herself to be, she feared their reproaches. To turn to the young countess and her mother in her trouble, and beg them to allow her to go back to her parents, seemed to her quite as impracticable, for the content and enjoyment of life which she had manifested hitherto would make such a request seem unworthy of attention. And although Baron Emanuel had offered her his protection, in this case she could not ask it; for to tell him of what had been said to her was simply impossible. There was no one left to go to but Miss Kenney, and this day of all others it seemed as if Miss Kenney would never come. Poor Hulda's distress and impatience waxed greater with every slow-moving quarter of an hour.

She walked several times to the window and looked out, but the evening was very dark, and the spark of light in the little hand-lantern that Miss Kenney used to light her way from the castle was nowhere to be seen. Something must be done to while away the weary time. Suddenly she remembered that her father had given her the translations of a couple of Lithuanian songs to copy for the baron, and since they must be done before she left the castle, she determined to finish them now. She seated herself at her task, but everything turned to melancholy this evening; these songs that she had heard her mother sing times without number, and that she herself had often sung with a light heart, seemed utterly changed. The verse,

"Gaily in my own dear home
  I sprang to life a flow'ret fair;
But now in stranger lands I roam,
  A withered leaf tossed on the air,"

had fallen upon her ear from childhood like some old cradle-song, without much meaning; now, when she tried to write it down, it touched her very heart. Before she could prevent it, a couple of tears fell upon the paper, effacing the last word she had written; and as the young delight to foster grief, since it possesses for them the charm of novelty, she painted to herself, in the most vivid colours, the contrast between the Hulda of yesterday and the Hulda of to-day, until, as she pictured her unhappiness when she should have left these pretty little rooms, and all those about her who had treated her with such kindness, her misery again overcame her and her tears flowed afresh.

Just then she heard footsteps upon the path outside. She arose, quickly dried her eyes, and opened the door to admit her protectress. But instead of her whom she expected, Baron Emanuel stood before her, and, throwing aside the cloak he had used to shield him from the rain, said, "Shut the door, that Miss Kenney may not feel the draught. I am coming in for a minute."

Hulda, greatly surprised at his unexpected appearance, since he had never before been there in the evening, rejoined that Miss Kenney had not yet returned from the castle.

"Am I too early, then?" asked the baron, taking out his watch as he entered. "She told me she would be here at seven o'clock to look through some letters and papers with me that belonged to my mother, in which frequent allusion is made to her children's education."

He sat down in an arm-chair beside the table; and as the light fell upon Hulda's face, he noticed the traces of tears upon it and the dejection that was expressed in her features. She saw she was observed, and turned away from him. But that did no good.

"Is anything the matter?" he asked. She replied in the negative, but that did not content him. "I have not seen you," he said, "for some time; you were not at the castle yesterday, nor have you been there to-day."

"Miss Kenney was not well yesterday," she replied.

"And to-day?" he asked.

"To-day I have been at my father's," was her answer.

He inquired after her father's health, and she answered his questions, but her heart was so heavy that the unwonted brevity and languor of her replies still further struck the baron. He leaned forward on the table towards her, and asked, looking her full in the face with his kindly eyes, "What has been done to annoy you? Has Ma'amselle Ulrika vexed you? Something has happened, I know, or else what have you done with your merry voice and laughing eyes?"

She hesitated, seeming to wish to tell him something, and then, suppressing it with an effort, sat down at the table, and leaned her head upon her hand.

Emanuel had never seen her thus, and did not know what it meant. Afraid to question her further, since what he had said had seemed only to deepen her melancholy, he arose from his chair, and, bending over her, looked down at the paper upon which she was writing, saying, in order to help her to compose herself, "Oh, you were busy in my service. I am very grateful to you." He took up the sheet of paper, and read the verse aloud.

"How simple and pretty it is in the adoption of the similes nearest at hand!" he remarked, again repeating the verse. "If the melody equals the words, it is a very model of a popular song. Was your father kind enough to write down the air for me, too?"

She shook her head, saying, however, that she knew the air, and that it was very soft and plaintive. He asked if he might hear it, and brought her her guitar from the corner where it hung.

It seemed hard to her to be asked to sing the very song that had already moved her so deeply; but the habit of obedience prevented any hesitation in complying with the baron's request, and, after a few chords by way of prelude, she sang the little song through. But the agitation which she had endeavoured to suppress now broke forth in the true expression of the words and music. Her voice trembled; all her grief —and the first grief of a young heart is always deeper and more passionate than its cause warrants—found utterance in the simple melody. Emanuel, quite carried away by the music and her singing, would have expressed his admiration of her her thoroughly artistic rendering of the air, but she suddenly arose, and, laying down her guitar, made as if she would leave the room.

He too arose, to bar her going. He did not understand her

behaviour, and, in spite of his knowledge of the world, he was not so much at his ease as usual. In the girl's entire freedom from affectation, in her maidenly reserve, there had always seemed hidden a passionate fervour which if it once broke forth would carry all before it. She had always seemed to him the embodied spirit of the poetry of her country. Her whole nature harmonized wonderfully, he thought, with the rare quality of her beauty; and all youthful beauty was doubly dear to him since he had so painfully lost his own. He could not suppress the sympathy he had felt for Hulda ever since the countess had brought her hither from the parsonage, and, involuntarily giving utterance to his thoughts, he said, "This is no place for you."

That was more than she could bear. "No, no!" she cried, and, seating herself, she hid her face in her hands. "I must go, I must go back to my father and mother! To-morrow, to-morrow! And you, oh, you will be kind and tell the countess?" She could say no more.

"What shall I tell my sister?"

"That I must go home," she said, almost inaudibly.

He shook his head doubtfully. "If you would only confide in me," he said, after a pause; adding, "How can I help you when I do not even know what troubles you?" He had taken her hand in one of his, and with the other he gently lifted up her bowed head. As she gazed up at him from out her beautiful, melancholy, child-like eyes, a sudden rush of tenderness, such as he had never known before, overcame him, and, bending over her, he kissed her brow.

At this moment Miss Kenney entered. "I have kept you waiting, baron, but it was not my fault." Then, noticing Hulda's agitation and Emanuel's emotion, she paused. She was too wise to ask any question the answer to which she would rather delay for the present, and Emanuel gave her no chance to say more.

"How glad I am you are come at last!" he cried, with a frank emphasis that dispelled her anxiety. "I have been impatient for your return. Something must have happened to grieve this poor child, and I could not make up my mind to leave her alone. You will understand far better than I how to discover the wound and apply the remedy."

He smiled, and gave his hand to his old friend, then said

a few kind words to Hulda, and added, as he left the room, "I will come to-morrow about my mother's letters, and then, my dear Kenney, you will tell me all about this matter, and whether I can be of any assistance."

CHAPTER XV.

THE countess had not been well for a few days, and had kept her room in the forenoon. Then no one was admitted but her old governess, unless upon special business.

On the morrow after Hulda's adventure, Miss Kenney appeared earlier than usual in her patroness's presence, and, with all due regard for the countess's peculiarities of disposition, recounted to her all that had occurred on the previous evening.

The countess listened, without either by word or by sign expressing any displeasure; but, before Miss Kenney had time to ask her opinion as to granting Hulda's request to return to her parents, she cried, "Then I was not deceived in that man. There is something sly in his look, something equivocal in his manner. I disliked him from the beginning. He must be got rid of. Not that I believe one word of his slander about his master," she added, hastily. "The prince sincerely loves Clarissa, and is a man of honour. He knows well what is due to himself and his position. I do not doubt him for an instant. But even an intimate friend always present in the house is a doubtful ingredient in the happiness of a young couple; and such a creature, half friend and half servant, is quite detestable. Besides, this fellow is too much of a Scapin for the peace of any household. He must go, and forever, as soon as possible."

Miss Kenney agreed with her. "And," said she, "the position that the young people intend to assign Hulda in her future home is matter for grave consideration, I think."

The countess looked up in surprise. "You did not think that I really meant to have her go with Clarissa?" she said.

"Why, both your grace and Clarissa have spoken to me of such an arrangement," the governess rejoined.

"Clarissa always talked very seriously of her plans even when she was a child, and very soon grew tired of them if no one opposed her," replied the mother. "You know that as well as I do. And the prince? He has at present but one desire—to call Clarissa wife. And for this reason he is bent upon gratifying every whim of hers. I certainly shall not quarrel with him for that. But I have no idea of allowing Hulda to go with them. She will remain under your charge, and she must not leave the castle at present; for I will not have the question asked, why, when we seemed pleased to have her, we so soon sent her away."

The countess's decision of character was always the object of her old governess's proud admiration, and she never dreamed of opposing her. Still, she seemed to have something on her mind of which she wished and yet hesitated to speak.

The countess had risen, and seated herself at her writing-desk. As her old friend did not withdraw, she turned to her again. "Do you want anything, dear?" she asked, "or what are you waiting for?"

"I am waiting," Miss Kenney answered, "because I cannot make up my mind whether it is best to speak or be silent."

The countess's clear eyes looked at her searchingly. "I thought," said she, "that you and I had known each other long enough to make any such doubt impossible. If it is anything I ought to know, tell me the worst at once. If it is anything that you or some one else can arrange without my assistance, leave me out of the matter entirely."

"It is only a suspicion of my own, which I will make known to you lest you should hereafter hold me responsible," said Miss Kenney. And then she added, in a voice even softer than usual, "I think Baron Emanuel feels more than a common interest in Hulda."

A smile flitted across the countess's grave features. "I too have noticed," she said, "that my brother treats her very kindly, and that he frequently watches her with apparent pleasure; and certainly it is well that it is so. With his views and the resolution he has unfortunately formed as to his future life, not to mention his cold reception of all feminine advances, let us rejoice that his fancy can be touched, and perhaps his heart warmed. We shall not stay here long." With these words she as it were dismissed her old friend; but before the door was closed behind her she recalled her.

"I trust the girl is not given to idle fancies," she said, gravely. "Remind her that there is no possibility of her remaining with us, whatever Clarissa may have hinted to the contrary." She paused a moment, and then added, "I did think that perhaps we might retain her in our household, but she is far too beautiful. All the men notice her. They pay her too much attention now; and Clarissa's affection for her would only make matters worse. She had better stay with her parents. So long as they live, her place is with them, if no suitable husband can be found for her. For the present, keep her with you. It would never do to send her away suddenly. She must learn to be more discreet—she and her parents also. Give her and them to understand this." Then, as if struck by a sudden idea, she asked, "Did you not tell me my brother was coming to you to see some letters of our mother's, and to hear what had happened to the girl?"

Miss Kenney assented. "Well, then," said the countess, "send him the letters, and sit down and write him just what you told me. But don't let him suspect that I know anything of the matter. He is the prince's friend; he presented him to us first, and Severin has a real respect and affection for Emanuel. Point out to my brother the mischief such a servant as Michael may do in a household. Tell him in your own name everything I have said to you upon the subject. You can do it all the more easily since Hulda is under your care and you are responsible to her parents. Add that you have taken him into confidence to spare me annoyance. I am to know nothing of the business. It is best left to the two gentlemen for settlement."

It was not the first time that the faithful old governess had been intrusted with a like secret commission, and she had a great degree of satisfaction in fulfilling all such, since to adjust, smooth, and arrange matters, without any violent collision of tempers or temperaments, was the work in which her soul delighted. Then, too, although the two countesses and their interests were the sun of her horizon, she was not without her own modest share of self-appreciation, and had not forgotten her own youth and the experiences of her first years of dependence. She had grown fond of Hulda. To keep her by her side, to caress and protect, was what she desired; and she was not at all doubtful, when she sat down to write, as to the tone she should take with Baron Emanuel.

CHAPTER XVI.

THE gentlemen had just finished a game of billiards, and were about to betake themselves to their rooms for awhile in the gathering twilight, when a letter was brought to Emanuel. The prince remarked that it must contain something special, since it was not post-day; but Emanuel, who recognized the handwriting of the address, quietly put it in his pocket. Then they ascended the staircase together, and separated in the corridor above.

Upon reaching his rooms, Emanuel opened the thick envelope, and scarcely had he cast his eye upon the first page of the enclosure and seen Hulda's name there, when he threw aside his mother's letters, and eagerly read through Miss Kenney's from beginning to end.

"That was the matter, then!" he cried, with an angry stamp of his foot. "This must be mended immediately." And, without waiting an instant, he hastily crossed the little antechamber that separated his room from the prince's, knocked at the door of the latter, and announced himself.

It was dark in the room, but candles were lighted in the adjoining bedroom, where the valet was engaged in some trifling service. When the prince heard the baron's voice, he arose to receive him, telling Michael to bring the candles. As it was the custom at the castle not to intrude upon its inmates when they were in their private apartments, Emanuel excused his visit. "But a most vexatious occurrence," he said, "has compelled my coming to you this afternoon."

Michael heard these words as he was placing the candles upon the table. He also saw the letter in the baron's hand; and some guilty misgiving may have arisen within him, for he asked whether the prince needed his further services, or if he might retire. The baron forestalled the master's reply. "Let him wait," he said. "We may have need of him."

"Wait, then," said the prince, rather surprised by Emanuel's words. Michael retired to the adjoining room; the prince begged his guest to be seated, and the baron, who noticed his friend's surprise, explained that it was on this man's account that he had come to him.

"I am in a very painful position with regard to you," said he. "I am forced to ask questions that do not become me, and of the answers to which I am perfectly sure. And yet I must hear those answers from your own lips."

This seemed still more mysterious to the prince. He grew grave, as every man will do who finds another, uninvited, on the eve of an inquiry into his personal affairs; but he looked frankly and firmly into the face of the uncle of his bride. "I am ready," said he, "to give you any satisfaction you can ask."

"Well, then, Severin, have you perfect confidence in your valet?"

"The question is comprehensive, and not to be answered by a plain 'yes' or 'no.' I have entire confidence in his honesty. For the rest—he is a servant. I use him with a due regard to his faults and failings. He likes to take airs upon himself, and I am forced to use the curb; but he is useful. But what can all this matter to you? I really cannot understand you."

"Another question. Has your valet ever heard mention made of Clarissa's plan of carrying away our pastor's daughter as one of your household?"

"Very possibly he has heard us speak of it," the prince replied, with difficulty restraining his impatience.

"And is it possible that you may have expressed in his presence your admiration for Hulda's beauty? Have you ever made use of an expression which could lead him to believe"—the words were sharply emphasized—"that you had a personal interest in the fulfilment of Clarissa's project?"

The prince started to his feet. "That question touches my honour!" he cried. Then, controlling himself by an effort, he added, "And you, Clarissa's uncle, you, my friend, can ask me such a question, knowing how I love her and her only?"

Emanuel grasped his hand. "Forgive me, Severin," he

said. "I told you expressly that I must hear the answer from your lips, although I knew perfectly beforehand what that answer would be. I was forced to put the question to you before I could show you this letter that I have just received from our good Kenney. Read it now, I pray you, and then do as you think best." They exchanged a few more explanatory words, and then Emanuel left the room, leaving the letter with his friend.

The prince stepped to the table and began to read. As he did so his colour came and went angrily, and when he had finished, he threw the sheet upon the ground and strode towards the door of the adjoining room. But he paused before he reached it; his dignity would not suffer his servant to know that it had been in his power thus to irritate and wound his master. He paced the room to and fro, perfectly clear in his mind as to what was to be done, but deciding how it should be done; and it was not long before he called his servant by name, in a voice from which all trace of irritation had vanished.

One glance at his master's countenance sufficed to tell Michael that he was called to judgment. He paused on the threshold to ask what were his highness's orders.

"Come here and read that letter!" was the stern command.

Michael would have taken it to a side-table; but such was not his master's pleasure. "Come here, and read aloud and distinctly," he ordered.

The blood left Michael's cheeks. He saw from a glance at the letter the nature of its contents, and he knew his master. It was easy to encounter his sudden bursts of irritation, but from this cold resolve there was no appeal. He knew that he must obey. Still, although his voice faltered as he felt the prince's cold glance resting upon him as he read, he did not give up all for lost. But when he reached that part of the letter that told of his allusion to his master's secret and unworthy designs upon Hulda, he ceased, and the hand that held the sheet of paper fell at his side.

"Go on! go on!" cried the prince, with a smile that boded ill to the culprit. "You can surely repeat to me what you were so ready to tell the girl yesterday."

"Your highness, it was only a jest of mine with the girl," the man stammered.

"Do you dare, you scoundrel, to jest with your master's

honour?" cried the prince. "You dare to coin lies for your miserable amusement? You dare to presume even to approach a girl who is under the protection of——"

A ray of intelligence shot across the servant's face. One bold stroke might yet set all to rights for him, and interrupting the prince, he exclaimed, "Oh, I did not know that the Herr Baron had appropriated the girl."

Before the words were well out of his mouth his master's muscular hand had forced him to his knees, while with the other he seized a riding-whip from the table, and the lash went stinging across Michael's face. Then, spurning him as he would have spurned a dog, the prince pointed to the door, saying, "Begone! and never show your face in my presence again. Johann will pay you what is due you. You leave the castle within the hour."

The prince turned away and entered his bedroom. Michael sprang from the ground, and made as if he would have followed him, then paused. The look that he cast after his master was full of hatred; but he controlled himself, stood erect before the mirror, and, passing his fingers through his curling black hair, "Free at last!" he murmured. "Dismissed, to be sure, after the brutal fashion that such men love. One day this distinguished foster-brother of mine, so ready with his whip, shall wonder indeed that I ever condescended to serve him. And there is one other who shall remember me and this hour."

CHAPTER XVII.

THE supper-table was already spread at the bailiff's when Michael entered. It was a habit of his when released from service to spend an hour or two in Ma'amselle Ulrika's comfortable room, although his visits were by no means desired by the bailiff. It was the bailiff's sister who was always ready with her welcome to one who answered all her ideas of what a "proper man" should be. "He knew how to talk and how to be silent," said she; "he had eyes in his head, and was ready to use them in the service of a friend."

But on this evening he declined her hospitable offers, replying to her invitation to sit down and rest, that he had come only for a moment to request her brother to place a conveyance of some kind at his disposal, as the prince, his master, desired him to fulfil a commission for him in the nearest post-town. The bailiff grumbled at the lateness of the hour, to which Michael replied, with a shrug, "You know they're all alike, bailiff. What difference can the lateness of the hour make to his highness, if the gratification of his whim is at stake?"

When the bailiff left the room to give his orders, Ma'amselle Ulrika again urgently repeated her invitation to her guest to take at least a glass of wine before his departure, inquiring at the same time about the nature of his errand and the time of his return.

Michael, glancing around the room, as if he did not wish to be overheard, and carefully wiping his moustache after emptying the glass she handed to him, replied, mysteriously, "I have always regarded you as my friend, Ma'amselle Ulrika, and I have the greatest respect for you as a woman who knows the world and what it is worth. I don't mind telling you that it is all over between the prince and myself."

"Impossible, Herr Secretary!" cried Ulrika. "What can you mean?"

"And, in fact," he continued, without heeding her surprise, "I am very glad of it. I have long been tired of playing the servant. I was born for something better, but habit is second nature, and I might have dragged on awhile longer, for he is my foster-brother; but really he has gone too far. I cannot stand everything."

He seemed to wish to say no more; but Ulrika had no idea of allowing him to depart without satisfying her curiosity, and was so emphatic in declaring that her secrecy could be relied on, that at last Michael determined, as he said, to confide in her.

"You were young yourself once, Ma'amselle," said he, "and there's no denying that the girl is pretty, and, one would suppose from her looks, innocence itself. So you will not wonder when you hear that I thought Hulda would make just the wife for me."

"Not Hulda?" Ma'amselle interrupted him. "Why, she is the merest child, and not worth ——"

"Child or not," Michael broke in in his turn, for he wanted

to come to the end of the matter before the bailiff's return,—"child or not, she is a confounded pretty girl. And since I wanted to change my condition, and really cared for her, and saw that there were others whose intentions with regard to her were not so honest as mine——"

"Others?" cried Ma'amselle, and her eyes sparkled. "What others? Tell me, Herr Secretary." And in her eagerness she laid her lean hand upon his arm. "Who are the others? I promise you their names shall never pass my lips."

"Nor mine either," was the reply; "for I shall have left his service before an hour is past. And he is not the only one. But I wish," he suddenly interrupted himself, "that the wagon would come. I fairly long to be where there is no danger of ever seeing her again." And he walked to the window.

Ma'amselle's malicious curiosity was fully aroused. "You owe it to me, Herr Secretary," said she, "as Hulda's guardian here, to tell me all that has occurred between you. I trust you more than I would the girl herself, for she is as hypocritical as her mother used to be."

Michael pretended to be annoyed by Ulrika's urgency. "What can I tell you?" he said. "I was walking in the park at dusk yesterday evening, when I came upon the girl as she was returning from her parents'. I was surprised to see her abroad so late, and offered to escort her to the castle; she said neither yes nor no to me. And as we walked through the park together, I—well, you know how it is, Ma'amselle Ulrika, when a man's heart is full—I told her how I felt, and then I warned her about—but there is no need to say whom."

"Well!" cried Ulrika, breathless with eagerness. "And what did she say?"

"Say? Why, she behaved as if I had insulted her. She fairly ran home, and I was fool enough to think it maidenly modesty. I soon found out what it all meant. She was not long alone when she did get home, and a pretty return she made me for my affection and well-meant warning. The hypocrite!"

His face grew so dark and angry that Ma'amselle Ulrika was delighted. This was the most interesting tale she had ever listened to. All that she understood was so touching, and what was hinted at seemed still more interesting.

"Poor fellow, poor fellow, you must have suffered indeed!" she said; "but tell me who was with her. I must know from you who it was, for I have long noticed his sly admiration for her, and of course, if she told him how you felt towards her, it is no wonder he should want you out of the way."

Michael, who had been gazing out into the night, now turned round, and asked, as if he did not understand her, whom she alluded to and what she meant.

His surprise was so well feigned that it embarrassed her. "I thought," she stammered, "that his highness——"

"What in the world put his highness into your head?" he cried, in the same tone of amazement. "Who told you that the prince had anything to do with it? I'm sure I never hinted at such a thing, nor even mentioned his name, except perhaps to say that he had had something of a quarrel with the baron this afternoon; after which, as I happened to overhear it, and could not help coming forward to declare that, however humble my station, I was a man, and a man of honour——"

Ulrika, utterly bewildered, and yet struck with a new idea, could not help interposing, "Then it was the baron? Did the baron tell her?"

But this seemed too much for Michael. He broke away from her, and, with a bitter laugh, said, "One of us must be dreaming. Do you ask if the baron told Hulda of my love for her? Hardly; I told her myself. But it is all the same, since she has other plans in her head and does not want to be an honest man's wife. 'Tis all for the best. She would have been only a drag upon me in the future life I propose for myself. I see clearly that Heaven arranges matters for us better than we could if left to ourselves."

Then, going into the bailiff's private room, he employed himself in various inquiries as to the route he was about to follow to the capital, until the conveyance ordered for him drove up to the door. After seeing that his luggage was all carefully disposed within it, he again approached Ulrika, and in a tone loud enough to be overheard by her brother, he thanked her for her great kindness to him, adding, "And pray forget what I have just told you. It is best that all should enjoy themselves after their own fashion; and it certainly will be none of my business in the future to meddle or mar in any of the castle affairs."

When the carriage was gone, Ma'amselle Ulrika turned to her brother, and, in a tone of triumph, cried, "Who was right now, pray, about Hulda? Who saw that she was just as false as her mother? Just think of that poor, good fellow! And the young countess to suffer so on the shameless creature's account; and our lady, too!"

Her brother's exclamations and interrogations were unheeded by her in the full flow of her gratified spite. One accusation of Hulda followed fast upon another. Her excited fancy had free play among all that Michael had said or hinted, and she went on weaving a web of calumny around the girl who had innocently incurred her ill will, until her breath fairly failed her, and she wound up with, "It is just incredible! I cannot believe it of the girl!"

"Well, then, don't believe it!" said the bailiff, settling himself comfortably in his arm-chair and lighting his pipe. "Don't believe it. It is the best thing you can do. I don't believe a word of it."

"You don't believe it?" cried his sister, as if he had charged her with falsehood.

"Not one word do I believe of what that scoundrel has to say," replied her brother. "And you, at your years, ought to know better than to swallow all the lies that come from beneath that waxed moustache of his."

But Ulrika was not to be thus vanquished. She went on, finding confirmation of her worst suspicions in slight incidents that had almost escaped her observation at the time of their occurrence. She exhausted her eloquence in lamentations over the want of morality among men, and the depravity of certain young women. Her brother said nothing more. He leaned back in his chair and gazed placidly at the face of the huge clock that was ticking upon the opposite wall. At last this seeming indifference was more than Ma'amselle could bear.

"You look as if you did not hear a word I say," she cried, in an offended tone.

"Oh, yes, I hear you," replied the bailiff. "Take time." And then rising and planting his burly figure just before her, he pointed to the clock, and said, "You have one quarter of an hour more in which to say and to believe whatever nonsense you choose. But when the men come in to supper, at seven o'clock, if you utter another syllable of all those lies that rogue has told you about that poor thing and our ladies at the castle,—one syllable,—mind what I say,—I shall take the matter in hand. And when I am in earnest you know there's no joking with me."

He turned and went into his office. At the door he turned again: "If I ever hear one word of all this from any other quarter, I shall hold you responsible. To-morrow I will speak further with you. And to-night you do not stir from this house. There shall be no running to the castle to gossip with Ma'amselle Babette and the rest."

And going out, he shut the door behind him with a bang.

Ulrika looked angrily after him. "All alike," she muttered between her teeth. "She has bewitched him, old as he is. She is just like her mother!" But she knew she could do nothing with her brother when anything had roused him from his usual phlegmatic humour. So, after allowing herself the relief of tears, she swallowed her anger as best she might, and seated herself in her corner behind the stove, to wonder what really was the truth concerning Hulda, and to confirm herself in her own evil suspicions.

CHAPTER XVIII.

The world below-stairs at the castle was greatly agitated by the news of Michael's departure. No one knew the cause of his sudden dismissal; but there were wise shakings of heads, and much gossiping of maids and men in corners—some insisting that they had always known that the Herr Secretary's airs would lead to his downfall, and others, that some especial neglect of duty must have irritated beyond endurance so kind a master as the prince.

Of course the matter was scarcely alluded to among the family themselves. The prince cursorily mentioned that he had sent Michael to town; and if his hearers bestowed any thought upon his remark, they probably supposed he had been despatched upon some confidential errand.

The matter was more annoying, however, to the prince than he cared to confess: he regretted that he had not dismissed Michael while Emanuel was present: it would have been a satisfaction to his own feeling of honour; and he could not help, besides, reverting to Michael's last insulting words with regard to the baron, and wondering whether they might not have contained a spice of truth. He remembered now that Emanuel had never cordially approved Clarissa's plan for transferring Hulda to her household, or even of the girl's leaving the parsonage, although he evidently liked her and wished that she should be made happy. And once or twice lately the baron had alluded to the possibility of his passing a winter in his sister's castle; the sea-air, he said, seemed to invigorate him. In addition to these uncomfortable thoughts, Severin was obliged now to discountenance what he had hitherto favoured, Clarissa's pet project for carrying Hulda away with them.

Emanuel was not, for his part, one whit more comfortable. The two men were firm friends, and neither would have suspected the other of baseness or treachery; and yet Emanuel was not sure that in the buoyancy of his youth Severin might not have permitted himself a certain degree of familiarity with Michael, which would have made expressions possible from his lips that the man might have misconstrued and cunningly misinterpreted. The world was not Paradise, and mortals were but mortals still, and he had no right to exact from others the life of rigid self-sacrifice to which he thought himself condemned by his sad destiny and the impossibility of his ever inspiring a disinterested affection.

The prince had immediately informed him of Michael's dismissal, and the two men had exchanged all the friendly phrases due to the occasion, but there was a constraint between them. All was not precisely as it had been; each was conscious of this, and yet was powerless to restore matters to their old footing. The baron was surprised to find that the annoyance caused him by Miss Kenney's letter did not wear off. He disliked the thought that a servant had ventured to find Hulda attractive, that he had spoken to her with such unwarrantable familiarity; he was infinitely annoyed that she should have been the subject of discussion between the prince and himself, and between the prince and his servant; and while Severin reproached himself for not discharging Michael in the baron's presence, the baron regretted that he had not ridden directly to the parsonage and advised the instant recall of the daughter of the house. Why, indeed, had he not opposed with more decision his sister's ever bringing her to the castle? Suddenly he asked himself why all this interested him so deeply; and finding no reply to this question, he cast about in his mind for some one upon whom to lay the blame of all the annoyance he had suffered. He had not far to look: his sister's love of rule was at the foundation of it all; he remembered now how she had resented his warning, on the afternoon when she confided her plans to him.

He was irritated against her, and when, in a by no means placid frame of mind, he presented himself rather late at the tea-table, he took amiss, and showed that he did so, some innocent remark that the countess made upon his tardiness. And although well-bred apologies followed, there still remained a slight estrangement between them that the guests did not fail to observe.

The prince, too, was not in the best of humours, and when his betrothed, desirous of restoring the usual cheerful tone of the party, proposed that Hulda should be sent for to sing with them a quartette they had been practising, he shook his head, and said, in a voice that betokened displeasure, "Is it not possible for you to live through one evening without that girl?" To be sure, he agreed instantly when he saw how surprised Clarissa was by his manner; but it was the first unpleasant evening that had been passed at the castle. The countess, as well as the prince and the baron, privately decided that Hulda could no longer occupy her present position among them; but all entertained their peculiar opinions of the whole affair.

There was one, however, who was determined to do the duty which lay nearest him, and that was the bailiff. The next morning, after his hour in his office was over, he put on his rough great-coat, drew his fur cap over his grizzled curls, and, stout walking-stick in hand, presented his burly figure in Miss Kenney's sitting-room.

The large embroidering-frame stood before the window, and Hulda and her preceptress were both working at it. A cheery fire was burning in the stove; the myrtle and monthly roses in the flower-stand were in full bloom; the little room looked like the abode of peace and comfort. But when Hulda arose to welcome the unwonted guest, he saw that her eyes were red with weeping.

"I beg pardon, Ma'amselle Kenney," the worthy man began —he had never been able to bring himself to pronounce the English "miss"—"I beg pardon, but I did not come for pleasure this morning, and those swollen eyelids tell me I was right in coming. To cut the matter short, do you know what occurred yesterday between Michael and Hulda?"

Hulda shrank at this question, and the tears rushed to her eyes as she cried, "Indeed, it was not my fault; and I will thank you on my knees if you will only send me home to my father and mother to-day. I have been begging Miss Kenney to do so, but——"

"But," the old lady interrupted the weeping girl, "Miss Kenney told you, my child, that you would only make matters worse by going home just at this time. What would people think of you if you should leave the castle simultaneously with that insolent man, especially since, as we see from this visit of the Herr Bailiff's, he has already said or done something that might call attention to you? The prompt kindness of Baron Emanuel, and the strict justice of the prince, have relieved you from any danger of further annoyance, and it is your bounden duty to allow no hint of what was in itself an insignificant incident to pass your lips, or to reach the ears of your noble benefactresses, whose refined natures it might well shock."

She spoke with her usual gentle dignity. Hulda stood by the embroidery-frame a pale image of submission. But the bailiff understood not one word of the whole affair. He raised the thick stick, that he held in both hands between his knees, once or twice an inch or two from the floor, and then gently dropped it again. He had much ado to keep from bringing it down with a bang; but the old Englishwoman spoke in "such a confoundedly soft voice." However, his silence did not last long.

"That is all very fine, and doubtless correct, from a certain point of view, but I must know the short and the long of it. What was it that happened yesterday? for that scoundrel's words in my house to my sister last evening, Ma'amselle

Kenney, had an evil flavour about them." He then proceeded to question Hulda, who replied frankly, assisted now and then by Miss Kenney; and the epithets with which the bailiff interrupted their account from time to time, always begging Miss Kenney's pardon for using such terms in her presence, testified to his faith in all that was told him. But Hulda was disappointed if she had hoped he would advise her return to the parsonage. He agreed with the governess, in saying that such a plan must not be thought of,—she must remain quietly where she was, never breathing a word, even to her father and mother, of what had annoyed her, never allowing the baron to perceive that she knew of the influence he had exerted in her behalf. Her calm continuance in her accustomed duties would effectually put a stop to any slanderous whispers that Michael might have put in circulation concerning her. After giving this advice to the girl, the good man arose, excused his visit once more to Miss Kenney, and then, patting Hulda upon the cheek, said, "Aha, my little fledgeling! you were ready enough to leave the nest; now persevere,—it cannot last forever,—and the nest will be ready to receive you after this trial is over."

Then he paused before the flower-stand, felt the earth in the pots, to see if it were moist enough, for his eyes were everywhere, and then took his way to the fields.

When he returned home to dinner, however, he was whistling. His whistle was like the moor-fowl's cry,—it betokened stormy weather. His sister was standing at the cupboard in the corner of the sitting-room when he entered, and she never looked round, or bade him good-day,—the previous evening was too fresh in her mind.

Suddenly he spoke: "Sister, what I thought was quite right; all that that cast-off scoundrel told you was just a pack of lies. I know all about it now, and mean what I say: if one word of it comes to the ears of the pastor or his wife, I shall hold you responsible."

"As if I were the only person to be found with ears and tongue in my head," she muttered.

"I don't care for that; I mean what I say," said the bailiff, who was immovable in such cases.

"I can't help it if the poor man has told his sad tale to others."

"But you can help calling such a rogue a poor man in that

tender tone. If he has talked with any others, it is your part to let them know he has lied. Enough! If I see one suspicious glance cast at Hulda, I have determined to take her home here to keep house for me, and you may retire to a single room in the village. It would not cost me much pain to make such an arrangement."

And again, as on the evening before, he left the room angrily; but Ulrika did not burst into tears to-night. The smile that took the place of tears on her face boded ill to poor Hulda.

CHAPTER XIX.

In every summer there is sure to be an hour when something in the air strongly suggests the approach of autumn, even although the sun is shining brightly and the flowers are in full bloom; and something like this hour had interrupted the summer-like serenity of the social life at the castle. Every one felt its influence more or less, but no one looked for its cause where alone it was to be found.

Matters had hitherto pursued such a smooth and even course that small obstacles were all the more perceptible. Michael's services were by no means indispensable to the prince, but he missed the man's readiness and ability in a thousand ways. He knew that he could not have retained him much longer about his person, but he did not like to be thus forced, as it were, to dismiss him suddenly. With all his follies, the man had known how to make his services valuable to his master. He had a decided talent for dramatic representation, and could transform the most unpromising material into all that was needed for an evening's entertainment of this kind. Whenever tableaux vivants, charades, etc., were the order of the day, Michael had always filled the post of director with great ability; and in a thousand ways he was now missed. And Clarissa, who had accustomed herself to depend greatly upon Hulda's society and her musical knowledge and talent, was annoyed to find that Miss Kenney's demands upon the girl's time made it impossible for her to spend many moments daily in the castle proper. Miss Kenney now found it but fitting that Hulda should attend church regularly and pay strict attention to her lessons and hours of instruction. Clarissa was obliged to acknowledge that her old governess was in the right, but none the less did she miss the entertainment that the girl had afforded her. Hulda, too, felt that every hour she passed with Miss Kenney was for her advantage, and yet there had come a break in the summer of content. The lovers no longer came to take lunch with their old friend. They had first been prevented by a slight cold that the young countess had taken, and then there had been several days of stormy weather; and, as Miss Kenney had never been heard to regret their absence or suggest the renewal of their daily visits, the custom died a natural death. Nor had Miss Kenney apparently observed the discontinuance of the baron's frequent visits.

Formerly he never passed through the garden, upon one of his long walks, without stopping at Miss Kenney's open window to exchange a few words with her, to ask about Hulda's progress, and what news she had from the parsonage. Later, when the luncheons were abolished and the weather had grown colder, he came from time to time, both in the morning and in the evening; but, although on the evening when he had found Hulda alone and in distress he had promised to return to hear how matters stood, and the girl knew that Michael's dismissal was due to his influence, he had not made his appearance since in Miss Kenney's room.

At first Hulda had hourly expected him, and sitting quietly at her work, had meditated upon how she should thank him. She had decided that it would be impossible to do so in Miss Kenney's presence, since her old friend would surely expect her to utter her gratitude in stiff, formal phrase. But why trouble herself to say anything, since the baron always divined what was in her heart before she spoke? How often had he guessed her thoughts, and kindly anticipated some wish to which she would never have dared to give utterance! In all the embarrassment and shyness that she had felt in her early intercourse with the great ladies at the castle, how had he always come to her assistance with words and looks that placed her at her ease! The protection that he had once laughingly offered had been accorded her without her asking. She had relied upon his presence in all that she had done; his approval had been the looked-for reward of all her services. She had often told herself that God had sent him to aid and encourage her: his existence was a blessing to her; and then Ma'amselle Ulrika's weird legend would recur to her, and the thought that he believed himself under the influence of a spell, —he, the kindliest of men, burdened with a curse! But the spell could be dissolved by love, and surely that must be his in richest measure.

It did no good to try to regard all such thoughts as folly,—an idle nursery-tale. There are certain things against which reason is powerless, so firm is their hold upon the human mind; and this fact she was learning to acknowledge. She herself seemed entangled in some mysterious spell, and everything around her was as if strangely transformed. "What does it mean?" she repeatedly asked herself. The castle still stood just where it had always been standing, but an invisible wall had arisen between it and her. The countess's maid brought no more messages to her, desiring her presence or her services. She only went there once a day, in the afternoon, to braid the Countess Clarissa's hair, and she too seemed to have lost her former merry humour. She was unaccustomed to the northern winter,—the mist, snow, and rain affected her voice, confined her within-doors, and depressed her spirits. Then, too, there were tidings with regard to the health of the prince's father which made it likely that the young man would have to curtail his visit; and if he should go away, the time of his return was uncertain; it was not decided whether it would not be better for the family to follow him to the capital. In short, everything suddenly grew uncertain, the old familiar aspect of the household was changed.

The maids nudged one another when they met Hulda on the stairs or in the passages, and once, as she passed through the dining-hall, the servants loudly regretted that Michael should have been dismissed so summarily, while others, who were slyer, had retained their places. The gardener's wife, a kindly-intentioned woman, asked the girl one day if it were true that she was to remain at the castle after the family had left, even although Miss Kenney went with them. And when Hulda, with a look of surprise, asked why she should stay, and said that of course she should return to her parents, the good woman begged her not to take the inquiry amiss, and declared that she had not herself believed the report.

If Hulda went upon an errand to the bailiff's, Ma'amselle Ulrika hardly deigned to look at her, and would always supplement the bailiff's kind words with some bitter remark. On one such occasion, when Hulda, wounded to the soul, burst into tears, and asked what she had done to provoke such anger, Ulrika replied, with a scornful laugh, "Such a beautiful young lady ought never to cry,—tears bring wrinkles and make your eyes red, and gentlemen don't like red eyes."

Even in church, and as she walked home, all seemed to regard her oddly. It was true that, owing to Clarissa's generous kindness, she wore much better clothes than formerly; the young countess had lately presented her with a pretty brooch and ear-rings, and of course it was natural that the farmer's daughters should ask her where she had got these new adornments. But there was something in their manner of asking that pained and embarrassed her, she could not tell why,—something that sent the blood to her cheeks and choked the words in her throat. And yet she had done no possible wrong, and it surely had not been her fault that the countess had brought her to the castle.

Her gayety and happy disposition could not keep ground against the ill-will that she encountered. She could not explain what distressed her; there was no one to whom she could tell how heavy-hearted she had grown, and how weary and spiritless.

As the season advanced, the weather grew more gloomy. Rain fell steadily day after day, with now and then a flurry of snow that did not yet lie long on the ground. The sun seldom appeared, except, perhaps, among heavy clouds at sunset, when with its pale-yellow light it illumined the dead leaves upon the bare earth, the stripped boughs dripping with rain, or the white wax berries upon the leafless spirea-stalks, and the gloomy groups of firs and hemlocks, above whose tall tops long trains of wild geese screamed their shrill farewells as they sailed away to the sunnier south. Thus several weeks passed. The number of guests at the castle had greatly diminished, visitors from the surrounding country were rare, on account of the bad roads, and within the castle, as without, all joyous song was at an end. The old prince's illness occasioned great anxiety; the time was occupied in looking for letters, and preparations were made for any sudden emergency.

The travelling-carriages were taken from their sheds and repaired. The morrow seemed uncertain; even Miss Kenney spoke of packing her trunks, and from time to time gave Hulda directions as to how she was to pursue her studies if the family should leave the castle and she return to the parsonage sooner than had been anticipated.

Hulda saw and heard it all like some dreamer who knows that the terror he is suffering is all a dream, and who yet finds it impossible to awaken, impossible to escape from the distress that oppresses him. For, with all her thinking, she never could discover the answer to the questions she perpetually asked herself, "What have I done to put an end to my happiness? Why should the baron, hitherto so kind, have ceased to interest himself for me?" She could not sleep at night or sit quietly during the day. Her eyes ached, and her heart beat all the while as if she were expecting some strange event. A spirit of unrest possessed her and drove her on to constant exertion only to add to her weariness.

"How pale you look!" said Clarissa, always kindly disposed towards her, one afternoon when Hulda brought her a little piece of work she had just finished. "What has become of your lovely colour? I trust you are not ill?"

"She grows so fast," said Miss Kenney, before Hulda could answer; "and perhaps the change in her whole manner of life has been a little trying to her. You are quite right; Hulda does not look well."

"It may be," said the countess, "that with the best will in the world on our part, it was not well for her to come to us when she did. She needed perfect rest while she continued to grow, but I thought she had attained her full growth when I first saw her. The repose of her father's house will restore her perfectly, I trust. If you do not feel very well to-day, child, and would like to pay a visit to the parsonage, you have but to say the word."

"Oh, I am perfectly well," Hulda replied. And yet her heart had never throbbed so painfully; for the baron, who was seated at the chess-board with the prince, turned slowly round, and, riveting his dark eyes upon her, said, "Do you remember our conversation, Adelheid, and the objection that I made to your plans? Horace was wise when he said, 'Let what is quiet stay so.' "

The countess apparently took heed only of his last words "An excellent and genuinely conservative saying, that: it should be engraved upon our crests and set up over our gateways," she said, "because it so admirably contradicts all those modern ideas that one hears so much of, and notably your own. I assure you I will take your admonition to heart, and try to be more prudent in future."

"I am sure of it," he replied. "'Tis a pity that our good resolutions cannot work backwards, and that for the most part they only benefit ourselves, whilst others suffer from our earlier errors."

He said this without looking up from his game—fortunately, the countess thought, since he must else have remarked Hulda's agitation. Her colour came and went rapidly, her lips quivered, and her eyes had a look of eager entreaty as she turned them towards the baron, as if to ask what significance his remark contained for her, and in what way he had, without her knowledge, influenced her destiny.

The countess looked at her keenly. What she detected was the reverse of welcome to her; but she concealed her annoyance, and kindly patting Hulda's burning cheek, she said, "You are too warm; the heat in my rooms is greater than you are accustomed to. Go back, child, and take some rest. To-morrow we will see what can be done for you."

Hulda would have obeyed, but Clarissa detained her. She put her own shawl around her, that she might not catch cold in going through the garden, and the baron, whose physical suffering had made him compassionate for that of others, arose, and, coming towards her, took her hand and asked whether she was in pain or had fever.

"There is nothing whatever the matter with me," she cried; but again her cheeks flushed and there was a strange glitter in her eyes. "I am perfectly well," she added, and tried to smile; but her emotion was too great, and, drawing her hand away from the baron's, she hurried out of the room.

Emanuel looked after her with anxiety. "The girl is ill!—very ill, I am afraid." And he proposed to send his groom to the village in the morning to fetch the pastor's wife and a physician. But the countess and Miss Kenney easily alarmed though the latter was usually, did not share his anxiety.

"Do not increase the evil that you have all occasioned," said the countess, with a degree of sternness. "Emanuel gave me to understand just now that I should have done better to leave Hulda in her father's house, and I could not explain myself in her presence. But if you had not transferred her from the sphere in which she belongs, and where I had placed her,—had not Clarissa, and you too, Emanuel, pleased with Hulda's pretty face, drawn her into our circle, where all is foreign to her, and where it is impossible she should be in future, her imagination and her nerves would not have been so excited, and she would have been as strong and well as at home. I will send for her mother to-morrow, and let her take the child home for a few days; then this little nervous attack will pass over, and she will remember her stay among us as a bright ray of sunshine, or some pleasant dream. Do not be unnecessarily alarmed about the girl. Life has enough of serious care without——"

"An express!" All interrupted her here as with one voice, for through the quiet of the darkening twilight the sound of a post-horn was heard in the distance, followed by the rapid galloping of a horse. The prince hastened to the door, and Clarissa accompanied him.

"Was I not right," said the countess, "in saying that we should not seek out unnecessary cares? Care is seeking us. What is it?" she asked, as the lovers returned with pale faces and anxious looks.

"We rely upon you, and your help, dearest friend," said the prince. "We must go this very evening—I and Clarissa, and yourself also."

"Since you ask this," replied the countess, "something very serious must have happened. Tell me what it is."

"My father writes himself. He has insisted upon hearing the truth from his physicians, and they have told him that his recovery is impossible, and that he may not live many days. He therefore wishes to see Clarissa my wife before his dear eyes are closed forever." He said this with calm self-control, but at the last his voice trembled, and Clarissa, turning, threw her arms around him and hid her face upon his breast.

The countess looked at her watch. "It is five o'clock now;

we will be ready to start by eight. Will that be in time for you, Severin?"

The prince and Clarissa gratefully kissed her hand; and the former was about to leave the room, that he might himself give orders to the postilion to have horses ready at the next station, when a sudden thought struck him.

"Fill the measure of your kindness to overflowing, dear lady," he said, "and let me go with you in your carriage. It will be much the quicker way to let my carriage follow to-morrow with the luggage, and thus not need all our horses to-night."

The countess pondered for a moment. It had always been resolved that the baron should supply the place of father at Clarissa's marriage, and give her away, and the young countess could not forego this arrangement. But there was some fear lest the hurried journey in a full carriage might be too fatiguing for Emanuel. He however, refused to be considered any longer as an invalid, and entirely approved of Severin's plan. The countess agreed to it all the more willingly as it necessitated leaving Miss Kenney at the castle, and made easy what she had some time since decided must be done.

CHAPTER XX.

The arrival of the express and the sudden departure of the family created great bustle and activity among the castle servants. The corridors and passages were instantly alive with ladies' maids and valets; trunks were brought out and packed, and it was plain that eight o'clock would find the party ready to start.

The countess sent for the bailiff to give him her last orders. Ulrika busied herself in her store-room in packing hampers and baskets. Even Miss Kenney exerted herself to the best of her capacity; but she was far from strong, and, as she sank fatigued into a chair, she said, "What a pity it is that Hulda should be of no use on this evening of all others!"

"I must run across to her, at all events," said Clarissa;

"and you must tell me in your first letter how she is. I thought her greatly changed to-day."

"As you are to be left alone, my dear Kenney, and the castle will be very quiet, do not send her home, but keep her with you. Rest will do you both good," said the countess, who was quite content with the turn things had taken. "Make yourself perfectly comfortable, and order what you please, until I know what our future plans must be."

These words seemed to bring up for the first time in Miss Kenney's mind a vivid sense of her coming separation from the two people to whom she had hitherto devoted her life, and, in spite of her habit of unmurmuring submission, she could not suppress her sorrow at being left alone at so unfriendly a season of the year in a country quite strange to her. But, exclusively occupied with other matters that circumstances forced upon her attention, the countess paid her little heed. Clarissa, however, said, soothingly, "Have Hulda with you all the time; she has so much talent, and is so sweet-tempered, and I will not be jealous even if she supplant me in your heart. I love her as if she belonged to us, and she does not even know that we are going."

The countess thought that the arrival of the express and the bustle in the court-yard could hardly have been unperceived by her, and wondered that she had not come to offer her services, since she really could not be very ill. She might be sent for, or they could stop in the carriage as they passed Miss Kenney's quarters, if Clarissa had set her heart upon bidding her good-bye.

But there was another besides Clarissa who had remembered that Hulda knew nothing of their departure, and that separation from those within whose circle she had been drawn through no desire of her own would be hard for her to bear. This was a double grief to him, since he reproached himself for not having seen so much of her lately as formerly, so disagreeable had been the impression made upon him by the affair with the prince's servant.

He thought of her continually while he was ordering and arranging what of his belongings was to be taken with him and what to be sent after him. He took out a couple of books that he meant to leave her as a remembrance, and was just about to write a few kind words of farewell in one of them, when he was seized with an invincible desire to see her. Yes, he must see her alone before he parted from her,—this girl whom he had first met in the perfect solitude of the fields, where she had arisen upon his sight like a vision of grace and beauty, and whose loveliness of character had so impressed him; he must see her once more, that her image might be stamped upon his memory; he must tell her that whatever lot the future held in store for her, she should always find in him a firm friend.

He threw his travelling-cloak around him and went into the garden. The evening was cloudy, but no sound yet stirred the air. The light from the window of Miss Kenney's little sitting-room sent out its peaceful glimmer into the darkness, and, as it grew more and more distinct, he hurried towards it. He reminded himself that he must not delay, that he must return immediately to the castle, that the moment of departure was at hand, and in the haste he made his heart throbbed fast, and a mysterious emotion possessed him. Why had he come out upon so silly an errand? Still, he could not turn back, for now her window was close at hand, and the girl's tall, graceful figure was visible through the thin muslin curtains. The old pang shot through his breast.

"So young! so fair!" he said aloud, and then started as if the words were not the utterance of his old doubts of himself; still, he must see her, speak with her once more.

In the profound silence she had heard the sound of approaching footsteps,—footsteps that she knew. As he opened the outer door and the gardener's dog began to bark, Hulda opened the door of the room. The gardener and his wife came from their room to see who was coming at so late an hour, but quickly withdrew when they recognized the baron. He observed this; but Hulda, in her agitation, saw nothing of it.

"Am I to come over?" she cried, as he entered and closed the door after him. "I have waited and waited for some one to come for me. I could not come else, since I was told to stay here. Is it true that they are all going to-night?"

"We go in accordance with the prince's desire," Emanuel replied. "In an hour we shall be gone."

"All?" asked Hulda, her eyes gazing into his. "All, Herr Baron? And you?"

Her look, the tremor in her voice, agitated Emanuel more than he had conceived possible. His habit of self-control stood him in stead, however, and he was able to reply quietly and kindly that he was going too, that he might give away his niece at her marriage.

The girl's face flushed and glowed. Stretching out her hands towards him with the gesture of one impelled by the instinct of self-preservation, she cried, "No, no, you will not go!"

Emanuel feared to trust his senses. "Child, child, what does this mean?" he asked, preserving his self-mastery with the greatest difficulty, while a sense of bewildering joy was stealing over him. "What does this mean?" he repeated, looking into her eyes as if to read her soul.

"I shall die if you go!" she gasped, and, utterly overcome by the violence of her emotion, she fell upon his breast.

"My darling, tell me—speak—do you love me, Hulda?" he cried. His face shone as in the days of his youth, and the eyes that she had seen in the picture gazed down upon her; but she could not speak. She was terrified at what she had done, and could not collect herself. Her head was leaning upon his breast; his arm was around her; he felt her heart beat against his own.

"And can you love me—me—changed as I am?" he asked.

Still, she could not reply; but she raised her eyes to his in mute adoration.

"Yes, yes!" he cried; "this is love, love pure and disinterested, for which I have longed, but never dared to hope. What I never dreamed of winning or possessing in my wanderings over the world you bring me here in my native country——"

"Deliverance!" she whispered. "Love delivers!"

He heard it, and it touched him, although he did not understand it as she had meant it. "Yes, it delivers and enslaves!" he cried. And their lips met in a long, first kiss. "It binds me in fairest fetters to my country and my home; for now I belong to you, and my place is here!"

CHAPTER XXI.

The heavy travelling-carriage was packed and standing before the hall-door; the lady's maid was arranging the cushions for the ladies; the outrider had consigned his horse to a groom, and was assisting the coachman in harnessing the four huge bays. The coach-dogs, released from their kennel, were careering wildly about, rejoicing in their freedom and adding greatly to the general confusion. The family were assembled in the great hall above the entrance, ready for departure; cloaks and furs were all provided, and the countess's casket of valuables was on the table before her. Miss Kenney, with difficulty controlling her emotion, kept near Clarissa, attending to the arrangement of her wraps, and giving her, meanwhile, many a silent caress.

Clarissa was much agitated. For her more than for the others the future seemed all untried; she could not tell when she should see this home of her fathers again. It was the first time, too, that her mother had ever left it except in her husband's company. Painful as her thoughts were, however, she gave no utterance to them; but now that the hour for starting had arrived, did all she could to accelerate departure. The baron alone was missing; and yet the servants reported that his preparations for the journey had been concluded for some time.

At last the countess gave orders that he should be informed that they were waiting for him. The servant who received her commands stated that he had seen the baron going through the garden towards the left wing of the castle; his portmanteau was already in the carriage.

"Then we will start," said Clarissa, "and take him up from there, and I can say good-bye to poor Hulda."

The proposal was not quite agreeable to the countess, whose face betrayed her annoyance at the servant's words; but, as she was chiefly bent upon getting away as soon as possible, she assented to it; and the wraps had just been gathered up, and the bailiff and Ma'amselle Ulrika admitted to say farewell, when the baron entered.

"We have been waiting for you, and had just determined to stop and take you up," said the countess.

"I am sorry to have kept you waiting," he said; "doubly so, since I must detain you a few moments longer to tell you why I cannot go with you to-night, but will follow you to-morrow or the day afterwards." Then turning to the bailiff and his sister, he requested them to leave them for awhile.

They obeyed; the servants followed; and Miss Kenney would have left the hall also, but Emanuel detained her.

"You, dear friend," said he, "are perhaps the only one who will be less surprised than I am myself at what I am about to say. For, in the hasty review that I have made of the past in these last few moments, it seems to me you must have divined the joy there was in store for me,—a joy so intense that I can yet hardly believe in its reality." He paused, and then added, in a firm, decided tone, "I have loved Hulda from the first moment that I beheld her, and she loves me: therefore I shall remain here until I can see her father and obtain his consent to our marriage."

The effort to be calm gave to his words and his voice a dryness and stiffness that were in strong contrast to the matter of his announcement, and that added greatly to the strange impression it produced.

"Impossible!" cried the countess; while the prince's surprise kept him silent; and even Clarissa, accustomed to regard her uncle's marriage as something beyond the range of possibility, joined in her mother's exclamation. She would have been delighted to appropriate Hulda as a dependent companion; but to regard the pastor's daughter as her uncle's bride, as her aunt, was repugnant to her.

The baron resented his sister's exclamation and the silence of the prince; and the self-distrust that was the morbid part of his character stirred within him and sent the blood to his cheeks.

"To what does your exclamation refer, Adelheid?" he asked. "Do you find it impossible to believe that I should yield to my inclinations and marry?"

At this the countess did as persons who are usually calm and self-controlled always do when taken by surprise: she lost her temper, and replied, "I find it impossible to believe that you should forget what is due to yourself and your ancient name, and that you are not alone in the world!"

"Certainly that last fact is not one I am in any danger of forgetting at this moment," he rejoined; "for I am most sensible how entirely alone I am, and how differently we feel. This, however, we can discuss at some future time."

A pause ensued that was by no means oil upon the waters. All had something to say, and all restrained it. At last the prince remarked that the time appointed for departure was already past. This was a relief to the countess, and yet she would gladly have said a few words alone to her brother. She signified this to him; but he would not understand her. When she made it a direct request, he declined.

"We are both agitated, and there is no time to lose," said he: "therefore neither of us is in a frame for a discussion which could in no case be productive of good."

This decided refusal offended the countess still more. She was used to plume herself upon her influence over her younger brother; and the step he was about to take wounded her pride and opposed all her convictions. That this disagreeable announcement should be made and discussed before her future son-in-law and Clarissa; that he should betroth himself to the daughter of a pastor,—a girl whose mother was born a serf,—just when he was about to give away his niece at the altar to her high-born bridegroom,—all this was intolerable. Wavering between the irritation that would have now sealed her lips on the subject and the desire to prevent, or at least avert for awhile, the threatened calamity, the countess, after the lovers, followed by Miss Kenney, had left the room, turned back to Emanuel, who was standing leaning against the chimney-piece. "Do you really mean to stay here? You will not come with us?" she asked, in a voice that testified to her desire for his compliance with her wishes.

"No!" he replied, in a decided tone; "but I trust I shall not long abuse your hospitality here."

"Then Michael was right, after all!" she exclaimed, scarcely knowing, in her irritation, what she said, and speaking so loudly that the bailiff and his sister, who were just outside the hall-door, heard her distinctly. Then, following the rest, she descended the broad flight of steps and got into the carriage.

The baron remained behind, entirely alone. His sister's

words had been daggers to him. They betrayed the fact that Miss Kenney had made him the instrument of a concerted plot. He had learned much within the last hour.

The doors were wide open, and the draught made the flame of the candles sway and flicker. Emanuel heard the closing of the carriage-door, the loud crack of the coachman's whip, and the adieux interchanged by the travellers and those remaining behind, soon drowned by the noise of the horses' hoofs and the rolling of the wheels. Then the gates were shut, and all was still, save for the wind that had risen and that went howling around the old castle and clattering at the windows. The soot blew down the huge chimney, and the owl that had its nest in the tower perched upon the balcony outside and hooted drearily into the night.

As the baron looked around and found himself thus alone in the hall, a feeling of pain stole over him. At the moment when a woman's love—a joy to which he had resigned all claim—became his own, his nearest of kin had turned from him; and the woman who had been to him more than a sister, whom he had regarded as his dearest friend, had wounded and grieved him. She, knowing well how the misfortune of his youth had oppressed and burdened him, calling him to resign all bright anticipations, should not have treated him thus. Was he not capable of directing his own actions? should he not carve out his life as he pleased?

Tender-hearted as he was in his affection for his sister, he could do nothing now but arm himself with anger against her. He was justly irritated that, as they were about to separate, she had hurled in his teeth the slanderous words of a dismissed lackey,—attainting not only his honor, but also that of the girl so soon to bear a name that the countess had been proud to call her own. It was true that he himself had never approved when representatives of ancient noble names had allied themselves with the bourgeoisie, thus sullying the purity of the noble blood which he, as well as his sister, had so highly prized.

He had never contemplated the possibility of choosing a wife not of noble blood. But had he *chosen* here? The love of this divine creature, who had been to him a presage of joy, had fallen upon him unsought, unhoped for, a gift of the gods. He had never been so reconciled with his lot as since the day when first he saw Hulda. She had seemed to him then a vision of the daughter of the blessing-bringing goddess; and what a blessing she had brought him, and would always bring him in ever-increasing measure, as her lovely nature developed beneath the fostering care with which his love would surround her!

Again he saw her in all the glory of her youthful beauty. Her soft arms were around him, her head rested upon his breast; the thought of her impelled him to seek her again, that in her presence he might forget the painful impressions of the past half-hour.

In the anteroom his servant met him, and asked for orders as to the unpacking of his portmanteau, and whether he would sup in the dining-hall or in his own room. Two maids were busy in the passage under Ma'amselle Ulrika's supervision. Everything reminded him that the life of the last few months was at an end, and he reflected that on the morrow at this time he should have left the castle. Well, he had passed delightful days here with his sister, the prince, and Clarissa, but, after what had passed, those days never could return. As he opened the door into the garden, the storm and wind from the sea came driving in his face and beat against him during his short walk. The boughs of the firs swayed to and fro with the violence of the wind that moaned through them, while their tall tops creaked and groaned, and there was a flurry of rustling leaves along the pathway. He was glad when his foot was upon the threshold of a protecting roof, and rejoiced in the prospect of so soon forgetting all save the new joy of being beloved. But here, too, disappointment awaited him. He had hoped that a fair girl would come towards him, her beautiful face beaming with the reflection of youthful love. Instead of this he found Miss Kenney sunk in silent grief in her corner of the sofa, while Hulda rose from her seat at the table and stood quiet and shy, without even looking at him.

"What is the matter? What has happened, my darling?" he asked, although he could well divine what the matter was. He took her hand, and threw his arm around her. She withdrew from his embrace, and, stooping to press a kiss upon his hand, she said, with an effort that was painfully evident in the trembling of her lips, "Forgive me, Herr Baron."

"I forgive you, dearest love? What words are these? Forgive you for making me happy, for loving me? What folly, what evil enchantment, is this? What could I have to forgive in you who are purity and love incarnate?"

"Forgive me for daring to raise my eyes to you, for bringing discord where I had received kindness,—for—for——" She could say no more, but hid her face in her hands.

"And is it thus my good Kenney has employed the time of my absence? Is this the lesson she has tried to teach you?" Emanuel said, with a laugh that ill concealed his annoyance. "It is lucky for me that your memory will prove a short one; you can never learn this incomparable lesson by heart. But I see clearly this is no place for you, or for me either. To-morrow morning early I will myself take you to your home. Till then, my dearest, farewell."

"Excuse me, Herr Baron," Miss Kenney interposed, in her softest voice and with her kindest look, "if I venture for the first time to oppose your commands. Hulda has been entrusted to my guardianship by her parents, and by the countess, from whom I have received directions to accompany her to-morrow to the parsonage. Until then she remains in my charge alone."

Emanuel winced. This opposition at every turn was intolerable. "The countess is exceedingly attentive to my future wife," he said; "but really she must allow me to adjust my own affairs as I think best. Wrap yourself up warm, my darling. I will return in half an hour, and you shall sleep this night beneath your father's roof: you never would have left its shelter if the countess had paid heed to me."

He went towards the door. Hulda stood in the middle of the little room, irresolute as a child. Her helplessness and the baron's annoyance went to Miss Kenney's heart. She knew not what she wished, or what to do. She had once been young and fair herself, and beloved by the son of the wealthy nobleman whose intendant her father was. Meekly resigning her love, she had left her home that she might ensure the peace and prosperity of her family, and had found repose and a new home with those to whose service she had ever since been devoted. Why should not this girl follow her example? Should she not once more by her advice and exhortations try to play the part of an angel of peace in a noble household? Submission and self-sacrifice were so much a part of her nature that she could hardly understand why every one could not find the most profound content in utter self-abnegation.

She rose and laid her hand upon Emanuel's arm to detain him. "Do not let me plead in vain," she said; "do not force me to transgress the countess's orders for the first time in my life. Does the thoughtless fancy of a child weigh more with you than do the sacred claims of a sister's affection? For—you know the countess as well as I do—she will sacrifice everything sooner than her convictions."

The soft, quavering voice of the old lady, and Hulda's evident helplessness, rasped Emanuel's high-strung nerves, and the last words made everything worse. "Then," he cried, "the countess will the more readily understand my acting according to my conviction. Be ready as soon as you can, my child; the carriage will be here in a few moments."

He hastily left the room, and Hulda sank into a chair, utterly stupefied. Good old Kenney wavered irresolute between kindness of heart and conscientiousness, between fidelity to duty and sensibility, between her regard for rank and her delight in making others happy. She told Hulda that the whole trouble was entirely owing to her want of a sense of decorum, while she tenderly and anxiously felt her pulse, fearing that she was really ill. She declared that Hulda should never go out into the stormy night with the baron, and demanded that she should herself refuse to accompany him, and should wait until the next day before she went home; and yet her very heart ached with pity for the girl, and for Emanuel, whose sensations she could well divine. But nothing that she said had any effect upon Hulda.

"I must go with him, and I must go home,—this very night," she said again and again, as if there were no room in her mind for any other thought. Then suddenly starting to her feet, as in positive terror, she added, "Oh, if he would only come! Something at my heart is drawing me to my home." She went into the adjoining room and dressed for the drive; then she stood at the window, looking out into the night, and then went to look at the clock. Her restlessness increased; Miss Kenney feared she was seriously ill.

"No, no!" she replied to her old friend's expressions of

anxiety; "but I am in dread,—in utter dread. I should have to walk home if I could not go otherwise; I never felt so before. Oh, if he would only come!" Suddenly she hastened again to the window and opened the casement. The wind flapped it wide open and extinguished one of the candles upon the table. Miss Kenney, chilled by the draught of air, inquired what she meant.

"Did you not hear it?" asked Hulda, looking wildly around. "I surely heard my mother call me! It pierced my very heart! Oh, such a wild, despairing cry for help!"

Miss Kenney closed the window, and drew her away from it. She was very anxious; she feared the girl was slightly delirious, so feverish was her desire to go home, her longing for her mother.

The baron, too, stood at the window of his room in the castle, and waited for the horses, with a devouring impatience which the surrounding loneliness increased to an intolerable pitch. He had ordered his carriage to be ready as soon as possible, and an outrider to be provided, since the storm and pitchy darkness made caution necessary even for so short a distance as that between the castle and the parsonage. His old valet had asked whether he should attend him, and when Emanuel replied curtly in the negative, the faithful fellow, who could not but see that matters were all wrong, and who was troubled that his master had not left with the rest of the family, still lingered in the room in hopes of some change occurring in the baron's plans.

Emanuel scarcely noticed his presence; his mind was in a turmoil. Left to himself for a few moments, he distinctly saw for the first time that the last hour had been a turning-point in his existence, and that he had chosen a future in direct contradiction to all his previous ideas and convictions.

He scarcely recognized himself. The joy of knowing that he was beloved had conquered his self-distrust; but the alienation from his family that threatened him cooled the rapture with which he dwelt upon the thought of Hulda, and it added to the annoyance occasioned him by the manner he had been obliged to adopt of securing his happiness, used as he was to a dignified and calm progress of events in his daily life, that he could not be for a moment in doubt as to how the step he had taken would be regarded in those circles forming his society, whose opinions he had been accustomed to regard with some deference.

His agitation increased with every moment of delay. He was relieved, indeed, when the carriage drove to the door, and Hulda, as he entered Miss Kenney's room, flew to him as if to a liberator, with a "Thank God, you are come!"

He scarcely knew how he put her into the carriage, or how Miss Kenney, carried away by her tenderness of heart and her love for Hulda, embraced and blessed them both. All else was forgotten in the sense of ecstasy with which he clasped his new-found treasure to his heart.

CHAPTER XXII.

THE night was profoundly dark, the wind coming from the sea swept, roaring, across the wide level, and the horses breasted the storm with difficulty, while the lantern carried by the outrider gave but a flickering gleam in the blackness. But Emanuel heeded neither the storm nor the darkness. He was supremely happy.

Innocent and confiding as a child, tender and submissive as a loving wife, Hulda nestled at his side. Her head rested upon his shoulder; he had thrown his large cloak around her as he clasped her in his arms and pressed his lips repeatedly upon her hair, brow, and lips. The gentle reserve with which she replied to his words of love, the child-like longing with which she spoke of her parents, and the quiet joy with which she pressed his hand as he told her that at her side he was young again—won to new life—so engrossed him that he hardly noticed that snow had begun to fall thickly, and that it was only with great care and caution that his people were able to keep their onward way. Suddenly Hulda started from his side.

"That is Pluto, our dog!" she cried. And pressing her face against the carriage-window, she asked if they could be at home already. The baron put down the window. They were still in the open fields. Hulda recognized by the light of the lantern the old sign-post pointing in three directions, towards the castle, the sea, and the village. Yet true enough it was the pastor's dog barking loudly that she had heard, and that now, when she called him, came leaping up wildly at the side of the carriage.

"Where can he have come from?" said Hulda, when the baron had closed the window again. "He is never unchained at this hour! And," she added, as they drove past the first houses in the village, "what is the matter here? The houses are all lighted up, and the people are standing out-of-doors! Oh, I hope there are no boats out in the storm!"

Just then the carriage stopped; some one was speaking with the outrider. "What is it?" the baron called to the men.

"They are asking," was the reply, "whether we have met the postmaster's chaise; but we came from the opposite direction."

"Why are they in search of it?" asked the baron.

Before his question could be answered, an old man wrapped in a huge cloak, his fur cap drawn over his forehead, and a stable-lantern in his hand, came up to the carriage-door, and without, in his agitation, seeming in the least surprised by the appearance of the baron and Hulda in such weather and at such an hour, exclaimed, as he recognized the latter, "Thank God, you are here at last! There is some one for the Herr Pastor to talk to!"

A deadly pang shot through Hulda's heart as she heard these words of the old sexton's.

"But where, then, is my mother?" she cried. "Herr Falk, where is my mother? She is not sick? Who was coming in the postmaster's chaise?"

"The pastor's wife was coming in it," said the sexton. "The postmistress is ill, and sent for your mother, Fräulein Hulda, this morning, and she drove away from the post-house at noon to return in time for supper at the parsonage, and she has not come yet."

"Perhaps she was detained at the post-house by the storm," said the baron, hoping to soothe Hulda's anxiety, although he himself was possessed by a gloomy foreboding.

"No," said the sexton; "she started long before the mail that drove by here at five o'clock."

Hulda uttered a cry of horror. In spite of the cold, her hands were burning hot. The baron ordered the coachman to drive on, and in a few minutes they drew up before the parsonage.

The garden-gate and the house-door were open. At the noise of the carriage, the pastor, the maid-servant, and a couple of neighbours hurried out of the house.

"Then you know it already?" cried the pastor, as Hulda threw herself into his arms; "you know it already?"

"No, we know nothing!" replied Emanuel, leading the father and daughter into the house.

"She started at three o'clock in broad daylight," wailed the pastor. "There is no hope; they got upon the quicksands. She is gone!"

Hulda uttered an agonized shriek. The whole force of the blow that her father had gradually experienced in the last six hours came upon her with a sudden shock and utterly prostrated her. Emanuel tried in vain to arouse some glimmer of hope in the two mourners; but his words of comfort fell upon unheeding ears. He would send out his groom—would send people in every direction upon the four carriage-horses—to search for the missing ones; but he knew perfectly well that the pastor was right in saying that until the sea gave up its dead they never would be found.

"The postilion who drove the mail," the pastor said, with the calmness of despair, "followed the track of their wheels for half a league, and then it ceased, just where the shore seemed to him strangely altered,—the sea came higher up, and he immediately altered his course and drove farther inland."

"The wind may have heaped up the sand and obliterated their traces," said Emanuel, soothingly, distressed by the rigidity in Hulda's features, knowing, as only he could know, how doubly hard it was for her to endure this shock at the present time.

The pastor shook his weary head incredulously. "The wind drive wet sand? Impossible! And where could they go to? We have searched every foot of land from here to the post-house. None could lose their way here." Then, bowing his pale forehead upon his folded hands, he cried, "God has so ordered it. His will be done! but it is hard for me and for the child. Such a mother! My poor, poor child!"

Tears rolled down his furrowed cheeks as he laid his hands upon Hulda's head; she had sunk upon the floor at his feet. Emanuel stood beside them, wrung to the soul.

"I am here, old friend. Hulda, am I not beside you?" he said, bending over her. But she turned from him and clasped her father's knees, crying, "Here, here is my place! I can never leave it!"

He did not venture to speak to her again, given over as she was to natural sorrow, and to have asked the father for the daughter's hand at such a time, to have mingled his hope with their despair, would have been a double desecration.

The villagers, whose sensibilities, however dulled by the frequency of such disasters among themselves, were aroused in behalf of their pastor, gathered about him; but he paid little heed to their rude attempts at consolation, and not until the baron's servant appeared to ask his master's orders with regard to the carriage did the poor man awake to the fact that there must have been some extraordinary cause for the appearance of Emanuel with Hulda at the parsonage so late at night.

He asked the baron for an explanation of his visit, and received from him the intelligence of the arrival of the express, and the sudden breaking up and departure of the family at the castle, leaving no one behind but Miss Kenney and himself. This the pastor heard with sorrow; and, when Emanuel saw that it seemed to do him good to have his mind diverted from his own grief even for a moment, he said, "I will tell you to-morrow, when we are not so bewildered by this sudden misfortune as at present, why I have brought home Hulda, who is as dear to me as to you."

"Then you really did not know of it?" asked the pastor, to whom Emanuel's presence seemed more of a riddle than ever.

"Yes," cried Hulda, before he could speak in reply; "yes, father, yes, I knew it. She called me once, twice, and so loud that I ran to the window and opened it; but I did not see her. But now, now I see her! There! there! Oh, mother! dear mother!" And with outstretched arms, and beseeching agony in her voice, she arose and was hurrying to the window, when she fell to the ground in a dead faint.

Her father, Emanuel, and the old maid-servant ran to her

assistance. They carried her to her little room and laid her on the bed. When she revived from her fainting-fit, she was perfectly delirious, and in her feverish ravings she soon betrayed to her father all that Emanuel would have told him on the morrow, all that could explain the baron's anxiety on her behalf. Any further confidence on Emanuel's part the pastor quietly declined to receive.

"God has sent the angel of death to my dwelling," he said, submissively. "How can we contemplate life and its demands whilst the dark wings are outspread above our heads? Why should we decide before the Lord has decided? Why should I listen to you before we know whether the mother will not call her child to follow her? It was hard enough for her to part with her here on earth. God will be merciful, I think, to her and to me. He will not long put asunder those whom he has once joined together."

Without, the storm had begun to subside. The window-shutters were open, so that the light streaming from them might signal the missing ones, if by some miracle they were still alive. Gradually the villagers withdrew,—nothing more could be done to-night in the way of search. They could not console their pastor, and they must take some rest to prepare for the ordinary duties of the following day. At last even the faithful old sexton went sadly to his home. But the house-door was not locked, and the faithful dog kept watch upon the threshold.

Emanuel had sent for the physician; but it was impossible that he should arrive before daybreak. Overwhelmed by grief, the poor old father wandered from the window to the door, and then into the open air. He looked around him, but his weary eyes saw not what he sought. The wind was slowly driving the clouds from the land to the sea; the weathercock upon the church-tower creaked and turned as was its wont; and when the moon broke through the clouds it illumined the garden and the pebbly pathway and the little house as brightly as if the faithful wife were still by her husband's side instead of far down in the depths of the heaving sea. He could not bear to see everything thus wearing its usual aspect; he wandered back to the house, where all was so changed.

Hulda was not aware of either his coming or his going. Her

thoughts were busy in the world of fancy, where they had so often lingered of late. She believed herself to be the little scullery-maid whom the king of the fairy-folk wished to marry, and she implored Emanuel not to allow it, nor to let her leave him. She had delivered him by her love from the curse; he was once more young and handsome as the picture in the castle. She would marry him and be his queen. All this she would say in short, broken sentences but too well comprehended by her father and by Emanuel, both of whom knew the old legend, and then in heart-breaking tones she would cry that her mother was coming, rising pale and dead from the deep, deep sea, whither she would carry her poor child back with her, since an evil eye had been cast upon her love and her happiness. It was a terrible night; it seemed as if day would never come, and when it did come, what could it bring but a sad certainty?

No traces were found of the pastor's wife, or of the horse, vehicle, or driver. They were gone forever. The physician pronounced Hulda to be suffering from a severe attack of nervous fever, and time alone, he said, would show whether youth and a good constitution would come off conquerors. In such days of suspense, what but the tender hand of a mother could truly minister to the stricken daughter?

Whilst the two helpless men were discussing what was best to be done—Emanuel talking of taking up his abode at the parsonage, and the pastor representing to him that in his present forlorn condition it was impossible that such a guest could be made comfortable beneath his roof—a messenger from the castle arrived, bringing a letter from the countess to her brother, and another to the pastor. A third had been sent to Miss Kenney. The countess had written them at the first station, where they stopped to change horses, and all three were quite short.

"I must entreat you, my dear brother," she wrote to the baron, "to forgive my hasty, unkind words, which nothing but the sudden shock of your announcement could excuse. You know that to see you married has long been my most fervent desire. But the girl whom you have selected for a wife is very young and in every way your inferior. Is the affection that you feel for her strong enough to outlast the years that must be devoted to her education, and to neutralize the inevitable embarrassment you will have in presenting her, nameless as she is, to our circle of friends? And do you not shrink from the thought that your children, their mother not being of rank, will be obliged to resign the entailed estates of the ancient family whose name we bear? You see, I am really disinterested, since those estates would in that case fall to my son as the next heir. These lines have no other purpose than to beg your forgiveness and entreat you to pause and reflect before you bind yourself further. At the same time I will not deny that the prospect of welcoming as my brother's wife a girl whom I had proposed to take into my own service is anything but agreeable to me."

She spoke still more plainly in her note to Hulda's father. Since he knew her, he would not be surprised, she said, to learn that her brother's intention had not met with her approval. She thought it owing on his part to a transient emotion, for which, doubtless, Hulda's ingenuous *naïveté* was somewhat to blame. For her own part, she acknowledged with regret how grave a matter it was to attempt, even in the interest of education, to remove a girl from the sphere of life in which she was born. Still, in this instance she relied upon the pastor's knowledge of the world, as well as upon his devotion to her family, and upon the gratitude of Simonena. She was quite sure that both parents would see the entire unsuitability of this connection, and do what in them lay to prevent their daughter's entrance into a family from which they themselves had received nothing but benefits, but which could never admit her gladly within its circle.

After a kindly fashion, but quite clearly, she gave Miss Kenney to understand that she held her partly responsible for what had already occurred and for what might happen in future. She added that she need not say how utterly distasteful to her, and how unsuitable in every respect, this intended marriage of Emanuel's was, and that she trusted that Miss Kenney would use her utmost efforts to open his eyes to his infatuation, and to remind the pastor and his wife of the duty they owed the noble family which had conferred so many benefits upon them.

Emanuel and the pastor read their letters, but while the dread struggle between life and death was going on there was no time to contemplate any possibilities save those of the present moment. It was clear that the baron could not stay at the parsonage, and that some one must be installed there to take charge of poor Hulda. Emanuel drove to the castle to seek what assistance could be found there. Upon his arrival he found every one filled with dismay and grief over the intelligence of the loss of the pastor's wife. Even Ma'amselle Ulrika had forgotten her long-cherished grudge against "poor Simonena." She was always to be relied upon in any misfortune or distress,—always ready then to aid and sympathize. The sunshine of others' happiness scared away her sympathies and aroused the antagonism of her nature.

She and her brother were all ready to drive over to the parsonage when Emanuel reached the castle. Every one crowded around the baron and his servants, with expressions of sorrow, to learn all that could be told of the poor woman whose unassuming loveliness of character had made her universally beloved.

Emanuel went directly to Miss Kenney, whose kind heart instantly decided what was best to be done. One of the younger maid-servants at the castle had shown herself especially capable and sweet-tempered, and Miss Kenney declared that she would take this girl with her and establish herself at the parsonage, to undertake the entire charge of her dear pupil until she was restored to health,—a consummation that might surely be expected, in view of her youth and strength.

It was far more suitable that she should be at the parsonage than that the baron should attempt to stay there; she could be of more use in every way, both with regard to Hulda and as a companion to the poor old pastor, who would feel the charge of her entertainment far less than that of the baron. She would immediately report to Emanuel any change in Hulda's condition, and, if she should shortly recover, it would surely be best that in the first stage of her recovery any agitating interviews with her lover should be avoided. The quiet influence of a teacher to whom she had been accustomed, and of whom she was fond, would surely be best for the girl at present.

All this was so sensible and kind that Emanuel accepted her offer with gratitude. Even Ma'amselle Ulrika remarked that it was odd that any one who had had so little to do with household affairs should understand so well the practical part of a matter; "not that Hulda," she added, "is worth all this fuss and worry; every one can see clearly now that matters had come to a pretty pass between the baron and the girl, and must acknowledge that poor Michael was treated with the greatest injustice."

Still, she packed up a large hamper of everything that was necessary for Miss Kenney or the invalid, and was soon on the way with her brother to inquire after the poor widowed pastor and to offer her services in the emergency.

CHAPTER XXIII.

DAYS of wearing anxiety in the castle, as well as in the parsonage, followed these hours of anguish and dread. Letters from his sister were the only interruptions of the baron's life. The great affection, strengthened by custom, that existed between the brother and the sister, made a superficial reconciliation easy, especially since the dangerous and continued illness of the girl whom he loved kept him at the castle and postponed the formal announcement of his engagement, at least until she could be pronounced out of danger.

In the mean time the weather, of course, grew rougher and more stormy; the roads were almost impassable. The noble proprietors of estates in the neighbourhood had almost all retired from them to enjoy the comforts of the capital; and the two or three who remained, with whom the baron had some acquaintance, lived so far across the country that it was too great an undertaking to seek them out. Even his daily drives to the parsonage occupied double the time they had formerly taken, but they were never omitted. Often during these drives, as he sat wrapped in furs in his carriage, from the windows of which nothing could be seen for the driving snow and sleet, he asked himself, "What am I doing here at this season of the year?"

Since his early youth he had never before spent a winter in the north,—had never lived in such profound solitude. He was as thoroughly used to southern skies, and to nature in her most luxuriant aspect, as to intercourse with men distinguished either by birth or by breeding. Suddenly he was deprived of both, and sometimes, while sitting at Hulda's bedside, watching her pale, worn face, and listening to her delirious cries to him to save her from dangers by which she believed herself surrounded, he seemed to himself to be wandering among the deceptive joys and sorrows of dream-land, or to be really a part of the wild legend to which Hulda perpetually alluded.

Without a thought of himself, without a hope for the future, he had, for his sister's sake, returned, after years of absence, to his home. Here, where he had least expected it, the flower of love had blossomed in his path, only to wither at his touch. Was this the curse that had rested for centuries upon his race, —this deceptive glow of happiness that mocked him, threatening to snatch from his grasp what he had so coveted, to bestow grief and desolation where he had looked for peace and repose?

The knowledge, too, that no one took pleasure in the love that he had gained pained him and made him silent. Even the girl's father, upon whom he could bestow all worldly prosperity, disapproved. He could, to be sure, scarcely blame the sense of honor that prevented the father from contemplating with satisfaction his daughter's entrance into a family whose aristocratic prejudices he was not only aware of but approved. And he could not disagree with Miss Kenney when she reminded him, with regard to Hulda, how prone youth is to give undue weight to sudden violent emotion, and how often such emotion fades or is overcome.

But when Hulda called him by name, when in her delirium she would have arisen from her couch in search of him if she had not been forcibly detained there, his heart was filled only with an unutterable longing to see her restored to health. Tender memories would arise of the moments when a dim suspicion of her love for him had arisen before his mind like a beacon-light. To himself he called her his deliverer; there was a sweet satisfaction in his care of her, although he had as yet known none of that familiar intercourse with Hulda which makes the presence of one whom we love a necessary part of our existence. He loved her fondly, and yet his own former ill health, during which he had been an object of tender solicitude to all around him, had produced in him a certain amount of egotism that unfitted him for any enduring, unselfish self-sacrifice. He really suffered more than any one suspected from the inclemency of the climate during his daily visits to the parsonage; but when his sister entreated him to leave the north, and the pastor and Miss Kenney proposed that he should go south before midwinter was upon them, and there await Hulda's recovery, he refused to listen from distrust of the motives of his advisers, as well as from a desire to be present to catch the first gleam of his darling's returning reason.

Thus Christmas passed by, after a melancholy fashion. The letters the baron received from his sister contained little to cheer him. The old prince had died shortly after his son's arrival and marriage; and the young people passed the first months of their wedded life in deep mourning. The countess had left them; she thought it best to withdraw to the capital, where she was awaiting her son's arrival. His recent appointment to a new diplomatic post facilitated his stay for some time with his mother, who was anxious for his assistance in the final winding up of the late count's affairs. But his coming, she wrote, had been delayed; he was not yet with her, and deprived as she was, for the first time in her life, of the society of all who were dearest to her, and even of her faithful old governess, her letters were full of sad reflections upon the solitude that age brings, the helplessness of mortals in carrying out their plans for the future, and the folly of expecting to reap where we have sown, or of receiving affection where we have bestowed it.

To rid himself of the depression caused by the arrival of such a letter from his sister, the baron drove over to the parsonage, the day before the first of the year, earlier than was his wont. For months now there had been no change for the better; there had been months of grief and illness, and for weeks no ray of sunlight had penetrated the heavy clouds that obscured the face of nature. He was unhappy, and, what was worse, out of harmony with himself. For the first time it had seemed to him a question whether, after all, he had not committed an act of folly in yielding to his passion for Hulda. He was certainly playing a very extraordinary part here, that of unwelcomed suitor to a dying girl of low birth; yes, his was so strange a position that he wished himself away, and yet there was something in his heart that held him here, in spite of all such thoughts and every argument against it.

"If I could see her standing before me once more as on that first spring evening," he cried, involuntarily, "how gladly would I wait!" Then suddenly as his carriage approached the beach, a bright sunbeam stole out through the clouds; the cold breakers glimmered and shone, and a huge flock of sea-mews soared up from the water, shrilly screaming and flying before him, circled around the church-tower and the parsonage, and back again over the sea, where they soon vanished on the horizon.

His gaze followed their flight. How gladly would he have soared aloft like them, far above himself! An indescribable longing for light and warmth and happiness possessed him. His heart was full as he entered the quiet little room, now illuminated by the sunlight, where the pastor and Miss Kenney received him, and he seated himself by the sick girl's couch.

Did the rare sunlight deceive him thus at the close of the year with a ray of hope? or had the rest of the previous night, the best since her illness, wrought a miracle of healing in Hulda? Emanuel had scarcely reached her side when she opened her eyes and riveted them upon him. Miss Kenney signed to him to be perfectly quiet. The girl gazed at him as if she could not trust her senses. Suddenly a smile flitted across her pale lips. The baron could keep silence no longer: he softly uttered her name. She listened, and held out a weak, weary hand.

"Ah, you are come! you are come!" she said, with a caressing tenderness that found an echo in his own heart. He kneeled at her bedside and lavished terms of endearment upon her, calling her his dearest child, his Hulda, his darling. He kissed her hands, her brow, her lips. She tried to raise herself from her couch, but she was too weak. It had been too much for her, and as the sunbeam outside vanished behind the dark clouds, she relapsed into insensibility.

CHAPTER XXIV.

It was late in the evening. The year had but a few more hours to live. Emanuel tried to occupy his mind with the studies and occupations in which his days were passed, but his efforts were vain. He longed for some friend to whom he could confide the hopes and fears that agitated him. But whence could such a guest arrive in this solitude and in the depth of winter?

All was quiet in the castle. The fire crackled in the huge chimney, down which the wind roared in fitful gusts that now and then sent a shower of sparks into the room. The antique clock upon the old oak cabinet ticked audibly, marking the last moments of the dying year, as it had done for so many of its predecessors, while without the snow was falling steadily.

How great a contrast this evening presented to the New Year's eve that had preceded it! That had been spent in Italy, in his sister's villa there, in the midst of a gay and brilliant circle, his brother-in-law then in robust health, Prince Severin lately betrothed to Clarissa, the old prince delighting in his son's happiness, and a number of noble Germans spending the winter in Italy, with some Russians from the provinces on the Baltic, who still proudly preserved the ancient traditions of their German origin. All in the little circle had been in harmony with themselves and one another. Two from among them were dead, and where were the others? Where was the lovely Konradine, who, in her pretty disguise of a youthful postilion, had bestowed upon every one present some charming gift, the value of which was enhanced by the sparkling verses, written by her mother, that accompanied it?

Emanuel had scarcely bestowed a thought upon those two people during the last few months, although they were among the friends with whom his life had very frequently brought him in contact. The mother was an early friend of the countess, had been married very young, and well deserved her reputation as a clever, brilliant woman.

Upon her husband's death, shortly after her marriage, she

devoted her time to travelling with her only child, a daughter, in various European countries, and was widely known at the several courts that she had visited. In spite of the gossip that inevitably attends the mode of life of a young, handsome, rather dashing widow given to eccentricities, she had preserved her reputation intact; and although, as she laughingly asserted, she made no claims to be considered the model of a Roman mother, the relations between herself and her daughter, now grown up, seemed to be of the pleasantest. Konradine was thought rather an original, especially since with all her beauty and wit, even now when she was nearer thirty than twenty years of age, she declared that she preferred freedom to the gilded bondage of matrimony.

It was these ladies who some years previously had first interested the baron in collecting the popular songs of Lithuania and Northeastern Germany. He had once heard Frau von Wildenau and her daughter speaking together in a language which, although not yielding one whit in melody or delicacy to a southern tongue, yet retained enough of northern vigour to indicate its origin, and in answer to his inquiries they told him it was the language spoken upon their estates in Esthland. He remembered distinctly the melancholy little love-song that Konradine had then sung for him:

> "Tio was so good and dear,
> Tio I loved above all here;
> Tio grew ill, my dearest bride,
> Tio faded, Tio died."

The simple words had a very different significance for him to-day from what they had when he heard them first, upon a sunny afternoon in Venice, in a balcony above the waters of the Grand Canal. Who could tell but that his Tio, grown so ill, might not also fade and sink into the grave? He went to the piano to try and recall the melody, when suddenly he thought he heard the sound of a post-horn. He could hardly trust his ears; what could be coming to the castle at this hour? The sound was repeated, now much nearer, and following upon it came the ringing of the huge gateway bell and the opening of the court-yard gate. In the stillness that reigned around, every sound was audible; the hoofs of a horse echoed upon the stone-paved court-yard, and the rider reined in his steed just below the windows of Emanuel's room.

With his mind full of the memory of the last evening upon which an unexpected express had arrived at the castle, his thoughts as he opened the letter handed to him by the servant were none of the pleasantest. It bore his address, in a feminine handwriting that seemed familiar to him, and its contents ran thus:

"Every bitter brings its sweet. Two of your friends entreat a welcome and shelter for the night at your hands. All else, with cordial good wishes for the new year, shall be said *vivâ voce*, provided always that the postilion who carries you this prove stronger and stouter than the one who was the bearer of good wishes to you last New Year's eve."

The note was signed with Frau von Wildenau's name, and was dated from the nearest post-station. The baron could not understand how the two friends who had just been present in his mind could possibly be at such an out-of-the-way place; but the prospect of welcoming them to the castle on this evening above all others was certainly very pleasant. Upon inquiry, he learned that the ladies' carriage had been overturned and seriously damaged a short distance from the station, whither they had retired to pass the night and wait until another conveyance could be prepared. Hearing, however, that the countess's castle was but two or three miles distant, they had changed their minds, had sent this letter on before, and were following it with their maid in one of the vehicles belonging to the postmaster.

Emanuel looked at the clock; the travellers, according to the postilion, would arrive in an hour, somewhat before midnight. Of course, all the servants in the castle and at the bailiff's were up and stirring on New Year's eve, and the baron knew Ma'amselle Ulrika well enough to be certain that nothing would be wanting for the comfort of the unexpected visitors.

He therefore ordered a horseman with a lantern to be sent to meet them, while Ma'amselle was told of the tidings he had received.

She was in her element in an emergency like the present. Here was a chance for bringing to light and use some of the delicacies stored away in anticipation of the Countess Clarissa's wedding and the lengthened stay of the family at the castle. She was quite tired of only packing up a few things every week to be taken to the parsonage, where she felt that very inferior fare would have answered the purpose quite as well.

It was easy to see how much she enjoyed thus proving herself equal to the occasion. Fires were soon lighted throughout the castle, and one of the smaller drawing-rooms was decorated with flowers. The supper was prepared, and the New Year's bowl brewed, with which, after northern fashion, Emanuel resolved to welcome his guests.

The last hour of the old year had not struck when their carriage entered the castle court-yard. Emanuel hurried down to meet the ladies in the hall, and their gay laughter at sight of him was a refreshing sound. It was so long since he had heard any one laugh; of late his days had been passed amid mourning and tears.

Exchanging expressions of pleasure at this unlooked-for meeting, they passed up the wide staircase to the supper-room, the cheerful aspect of which called forth renewed exclamations of delight from the ladies. They would not hear of retiring to the apartments provided especially for them to make any alteration in their dress.

"How can we change our dress, my dear baron," cried Frau von Wildenau, "when all our trunks are in our carriage, and that is at this moment lying in a ditch three miles off, and Heaven only knows how it can be got out and put in order again? We left our servant with it, and came to you all forlorn as we are, ready as you see to act the *proverbe*, 'Man proposes, Heaven disposes,' for your New Year's eve entertainment."

As she spoke, they had thrown off their furs and wraps, and both mother and daughter, each so like the other that they were continually taken for sisters, seemed to him more blooming and lovely than ever. Frau von Wildenau had grown stouter, and looked younger; and Konradine, in her heavy black cloth travelling-dress and velvet jacket, a many-coloured silk scarf wound about her head, after a Lithuanian fashion, concealing her hair and forming a frame for her lovely features, was a dazzling picture of perfect symmetry of face and form. She went to the mirror to take off the scarf, and as she unwound it the comb that confined the coils of her hair fell out, and the mass of golden "rippled ringlets" was shaken down over her shoulders, while her mother hurried to her assistance in coiling it up again.

Emanuel could not refrain from admiring the beauty of her hair. Konradine called it the trial of her life. "I cannot lean my head back or sleep if it is braided," said she, "and therefore I am obliged to wear it unbraided when I am travelling, and am always in danger of just such annoyances as the present."

But when, a few minutes later, they were all seated at the supper-table and the first glasses of wine had been tasted, Frau von Wildenau, looking around at the blooming flowers, the blazing candles, and the cheerful fire, declared that this was the most charming adventure that could be imagined. "Who would have thought, when we suddenly found ourselves frightened out of our wits at the bottom of that ditch whence we extricated ourselves with difficulty, that we should celebrate so delightful a New Year's eve?"

The baron, pleased at her evident satisfaction, asked how she had known of his residence at the castle; and she gaily related how they had no sooner found themselves beneath the sheltering roof of the post-house than she summoned the postmaster to her presence to learn from him whether there was any mechanic in the neighbourhood who could undertake the repair of their carriage, how the man had declared that such repair would certainly occupy a couple of days, and that then she had suddenly remembered how near the castle of her friend the countess must be. She told of her joy upon learning that the baron was at present in possession there, and described with much comic effect the consternation of the postmaster upon hearing that they should immediately betake themselves thither, regardless of the entertainment provided for their refreshment, and which would now doubtless form a New Year's eve banquet for the inmates of the post-house, worthy people who she was glad should be feasted at her expense; and she concluded with, "And now that you know all about us, pray solve me the riddle of your presence here in the north alone. Were you not at Clarissa's marriage? I thought you spent every winter in your villa upon the Lake of Geneva."

"More questions, dear lady, than I shall be able to answer this year," Emanuel replied, as the clock began to strike twelve. Then, raising his glass, he said, "May this unexpected meeting be an omen of good for the coming year, a sign that it will bring fulfilment to our desires!"

"So far as those desires are reasonable and consistent," Frau von Wildenau lightly remarked, as they touched glasses. The words were commonplace enough, but they arrested Emanuel's attention as coming from one not prone to remarks of the kind; and, looking at Konradine, he imagined that a change passed over her countenance,—the thanks that she uttered for the bouquet which he handed to her as a New Year's token were spoken in a constrained voice; nay, he even fancied that he could detect tears upon her long eyelashes as she bent her face over her flowers to inhale their fragrance.

Frau von Wildenau, with all her vivacity, was not to be lightly turned from pursuing her inquiries; and again she asked what miracle had been the cause of Emanuel's stay in this northern castle.

"A miracle it may be called," Emanuel replied, "if by miracle we understand something lying beyond the range of human probability. I am an engaged man; but my future bride is very ill, and I am here to await her recovery in her near neighbourhood."

"Why, everything delightful and unexpected is happening at once!" cried Frau von Wildenau, and Konradine's lovely face brightened and her eyes beamed as she held out her hand to congratulate him. "What an admirable step you have taken!" continued the baroness; "one, too, that will rejoice your family, and especially the countess,—how pleased she must be!"

"Much less so than you imagine," Emanuel rejoined; "for my choice, unfortunately, does not accord with my sister's desires. I am betrothed to a girl of no rank; she is the daughter of our pastor, and——"

"But what becomes of your family estate, my dear baron?" Frau von Wildenau interrupted him. "Can you make up your mind to relinquish, by your marriage, all claim upon that?"

He did not allow his annoyance at her question and tone to become apparent. "Can you blame me," he said, "if I admit that in the choice I have made I think more of my future happiness than of a family estate, by which some remote ancestor of mine entailed upon his posterity the curse of a slavish conformity to his own prejudices and to those of his time?"

"Oh, I think I could support the curse of an income like that from your family estate," replied the baroness; "and that without considering myself an object of pity."

"But I never desired the possession of this estate, which is at present my brother's," was his answer. "On the contrary, I have always regretted that he had no children to inherit it."

"Of course," cried Frau von Wildenau, "your own independent fortune is so very great; but your brother has no children, and your views would alter if you should ever have children of your own. An ancient name, handed down to us through centuries, is a very fine thing, and its importance is daily on the increase among all these parvenus, who, with their huge and too often visionary fortunes, think themselves entitled to all our privileges. I have always believed that the peace of a household must be greatly endangered when the sons learn that their bourgeoise mother stands in the way of their inheritance; and their father, too, must sometimes regret his sacrifice of real, enduring interests for the sake of a fleeting satisfaction. For what reasonable being imagines that at the end of ten, or even five, years a man cannot reconcile himself to the loss of a bride, or a girl of a bridegroom, without whom life at one time seemed worthless, and be infinitely content with another choice? Say what you will, baron, one is either fit or unfit for matrimony. If you are fit, that is, of an easy disposition, patient and unselfish, you will be content however you may marry. If you are unfit," and she laughed, "why, then, if your choice is the Venus of Milo, with the moral qualities of a saint and the wit of a Corinne, at the end of three years you will have found your dear perfection full of faults and failings. You will tire utterly of your ideal, and find any commonplace Maritorna more fascinating than your once-adored idol. There is nothing so deceptive as what we call love, and nothing less worth examination than the one whom we marry. It is ourselves that we must examine carefully to discover our fitness for matrimony, or the reverse, and then let our choice be made with regard to solid advantages. Whoever acts otherwise must suffer from disastrous consequences. The time is not far distant when the world will laugh at what we call love-matches, as at some child's plaything, and no one will believe in the possibility of pining or dying for love."

She said all this lightly, and in a fashion peculiarly her own of uttering on the instant her sudden conceits. But Emanuel could not understand how she could talk thus to him just at the moment when he had announced his own intention of making a "love-match." Nothing could excuse her want of consideration for him except her warm friendship and sympathy for the countess, especially since she was very fond of saying flattering, pleasant things to every one. There must be some reason for her severity; and Konradine's remark, following her mother's, equalled it in this respect. "It is a pity," she said, "that enjoyment of life and careless gaiety do not suffice to content every one; some natures require something more."

Then she suddenly changed the topic of conversation, warmly expressing her interest in Emanuel's betrothal. Her mother joined her in inquiries as to his future bride, her name, her present invalid condition, and declared that he was a man fitted by disposition and nature to make a wife supremely happy. Their interest warmed his heart; he felt as if the spell of silence lately woven around him were broken. He gladly expatiated upon Hulda's beauty, and her musical talent, telling of how charmingly she sang the national airs of Lithuania. Naturally enough, Konradine went to the piano to sing for him the little verse about poor Tio, which had recurred to his memory with such sad significance an hour or two before. He thought it prettier than ever; the voice of the singer had gained in tenderness since last he had heard it; the tones were softer, the rendering more natural.

Once at the piano, song followed song—French and Spanish romances, Italian ritornelle and canzonette, and German and Russian national airs, so that the first hours of the new year passed gaily and happily.

Emanuel conducted the ladies to the antechamber when they retired. Here Konradine gave him her hand. "Good-night, dear friend," she said; "for you, at least, I trust the coming year may be a happy one!"

Her grave words, and the firm grasp of her hand, did him

good. But what had happened, that she should thus seem to have resigned, in her own case, the happiness she trusted would be his? What significance for the daughter had there been in the mother's words? The relation between the two had always been peculiar, and now the daughter's independence of the mother was more striking than ever. Had any love-experience so changed Konradine, lent such tenderness to her voice, such new lustre to her eyes? He could not answer this question, and he pondered upon the lovely Konradine until he fell asleep.

CHAPTER XXV.

Before parting for the night, it had been agreed that the ladies were not to be disturbed the next morning until they were thoroughly rested and their luggage had arrived at the castle. The baron, therefore, would be left to himself during the forenoon. Bright sunshine and the finest sleighing ushered in the new year, and the sleigh was ordered to the door that he might drive to the parsonage.

In passing through the antechamber, to his surprise he encountered Konradine. She looked quite rested, and as brilliant as the morning, as she assured him that she had been up a long while, and had been calling herself and the new year to account. Noticing that he was prepared for a drive, she asked if he was not going to the parsonage, and if she might accompany him. He assented gladly. Her furs were brought, and in a few moments they were gliding along the avenue, where the snow-laden trees looked more majestic than ever beneath their white burden, and the glittering boughs scattered sparkling powder along the path.

"How splendid it all is!" said Konradine; "how glittering and shining, and yet so cold, and melting to nothing at a touch! But we live only in appearances, and they suffice us until some rude reality opens our eyes. Then indeed we are to be pitied."

Emanuel could not help connecting these words with what

her mother had said on the previous evening, and so framed his reply as to give his companion an opportunity, if she desired it, to disburden herself of what evidently lay heavy on her mind.

"Perhaps we sometimes stigmatize as mere show what is actual reality,—some genuine characteristic. Beauty, for instance, is so necessary to me that I cannot forego even its semblance. I ask you, frankly, could you be yourself without the beauty that we so much admire, or the semblance of constant gaiety which we find so attractive, even although this last quality be a habit formed only by education?"

She made no answer to his flattering words, strange to say, for she had a ready wit; but, waiving the making herself the subject of conversation, said, "Your betrothed is beautiful, then, and sweet in disposition?"

"Yes, she is beautiful," he replied; "and her chief charm lies in her child-like and entire naturalness. She is the very 'wild rose' of the poet."

"And you will break it from its stem," said Konradine.

Both the words and the tone grated upon Emanuel. "What do you mean?" he asked.

"Nothing, and everything!" she replied. "I spoke without consideration."

"But you must have had some meaning?"

"Nothing but that I cannot believe in the happy issue of a love in which a sacrifice is required of the man; and you might have learned from my mother yesterday evening that even women think that love should be subordinate to the possession of rank and wealth."

As she spoke, she threw back her head haughtily, and her lip curled so with contempt that her forced smile was as bitter and defiant as a man's. Emanuel had never seen her thus, or believed her capable of such strong emotion. The change in her that he had remarked the evening previous was more apparent than ever.

"You speak in riddles that distress me," he said; "give me the key for which friendship seeks in vain. Since we saw each other you have passed through some painful experience. I fear you are no longer happy, Konradine."

"Happy?" she cried, throwing back her dark veil from her face. "Is any one happy? Are you happy? I cannot believe so. But I will lay bare my heart to you. It seemed to me last night that Heaven itself, at the close of this last wretched year, had guided me hither to you,—to you, a betrothed man; for I must tell some human being how intolerable is my burden. I must talk with some one who will not despise me because I gave my whole heart to a man who, simply because he stood upon the steps of a throne, felt himself justified in playing with the poor toy and tossing it back to me. It was no more to him than the 'wild rose' that Schiller's boy broke from its stem." And she laughed, while her lip trembled. "That I could not wound him with my thorns, that even now I cannot hate him, that I am laughed at, that my own mother blames me for believing I could be preferred to a woman of royal birth, all this crushes me and makes my life wretched. I am weighed down by my own splendid, humiliated pride; I bend beneath the burden of it; I cry shame upon myself; I hate myself for loving so like a child and a fool, and every one passes me with a shrug. No one holds out a hand to me and bids me rise and walk. I could worship the human being who would give me even a hope that to arise and walk would ever be possible for me again."

Her face flushed; she suddenly broke off, and, in a tone of indifference shocking by its contrast with her former burst of feeling, said, "How useless to heat one's self in all this cold! It is really quite ridiculous!"

"What a word to use!" cried Emanuel. "No word for either you or me. Volcanic fires bursting forth to heaven from the midst of a snowy plain are terrible, but never ridiculous. Do not add to your suffering by cruelty to yourself. Respect your own grief, as I respect your confidence. You will tell me more, you will tell me all, Konradine,—you know how thankful I should be to help you to endure, to offer you any consolation."

"I know it," she said, and then both were silent, for they had reached the village, and Emanuel drew rein before the parsonage. But as he handed his companion into the house he regretted her presence. She was a stranger, and to present her to the pastor in the only sitting-room, adjoining the one where the invalid lay, the door of which was always open, was neither desirable nor fitting. Chance, however, came to the rescue.

The pastor was still detained in church by the New Year's service, and Miss Kenney had known Konradine from a child. The old governess's joy at seeing her, the mutual asking and answering of questions, helped Konradine to regain her self-possession, and the announcement that Hulda was much better, that she had for the first time alluded to her mother's death intelligently, and had expressed her desire to see the baron, was cheering news for Emanuel, who went into the chamber of the invalid, leaving Miss Kenney with her guest.

The window-curtain opposite the sick girl's bed was slightly open, admitting a ray of light through the frosty panes to play upon Hulda's small white hands, that held a freshly-blown monthly rose, which she held out to him as he approached her, with a softly-breathed wish for his happiness in the new year.

"Is it not enough of happiness," he said, taking both her hands in his, "that you still live, and that you know me once more?"

"Yes," she answered; "but my poor mother has gone!"

He did what he could to soothe her. At last he took from his pocket a small box, and, opening it, he held it towards her. It contained a simple hoop of gold, like the one he always wore, except that in the place of the ruby there was a turquoise set in diamonds. On the inside were clearly engraved the words—

"Thee and me shall no one sever."

A happy smile flitted over Hulda's pale face as he repeated the words to her; she had often sung them to him in the little Lithuanian song:

"Firmly bound, my darling, now,
As unto the tree the bough,
As to the ring the diamond ever,
Thee and me shall no one sever."

"No one! no one!" she said, tenderly, as he put the ring upon her finger; "but," she added, "I cannot go away from here. Who will stay with my father? He is all alone."

Emanuel comforted her by the assurance that her father should not be left,—he should always live with them. She scarcely heeded him, and seemed to be searching her memory for something. Suddenly she said, "I must have dreamed it, but, oh, so vividly! I was kneeling before the altar, as if—as if—for my marriage; but I was alone in the church. I heard the words of the service, but I saw no one. When the rite was ended, I looked up, and my father was standing by me, while my sainted mother hovered above us and blessed us, whom she had just united."

She shuddered, and Emanuel was sensibly impressed by what she said, although he tried to divert her mind from such sad thoughts. Slowly and gently he spoke to her of the coming spring and her recovery; how he would take both her father and herself to his home in the south by the blue waters of the mountain-lake; and she listened to his words with a smile until she fell asleep with her hands clasped in his.

He sat perfectly still, that he might not waken her. There she lay, white, lovely, motionless, as if carved in stone. He, too, had passed the winter beneath a benumbing spell, and it was high time to break it. He must deliver Hulda, who had already been his deliverer. As soon as possible he would carry her away from this place, where everything reminded her of her mother's tragic fate, from these contracted surroundings which her vivid fancy informed with ghostly, legendary creations. But some time must yet elapse before she could be moved with safety.

He looked at the ring that he had just given her in pledge of his love and fidelity, and his thoughts grew so restless and wandering that to sit still became most irksome. He took out his watch. Was it so early? He had supposed it was much later. He looked at Hulda's calm sleep, and thought of Konradine's passionate words. At last he gently rose from the bedside. He could not let Konradine wait any longer, and, as he emerged with her into the open air and the bright sunshine, he seemed lightened of a load and breathed more freely.

The horses neighed and tossed their heads as they sped like the wind upon the homeward way; and Emanuel himself felt the exhilarating influence of the sunny day and the glittering landscape. It was a pleasant return to the old castle.

CHAPTER XXVI.

Frau von Wildenau was sitting at the breakfast-table, while Ma'amselle Ulrika herself waited upon her, regarding such deference to the countess's guests as her special province in the absence of the mistress of the castle. Certainly the majestic appearance she presented in her flowered chintz gown, massive gold chain, and high cap with broad yellow ribbons, was by no means lost upon Frau von Wildenau, who was not at all averse to whiling away a lonely hour in half listening to the talk of an old family retainer, evidently an original.

A few complimentary expressions from the lady as to the great comfort of everything about her was enough to place Ma'amselle upon a pinnacle of serene self-complacency and unlock her tongue, so that before breakfast was ended the countess had heard the history of the castle from the time of the French occupation until the day when the express had arrived with tidings of the old prince's serious illness.

"They were gone in three hours after the news came," said Ulrika; "but indeed your ladyship is quite right in saying that those who live in the world must not be taken too much by surprise either by deaths, births, or marriages. It is the will of God,—no one can gainsay that. Still, when we heard that the baron was not going away, but would stay here, and his reason for staying, and when the pastor's wife disappeared that very night, so that every one saw that matters were not as they should be, it did seem as if I could not tell which way to look."

"Yes," said Frau von Wildenau, "the manner of the poor woman's death must, indeed, have filled every one with horror."

"To be sure, to be sure," Ma'amselle interposed, hastily; "but, good heavens! that often happens here. I didn't mean exactly that. God calls us when he pleases, and many a one has perished in the quicksands. But that the baron should betroth himself as he did, after having given up all idea of marriage,—depend upon it there was something wrong there.

Your ladyship of course knows all about the baron's family and the ruby ring and its history?"

Frau von Wildenau, more fatigued by the adventures of the previous day than she had at first been aware of, had thrown herself upon a lounge, and was idly listening to Ulrika's words, when the last sentence attracted her attention. She had often heard the countess allude to her brother's determined opposition to all idea of marriage, and had sympathized with the grief it caused her, all the more since, in spite of the disfigurements which he himself so exaggerated in imagination, he was well fitted by birth, culture, and address to gain a woman's favour. Only the evening before, both she and her daughter had spoken of the charm of his manner and conversation, and it was real interest, not idle curiosity, that now prompted her to ask Ulrika what she meant.

Ma'amselle shrugged her shoulders. "Mean, my lady? Only what every one in all the country round means, with the exception perhaps of my brother, who always thinks himself wiser than all the world beside, and whom she has in her toils like all the rest of the men." Thereupon followed a long and involved narrative, in Ma'amselle's peculiar vein, a perverted account of Michael's departure from the castle, and of the baron's interference, all strongly tinged with Ulrika's superstitious fancies, ascribing the attractions of Hulda to some dark art which she had inherited from her mother, who years before had played just such a game with the poor Herr Pastor.

Long before she had ended, the lady was wearied with what had at first amused her; but nevertheless she gathered from it enough to increase greatly her sympathy with the grief of her friend the countess in seeing her brother bent upon marriage with a girl not only vastly his inferior by birth and education, but of a low, designing character, and whose conduct seemed to have made her the common talk of the country around. All her own pride of rank and position was enlisted against such a *mésalliance;* all her own influence should be brought to bear upon its postponement, at least for awhile. Pity for Emanuel soon mingled with her affectionate sympathy for her friend the countess, as she reflected how powerless he had been, gifted though he was, to escape from the crafty toils of this village beauty. She really was as much interested in the whole affair as if he had been her own brother.

She had just dismissed Ulrika when Konradine and the baron returned from their drive; and the bailiff almost immediately afterwards requested an interview.

By the baron's orders, he had visited the post-station, and the news he brought thence was very unfavourable as to the possibility of the ladies' speedy departure. The carriage had been found to be much more injured than was at first supposed; and although the village smith declared that he could make it fit for use in a couple of days, it would be much better, the bailiff thought, to send it on a sledge to the nearest town, where it could be thoroughly repaired, although at a cost of the loss of five or six days.

Konradine exclaimed that this delay would cause the breaking of several engagements with friends; and her mother was inclining to trust to the skill of the village smith, when the baron said, "You put my unselfishness to the proof, dear lady; but, in truth, my travelling-carriage is at your disposal, if you must be in such haste. Can you not possibly decide to lighten my solitude by your presence here for a few days longer?"

"Permit me also to suggest to your ladyships," said the bailiff, "that, as the barometer is rising higher than I have scarcely ever seen it before, the cold for the next few days will be intense; and, if your ladyships are not accustomed to travelling in such weather, it would be wise to wait here until the bitter cold abates. And," he added, "the Herr Baron also must allow me to warn him against exposing himself to this northeast wind; it is especially injurious here on the coast to those who are accustomed to pass their winters in the south."

Frau von Wildenau agreed with him there; and, laying aside the consideration of her own plans for a moment, she said to Emanuel, "I have regretted all the morning, my dear baron, that you drove Konradine to the village in an open sleigh. It was unpardonable. For your own sake, for the sake of your friends, you should long since have departed for your winter home on Lake Geneva."

She knew, he replied, what anxiety, what duty, had detained him in the north, although he was by no means insensible to the severity of the climate.

"But," persisted the lady, "the preservation of your life is your first duty, which, as well as charity, here begins at home. And since I am determined not to be one of those who have so unnecessarily kept you here——"

"Pardon me," interrupted Emanuel, quick to resent the implied reproach to Hulda and the pastor; "no one thought even of keeping me here. Quite the contrary, I assure you."

"As you please! In that case I must protect you against yourself, my dear friend," she said, gaily; "I will try to compromise matters in a way that will please us, and that I hope you will not oppose. We will stay here by your bright fires until our carriage is thoroughly repaired, and keep you within-doors, if you will consent, when we go, to accompany us to the city, where the blasts are certainly not so biting, and where we will leave you, unless you decide to go south with us."

Emanuel thanked her for her kindness in consenting to stay with him, promised to take care of himself, since he was certainly vulnerable to the cold, but waived all further decision for the next few days as to his movements, only engaging that the injured carriage should be put in complete order.

The lady was satisfied, and in the gayest humour gave her directions concerning the carriage to the bailiff, who, seriously alarmed as he had been for the baron's health, was relieved by the turn matters had taken, and showed great alacrity in Frau von Wildenau's service.

The luggage arrived from the broken carriage, and the guests established themselves for some days, taking evident delight in the comfort and beauty of the castle and its appointments. They talked of erecting an altar to the god of chance, who had decreed this romantic adventure; and, as they sat at luncheon, Konradine declared that, if they appreciated their advantages, they certainly should keep the whole matter a profound secret, since the charm of mystery was all that was needed to make the meeting a perfect success.

Her mother, evidently pleased to see her in good spirits, declared that the proposal was quite characteristic. "From her earliest childhood," said she, "Konradine has always shown a desire to conceal and suppress everything of her own,—personal possessions or mental gratifications. She is in a certain sense very exclusive."

"And," Konradine rejoined, "life has punished me severely for it, by dragging into the garish light of publicity all my most sacred emotions." And she tossed back the long golden curl that fell upon her shoulder, and busied herself with the clasp of her bracelet.

Emanuel saw that her whole manner was painful to her mother. He, too, disliked her sudden exclamation, which, in its ruthless want of reserve, impressed him as indelicate,—unfeminine,—even while it interested him. To break the silence which ensued, and which might have been embarrassing, he said, "The truth is that every one likes to possess something that is especially, exclusively, his own. I really think it is this that makes diplomacy so attractive: there is the constant charm of mystery, wherein those who walk gain—there is no doubt of it—a degree of consideration in society. It is an easy way of obtaining the respect of the crowd."

In support of his assertion of this charm in mystery, Frau von Wildenau told of one of her friends, who, owing to an entirely unfounded mysterious report that she had forsworn matrimony in consequence of an unfortunate love-affair, was so sought after and admired that it ended in her contracting an advantageous and happy marriage.

And so the talk went on happily enough, until Frau von Wildenau thoughtlessly remarked that she had a horror of affection in excess, a positive dread of those powerful emotions that constitute a grand passion.

"Yes," Konradine said, with bitter emphasis, "my mother is perfectly right; they are terrible, these grand passions, with their 'Le jeu est fait, rien ne va plus!' when one has risked all and is left with absolutely nothing. But a small venture of love, risking but little, neither winning much nor losing much, is certainly a capital pastime. Now that I think of it, you and I, my dear baron, ought to bring this adventure of ours to perfection, by immediately falling in love with each other. Think how delightful it would be! We have known each other for years, and our friendship has been of the calmest, but now that we are thrown together as if wrecked upon a desert island—why, the situation is all that a poet could desire. And, to tell you the truth, I think my fervent gratitude for your amiable care of us must have made a certain impression upon you already."

He declared that the impression had been made upon him long since, but that he had never ventured to claim a place in the glittering ranks of her adorers. She gracefully acknowledged and returned his flattery, and thus they were gaily tossing to and fro the shuttlecock of social gallantry, when Frau von Wildenau shook a warning finger at them, bidding them be careful how they played with fire. "For," said she, "I am superstitious about challenging our fate,—it is dangerous to jest thus with the unknown."

Emanuel refused to heed her warning. He had for so long been deprived of all society but that of his books, with now and then a few words with the grief-stricken pastor or kindly old Kenney. Now Konradine gaily threw down the barrier that had been interposed between him and the world, and he was surprised to find how strongly, in spite of his disapproval of much to be found in general society, the habit of years had attached him to the great world from which he had lately withdrawn himself.

The light from it was garish, and the tone that sounded in his ears shrill, but they excited him pleasurably, like the taste of wine to one to whom it has long been denied.

Konradine's nature and opinions were by no means similar to his own, but their social position had always been the same, they had developed themselves individually within the same limits. The rules of what is called society concerning decorum and indecorum, manners and morals, in the full significance of the words, were to them a native tongue,—here they were perfectly at home together. Emanuel could easily distinguish in all the exaggeration that Konradine allowed herself how much was conventional, coloured by what she had seen and heard, and how much the result of her own individual character. What was borrowed displeased him less, therefore, and what was native to her interested him and piqued his curiosity more, than ever before. He could even understand the sudden exercise of self-control that enabled her to follow up some remark of her own which betrayed bitterness of soul with an easy, indifferent observation, for not only did he know that such concealment of all genuine emotion was one of the first requisites of society-life, but he had frequently practised it himself.

He would never have begun this conversation; but since it seemed to afford her a momentary diversion, he found pleasure in continuing it, mingled with a certain satisfaction that he had not lost in his retirement all power to bear his part in the gay world.

"Everything is dangerous and serious for the unskilled," he said, gaily. "Fire and powder are dangerous things in a child's hands; but how charming are the rockets and balls of fire that soar into the air from a grand display of pyrotechnics! And the Carnival is just at hand, and I can have no merry masks here, as in the streets of Rome or upon San Marco. Therefore Fräulein Konradine's idea seems to me an especially happy one. We will improvise a little comedy for the few days that we are to pass together. She is mistress of the part she has chosen. I will do my best in my novel position. You, my dear friend, are our public, and when the curtain falls you both leave the theatre and I pay the cost, if there be any, of our play, for I am the only one who can possibly be exposed to any danger."

"You?" cried Konradine. "As if you were not cased in the armour of your love, your betrothal. You may think all the while of your lovely suffering bride and of your marriage, and I will think of the cross of the order that is to be offered me, for the worthy wearing of which I am already practising daily a dignified carriage before my mirror, and thus, as we are both preoccupied with entirely foreign thoughts, our play will be a genuine and perfectly harmless farce. But really we ought to dress in costume."

"Which will you have, Watteau or Renaissance?" asked Emanuel. "Both are ready in the castle."

The ladies were incredulous. Ma'amselle was ordered to bring the antique costumes from the old robing-room. They very shortly made their appearance, and were much admired in their ancient splendour, which had been well preserved, especially since they had only lately been brought into requisition for charades and tableaux. Comparisons were made between them and the fashions of the present day. Frau von Wildenau told amusing anecdotes that she had heard of the inconvenience which had been caused in the beginning of the century by a close adherence in the cold northern courts to the Greek fashions introduced into France in the time of the First Empire. This led to an account of the interviews she had had when very young with the mother of the reigning Emperor of Austria; and thence both ladies passed to a discussion of the present customs of the court of Russia, at which for the second time they had resided during the preceding autumn. Thus, when they rose from table, the costumes were forgotten, as well as the proposed comedy, with which the conversation had begun, although its discussion, like a rocket blazing for an instant in the air, had revealed here and there much hidden thought and feeling. All was quiet now; but the impression left upon Emanuel's mind was that either he had not rightly understood Konradine formerly or that her unfortunate love had produced a radical change in her.

CHAPTER XXVII.

THE barometer and the bailiff proved to be true prophets,—the cold became intense. Emanuel could not possibly visit his betrothed the next day, and it cost him a pang as the usual hour for seeing her drew near, especially as he had been guilty of a slight neglect on the previous day which he feared might have wounded her sensitive nature. He had left the rose she had given him for a New Year's token lying upon her bed, and he would have given much to be able to recall this act of forgetfulness. There was nothing to be done, however, but to express his sorrow in the note that he wrote her to tell of his inability to come to her, and to dwell upon the bright future that was in store for them. He added that his guests prevented his solitude from becoming intolerable, and he proposed to send a covered sleigh to the parsonage every afternoon to bring the pastor or Miss Kenney to take coffee at the castle. Then he prayed her to send him the rose he had left, for which he offered her in exchange a basket of rare exotics; and although as he despatched his note and gift he knew how his presence would be missed, he was not perhaps very much disappointed at being obliged to omit one of his visits. Just to-day he was not exactly in the mood to sit still by the bedside of a sick girl who must be petted and caressed like a child, and he knew that he should hear tidings of her state of convalescence from his returning messenger, and from her father or faithful nurse later in the day.

When he had seen his groom depart, he sought the society of his guests. Frau von Wildenau was busy with letters in her own room; but Konradine received him in their little morning-room. She was in a charming toilette, and had a lace kerchief thrown over her head and tied beneath her chin, showing to great advantage the pure outline of her face.

Emanuel excused his early visit by declaring that his long solitude had made him positively thirsty for such delightful society, and perhaps unreasonable in determining not to lose, if possible, one moment of the short days of their stay.

"If you can call yourself unreasonable, what must you have thought of me all day yesterday and in our last evening's conversation?" she said. "I was hardly my own mistress, I confess, and my remorse kept me from sleeping well, and yet it was the only way in which I could banish the thoughts that would arise on seeing you once more and remembering our happy, innocent gaiety together last year with the countess. What a contrast were the terrible months that followed! My health has suffered. I should be utterly overcome—lie prostrate sometimes—if I did not boldly leap the abysses that yawn before me whenever I permit myself to dwell upon the past year. You must find me greatly changed."

As he had admitted this to her on the previous day, he answered without hesitation. "You are not what you were," he said; "but you are far more attractive. I am only afraid that you have paid dearly for the depth of character that you have gained."

"Very dearly," was her reply; "and it does not atone for the loss of that self-complacency that formerly made life dear and easy." They sat on opposite sides of the fireplace. Konradine, leaning back in her arm-chair and gazing into the leaping flame in the chimney, seemed lost in thought. Emanuel did not venture to disturb her.

"One comfort there is," she suddenly began; "everything is transitory,—everything fades and dies out like those flames, and we lose interest in ourselves, since, if we are not wilfully blind, we must admit that even suffering and anger and despair cannot last in their original intensity. And what does it matter if so perishable a being as man be happy or miserable?"

She would have fallen again into reverie if Emanuel had not said, "You permit me to follow your train of thought, you show me your wound, but I do not know whence you received it, although you intimated yesterday evening that it was no secret from the world."

"I see in what retirement you must have lived," she replied, "not to have heard of it. The story is very commonplace, very human, and as pitiable as is much else that is human. I need not tell you that I was never a coquette. You have known me long, and can well believe that the exchange of the small coin of affection that passes current for love in society was never to my taste. It made the whole matter one that I considered beneath my attention. Matrimony, too, as I saw it among my friends, had no attraction for me. I shared the freedom of which my mother was so fond, and ordered my life as I pleased. I had admirers, suitors,—lovers, if you will,—and contrived to retain them as friends even while proving that I did not consider them irresistible. I should have thought it folly to sacrifice my freedom except at the imperative bidding of my heart.

"So I lived on, and enjoyed existence, until we decided last autumn to leave our estates and spend a few weeks at St. Petersburg, since the emperor encourages those families of rank who live in the southern provinces to present themselves at court from time to time. Upon our arrival, we were graciously received. Several Germans of princely birth were guests at the court, and the 'season' began earlier than usual, and most brilliantly.

"Among the German guests was Prince Frederick von ——." And she mentioned a name of far greater importance in those days than would be credited at present. "The rest," she said, with a bitter smile, "is soon told. It might be taken from a popular romance. My fault was that I imagined that Prince Frederick differed from all other princes, and that I overestimated the power of love,—of my love.

"The prince was not the direct heir to the throne; he enjoyed the privileges of his rank without enduring its burdens, and this liberty he greatly prized. He used to declare that his chief delight lay in the fact that he should never, like an Atlas in shako and uniform, bear upon his shoulders the cares of government. Such a declaration became him well, proud as he was and as he knew himself to be. I never saw a handsomer man, and never a man whose every word and look seemed to bear so much the impress of truth. He is more than attractive: he is convincing and irresistible when he chooses to be so.

"He was a great favorite with the emperor, and women sought to attract his attention. I acknowledged his incomparable merit, and from the first he singled me out. A sympathy in all intellectual pursuits attracted each to the other. We were no novices, ignorant of our own hearts. I was entirely free, and he said he was master of his actions. There was no reason therefore why we should conceal from each other the sudden passion that sprang into life between us. Oh, what a delicious, glorious time it was!"

She had told it all as if it were the story of some third person, nothing betraying her emotion except now and then a slight tremor in her voice. At the last words she paused.

Emanuel was fascinated by her self-control,—her beauty. He had never accorded any woman credit for such capacity to sit in judgment upon herself, and, giving involuntary expression to his thought, he exclaimed, "Enviable man!"

Konradine looked at him with flashing eyes. "Yes," she said, "he was to be envied." Then she arose, and Emanuel followed her example. Together they went into the adjoining saloon, where it was cooler, and there they walked to and fro for a few minutes in silence.

"The prince," Konradine then began again, "could not contract a marriage without the consent of his family, especially with a woman not his equal in rank; but, as the succession to the government was assured in the direct line, his desire to form a connection where there was no danger that his possible heirs might have to be supported from the ducal treasury, met with no opposition. He signed the usual act of relinquishment for himself and any children that he might have, and on the same evening our private betrothal was celebrated in an assemblage of our intimate friends. A few days afterwards we were to be publicly presented at court as a betrothed pair. The emperor, who had always been extremely gracious to my mother and myself, approved the prince's choice, and the future seemed a paradise. There seemed no end to my happiness.

"On the day before our presentation was to take place, a courier arrived from the prince's uncle, the reigning duke. Brilliant prospects had suddenly opened for Frederick, and his uncle wrote that whatever had taken place with regard to our betrothal might be considered null and void. The daughter of one of the foremost of the reigning houses of Germany was of an age to marry. She, with her mother, had met the prince the previous summer at a celebrated watering-place, and the young princess had had the eyes and the wit to find him superior to every one else, a preference which her mother had regarded with approval. The thought of a marriage of affection upon the steps of a throne possessed a double charm for the mother, who had been unhappy in a marriage contracted in defiance of her own inclination. Her desire that her only daughter should lead a happier life was natural enough, and Frederick, as well as the house to which he belonged, could not view her preference in any other light than as a distinguished honor.

"He himself brought me his uncle's letter. I read it perfectly calmly and handed it back to him. This surprised him, and he expressed his surprise. 'You do not seem to rate very highly the advantages that I am about to sacrifice to you,' he said; and his whole manner, as well as his words, betrayed that the possibility of an alliance with that powerful house had aroused his ambition. His words were a blow to my love and to my pride. 'Yesterday you called yourself the happiest of men,' I said; 'if to-day can offer you anything more desirable than all that we hoped to enjoy together, our hopes are proved an illusion, and my love for you is too great to be any obstacle to the attainment of what is at present apparently more precious to you.'

"I had thought thus to recall him to a sense of what we were to each other; but he reproached me for indulging in sarcasm, for want of depth of feeling.

"'A woman who truly loved,' he said, 'would be incapable of such a thought; but I really believe that in your case ambition might easily outweigh love.' I could scarcely trust my ears. He accused me of ambition, while his own was already causing him to repent that he was no longer free. He seemed to forget all that we were to each other, all our mutual vows. I tried to control myself, but in vain. In reproaching him, I revealed to him how deeply he had wounded me. He was cold and calm. 'Can you not see,' he said, 'that I share all your feelings? Do you not know that I came to you just now with a bleeding heart? But I am not able, unfortunately, to think only of myself and of my love. My family and my country have claims upon me to which I must pay some heed. A connection with this powerful royal line is of the greatest importance to us. I have no right to consider myself where much more important interests are at stake. It is no trifle to reject the overtures of this princess. She is the niece and granddaughter of kings. She is——' I could bear it no longer. 'She is younger than I, and one of the wealthiest heiresses upon the thrones of Germany,' I cried. He made me no answer. After a long pause he resumed. 'I came to advise with you how to conduct myself in this matter. I had hoped that you would understand the delicate and difficult question that I am called upon to solve. I relied upon your understanding, your love and friendship for me, and your worldly wisdom. Yes, I thought so highly of you that I trusted to find in you a support for my own weakness. But your violence is deaf even to the most reasonable claims of justice and forbearance.' I could not endure this farce any longer. He and his love were both lost to me; there was but one thing to be done: to take the loftiest possible stand, and at one cast return to him all that he contemplated recalling from me—and I did it. This was what he had hoped for, but had scarcely expected. He stood there in my presence, in all the pride of his manhood, as if he had not just deeply injured me, and received, in return, a most humiliating reply. But I saw he was undecided whether he should give the reins to his vanity, and betray what he could not help feeling as a man, or whether, as a prince, he should soar above all human feeling, above any consideration for my heart or his own,—for I know he loved me as he can never love again,—and forgive me for the treachery and breach of faith of which he himself was guilty. At last he took another, a still loftier tone. He threw himself on his knees before me, and seemed overcome with grief. He begged me to forget that he had for one moment failed to appreciate me, to doubt my magnanimity. He praised the admirable strength of mind that had enabled me to point out the path of duty to him, and so convincing is the illusive frankness with which nature has gifted him, that I parted from him in a burst of sympathetic grief, and almost forgot for the moment, my own sufferings."

She suddenly paused in her narrative, and walked on silently, with her hands clasped in front of her, at Emanuel's side.

"Now I understand you," he said, after some moments of silence.

She seemed scarcely to hear him. "That very evening the prince had an interview with the emperor, and the next day he left the court. My mother and I were invited to the royal table, and treated with distinguished consideration. The report of my generous renunciation," and she laughed as she said these words, "was freely circulated, and met with the belief that it merited. I had been greatly envied. There was a certain amount of satisfaction in pitying and consoling me. The ground upon which I stood seemed unstable; the air of the rooms where I had so continually seen him stifled me. I could not look at the objects he had touched, upon which his eyes had rested. I was possessed by the single desire to get away, but for decorum's sake I was obliged to remain. All the world flocked around me. They wished to see me play my part, drape myself in my veil of forced self-abnegation. The prince was thought to have strictly obeyed the dictates of duty. Even my mother agreed in this view, and pitied him quite as much as she did her child. All understood his ambition, and thought it perfectly natural. No one understood me or my love. The prince's uncle offered me the position of canoness in one of the richly-endowed sisterhoods of his realm. To my mother this was a great satisfaction. She actually almost believed in my magnanimity, since the empress had praised it and the reigning duke admired it in his letter to me. All that was wanting was that I should believe in it myself, that I should forget in how cowardly and cruel a manner I had been treated, how I had been forced to summon up all my courage to avoid being trodden under foot. Oh, what a farce it was! And now, now, my dear friend, I think you no longer wonder that I am not the same Konradine you knew last year."

She threw herself upon a lounge, and took the kerchief from her head; her cheeks glowed; even her brow was flushed. Emanuel pitied her; but he admired her more. She saw this, and held out her hand. He grasped it cordially, and she returned the grasp.

"Do not look back any longer. Konradine. Look forward!" he cried, not daring to say any more at present, while she was so much moved; and just then a servant brought the news from the parsonage.

Miss Kenney promised to come to the castle in the afternoon. She sent word that Hulda was better, and rejoiced that the baron had not risked coming into the cold. Also the sick girl sent him his rose, with her morning greeting. He opened the little package, but the rose was faded and almost without fragrance. Konradine looked on as he put it into his pocketbook.

"It is late, and time to dress," she said; "but you owe me a long account of yourself, my dear friend, and I shall ask for it in the first quiet hour that we have together again."

"It will be soon given," he replied. "I never dreamed of the possibility of creating an interest in any woman, and I will not deny that I resigned with pain all hope of doing so. Hulda's innocence and artlessness betrayed to me that she loved me, and——"

"As if there were anything wonderful in that!" Konradine exclaimed; and then she repented the exclamation, for Emanuel's pale face flushed crimson, and she could not understand his confusion, or why he suddenly broke off his communication.

CHAPTER XXVIII.

Emanuel was occupied with letters that must go by the next day's post, when Miss Kenney arrived in the afternoon at the castle to visit the guests so unexpectedly established there. But his absence was hardly noticed. So much had occurred in the time that had elapsed since the good old governess had seen her friends, so much about which she was better fitted than any one else to answer questions and give information, that there was no lack of interesting conversation, and, naturally enough, the baron's betrothal was the grand interest of the hour.

Concerning this matter, however, Miss Kenney was in a state of ever-increasing doubt and uncertainty. Hulda had become far dearer and more precious to her during her illness. She delighted in expatiating to the ladies upon her darling's fine qualities of mind and soul, in thoroughly obliterating from their minds any bad impression produced by Ma'amselle Ulrika's malicious speeches. She told how, in her estimation, there was something infinitely touching and lovely in the confiding, humble affection that the girl entertained for Emanuel. And yet all this only increased her sorrow at the undeniable unsuitability of the marriage; she saw it all,—although she was half disappointed when Frau von Wildenau, and Konradine too, entirely agreed with her in this respect.

"Indeed," said Konradine, "in my opinion the difference of social position is by no means the chief objection to this marriage. If a man chooses to resign for himself and his children certain privileges to which he is entitled by birth, it is his own affair. His native egotism will usually prove his best adviser in the matter. But Miss Kenney praises the poetic tendencies, the vivid fancy, of the pastor's daughter, and these are just the qualities in contact with which a man's vanity makes him thoughtless, and even blind. They are the most dangerous dowry that a woman can have. How can any man answer the demands made upon him by an imagination that regards him in the light of a fairy prince, as it were? She dreams of a paradise in the future, where she will dwell with her lover in the freshness of an eternal youth, whereas the year really is made up of four seasons, liable to sultry heats and dreary tempests, as the case may be, and each year makes us all older and more disagreeable; and poor human beings are held responsible for what is a simple consequence of the prosaic laws of life. Your poetic feminine nature weeps bitter tears when it finds itself disenchanted, and that we live not in heaven, but upon the earth, where the reigning deity is not love, but selfishness. And Baron Emanuel is the very man to disappoint the inexperienced fancy of such a girl,—the very man!"

Miss Kenney remarked that Baron Emanuel himself was an idealist.

"So much the worse!" said Konradine.

"And," Miss Kenney added, driven by Konradine's plainness of speech to defend what she herself had declared unsuitable, "Baron Emanuel is not selfish."

"Then he should be exhibited as a lusus naturæ," laughed Konradine. "A man, and not selfish! To be sure, he is no coarse egotist. But the refined egotism of such a man is all the more dangerous since it deceives both himself and us. Can you not see, can you not hear in his every word, that it is the divine delight of conferring happiness that attracts Emanuel to this girl? What can so elevate him above all prosaic reality as the constant companionship of a being who owes him everything, adoring in him, as does the Greek Church in the apostle John, her enlightener and illuminator? But who can warrant the baron that it will always be so, that he will continue to be the girl's ideal after she has seen, in the world of which she now knows nothing, men far more brilliant and attractive than he? And what man is patient enough not to be impatient when he sees that all the sacrifice he has made is of no avail, that the happiness he has intended to confer does not exist? Why," she cried, "those who know what life is ought to vow before the altar not to look for special happiness in marriage, ought to adopt as their motto Dante's 'Leave all hope behind,' if they wish to attain a contented future. But what content can ever spring from the marriage of two idealists?"

Her mother remarked with disapproval that Konradine appeared to delight in extravagant assertions, and Miss Kenney, who of course knew nothing of the events of Konradine's life during the last year, observed that she judged far more harshly of matrimony than she had done formerly.

"Formerly, formerly!" Konradine repeated, "long ago, indeed. And do you suppose that I do not often long for those old times, when I trusted, believed, and hoped like a child? But I cannot reverse the wheels of my experience. I cannot command my penetration not to see, not to understand. Nor can I condemn myself to dwell in an illusion sooner than undeceive others. If Baron Emanuel were to ask me my opinion, I would not refuse to give it to him; indeed, he is far too clever not to feel the ground beneath him somewhat unsafe."

This Miss Kenney would not admit. She declared that he had refused to listen to anything that could be urged in opposition to this marriage, and had, indeed, resented as an insult the idea that he could possibly break his word. Nevertheless, she had often wondered what would be the effect upon Hulda's sensitive nature if she should ever feel that she was no longer a necessity to the baron. To prevent him from fulfilling his engagement would be utterly impossible.

"Of course it would be impossible by open dissuasion," Frau von Wildenau remarked. "But it would be worth while to try what effect separation from the girl would have. Many a tie has been severed by absence, and the baron has half promised to accompany us a part of our way when we leave here."

"He will not go!" sighed Miss Kenney, hovering between her convictions and her desires.

"A woman who loved him would be very foolish not to keep him!" Konradine remarked.

"Hulda keep him?" cried Miss Kenney, and her tone indicated the entire confidence she had in the girl's character,—"keep him, if she thought his leaving her would be of service to him? You do not know Hulda!"

"You make me long to know her!" said Konradine. Miss Kenney looked grave, but Konradine persisted, and again expressed her desire when the baron had joined them. Emanuel replied that he wished he could show her Hulda as he himself first saw her, but she was now only the shadow of her former self, although illness could not destroy the delicacy and purity of the outlines of her face. He hoped to be able before very long to present her to his friends in all her youthful freshness. But to this postponement Konradine would not listen.

"Who knows," she said, "when we may meet again? A little distraction is good for every invalid, and Hulda will be pleased that a life-long friend of the baron's wishes to see her. Tell her, my dear Kenney, that since the cold must prevent him from coming to her for a few days, I will be his messenger on some bright morning."

Emanuel was pleased with her persistence, and Miss Kenney was inclined to consent to the interview, upon which she founded some vague hope. The pastor was to bring word the next afternoon whether his daughter felt strong enough to receive the visit of the baron's friend.

But the cold, unusually severe even for those northern latitudes, kept both the pastor and Miss Kenney housed for the next few days. The daily messenger sent from the castle, however, brought back good news, and Miss Kenney wrote that Hulda would gladly receive Konradine's visit. The latter, with her usual vivacity, was ready to go at any moment, but Emanuel advised delay, and thus several more days passed, until news arrived from the neighbouring town that the travelling-carriage was once more ready for use.

Although during the stay of his guests at the castle some allusion to their departure had been made every day, Emanuel felt quite a shock when Frau von Wildenau announced the day and hour when they must leave. The time had passed so pleasantly, he had found the mother so much more serious and thoughtful than ever before, and the daughter's misfortune, her anger at her own inability to conquer the grief that a fate she had been so powerless to prevent had caused her, aroused in him such a sympathy for her, that he did all he could to induce their longer stay, without, however, effecting anything except a renewal of their entreaties to him to leave the castle as soon as possible for a warmer climate.

"I have never in my life paid much heed to the opinion of the world," Frau von Wildenau said to him when they were alone together, "but just at present it behooves us to be somewhat upon our guard. The breaking of Konradine's engagement has made a good deal of noise, and, although many of the kindly-disposed pity her, there are others who always envied her and would be very glad now to have any excuse for declaring that she was only suffering from disappointed ambition. Who can tell what plans might not be ascribed to me if we were to accept for a longer time than is absolutely necessary the hospitality of an unmarried man, who is not even master of the house where he receives us? There are people who would discredit our ignorance of your presence here, or that an accident was the cause of our detention, and of all the silly and unworthy parts ever played in this world by women, I hold that of a match-making mamma to be the most detestable. In this direction I would guard from even the shadow of suspicion both myself and Konradine. For the rest, they may think what they please of me and my daughter. We must act as we think fit, and whatever each may wish different, perhaps, in the other, we mutually rely upon each other; and that is a great deal, in this world that we live in."

Frau von Wildenau's frankness so astounded Emanuel that at first he could hardly reply to her. That she should regard him as a man whom the world might suppose capable of indemnifying her daughter for all she had suffered flattered his vanity, although he was unconscious that it did so. Involuntarily he recalled Konradine's exclamation when he told her of Hulda's affection for him, "As if that were anything wonderful!"

Was it possible that he had overrated the disadvantages under which he laboured? Could he interest and awaken affection, and was it really nothing wonderful that youth and beauty were attracted by him?

These thoughts shot like lightning through his mind, and at the same time he reproached himself for trusting to the judgment of superficial people in his former estimate of Frau von Wildenau. He had misjudged her, had refused to perceive that what prejudiced others against her was her vast superiority to commonplace mediocrity. His relations to his guests underwent a change, as it were: he no longer urged their further stay; he simply expressed with much warmth his pleasure in their presence, and the regret that their departure would cause him. Frau von Wildenau replied by hoping that they should soon meet again. The baron said that he was, as she knew, not the master of his own movements in the immediate future.

The baroness was silent for awhile, and then said, "I have spoken so frankly to you, my dear friend, with regard to ourselves, that I am emboldened to go on and entreat you more seriously than before to leave here as soon as possible. You should upon no account brave the stormy spring of this climate; and, since the impulse of a moment—a mere accident, I might almost say—was the cause of your betrothal, it seems to me imperative that you should put to the proof, amidst old, accustomed scenes and modes of life, the actual importance to yourself of this girl's affection and the tie so suddenly formed. In the joy of meeting you again, I proposed that you should accompany us upon our departure; but the same reasons that prevent our longer stay here make it impossible that this plan should be carried out, and I can only pray you to go away from here as soon as you can. Do not be too anxious about Hulda. Even Miss Kenney, who certainly is a sympathetic soul and devoted to the girl, has begged us to persuade you not to stay here longer for the present. You can come back whenever you please; and if you do not please?—Well, no one dies for love, whatever you men would like to think. But many of the truest and best have been destroyed by an unsuitable marriage. Nothing truer was ever said, never was better advice given, than in Schiller's

'See ye who join in endless union—
For Fancy's brief, Repentance long.'

In my opinion, there are no sadder marriages than those into which men have been hurried by some ebullition of child-like enthusiasm; and—pardon me, dear friend—this is a little your case."

She smiled as she said these last words, but she had gone a little too far, and they offended Emanuel and destroyed the impression she had begun to make upon him. He put restraint upon himself to prevent his annoyance from becoming evident; and whereas he had shown very little interest hitherto in the visit that Konradine had proposed paying to Hulda, he suddenly felt anxious that it should be made, and sent to know whether she would not take advantage of this sunny noon to drive to the parsonage.

Konradine was soon ready to go. To her surprise, when she descended to the hall she found Emanuel equipped to accompany her. To her remonstrances he replied that as there was no knowing when the intense cold would subside, he could not restrain his desire to see Hulda; indeed, he reproached himself for having allowed a selfish consideration for his own health to keep him so long absent from her.

Frau von Wildenau understood the significance of this remark, which she received with great composure. Conscious of having spoken with the best intentions, she could not reproach herself, except for too great zeal in her friend's service; and she never confided, even to her daughter, the reproof that she felt was conveyed in Emanuel's words. But the conversation had disturbed Emanuel, and as they skimmed along over the white, level plain, as on the morning after the arrival of the ladies at the castle, he felt that a gulf of time had opened between then and now, and as though he were on the eve of some unavoidable suffering.

The sensation confused him, and he took himself to account for the weakness that from his boyhood had made every leave-taking so painful to him. Then, thinking that he owed his companion some apology for his silence, he frankly acknowledged its cause, telling her cordially how much he had enjoyed her society.

Her fine eyes looked gravely at him. "I am very glad to hear you say so," she said, "for when one has ceased to interest one's self, it is some satisfaction to know that one is not equally uninteresting to others, and I will not deny that I regret to leave here. In order to enjoy a wandering life like ours, one must have desires, love of life, and hope; and all have failed me. Nothing is left but suffering. Rest here with you has so refreshed me that I long for a settled home where I can really remain; I am so tired, that the sisterhood, which seemed to present but a dreary prospect a few weeks since, is gradually becoming attractive to me."

When they arrived at the parsonage, the pastor was absent, called away to the next parish, and Miss Kenney received Konradine, while Emanuel went directly to the invalid's room.

He found Hulda expecting him. She had heard the approach of the sleigh, and recognized his voice. "Ah, how I have longed for you!" she cried, as he entered; "but it is so cold, you should not have come!"

He held out his hand, and she pressed it to her lips, then, with a shy smile, offered him her lovely mouth.

He kissed her gently, told her how it rejoiced him to see her so much stronger, and then asked her how she was.

"How shall I tell you?" she replied; "I cannot understand it all. Now that I can collect my thoughts, I seem to be dreaming. But I trust the cold will do you no harm. What should I do if you were ill and I had to lie here and leave you to strangers?"

Her whole soul was in her words. Emanuel assured her that he was perfectly well, the cold had done him no harm, and that he hoped now to see her every day again. But what had been said during his drive with Konradine still filled his thoughts; he could not make the response to Hulda's tenderness which it merited; and to conceal the wandering of his thoughts, he replied by a question, asking her if she were jealous.

"Yes," she replied, with her accustomed ingenuousness. "They are all so much more than I." Her simple words cut him to the soul, but he made her no rejoinder. This troubled her, and she asked if she had offended him by her avowal.

"No, no," he replied, "but I am sorry you give way to such emotions, for it makes me uncertain whether you really would like to see the lady who has come here with me to-day."

"Why, I have looked for her every day," said Hulda, raising herself in bed, as Emanuel opened the door, and Konradine, accompanied by Miss Kenney, approached her. A burning blush crimsoned Hulda's pale cheeks; she looked first at the stranger, and from her to Emanuel, who sat by her bedside; then, suddenly throwing her arms around his neck, she cried, "Emanuel, I cannot see any one but you—only you! Send her away! send her away!" And she hid her face upon his breast.

Both the baron and the ladies were much alarmed. Miss Kenney withdrew, and Konradine followed her. Emanuel held the agitated girl in his arms, trying in vain to soothe her. She wept, and entreated him to forgive her. She called him Emanuel, and lavished upon him such terms of endearment as she had never used towards him before, even kissing him passionately. Again she desired to see Konradine, asking when the strangers were to leave the castle, and then with a fresh burst of tears she cried, "They all wish to tear me from you, the countess, and my father, and Miss Kenney, and now the strangers too. I have no one in the world but you—only you. You must not forsake me, and I will not give you up; is there not written in the ring 'Thee and me shall no one sever'?"

She seemed beside herself, and Emanuel was deeply moved. He did all that he could to compose her, and Miss Kenney offered to assist him, but Hulda repulsed her.

"No, no one but you! no one but you!" she continued to repeat passionately. She scarcely heeded his soothing words, and finally swooned from exhaustion.

There was no doubt that it had been a great mistake to yield to Konradine's wish to see the baron's betrothed. Emanuel could not forgive himself.

The homeward drive from the parsonage was by no means so gay and cheerful as it had been upon New Year's day. Konradine made a few remarks concerning Hulda's beauty, they exchanged a few words with regard to the error they had committed, and when they arrived at the castle separated in silence.

CHAPTER XXIX.

THERE was but one day more to be spent by the ladies with the baron at the castle, and to all outward appearance matters were precisely as they had been. They assembled at the usual times in the usual places, but there was no longer the cheerful ease and freedom from restraint that they had hitherto enjoyed. Frau von Wildenau had taken pleasure in imagining the pleasure of her friend the countess when she should have succeeded in influencing the baron to take his departure from the castle, thus inaugurating, she hoped, the breaking of his engagement to Hulda; and, accustomed as she was to succeed in her attempts to influence others, particularly those of the opposite sex, she was by no means pleased at the failure of her attempt. Konradine, on her part, was reluctant to return to the world, and regretted the loss of the baron's sympathy and companionship; while Emanuel was profoundly preoccupied.

The depth of Hulda's passionate affection, the recklessness she had shown in testifying it, the native enthusiasm of her nature—all this, that had always so powerfully attracted him, had again asserted its power. Her jealousy had enabled her to read his very soul and to divine what he had never even confessed to himself. Still, he felt that he loved her with an unaltered affection, although Konradine's fate had enlisted his warmest sympathy. Hulda's incapacity to feign or to suppress the expression of her emotions belonged to the image of her that was stamped upon his mind, and yet there was something startling, almost terrifying, for him in this wild self-assertion, as there is for us all in every untamed force of nature, and he could not conceal from himself that Hulda's peculiarities, constituted as society was, might be in their future life a fruitful source of suffering both for herself and for him.

He thought continually of Hulda even when he was with Konradine and her mother. He was content that his guests should depart on the morrow, and nevertheless he was sorry to be separated from the possibility of seeing Konradine and aiding her to the extent of his power.

It was hard for him to play his part of attentive host on this last day. Conversations were begun and dropped; nothing seemed to interest. They tried to form plans for future meetings, but this was impossible, since the baron's movements were so uncertain. In the evening they attempted some music, but Konradine did not feel like singing, and it was soon given up, and they retired earlier than they had ever done before, excusing themselves on the plea of the early hour at which they were obliged to breakfast on the following morning.

Emanuel slept little; the rude north wind rattling his windows made him envy his friends going south. In the morning when they met at the breakfast-table it was still perfectly dark. Fortunately, Frau von Wildenau had recovered her good humour in the prospect of shortly finding herself beneath warmer skies and amid more congenial society. The pleasant little episode at the castle had lasted long enough, and since she knew that the last hours of all such episodes are those that dwell longest in the memory, she strove to make those last hours as agreeable as possible. But her efforts were hardly crowned with success. Neither Konradine nor Emanuel spoke much, only the latter exerted himself to make such provisions for the comfort of his parting guests that they could not but be grateful. By no word from any one was allusion made to Hulda.

As the baron handed the ladies into their coach he was far more depressed than upon the occasion of the departure of his sister's family. Then he had been exhilarated by the novel consciousness that he was beloved; to-day he was weighed down by many anxieties.

The stars were still sparkling in the heavens; it was bitterly cold; the snow crackled beneath the tread of those busy with the last preparations for departure. The bailiff was there in his fur coat, and Ma'amselle in her black velvet hood. The kindness of the strangers, so unlike the haughty reserve of the countess, had pleased the bailiff; and the costly gifts presented by them to Ma'amselle had greatly increased her admiration for them. Quite as if she had been the mistress of the castle she entreated them to honour her by their presence if ever they came that way again.

She was out of breath in her zeal to serve them as Emanuel handed the baroness into the carriage and Konradine held out her hand to him from the window.

"Farewell, my friend! do not forget me," Konradine said.

"How could I?" he replied, and the carriage rolled away.

He went silently back to his apartments. Ulrika looked after him and shook her head.

"That lovely Fräulein Konradine," she said, "would make a very different wife from the pastor's Hulda for our baron."

She said it to her brother in a low voice; but Emanuel heard every word distinctly, to his annoyance; for he was already taking himself to task for finding this parting so hard to bear, that he found himself wishing either that he had known Konradine as well as he knew her now, before her life had been so blighted, or that he had not met her again.

He walked through the empty apartments, so lately enlivened by her presence. How lonely it all looked! He sat down at his writing-table and began to arrange his papers, but he could not sit still. He was depressed and sad; and the day dawned so slowly.

Lost in reverie, he looked out into the glimmering daybreak. Thoughts flitted through his brain like shadows; he was conscious of them all, but could not retain any single one; and if he could, he did not wish to.

When the cocks began to crow, when the wind lulled and the pale-yellow streak on the horizon began to flush and crimson, while the sea beneath it grew aflame, he breathed more freely. He must pause before beginning a new day; and, as he threw himself upon his couch, to snatch, if possible, an hour of repose, he said, involuntarily, "That is over!" and then started at the sound of his own voice.

CHAPTER XXX.

As the previous day's drive had done him no harm, Emanuel was anxious to go to Hulda again as soon as possible. He was sure that she must long to see him; and he earnestly desired to efface their last painful interview from her and his mind by a quiet hour with her. Now that she was fairly convalescent, he had much to say to her; and he was also very anxious to obtain her father's consent to her betrothal, a consent that had hitherto been withheld; since, as the pastor said, human decision was useless until Heaven had decided.

Contrary to all precedent, however, the pastor arrived at the castle quite early in the morning. He said that he had availed himself of the postmaster's offer of a seat in his vehicle in order to speak with Emanuel, to come to an understanding with him that might save both him and Hulda from new cause for agitation.

Many days had passed since Emanuel had seen the pastor, and he found him sensibly altered. He looked bent and old, and the former clear light of his eyes was dimmed and sad. Emanuel could not but see that he was oppressed by other cares besides grief for the loss of his wife; nor could he forbear telling him of the change that he noticed, and of his hope that repose from the duties of his office, and a removal for a time to a warmer climate, might restore to him the health of which his grief had robbed him.

The pastor looked at him kindly. "Yes," he said, "I know that to stand such a shock as I have had requires youth and strength. It was too hard for an old man. But Heaven has sustained me. I have as yet omitted none of the duties of my office, in which I hope to have the strength to continue until the end, which cannot be far off."

Emanuel refused to entertain this view. "Let us hope, my dear old friend," he said, "that you deceive yourself with regard to your strength, although you surely must see that it is best to give up work for awhile, and live quietly with us; thus sparing your daughter the pain of separation from you."

The pastor shook his head. "I pray you, Herr Baron," he begged, "do not compel me to refuse in set phrase the magnanimous offer that you make me for Hulda and for myself. Do not tempt me in the weakness of paternal affection to forget the gratitude which we have owed for three generations to the countess's family, or, in obedience to my child's desire, to forsake my post of duty before Heaven calls me hence. I cannot consent that my daughter should be your wife; and I cannot possibly retire from my office while I have strength, as at present, to perform its duties."

"But your daughter loves me," Emanuel interposed, "and you have known of my hopes and wishes since first they were formed."

"Your reproach is just," the pastor gently replied, "and I have come to you to-day to declare my resolution and entreat your forgiveness for my weakness. I was overpowered by the blow that had just fallen upon me when you brought Hulda to me. At such times we cannot look beyond the present moment. Then my child fell ill, and looked to you in her bitter woe, calling for you perpetually; and because I doubted her recovery, because, too, it was a consolation to me to have your sympathy in the care for her young life,—I frankly acknowledge my weakness,—I allowed your visits, and let matters go on as I ought not to have done, for which the countess, in her New Year's letter, which she did not withhold this year, in the face of all that has occurred, justly reproached me, seeing that she had already made known to me her pleasure upon the subject of this connection, and that she could never approve it."

In spite of the pastor's humility, his words offended the baron; and the certainty that his sister had secretly endeavoured to thwart his desires, irritated and annoyed him yet more. "You seem in your devotion to your patroness, my friend," he said, hastily, "entirely to overlook that all this is my affair, and not the countess's."

"I know that, Herr Baron. But how can I preach to my flock self-denial, self-control, humility——"

"Your humility is not, apparently, inconsistent with a very proud self-assertion," Emanuel interrupted him.

The pastor's pale cheek was slightly flushed, and he said, "Can you grudge this pride to one who possesses nothing beside it? Or would you have me force my child upon those who have been my benefactors all my life long, when they are unwilling to receive her?"

"Rest assured," cried Emanuel, his annoyance increasing every moment, "that my wife shall never cross the threshold of a house where she is not received with open arms and hearts."

"I know that, Herr Baron; and there is where the difficulty lies. Shall your marriage be solemnized upon the ruins of brotherly and sisterly love, of united family affection? You do not separate yourself from the countess only, but from your brother also. You resign large estates and great advantages, that might be made instruments in your hands for the benefit of others; and all this for the sake of a child who has no way of indemnifying you for such a sacrifice. What Hulda instinctively felt yesterday, in a moment of passionate emotion, she will always feel in future, when confronted with women of rank and social position."

"I knew what I was doing," replied Emanuel, "when I entrusted my future to Hulda. I know what my choice entails upon me, but I also know Hulda, and how she will develop in my hands. You had the same experience in your own marriage."

The pastor shook his head. "Not the same. I stood entirely alone. I had no relatives to object to my choice and whom I was obliged to sacrifice. The ties of relationship are never severed without terrible suffering. And therefore, a few days ago, I informed the countess, voluntarily, that I was convinced that your marriage with my child was most undesirable, and that I should never consent to it. Surely, standing as I do on the brink of the grave, you cannot ask me to break a voluntary promise made to my benefactress."

"Would you rather destroy the happiness of your child? Would you rather play the traitor to the man who trusted you like a friend and offered you the affection of a son?" Emanuel cried, angrily, irritated beyond endurance by the old man's meek persistence; and strengthened by opposition, his love for Hulda asserted its full power over him, and all the vague doubts and wandering desires of the last few days vanished.

The pastor bowed his head at these words. "I was prepared

for your reproaches, for your anger; I deserve it all for my weakness." Emanuel was thoroughly disarmed. He held out his hand to the old man, who grasped it firmly. "Let this be a pledge," he said, "that you will give heed to what I say. Trust to my care for my child. I shall know how to lead her gently back to the life she never would have left had I not followed the suggestions of my own worldly wisdom and her childish love of change, rather than the counsels of her sainted mother."

Emanuel withdrew his hand. "That pledge I cannot give you, and you should not ask it," he said. "You must not force Hulda, force us,"—and he paused for a moment,—"to look forward with hope to the time when you will leave us. Do not force upon the dear girl a choice between her filial duty and her love—between me and you. Indeed, it would be wrong."

"No," replied the father, "I would not put her to such a proof. I have not done so." Emanuel looked at him inquiringly. "Early this morning she sent for me, to pour out her heart to me—to tell me of the passionate outbreak of yesterday. She wished to write to you, and to your friend, begging for forgiveness. I talked long and earnestly with her, and Heaven gave effect to my words."

"Ah!" cried the baron, agonized by the confidence expressed in the old man's look and tone. "You have persuaded Hulda to renounce me."

"I simply reminded her that my office would make this place my home as long as I lived, and that I was old and lonely. I begged her not to leave her old father; and she promised not to do so."

Bitter words of reproach trembled upon the baron's lips; but respect for the old man suppressed them. He stood up, and turned away to collect and clear his thoughts, which one moment dwelt with respect upon the pastor's conduct, and then stigmatized it as treacherous and jesuitical, prompted by his sister, the countess. Sympathy for Hulda, of whose love for him he felt convinced, mistrust of her father and Miss Kenney, and irritation with his sister, strove within him for the mastery. One thing only was clear,—as Hulda had delivered him from the spell of loneliness that he believed had been cast around him, he must now deliver her from this self-imposed renunciation, in which, he was sure, her heart had no share.

He told the pastor that he must speak with Hulda, that he must see her, before discussing the matter further. The old man replied that Hulda desired much to see him, and begged him to come to her on the morrow, since her conversation with her father had left her too weak for further exertion on the same day.

As the pastor was about to take his departure, Emanuel detained him for one moment. "I had hoped," he said, "that after to-day's interview we should be fast friends, never long separated for the future. Together we would have trained and developed Hulda's rare nature. But your entire subjection to my sister's wishes forces me to a conflict, in which I do not struggle for my own sake only, and I must trust to your honour. Your daughter's heart is in your hand. You will see her to-day, while I am away from her. Promise me that you will not seek to influence her, until to-morrow, when I can see her and speak with her myself."

The pastor readily promised, and Emanuel declared himself content until the morrow.

CHAPTER XXXI.

Twenty-four hours spent in solitude and meditation drag their "length along" very slowly, and Emanuel was glad when he found himself, the next morning, on the way to the parsonage. The day was bright, and the air exceedingly clear; and as he pondered upon the time passed here at the castle, and upon his relation to Hulda, he shook off the depression that had weighed upon him, and looked forward to seeing her, and dissipating, by his presence and words, all her gloomy prognostications for the future, much as one looks forward to the happy ending of a book or poem of absorbing interest.

Upon his arrival at the parsonage, the pastor and Miss Kenney came forward to receive him. There was a kind of Sabbath calm in the bearing of each; they looked more cheerful than they had done for some time, as they told him that Hulda was much better and perfectly calm. Still, there was something in their ease of manner that made him uncomfortable.

Her father led him to Hulda's room, and left him alone with her. She lay propped up by pillows, her eyes full of expectation. Her voice had its old melodious sound as she bade him welcome; but she did not, as was her wont, hold out her hand to him; there was something strange in her manner. As he looked at her, he could not but think of Shakespeare's words,—"She sat like Patience on a monument."

He told her how rejoiced he was to hear that she was really better, and he would have pressed his lips, as usual, upon her brow, but she gently repulsed him.

"Yes, I am well again," she said. "I have not been able to pray for so long; all those last weeks in the castle I could not. And then came my poor mother's death and my illness. I have not been myself; least of all was I myself the day before yesterday." And she timidly looked up at him.

He begged her to think no more of it. It had been all his fault. He was wrong to let Konradine come to her: Konradine herself had been convinced of that. "And do not," he added, "repent that outbreak, my darling, since it revealed to me the strength of your love for me."

"No," she replied; "Heaven permitted it that I might really understand myself." She paused in thought for a moment, and then continued: "I told you the other day how like a dream it all was; and when I saw Fräulein Konradine with you, so beautiful, so dignified,—like Countess Clarissa,—and thought of myself, then—then"—she brought out the words with an effort—"I knew it could not be, and for a moment I could not bear it."

"Hulda!" cried Emanuel, with emotion, "think what you are doing! You are speaking to me,—to your lover; your heart has no part in what you say. Look, I am here beside you!" And he threw his arm around her. "Have you forgotten that you are my love, my bride? Have you forgotten everything?"

"Yes!" she answered, "I had forgotten everything! But that is all past, for my father's words have recalled me to myself. I have been thinking only of my own happiness, not of him, and of my duty and his. I cannot leave him."

She passed her hand across her eyes; her voice grew feebler. Emanuel gently but earnestly attempted to win her to his views without agitating her. She listened to him with a smile, but when he thought he had convinced her, she shook her lovely head sadly and decidedly.

"It cannot be," she said. "It must not be. I have had no peace since my mother called me once, twice, just as she was dying. Through these long nights she has called me again and again, and when you left me the day before yesterday, she came to me in my dreams. She never wished me to leave the parsonage, and she wishes it now less than ever, and my father, too, does not wish me to go."

"Your father is old!" Emanuel interposed.

"All the more reason why I should stay with him, now that he has no one but me. When he told me this, and I remembered how my mother had united me to him in my dream, I felt that I could never leave him."

"And will you, then, leave me?" asked Emanuel, convinced that Hulda must obey the voice of her love. "Have you not given me your heart? Have you not delivered me from the curse of want of faith in myself? Do you love me no longer, then?"

"Oh!" she cried, in accents that cut him to the heart, as she snatched his hands and pressed them close to her breast, "do not make it harder for me; indeed, it is hard enough. If he were to die, and to call me in his last moments as my mother called me, and I could not be with him, now that he has no one but me in the world, I could never be happy again,—no, not even in heaven. I took the sacrament this morning,—I begged my father, and he gave it to me,—and I vowed to God and myself, with my father's hand in mine, that I would never leave him, but would live for him alone," and there were tears in her voice, "and not for myself, while his life lasted."

She leaned back, and closed her eyes. Emanuel knew not what to do. His love for her had never been greater, but he dared not urge her further at present. He felt the deepest sympathy for her.

He saw her spending day after day, it might be year after year, in this desert, in voluntary self-renunciation, at her father's side, and he looked forward into his own future, and it was gray and colourless, as the visions with which he had peopled it faded away.

As he still sat there with her hands in his, the pastor entered. Emanuel half arose, and Hulda, thinking he was preparing to leave, cried, in terror, "Are you going, Emanuel?"

"Tell me that you will follow me, and I will stay," he said, tenderly.

"Be merciful," said her father; "do not put her to the sharp test that you yourself called cruel. She found peace when she looked for it this morning, and it will be hers and dwell with her when all agitating causes are removed."

Hulda had folded her hands, and her eyes were fixed in entreaty upon her lover. It was almost more than he could bear. He rose to go. With a trembling hand Hulda drew from her finger the ring that he had given her. That was too much.

"No!" he cried, "this parting is not forever! The ring is yours,—a pledge that we shall meet again!" And, imprinting a kiss upon her brow, he hurried away.

He never heard the pastor's words as he accompanied him to his carriage, or Miss Kenney's promises that she would "tenderly cherish the dear girl." He reached the castle and his own apartments, and still his mind was filled with the image of his darling, her eyes heavy with tears, and her lovely mouth quivering, yet firm. He was profoundly sad. The fair vision of hope that had hovered before him had faded, and his confidence in those nearest to him was destroyed. His sister, the pastor, Miss Kenney, seemed leagued against him, and it appeared to him that a true love—a genuine affection, like that which he had hoped Hulda felt for him—would have heeded no oath, no parent's bidding, would never have hesitated between a father, and a lover who had entreated as he had done. And when these thoughts assailed him, he was heavier-hearted than ever.

He rang for his servant, and had all things prepared for his departure. Why should he linger here a moment longer, now that there was nothing more to hope or to expect?

In a few hours everything was ready, and towards evening his carriage stood waiting for him. Once more he walked through the long suites of rooms as he had done on the day when he had awaited there his sister and Clarissa. What length of years seemed to have passed since that summer day and this dreary nightfall! How different his present pain from the calm self-abnegation of that former time! To-day he could understand the antipathy that Konradine had expressed for society and the world, and yet it would be torture to remain in this solitude.

The bailiff and Ma'amselle Ulrika duly made their appearance to bid him farewell. They were greatly surprised at his departure, since nothing that they knew of had happened, and no letter had arrived to warrant so sudden a resolve. Ma'amselle declared that it made one feel like a fool to have such things happen without any reason, and the bailiff remarked that he should surely not busy himself about what did not concern him, but it was a pity that the Herr Baron should start off in such terribly cold weather.

Before the baron got into his carriage he called Ulrika, and reiterated his injunctions as to the attention that was to be paid to Hulda's every want.

"To be sure, Herr Baron," Ma'amselle eagerly interposed, glad of any excuse to ask a question. "You shall certainly find on your return that everything has been done that I could do. But when do you intend to return, Herr Baron?"

"I shall give you due notice," was the reply.

"They will know, at all events, at the parsonage, when you write to them, Herr Baron," she persisted; but to this last attempt Emanuel made no answer whatever, to her great disgust.

"A poor enough office it is," she grumbled, when the courtyard gate was closed upon the carriage, "this shutting up and putting away after every one has gone. Lonely enough it will be, and time enough I shall have on my hands. But," she added quickly, and her tone was far brisker, "everything is at an end between the baron and your Ma'amselle Hulda, brother. The pastor here the first thing in the morning yesterday, the baron at the parsonage the first thing in the morning to-day, and then up and away in this freezing weather, and not a word out of his mouth when I speak of his writing; not even a 'certainly!' or 'yes, indeed!' There is a screw loose somewhere! It is all up with the grand marriage!"

"For Heaven's sake, sister, keep your wisdom to yourself

until it is wanted!" growled the bailiff, and she judged it wise to go her ways and be silent.

Meanwhile Emanuel drove through the night, lost in melancholy reverie, across the white, dreary plain, and poor Hulda waked and watched in the parsonage, striving in vain to think only of the duty that lay nearest her, and to look her future life, now colourless and blank, bravely in the face.

PART II.

CHAPTER I.

EMANUEL, travelling by slow stages, did not arrive at his villa until the early spring had begun to burst into bloom; but the balmy air, and all the witchery of his southern home, failed to cheer him or to lighten his heart of the load that weighed down his spirits.

He avoided a meeting with his sister, only notifying her that he had left the castle, and adding a few words of bitter reproach for her unjustifiable interference with his plans and hopes. She attempted some explanation and justification of her conduct, but Emanuel refused to pay any heed to her, and the pastor's heroic design of restoring peace and affection between the brother and the sister at the cost of his child's happiness was utterly foiled for the present. His child's sacrifice had benefited no one but the countess, who saw not only the odious engagement broken off, but all her plans with regard to Hulda and Miss Kenney carried out, since the latter declared of her own accord that her charge had grown so dear to her that she could not think of leaving her until her health should be perfectly restored.

But what a dull, joyless existence was that to which Hulda awoke in the parsonage upon her recovery! Spring returned, and the cherry-trees were once more in full blossom; but Hulda's white dress no more fluttered gaily from the line as on the Easter gone by,—there was no preparation for the yearly visit from the bailiff's. Hulda sat quietly at her work, in deep mourning, and although the roundness and bloom had returned to her cheek, her eyes had lost their eager, hopeful, child-like expression. It was upon the past that she pondered now,—memory had superseded hope. Every day she asked herself, "Was all that really so? and if it were, why has it passed like such a fleeting dream? How can he stay away from me when my heart is crying after him every hour, and his ring tells me over and over again, 'Thee and me shall no one sever'?"

The bailiff's visits were continued the same as ever, although there was no Easter invitation extended to his sister, who annoyed both the pastor and Hulda with her questions and remarks. Miss Kenney had returned to her old apartments in the castle, but often visited the parsonage, especially since, by the countess's desire, a light carriage and pair had been placed at her disposal.

Hulda never went to the castle unless at her old friend's particular request. She did not like to leave her father or to meet Ma'amselle Ulrika, and the place was full of associations that she would fain have forgotten. Unless some errand called her to the village, the week would pass without seeing her beyond the boundaries of the little parsonage garden. There was nothing to hope or to expect in the world beyond it. And yet she waited and watched day after day, and each was so like its fellow that she wondered, when the church-bells tolled, whether a week had really passed since the previous Sunday and without bringing her a sign from him who was all the world to her.

The countess had written to the pastor after the baron's departure, commending the old man's ready compliance with her wishes, and assuring him that both he and his daughter might rely upon her patronage and protection; asking that she might be made acquainted with any of Hulda's plans for the future, and declaring her readiness to further them. But Hulda had no plans, no hopes, except the one which the countess would have been the last to sympathize with. Even the feverish longing that sometimes possessed her to see something of the world in which he moved was suppressed by her as sinful; indeed, what could throw down the barrier between her and that world except her father's death? And she shuddered at the idea of looking forward to that, or of founding any hopes upon his grave.

Work, hard work, was the only prop left her, and her father's learning and Miss Kenney's accomplishments stood her in good stead. Study kept her from absolute despair, although it could not lend her wings to soar aloft into the atmosphere of eager hope that is the birthright of youth, and which the changing chances of the world may restore to the young even when they think it gone forever.

CHAPTER II.

KONRADINE was happier than Hulda.

Her appointment to the sisterhood, which had been graciously granted her by the grand duke, was awaiting her upon her arrival at the capital. It was undoubtedly a great honour. The order was a noble and wealthy one; and she immediately retired to its cloisters, where she donned the habit that betokened her separation from the world during the few months of the year that its inmates were expected to pass within its quiet walls. She could not deny, as she surveyed herself in her mirror, clad in the black, flowing woollen robes, the white face-cloth, black veil, and cross of the order, that the dress added a grace and dignity to the pure outlines of her face and form; and since it clearly testified to her departure from the world where she had so suffered, she could not but hope that her resignation for a time of the life she had hitherto led might add strength and force to her power of self-control and renunciation. Of course, in the little community in which she now found herself, there were no secrets as to the motives or circumstances that had influenced its various members to adopt their present mode of life. Konradine's previous history made her an object of eager interest and admiration to old and young; and her efforts to comport herself with gracious kindliness to all called forth willing homage from her associates. The praise and high esteem that might have fostered self-conceit in a shallow, frivolous character aroused a noble ambition in Konradine, who found it much more consonant with her dignity to endure her fate with content and cheerfulness, than to present to the world the spectacle of a deserted and inconsolable mourner.

It was a satisfaction to her that none of her present associates were familiar with the details of her past. No one could surround her with the anxious care by which her mother had sometimes annoyed her, or care to know whether she had slept well, or had passed the night in tears; and before long she even began to regret that she had so unveiled her inmost heart to Emanuel. What good had it done her? What good could it do her? She wished she could make him forget all she had told him when she was in such an agitated state of mind. She could not understand why she should so have craved sympathy; and now that all around her were disposed to revere and look up to her, it was irksome to reflect that Emanuel was thinking of her as deserving of pity and compassion.

There had been no special agreement between them to write to each other; but it had been the natural consequence of their mutual confidences that they should do so, and their letters were free and unconstrained. Emanuel, in the quiet of his home, had an increasing sense of disappointment in the failure of his hopes and plans; and, however he might strive against it, a dawning consciousness that he had been in fault oppressed him at times.

Often, as he paced his broad terrace in melancholy mood, the thought of how he had hoped to see Hulda wandering here by his side, of the joy it would have been to him to see her delight in the beauty and majesty of nature in his southern home, would arouse a yearning for her that was not to be stifled, until overborne by the painful thought that her love for him had not been strong enough to overcome her sense of filial duty. But should not he, the experienced man of the world, have known how, in spite of all her scruples, to persuade her to be his, convinced that her father, in the end, would find his own happiness in the happiness of his child? But here again his old mistrust of himself asserted itself, and his pride of birth would prompt him to ask whether it were fitting that he should persistently sue a village maiden to accept a name that the proudest in Europe might be glad to bear. Thus he was tortured and torn by doubts and longings, until time and the constant interchange of letters with Konradine brought him a degree of calmness and content.

Scarcely a week passed without bringing him news from his friend and confidante, and her letters all told him of the repose that she enjoyed, a quiet contentment of which she had hardly believed her nature capable. She spoke of her attachment to the prince as of a thing of the past, which time and an altered mode of life had enabled her to regard as the experience of a third person, and she congratulated herself upon her power to think of him now without anger, or even irritation; her present satisfaction proving to her that the highest happiness lay, not in being beloved, but in loving, and, above all, in reliance upon one's self.

These statements and assurances might perhaps at first have been the result only of her desire that they should be true. They were perhaps only a picture of the state of mind that she hoped to attain. If so, they certainly conduced to bring about the desired change. She became thoroughly mistress of herself once more, and delighted, as she said, to find the former Konradine awake to life again.

Prizing, as did both she and her mother, the advantages of birth, she had always protested in her heart against the baron's choice; but, herself a victim to the prejudices of rank, she had never declared her disapproval. Hulda's conduct on the only occasion of her seeing her had hardly prepossessed her in her favour; and now she no longer refrained from expressing her aversion to such a *mésalliance.*

In her letters to Emanuel she openly avowed that she thought his pity and grief upon Hulda's account exaggerated. She herself—so she wrote—attached no special importance to what was called first love. Love was the highest expression of a fully-developed nature, and the heart must first learn to test and prove its force before it could become capable of a love so great as to absorb the entire being. Let him honestly ask himself whether he believed that young girl, scarcely more than a child, capable of such a love, or if he imagined that Hulda's life might not, in time, be truly happy and contented without him. And did he believe that such a child could find it impossible to forget what had been to her a bright morning dream, when she herself, Konradine, a woman ripe in knowledge of the world, had found peace and repose after the shattering of her hopes?

To these questions Emanuel made no reply even to himself. For him, with his knowledge of her, there was a difference between Hulda and all other young girls. He could not judge her by the common standard. But he continued to keep up a lively correspondence with Konradine, and Hulda became more and more a vision of the past.

A letter that he had addressed to her shortly after his departure from the castle had been returned to him by her father, unopened, with a request that he would spare his daughter; and Miss Kenney, to whom he applied some time afterward for news of Hulda, assured him that she was improving every day, and that youth and a good constitution were fully asserting their power in her restoration to health. She informed him that Hulda had accompanied her upon a visit of a week to the capital, and that she had been wonderfully impressed, quite carried away, in short, by the musical and theatrical entertainments she had there enjoyed. The baron would certainly be glad to know that the girl in whom he had taken such an interest was again restored to life and health. Doubtless, a little more time, with suitable amusements and distractions, would suffice to cause her to forget the hopes that had flattered her youth for awhile; but she must be allowed to forget them,—to which end Miss Kenney entreated Emanuel not to write to her.

He read and re-read this letter, and it shook his faith; especially as the bailiff, who wrote to him upon business at midsummer, added his testimony to Miss Kenney's, by mentioning at the end of his letter that all were well at the parsonage, and his god-child was as blooming as a rose again. The good man had his own ends to answer in this intelligence. He was very fond of Hulda, and could not allow the baron to believe that she was grieving or pining for his sake.

It did not need much to persuade Emanuel that a young and beautiful girl could forget both himself and his love. It pained him, but it relieved him of a great care, and of a certain amount of remorse. It quieted his conscience.

CHAPTER III.

THUS the summer glided by; and after harvest, when autumn had set in, Miss Kenney began to declare that care for her health, and her frequent need of the advice of a physician, would prevent her from spending another winter in the retired castle. The countess, who was visiting her daughter in her new home, proposed to her old friend to take possession for the present of her town-house, where she might possibly join her before the close of the winter.

To this Miss Kenney agreed, and she made haste to communicate her plans to her friends at the parsonage. The pastor, and even Hulda, appeared to think her departure but natural, since they could not hope to retain her forever in their solitude; and, besides, Hulda was beginning to be absorbed by a fresh anxiety.

Her father's health was failing, and there had lately appeared a weakness of his eyes that filled her with alarm. The physician advised his removal, if possible, for a time to town, that he might place himself under the care of an eminent oculist. But how was this to be done? A substitute for his office must be secured, and their limited means made any stay in the capital a matter of grave consideration. The countess, however, as soon as Miss Kenney informed her how matters stood, smoothed away all obstacles in the way of a change so desirable.

She begged the pastor to accompany Miss Kenney to town, and, of course, to take Hulda with him. There he could establish himself in the same rooms in her house that he had long ago occupied as her husband's tutor, and remain there as her guest for so long as seemed to him best. She furthermore insisted that it was her right, as well as her desire, to provide a substitute during his absence from his parish, and to defray all extra expenses consequent upon the residence in town, since she was certainly more interested than any one else in preserving the health and life of so admirable a pastor for her tenants, so valued a friend of her family.

All difficulties were thus removed, and the good old man, accustomed from his earliest years to dependence, was glad to know that the patronage that had never yet failed him was still extended towards him in fullest measure, and would probably be his daughter's after his death. But the countess's benefactions produced a very different effect upon Hulda.

She knew well that the countess's offer should be gratefully accepted, but yet, frequently as she recurred to the fact that her father's eyesight, perhaps his life, was at stake, she could not conquer her aversion to partake of the great lady's hospitality. During the few days that she had spent in town with Miss Kenney, she had reluctantly visited those spacious apartments, and even the prospect of delights and novel experiences, of which the mere thought was intoxicating, could not soothe her wounded pride.

The leaves, however, had hardly fallen from the trees before the pastor found himself once more amid the scenes of former years, and, from the windows of the rooms he had occupied as a young man, looking out into the gardens, along the formal alleys of which Miss Kenney took her daily morning walk with Hulda by her side. Exemption from duty and change of scene had a beneficial effect upon the old man. Miss Kenney, too, was glad to visit the capital once more, where she was greatly valued by the countess's circle of friends, who showed her much kind attention; and the pastor did not shun society. The old governess was very fond of dramatic representations, and Hulda had an opportunity, under her escort, of becoming acquainted with the best theatrical performances.

At such times the girl forgot everything, the danger that threatened her father, and her own wretchedness. She was no longer herself; she lived and suffered in the persons of those who moved upon the stage. She envied great actresses, who might utter and express what she was doomed to suffer and feel in silence. She could not help reading aloud to her father such parts as affected her most deeply, and he took delight in the enthusiasm that noble thoughts and emotions awakened in his child, and was glad to see her relinquish, even for a few hours, all saddening memories.

They had passed a couple of months in town, when every lover of the drama was filled with joyful expectation by the announcement of the appearance of one of the greatest actresses of the day. All who had ever seen the celebrated Gabrielle upon the stage remembered the occasion as one of the great enjoyments of their lives. Not only was she incomparable in tragedy, but her success was equally great in comedy, for she was still young and beautiful. And those who had seen her in private could not sufficiently praise her natural grace, her talent, her noble pride in her art. Among these was Miss Kenney, who had first admired her upon the stage, and afterwards had had frequent opportunity of seeing her at the countess's Italian residence, where she had been, during one of her rests from work, an almost daily visitor.

One evening, in a small gathering of friends in Miss Kenney's room, Gabrielle formed the subject of discussion, and some one present, after alluding to her age, said to be considerably past thirty, mentioned the various stories afloat concerning her.

She had seen, so ran the rumour, the most distinguished men, artists, authors, and princes, at her feet. A gifted young actor had committed suicide for her sake. Then she had been jilted and forsaken by a famous artist, for whom she had made immense sacrifices; and, after all these reports had been discussed, it was firmly maintained that she had been privately married for some years to a reigning prince, and that this morganatic marriage was kept a secret, because Gabrielle loved her art beyond all else, and had expressly stipulated that she should remain upon the stage as long as she felt herself called upon to do so.

Forbearance to judge harshly, and the aversion that well-conducted mediocrity always thinks fit to display to anything out of the usual way, worldly-wise liberality, and a severe sense of decorum, all found their advocates in the small circle here assembled. There was, however, one lady, an elderly relative of the countess, who did not unite with the rest in admiring the great artiste's qualities of mind and heart, but condemned her unsparingly, denouncing as demoralizing the latitude in manners and morals which is generally allowed to actresses.

The severity with which she maintained her views irritated to determined opposition the admirers of the artiste; and since in such an argument as now arose the extremest opinions are apt to be advocated, the old lady soon declared emphatically that in her estimation every woman who went upon the stage lost, by such a step, all claim to be received in good society. She, for her part, would never condescend to personal intercourse with a woman at whom every one could take public exception who had purchased the right to do so by paying for a ticket. This called forth extravagant opposition, and some of the disputants were almost in danger of transcending the bounds of good breeding, when the pastor put in his word.

He had been listening to the discussion, his eyes shaded from the light by a screen, without taking any part in it. Although his ill-health prevented him from visiting the theatres, he was remarkably fond of dramatic representations, and his recollections of the great histrionic stars, with whose performances he had been familiar in his youth, had made many a lonely evening delightful for his wife and daughter. His liberal culture, no less than his gentle, kindly heart, rebelled against any denunciation of the great actress like that to which he had just listened.

"I need not tell you," he said, at last, "that I share the usual prejudice, if prejudice it be, against a woman's seeking notoriety of any kind. It seems to me that a woman's sphere is home, and this not because I would limit her influence and power, but rather increase it. Doubtless, every woman who goes upon the stage, and is obliged continually to give expression to emotions and passions that she would otherwise suppress, loses what constitutes one of her chief charms, one of her most feminine attributes. But——"

"Really, Herr Pastor, I cannot see how we differ in the slightest degree," Gabrielle's accuser here interrupted him. "You apply to a class what I have declared with regard to a single person."

"No!" replied the old man, "I should never condemn, but rather pity, those women who, in obedience to a call too mighty to resist, have chosen a path in life where they must of necessity lay aside a woman's chief ornament and surest safeguard. And I would doubly honour those who, like the great actress of whom you have been speaking, have known how, amid all the temptations and pitfalls of a dramatic career, to preserve in unblemished purity the jewel of their reputation."

The conversation continued for some time to be occupied

with the theatres and dramatic performances; but Hulda scarcely heard anything more. She was pondering her father's words, which, gentle though they were, had seemed hard and unfeeling to her. Surely he, too, was prejudiced. What could there be unwomanly in the representation of emotions that could only ennoble? All actresses need not of necessity become hardened and unsexed. She was convinced that there were many exceptions to what her father considered the rule in this case, and surely Gabrielle must be one of them.

She had seen the actress's portrait in the shop-windows, and had been greatly impressed with her noble cast of countenance. The large eyes seemed to look abroad into the world in consciousness of a power to overcome it. Even the smile upon her lips was full of a proud security. Such a majestic carriage, in Hulda's opinion, could be the result only of genuine self-reliance and a good conscience.

With the warm enthusiasm of youth she had created for herself an ideal, and the more it was attacked the closer did she clasp it. Young and inexperienced though she was, she knew already how entirely unprovoked may be the assaults of envy and ill will, and how easily they may touch a woman's reputation.

All that had been said around Miss Kenney's tea-table had but heightened her intense desire to see the great actress; and with delight greater than any she had experienced for a long time, she heard that she was to accompany her kind old friend to the theatre on the night of Gabrielle's first performance, when she was to appear in Goethe's "Tasso."

CHAPTER IV.

It was a dark, cold winter evening when Miss Kenney and Hulda, wrapped in furs, drove to the theatre that appeared to absorb within the charmed circle of its brilliant lights all the life and bustle that had forsaken the gloomy, deserted streets. The first notes of the overture greeted their ears as they entered their box.

The house was crowded; and when the curtain rose, when

the bright sunshine of an Italian landscape effaced the remembrance of the northern storm without, and the figure of Gabrielle, who personated the princess, advanced from the terrace, she was greeted with enthusiastic applause. Her appearance justified all that had been said in her praise. Walking forward, as if unconscious of the presence of the audience, she addressed her companion.

Surely there was magic in the words to transport one far away from every-day life. One breathed another atmosphere. All that could distress or annoy was banished from this ideal realm.

Even those among the audience who had supposed themselves thoroughly familiar with the drama, found it invested with a beauty of which they had not dreamed. This was the Princess Leonora that had inspired the poet. So full of noble grace, of lofty and yet simple dignity, was every gesture and tone of the actress, that the applause of those who hung upon her accents was tempered by a kind of awe. And the confidence that Hulda had reposed in Gabrielle as a woman before seeing her, grew into affectionate regard with every moment.

For the first time since her parting from Emanuel her heart beat light and free, inspired as it was with a desire that bore no relation to him. She wished to speak to Gabrielle, although she hardly knew what she should say to her. She felt as if she must give expression to her reverence for her, which was akin to the emotion with which a devotee regards some wonder-working picture or image; and vague hopes arose within her when Miss Kenney, who had been greatly delighted by the performance, proposed to write to the artiste thanking her for the pleasure she had received, reminding her of their former intercourse, and expressing a hope that it might be renewed.

The note was instantly answered. Gabrielle cordially thanked Miss Kenney for her kind expressions, and, since she could not possibly, among her numerous engagements, appoint any time when she should be at leisure to receive a visit at her hotel, proposed, when opportunity should offer, to present herself in Miss Kenney's rooms, to renew an acquaintance mutually so agreeable.

Miss Kenney did not fail to be present at all her performances, each of which was a fresh triumph for the actress.

Upon her return from the theatre the governess would seek the pastor's room, and there delight her friends with a description of what she had enjoyed,—for Hulda spent these evenings reading to her father,—until at last the old man's eager desire to see this star in the dramatic world was almost as great as his daughter's.

One evening when Gabrielle did not play, Hulda and her father were seated at Miss Kenney's tea-table, when a carriage drove into the court-yard; and before they had had time to wonder at the unaccustomed sound, the door opened to admit a brilliant visitor indeed,—Gabrielle herself.

"I am sure you must have thought I was never coming," she said, advancing with inimitable grace, and taking both Miss Kenney's hands in her own; "but upon these theatrical tours my time is never my own; and it is rarely indeed that I can do what would please me most. To-night, however, I dressed early for a ball, where I must go to be stared at and questioned, and for which I shall indemnify myself by a quiet hour with you. Pray give me a cup of tea, and tell me where the countess is; and how Clarissa and the young count are; and why you are here without them."

She said it all perfectly naturally, and yet with the air of a princess who involuntarily feels that her presence and sympathy confer pleasure. Then turning to the pastor and his daughter, she expressed her satisfaction at finding that her old friend was not alone.

Miss Kenney presented them to her guest; and while the pastor joined in the conversation that ensued, Hulda, as she silently made the tea, gazed at Gabrielle in a kind of rapture. She seemed to her even younger than when she had seen her upon the stage; and, although she could hardly believe that this charming creature in her modern ball-dress, with jewels sparkling on her neck and arms, who was going to dance at a ball, was the Leonora whom she remembered, she was completely fascinated by her; every look and gesture seemed full of artistic beauty.

As Hulda handed her a cup of tea, her eyes for the first time rested full upon the young girl. A look of surprise passed over her features; and, turning to Miss Kenney, she said, "You knew me ten, twelve years ago. Do you not think this child resembles me as I was then?"

Miss Kenney could hardly admit this, although there certainly was a similarity in the colouring of the two faces. But Gabrielle liked to justify her assertions; and, rising and taking Hulda's hand, she led her up to a tall mirror, and standing side by side with her there, said, "Indeed, you are strikingly like me, my dear child. But don't cast down your eyes and look so distressed; you need not let the resemblance terrify you." Then, leaning towards her, she kissed her brow, and added, kindly, "Now that I find you so like me, I shall not be able to say that I admire you."

Returning to the tea-table, she asked the pastor, who was pleased by the notice taken of his child by the great actress, whether he had educated Hulda in the country; and Miss Kenney, who was always true to her governess instincts, thinking that more attention was paid to Hulda than was quite good for her, led the conversation away from her by declaring that Gabrielle herself had done much to arouse a love of the beautiful in the child, who had lately enjoyed the delight of seeing her in her rôle of Leonora.

"And in what other parts have you seen me play?" asked the artiste, turning to Hulda, who answered that she had been to the theatre but once, great as had been her desire to see her as Juliet. The pastor here expressed his regret that the state of his health prevented his enjoying so great a pleasure; and Miss Kenney was eloquent in her admiration of the artiste's rendering of certain passages of Romeo and Juliet.

Gabrielle was gratified by such genuine homage, and turning again to Hulda, who evidently prepossessed her greatly, she said, "I am sorry that I shall not play Juliet here again, for I consider it one of my best parts, and am always pleased when others agree with me. Meanwhile, since you wished to see it, and since I would gladly atone to the Herr Pastor for depriving him of his reader during this hour, if you have a Shakespeare at hand,"—and she looked at her watch,—"I still have half an hour to spare, and I shall be glad to read you a few scenes, if you will take a part with me."

"I? For you? Oh, how can I?" cried Hulda, who seemed to be living in some improbable dream.

"Only try; it can do you no harm," said Gabrielle, with a smile; "and get the book quickly, for really there is no time to lose."

The tragedy was soon produced. Hulda had been reading it lately, on the day when Gabrielle was to perform it. Gabrielle opened it at the first scene between Romeo and Juliet, telling Hulda to read Romeo's part, while she recited her own, of course, from memory. She was in her happiest mood. Through scene after scene she led her hearers entranced; and in the soliloquy, before Juliet drinks the sleeping-potion, both Miss Kenney and the pastor were in tears. As for Hulda, her emotion was too deep to be thus expressed.

Her heart had throbbed loudly at the first words that she was obliged to read, but by degrees she had entirely forgotten herself: her whole soul was lost in admiration of Juliet. As in a dream one performs actions that seem impossible even to the dreamer, so she resigned herself to the poetry and its representative. She read on and on, until she sat gazing, absorbed, at the actress, as she spoke the final words:

"O happy dagger!
This is thy sheath. There rust, and let me die."

Then Gabrielle rose quickly, with a smile, and turning to Hulda, with an evident desire to break the spell of silence cast over her hearers by her matchless rendering of the part, held out her hand, saying, "Well, did you like it, dear child?"

"Yes," was the reply; but even that one word was difficult of utterance; and while her father and Miss Kenney were expressing their thanks, she bent down and kissed Gabrielle's hand, tears streaming from her eyes.

"You feel deeply," said Gabrielle, pleased with the girl's passionate admiration. "Your daughter reads extremely well, Herr Pastor," she added; "really, uncommonly well. She did not annoy me by one false tone, and sometimes she surprised me. As a reward, she shall see me to-morrow night in my farewell part, Donna Diana. You are a country girl," she said to Hulda, with a smile, "and can rise early. Come to me to-morrow morning at nine o'clock, and I will give you tickets of admission for Miss Kenney and yourself."

Then she wrapped herself in her fur cloak, and left her grateful friends, assuring them that their enjoyment had been a greater satisfaction to her than the applause of a large audience.

CHAPTER V.

The sun had not even peeped over the tall roofs of the old houses in the narrow streets the next morning when Hulda, in her picturesque fur jacket and close velvet cap, betook herself to Gabrielle's hotel. A carriage stood before the door, and the lights were still burning in the lower story. The concierge to whom she addressed her modest inquiries told her that Mademoiselle was up and at breakfast, and that she had given orders that if a young girl inquired for her she should be shown up to her rooms immediately.

As Hulda entered, Gabrielle, attired in a dark silk morning dress, was sitting at the breakfast-table before a bright fire, while candles burning in silver candelabra lit up the breakfast equipage with a cheerful glow that was still wanting in the tardy day. In spite of the frosty panes, flowers were blooming in the windows, and vases filled with flowers were abundant in the room. Books, papers, and a variety of graceful trifles lay about on the tables; and a maid was just carrying into the next room a gorgeous crimson velvet robe embroidered with gold.

Hulda had been accustomed in the castle to all the appliances of wealth; but everything here had a different air. It was freer, more romantic. The impression it made was pleasanter, in the hasty glance the young girl cast around her, as Gabrielle greeted her kindly and insisted upon her laying aside her furs and breakfasting with her. She poured out a cup of chocolate and handed it to her, saying, as she looked her full in the face, "Now that you have such rosy cheeks from your early walk, I can see how very young you are. Your mature figure deceived me yesterday. How old are you, my child?"

Hulda replied that she was in her eighteenth year.

"And have you always lived in the country, and with your father? Where, then, did you get those deep tones in your voice,—tones that are not learned in the nursery?"

Hulda looked at her as if she did not understand her question. "Have you been accustomed to dramatic reading, like that which I asked of you last evening?"

"Oh, yes," said Hulda; "they often sent for me last winter to read for them at the castle."

"And who were 'they,' my child?"

"Sometimes there were guests present, and sometimes there were only the Prince and the Countess Clarissa, and"—she hesitated—"the Herr Baron."

"What Herr Baron?"

"Baron Emanuel!" said Hulda, as a crimson flush suffused her cheek, and she scarcely dared to raise her eyes, for fear they should betray her.

"Indeed! now I understand, my child, whence come those wonderful tones in your voice that cannot be taught!" cried Gabrielle, holding out her hand to the young girl, and looking at her with a clear, penetrating gaze that was more than Hulda could bear. All the past, with its hopes and fears and shattered joys, came rushing over her soul, and, carried away by the kindly sympathy in Gabrielle's tone and manner, she threw herself at her feet, and hiding her face in her lap, burst into tears as she sobbed out, "Oh, forgive me, I cannot help it! I am so unhappy!"

"Stand up, my poor child, stand up!" Gabrielle exclaimed, as the weeping girl strove to regain her composure. The artist's sympathy, aroused at first by a fancied resemblance between Hulda and herself, was now thoroughly enlisted. "Do not try," she said, soothingly, "to check your tears,—cry, cry, my dear child. There are tears which we hide from a father or a mother, but which must have free course some time, and which flow more gently when some one who cares for us stands by And I do care for you, my poor little flower! Tell me all; I shall understand it, for I too have suffered and endured. You may tell me everything without fear."

And Hulda told her everything, with all her native ingenuousness. It was an infinite relief to her to utter what she had never even dared to say to her lover; to tell of how her heart was full to breaking, and how her lips had been sealed to all the world until this moment.

Meanwhile the advancing day grew bright. The sun came shining in at the windows, but neither of the occupants of the apartment had thought of extinguishing the candles burning on the table. Not until the young girl's tale was at an end did Gabrielle address a question to her. "And what do you expect now? What are you going to do?"

Hulda looked sadly up at her. "What can I do, but fulfil my duty, and pray God that he will enable me to do it?"

"Yes," replied Gabrielle. "I too see that you must not leave your father. But I could not have acted thus, and the baron will not account your filial love a virtue. I have known him for years." She saw the girl's eyes kindle at these words. "I know Baron Emanuel well, and I know his tender enthusiasm of character, and can understand that you love him and that he loved you. But, as he is an enthusiast, he has all an enthusiast's sensitive and suspicious egotism. Such a man requires other proofs of affection than those you have given him. He was ready to sacrifice much for your sake, and you owed him a corresponding sacrifice. Doubtless he thought that a genuine love would cause you, as the Bible says, to leave father and mother and cleave to the husband. You disappointed his hopes. He cannot believe in a love which when put to the test proves weaker than filial affection."

Hulda had not expected such a reply, and it pained her. "Could I disobey my father?" she asked. "Could I——"

Gabrielle did not let her finish the sentence. "Most certainly you could, most assuredly you should! And the baron would have cherished you so tenderly in return. Just such a proof of love was what he demanded. But you read your poets and learn them by heart, yet never understand them. 'The highest price alone will buy those treasures that we rate most high.' And then again, 'No eternity can restore what a moment can lose.' But I will not pain you, child; I only wish to show you that all you have suffered is the result of your own actions, for which I hold you in no wise responsible. Your training has deprived you of all power to do otherwise. You thought you could break the spell cast upon your lover, but you had not strength to break spells which have been cast around you from childhood, and which should be regarded, within certain bounds, as sacred. But we all have rights as individuals in this world. If love is the strongest force of a woman's nature, I hold the courage that it inspires her noblest attribute." She paused, and then added, "You read Romeo so well, and understand Juliet not at all. And yet, as I look at you, I am reminded of my own youth."

"Were you forced to leave your home and your parents?" Hulda asked, timidly.

"I? I never knew either parents or a home. Whatever I am, I made myself!" said Gabrielle, proudly. "My mother's sister, a dancer like myself, took me when my mother died. I grew up, that was all,—shifting for myself, like a young duck in the water; and the water in which I swam was not always of the clearest. I had to work out everything for myself, even my sense of duty and of self-respect. At last my hour of redemption arrived, in the noble confidence reposed in me by one human being. I was born anew into the world. Such an hour, thank God! there comes for most of us, if we only know how to profit by it." She stopped, as if surprised that she had so spoken of herself, and said, "But this has nothing to do with your affairs. You tell me that you have entirely relinquished the hope of ever again seeing Baron Emanuel, and I think you are wise; such 'hope deferred' is too much for any woman. But is there any one to whom you can turn when you shall need a friend,—when your father, who seems to me very feeble, shall have closed his eyes upon this world?"

Scarcely a day passed in which Hulda did not ask herself this question, and for months she had told herself that she did not entertain the slightest hope of Emanuel's return, and that she would go forth into the world and earn her bread as best she might. But now that Gabrielle gave utterance to what had hitherto been unexpressed in words, she suddenly felt how, in spite of herself, all her hopes were centred in her absent lover, and she cried out, involuntarily, "He cannot have forgotten me!"

The tone in which these words were spoken quite charmed Gabrielle, and greatly increased her sympathy with Hulda.

"Forgotten?" she repeated. "What is ever forgotten, or who can forget? But even what we cannot forget, my child, we must often forego; and the sooner the better."

Her servant here announced the name of the director of an important theatre in a neighbouring province. He had already entreated Gabrielle for one or two appearances at his theatre, and had now come in person to follow up his request. Hulda would have taken her leave, but Gabrielle asked her to wait, since the cards of admission for the evening had not yet been sent her.

The director was a tall, handsome man, although now nearly sixty years old. Hulda had often heard her father speak of him, for he belonged to a family of celebrated actors, and during the time of her father' residence in the capital had appeared upon the boards himself, taking the parts of the young lovers. He seemed still to aspire to the same rôle, was dressed with great care, in the extreme of the fashion, and every word was evidently studied. Art had quite superseded nature in his case.

"I hope, fairest lady," he cried, when Gabrielle had expressed her surprise at seeing him, "that you are not cruel enough to mean what you say. Could I so far forget myself as to know you so near without an attempt to kiss this lovely hand, even although not only fields of snow, but 'a sea of troubles' interposed between us?" And he drew off his glove, and, with extravagant gallantry, touched Gabrielle's hand with his lips, saying, as she laughed and shook her finger at him playfully, "Still the same enchanting grace, the same irresistible laugh. Every one of them can weep,—but who can laugh like Gabrielle? To hear that laugh once more is well worth the journey hither."

She laughed again, amused to see how years had passed over his head without altering his theatrical manner, and replied, "Then you can return content, my friend; and, as you leave the room, you will hear me laugh again at the fruitless errand that brought you here. Jesting aside, why did you come when I wrote you how impossible it is for me to play for you at present?"

"Why did I come? Shall I tell you, and will you not scold me? My knowledge of your sex, and my conviction that you are no exception to the rule in this instance. It is so easy for women to say 'no' on paper. But when a suppliant appears in person before them, their tender hearts can hardly permit the ugly word to be used. And," he added, hastily, "you shall make your own terms. I accede to them before hearing them. The half, three-quarters, of the profits if you will. The public is frantic to see you. They will cheerfully pay double prices, and every seat will be engaged beforehand. Your lodgings shall be all ready for you. You shall choose your own rôles. I must go back empowered to say, 'Gabrielle is coming!' How about Eboli? Do you remember what an effect we produced when I played Carlos with you? Or Thekla? You will be delighted with your Max. An admirable young fellow; rising talent, fine voice, capital figure. Let me entreat you, fairest lady."

Gabrielle heard him quietly; but when he paused, she said, "Indeed, I am very sorry that stern necessity obliges me to falsify your estimate of feminine nature. I am bound by my contract, and although you were to build me bridges of gold and promise me an angel to play with me, I should still be forced to say no. I am really tired, and, with the long and tiresome journey that I now have in prospect, dare not make any extra exertion."

Still, the director would not consider his cause lost, and so well did he plead it, now as an enthusiastic admirer, now as an eager man of business, that Gabrielle at last yielded so far as to allow him to hope that she would appear two or three times upon his stage when she had concluded her present professional tour. He was all gratitude and delight at the prospect. Then the conversation turned upon other theatrical and dramatic matters; there was a good deal of gossip concerning stage-life, and those then connected with it,—all carried on in a free and easy tone that at times almost startled Hulda, who was sitting meanwhile, quite forgotten, in a corner. At last, when the servant entered with the cards for which his mistress had sent him, and Gabrielle arose to dismiss her visitor, he became aware of the young girl's presence.

He approached her, and, with a look of scrutiny that sent the blood to her cheeks, asked, "A young colleague? A relative? She is very like you. Admirable! With all that beautiful hair, what a Käthchen von Heilbronn she would make! Really, an ideal Käthchen!"

Hulda scarcely dared to lift her eyes; her shy blushes heightened her beauty, and Gabrielle's pleased glance rested upon her with all the interest she had inspired from the first moment of their meeting.

"No colleague at all," she said. "Mademoiselle is a country pastor's daughter. But you see the likeness to me, do you not? It quite surprised me yesterday; and you are quite right, she would make a lovely Käthchen. I think she has talent, too. I heard her read yesterday, and she did extremely well."

She held out her hand to Hulda, beneath whose feet the ground seemed fairly trembling. The director had put his eye-glass in his eye and was staring at her.

"High praise, Mademoiselle! praise that many a tried actor would be proud to earn. Are you desirous of going upon the stage?"

"I?" cried Hulda. She could say no more; and Gabrielle explained to the director what had brought the young girl to her room.

But this did not appear to make much impression upon the man. "Some one in Faust says," he said, "'An actor may instruct a parson;' many a man destined for the pulpit has gone upon the stage; all roads lead to the stage as well as to Rome, and the road thither is no longer from a parsonage than from any other place. So, if you think mademoiselle has talent, and if she thinks——"

"And if—and if," Gabrielle interrupted him. "Let it rest there, I pray. Don't you see you annoy and embarrass the poor child? Don't carry the jest too far. You find us play-actors uncomfortable people, do you not, Hulda dear? And you are not very far wrong. Fortunately, here are the tickets."

She handed her the tickets, and, with kind remembrances to Miss Kenney and the pastor, dismissed her, bidding her remember that she must turn to her if ever she needed a friend, promising to do all in such case that she could for her; and then she retired to dress for a rehearsal, whither the director, by her permission, was to accompany her.

CHAPTER VI.

HULDA could scarcely have told how she reached her home, and all through the day she walked in a kind of dream. In the evening, at the theatre, she could hardly enjoy Gabrielle's performance, for the director was in the proscenium-box, and stared at her frequently and fixedly, and as they were leaving the theatre he bade her good evening in a tone of familiarity which made her glad that neither Miss Kenney nor her father had heard him. She could not bring herself to tell them of what had occurred during her visit to Gabrielle, but she dreamed of it at night, and every word of the conversation seemed burned into her memory; she repeatedly asked herself what Emanuel would say if he could hear that she was thought like Gabrielle, or how a stage career had been offered her.

The days, weeks, and months went their accustomed way. Hulda's diligence and renewed interest in her studies pleased her father and her old friend, leading them to hope that old wounds were rapidly healing, especially since no one about them knew of Hulda's former relations to the baron, or ever mentioned his name.

Unfortunately, the pastor's eyes grew no better. It was found impossible to perform the operation that had been thought advisable, so great was the feebleness that old age and grief had wrought in the old man's constitution. The amusement and distraction that change of manner of life had at first afforded him, gave place to a desire to be once more among familiar scenes, before his eyesight should leave him entirely, and to perform those duties of his office for which he trusted, with the assistance of the curate whom the countess had provided for him, to find strength while life lasted.

Miss Kenney at first opposed his return. She had become fondly attached to Hulda; the home-life in town was very pleasant to her, and she liked to contemplate her future, now that old age had come upon her, as divided between the castle in summer and the countess's town-house in winter, wherefore she hoped to persuade the pastor to remain where he was until the spring should be sufficiently advanced to allow of her accompanying him and his daughter on their return to the country; but unexpected circumstances induced the countess to make another demand upon her old governess's time.

Her son-in-law was obliged to go to Paris, and was desirous that his wife should accompany him. Clarissa was rejoicing in her first-born, now only a few months old, and could not bring herself to leave him among servants, since her mother was to accompany her, and the journey was a perilous one for so young a child. Therefore the countess proposed sending for Miss Kenney, whose devoted care of the boy would relieve his princely parents of all anxiety. This was immediately done. The countess's letter requiring Miss Kenney's presence contained every direction that could be imagined: times for starting, hours of arriving; the whole matter was arranged with the exactitude that characterized all the great lady's movements. And yet the tardy pulses of old age harmonize so ill with the quick decisions of earlier years, that poor old Kenney was utterly bewildered by the sudden change in her plans, and even the delight of once more seeing and being of service to her dear Clarissa scarcely atoned for the bustle and hurry of preparation into which she was plunged. Hulda's clear head and skilful hands, however, came to the rescue, and in the course of a single day all was ready for an early departure on the morrow, and the three friends sat together in the evening for the last time.

The old pastor resigned himself with his wonted patience to the sudden parting from his valued friend; but the thought of his daughter was evidently uppermost in his mind. "Do not forsake her!" he said, pressing Miss Kenney's hand as he bade her good-night.

"Hulda knows," she replied, "that she can rely upon us. She shall never be forsaken while she is as true and good as at present."

Hulda arose early, that she might take breakfast with her departing friend, who handed her a list of matters that she wished attended to at the castle; and then, while she was putting the last articles into her travelling-bag, she said, "I reproach myself, my dear child, for never having made your future the subject of special conversation between us, but I so dreaded to give you pain by alluding to the inevitable termination of your father's life, that I postponed it from day to day, and now there is no time to say half that is on my mind. Besides, I had hoped to be by your side when the time came for you to be thrown upon your own resources. That cannot be now; I can only pray Heaven to sustain you. The curate whom the countess has provided for your father seems to be an excellent man, but his presence in the parsonage will make your stay impossible when your father is no longer there. Go to the bailiff's; he is fond of you, and you can stay with him until we have provided a situation for you, which we will certainly hasten to do." As she spoke, she went on packing in her warm overshoes, and seeing that her vinaigrette and ether-bottle were in their places. Hulda made no reply.

Not long before, Gabrielle had asked her what she intended to do when her father should be no more. Painful as this question had been to her, it had not produced the actual distress that Miss Kenney's words occasioned. Gabrielle had not known how clear a sun of joy had arisen for a few short days above her future, and could not see how incredible a thing it was to the girl that all that love and hope and happiness should fade, that her trust should be betrayed in one in whom she had seen personified truth and honour. But Miss Kenney knew it all, and yet snatched all hope from her! Miss Kenney, who had so often told her that she felt a mother's love for her, could go on attending to her vinaigrette and all her little travelling-conveniences while she calmly pronounced the doom of a fond, faithful heart.

In vain did Hulda struggle with herself; in vain did she remind herself how much she owed to Miss Kenney's tender care and wise instruction. The thought, "She robs you of all hope; she thinks all you have suffered but just and right, and would, without a pang, leave you to a gray, desolate, dreary future," deprived her of the power of utterance. If she had opened her lips she must have shrieked aloud.

Fortunately, good Miss Kenney was too busy to notice her silence. As she got into the carriage she gave the young girl many a parting injunction to go on with her music and languages, and not to neglect her drawing,—in which accomplishment she was quite proficient,—and assured her that she should carry the best possible report of her health and improvement to the countess and the Princess Clarissa, who would not fail to continue their kindness towards her, and to see that a suitable situation was provided for her as soon as it should be necessary. Then she kissed her with much emotion, begged her to write to her, and drove off, wiping the tears from her eyes as her maid drew up the carriage-window.

Hulda stood in the doorway and looked after them. "She will soon see Baron Emanuel," she thought, "and she will tell him that I am happy!" And at the thought the tears that were burdening her heart rushed to her eyes.

CHAPTER VII.

A FEW days after this the pastor's curate was paying a visit to the bailiff and his sister, when a letter from Hulda was brought in. She wrote, by Miss Kenney's desire, to tell the bailiff of her departure at the countess's request; and then she informed her old friend of the physician's opinion with regard to her father, and begged him to send a conveyance to town for them, since the pastor was longing to return to his home.

The bailiff, after reading the letter, folded it and put it away in his large leather letter-case without imparting a word of its contents to his sister, who, recognizing the handwriting of the address, could scarcely for curiosity continue the conversation she was having with the curate with regard to "a stricter observance of the Sabbath."

This man whom the countess had appointed as the pastor's assistant and successor was an earnest young fellow, upright, frank, honest, the child of respectable, God-fearing parents, but as yet thoroughly inexperienced in the ways of the world, and entirely unaware of the petty jealousies and envy that often make the life of a country clergyman so wearisome. Ma'amselle was very well inclined towards him; she made quite a pet of him, and, influenced by his gentleness, did not as yet dare even to give to her voice, in his presence, its usual shrill tone either of command or of complaint.

"No, no," she now said, in her mildest tones, "you will find no assistance from my brother, Herr Curate. He thinks of nothing but work, work, from morning until night,—Sundays as well as weekdays. A quiet day is his abomination."

The bailiff burst into one of his heartiest laughs. "There she is not far wrong," he said; "but what miracle is this? My sister sounding the praises of the quiet and sacredness of the Sabbath! Well, well, Herr Curate, if you convert her to meekness and submission, you are the man for me."

Ulrika's face was aflame. "Instead of sneering and laughing at the Herr Curate, you had better——" She paused, and bit her lips.

This bickering between brother and sister was very distasteful to the young clergyman, who appreciated the bluff honesty of the bailiff's character, and yet was too gentle and unsuspicious to doubt the sincerity of the interest in serious matters expressed by Ulrika. He was about to put in a word in her behalf, when the bailiff forestalled him, saying, "Come, then, out with it; what had I better do?"

"You had better remember," said Ma'amselle, no longer able to contain herself, "that I detest above all things to have you hide away Hulda's letters as soon as you receive them, without saying one word to me about them, as if they were filled with important secrets."

"No secrets at all," laughed the bailiff; "but I thought perhaps you and the Herr Curate might not like my sending a conveyance to town to-morrow, since it will be Sunday."

"What conveyance?" asked Ma'amselle, tapping the table impatiently with her finger, while her brother knocked the ashes out of his pipe and filled it again.

"Why," he said, at last, "the countess has called Miss Kenney away, and she has gone to the Princess Clarissa."

"And you were not going to tell me such news as that? Such good news? Thank Heaven, there'll be an end of her ordering hither and thither, and her fine lady airs! And what else did the letter say?"

"Nothing pleasant to hear," replied her brother. "I was afraid that there was little to be done for our good pastor. Hulda knows now that there is no help for him in this world, and the poor man wishes to be once more among old familiar objects as long as there is eyesight enough left him to distinguish them. So Hulda begs me to send for him as soon as possible; and I shall do so to-morrow, before the roads are worse."

"Since they have been away so long," said Ma'amselle Ulrika, "they might as well stay until——"

"Until the roads are impassable," the bailiff interrupted her, "or until the poor man cannot see the home to which he returns. No, the girl is right. He must come back; and the sooner the better."

The bailiff was quite affected at the thought of his old friend's sad fate. "It will be a good thing for you too, Herr Curate," said he, "to have them both at home again. The pastor was born here, and knows the people and their ways. And his daughter—well, you have seen her; you were in the parsonage three days before they left. I think a great deal of her; she is good and true. And her mother, too, was an excellent woman, who knew how to keep house thriftily upon the little that they had."

Ulrika had scarcely been able to keep quiet while listening to Hulda's praises; but since she had resolved to display only Christian forbearance and gentleness in her intercourse with the curate, she regarded the pastor's late wife as one of those innocuous people of whom she had nothing ill-natured to say. "Yes," she sighed, "Simonena was a good woman, and was well taught here. Both she and I did our very best for Hulda. But the girl is lacking in what no teaching can give her; nothing but a change of heart can do any good."

"And what does Hulda lack, pray?" asked the bailiff, irritated.

"Humility! she lacks humility!" replied Ulrika. And then she added, in an undertone, "No one but a baron is good enough for her."

The bailiff knitted his brows, and gave his sister a look that sent her from the room, rattling the bunch of keys at her girdle as she went. Her brother walked once or twice to and fro in the room, then suddenly confronted his guest and said, "I know the people hereabouts well enough, and I know my sister well enough, to be sure that you have heard all kinds of silly gossip. Do not believe one word of it. Lies and slander from beginning to end. The poor child is greatly to be pitied, and pray let her see a friendly face to greet her in her home."

There was so much honest kindness in his voice and manner that the young curate was overcome and convinced by it, and he opened his heart forthwith.

"I have, it is true," he said, "been distressed to find so many of the better class of our parishioners, besides Ma'amselle Ulrika, not well disposed towards the pastor's daughter. So far as I was able to judge in those three days, she is very simple and gentle, and the poor people are devoted to her. No open accusation is made against her."

"Because there is none to make. Because even envy itself cannot find anything to bring against my poor Hulda."

The curate rejoiced to hear this. It had been hinted to him that she was ambitious, vain, and cunning. When he had said that to him she seemed very different, there had been meaning smiles, and allusions made to the prince's handsome secretary, to his grace himself, and to the Herr Baron, who could tell true tales as to her great innocence. He had forborne to ask any questions; but he had looked forward with anything but pleasure to daily intercourse with a girl whose character was in such ill repute. The bailiff's hearty praise of her took a burden from his mind, and for the first time he asked for some explanation of the origin of all these vague reports. In reply, the bailiff told him all that he knew of poor Hulda's trials.

Meanwhile Ma'amselle Ulrika had been laying the cloth in the next room, and she now called them to supper. No further allusion was made to the pastor, or his daughter, until, as the curate took his leave, Ulrika pressed his hand, and said, in a whisper, "You will open your eyes, Herr Curate; but I have no fears for you."

He feigned either not to hear or not to understand her. She had grown repugnant to him, and he was oppressed by his want of worldly wisdom and experience. As he walked home, he wished his duties in this place had fallen to the lot of an older man, and he resolved to close his ears to all slander and evil-speaking.

CHAPTER VIII.

The vehicle that the bailiff had sent to town was ordered to remain there twenty-four hours; and at the end of that time the pastor and his daughter set out for their old home. The spring thaw had come on, and the roads were heavy, so that, although they left town very early in the morning, night had fallen before they drove past the massive walls of the castle, standing out against the gray sky.

The day in the half-covered carriage, in the cold and damp, was a very trying one for the pastor; but he uttered not one word of complaint, only expressing his satisfaction at once more approaching the scene of his duties, and, as they passed the castle, dwelling with gratitude upon the kindness of the countess, who, in addition to her other benefits, had provided him with an assistant in his office.

His patience, submission, and gratitude shamed Hulda, who could not emulate them, struggle as she would. She could not pass the castle without remembering all she had undergone within those walls; and as it grew darker, the memory rushed over her of that wild autumn night, when she had driven along this very road, her head pillowed upon her lover's breast, encircled by his arm, in a dream of happiness, from which the horror of her mother's death had roused her. All that she had since suffered and experienced swept through her mind like a dark storm-cloud, and the struggle between duty and desire was as fierce as ever. She was at war with herself, assailed by fear for a future illumined by no ray of hope. Such a mood rarely comes, except to older people; but Hulda, with her eighteen years, felt as if her life already lay behind her.

It was dark when they drove through the village; the cottages were closed, and the only welcome extended to them was from the schoolmaster, who, happening to be abroad, recognized the carriage, and shouted a cordial greeting to them.

But a bright light was shining from the windows of the little parsonage, and the curate was at the carriage-door as soon as they arrived. He helped the pastor to alight, and gravely held out his hand to Hulda. Within, the fire was crackling merrily in the green porcelain stove, and, with a sigh of satisfaction, the pastor settled himself in the old arm-chair that the sexton wheeled before it for him. Opposite the door hung the profile of his wife, which the curate had wreathed with fresh green. Evidently there had been kind hands at work here; and Hulda was almost startled to find how little pleasure she took in the thought. Amiable as the young curate seemed, the idea of living beneath the same roof with a stranger oppressed her. The house had never seemed to her so small as now, when she saw it again after an absence of several months. It locked her in like the walls of a prison. She longed to flee away through the night and gloom,—away to him whom she could not forget, far as he was from her, and little as he prized her.

She was glad that her domestic cares called her from the room and gave her a chance to brush away her tears; and for many ensuing days the necessity for exertion proved her best friend. Work, daily routine, helped to close the wounds that were ready to bleed afresh at the slightest cause; she learned gradually to bear her lot patiently, but she could not rise beneath it.

Meanwhile, the curate quietly accommodated himself to the home-life at the parsonage. His conscientiousness caused him to reproach himself with the injustice he had done to Hulda in listening for one moment to any reports to her disadvantage, and made him anxious to atone for it by all the kind attention in his power. The pastor took great pleasure in his society, and Hulda directed her little household with a prudence and feminine tact and grace which were peculiarly her own, and which to the curate, whose poverty had made his life one of the greatest retirement, seemed almost miraculous. Her culture and refinement were far beyond what he had been accustomed to meet with among the daughters of his clerical friends. He had never had a sister, and every day seemed to him to reveal fresh delight in this new companionship. Everything that she did, and her manner of doing it, every occupation that he could share with her, added to his happiness. He enjoyed reading aloud to the pastor, for Hulda would sit by with her sewing. Hulda's eyes raised to him on Sunday, when he officiated in her father's pulpit, inspired him and lent him eloquence. The mere walking to and from the little church with the old pastor was a delight, for she walked beside them. Many of his hearers assured him that they hardly missed their old friend when they could listen to him; but of late Ma'amselle Ulrika's words of commendation had been wanting, and she rarely appeared at church, although the year had turned and the skies were once more blue.

Easter had come again; the inmates of the parsonage scarcely knew how; each day glided by so like its fellow. But when days thus resemble one another, the measure of time in the retrospect grows vague and uncertain. Hulda could hardly believe sometimes that two years had not yet passed since she first saw that picture of Emanuel, that scarcely fifteen months had flown since she had parted from him. Sometimes she asked herself, how long since she had seen Gabrielle? She found it difficult to remember that there had once been a time when she had not thought of Emanuel, had not felt his ring upon her finger. Since her love was her all, it seemed without beginning and without end, like eternity. What signified days and weeks? She loved,—and the days glided silently by.

Half an hour before the ringing of the church-bell on the morning of Easter Sunday, while the pastor was still busy in the study with the sermon, which he had set his heart upon preaching himself on this day, Hulda went out into the garden to bring in her flower-pots, that had been enjoying for the first time this year a breath of fresh spring air. The curate was already there, walking slowly about among the flower-beds, now stooping to look for something among them, now gazing up at the firs and cherry-trees. He offered to Hulda, as she stepped across the threshold of the door, a few snow-drops and some willow twigs upon which had appeared the silver-gray buds that the country-people called "palms."

"It is real resurrection weather to-day," he said. "The first 'palms' are out, the hazel-twigs are budding, and even a few snow-drops are to be found." She took the twigs and the flowers, thanked him, and brushed the soft gray buds across her cheeks.

"I hesitated to pick those," he added, "lest I should deprive you of the pleasure of finding them; but I always used to take some to my mother at Easter, and I could not resist the temptation to bring these to you. It always pleased her."

"And it pleases me, and I thank you. I really enjoy them," she replied.

"You so seldom seem to enjoy!" he said.

"Does not each day bring me fresh anxiety?" she asked. "My father is so weak!"

"But God is so strong and loving!" he rejoined.

"This is no age for miracles; we must endure, we must suffer——"

"And trust, and hope," he added.

She shook her head. "I know what is before me. Hope?—" She suddenly paused. He stood embarrassed, not knowing whether to speak or be silent. He so wished to say to her that the bailiff had told him of her sorrow, but it gave him such pain to allude to it, and the thought of Emanuel was so repugnant to him, that his lips were sealed.

"It seems to me," he began, at last, "that you hardly share that entire submission to the will of God which I so reverence in your father."

This was not what he meant to say, and evidently did not please her, for she replied, with a kind of remonstrance in her tone, "God has not endowed me with a submissive spirit."

Her words startled him out of his usual self-control, and he exclaimed, "Oh that you had never left your home!"

The words were wrung from his heart, and the tone in which they were uttered showed that they were so. Hulda looked up at him in surprise. He could not bear her eyes thus fixed upon him, and he stammered, while the blood rushed to his forehead, "Forgive my presumption!"

But now Hulda blushed in confusion, for just as the curate was standing before her now had she once stood in the baron's presence, and she knew what it boded. In a flash a thousand looks, words, actions of the curate's, during the past few weeks, but little heeded at the time, arose in her memory and fitted themselves together, like the bits of glass in a kaleidoscope, into a distinct, regular shape, which she could not ignore, and in the presence of which she veiled her eyes as before some sacred mystery; but her ingenuousness left her no choice, and, quickly controlling herself, she said, "What have I to forgive?

That you take an interest in me and my life,—that you have heard what I suppose is frequently spoken of here in the country?" She hesitated, because it was hard for her to say to another what she daily repeated to herself; but the emotion that she read in the curate's face urged her on and helped her to conquer her maidenly timidity.

"It is true," she said, "that I am not happy, and perhaps it would have been better, as you say, that I had never left my home. But, believe me," and there was a clear, full ring in her voice, "there is a grief more precious than many a joy,—a grief that, with all its pains, is dear to us. Yes, if I could buy what is called a calm, untroubled existence, with forgetfulness of my suffering, I would say, as did the chivalric king, 'Mieux aime mon martyre!' for it is my life, my very being."

She turned hastily away and went into the house. She would not let him see how her eyes filled with tears, still less did she wish to look in his face. As for him, he stood like one spell-bound. If his double had suddenly arisen by his side, himself and not himself, as much a stranger as he now seemed amid all around him, it would not have so agitated him as did this sudden glimpse of his own and of Hulda's heart.

The church-bells roused him. They sounded dull and discordant in his ears, as if they were cracked,—and he had formerly thought them sweet. He could not stay out in the free, sweet air. The day,—the sunlight,—every tree and bush, gazed at him with clear, searching eyes. He could not bear it. He must be alone and collect himself. How could he perform the baptismal rites that were his duty for the day?—how talk to the people of holy Christian communion at a time when he felt thrust out, forsaken of God? He hurried up to his room to try to reflect upon what had happened, to collect himself; he folded his hands as if to pray,—in vain. The gates of heaven seemed closed against him. Those wretched words, "Mieux aime mon martyre," with their strange foreign sound, rung in his ears. He heard them, he saw them written in letters of flame. They were branded in his brain, scorching and drying there the fount of tears, and yet he so pitied both her and himself.

But it was time to go to church. He had always conducted the pastor thither since his return; he would not fail him to-day. With Hulda on her father's other hand, he passed through the garden down the village street and through the church-yard to the church. All went on to-day as on every other Sunday.

Hulda spoke of the lovely weather, and of how good it was for her father, and for the children who were to be baptized. The curate heard and did not hear. "Can I stay here? Ought I to stay here? And how can I go away, away from her?" These were the only thoughts that were clear in his mind.

He heard the pastor enjoin upon his hearers that they should crucify within themselves every evil inclination, thereby redeeming their souls, which should rise again, made fresh and white through Him who for the sake of all had been nailed to the bitter cross. Hitherto the curate had, as he thought, done all that he could to bring to his sacred office clean hands and a pure heart, and had given his whole soul to the performance of his duties in church, esteeming as sinful whatever could distract his mind; but to-day he could not banish from his thoughts the image that usurped the place of all holy aspiration.

He loved her as she loved her suffering; he understood her very soul; he gazed at her and her only; and when from the organ sounded the solemn strains of the closing hymn,

"After this life of mortal pain,
Thou too, my soul, shalt rise again;
From stain of sin and sorrow free,
Immortal life awaiteth thee,"

the lips of the young divine joined in the words, but his soul was vibrating to Hulda's "Mieux aime mon martyre."

Distracted and wretched, he went to the altar, after the Easter service was ended, to baptize the children assembled to receive the holy rite. There was quite a crowd of well-to-do people, for the intendant of the neighbouring royal domain had brought his twin boys, two months old, to be christened, and the bailiff and Ma'amselle Ulrika were their sponsors. And even the poorest of the parents present had been glad to ask those better off than themselves to stand god-parents to their little ones; so that Hulda, beloved as she was by the poor, was of course among the number, and her presence completed the poor curate's misery.

Between his desire not to look at her and the impossibility of avoiding it, he grew awkward and uncertain in his movements, and his discourse became rapid and incoherent. Ma'amselle Ulrika was not the only one who noticed how unlike the curate was to himself, how wanting in unction were his words; but it was she alone whose sharp glance, made keen by dislike and malice, detected the presence of a disturbing cause.

Cold drops stood upon his brow as he left the altar to go to the sacristy, where the intendant and his wife were waiting to thank him, as was customary, and to tell him that the carriage would stop for him at the parsonage to take him to the christening feast, to which he, as well as the pastor and his daughter, had been invited. The old man had excused himself on the plea of his health, and Hulda naturally stayed with her father; but the curate had accepted the invitation. Now, however, he begged leave to decline, alleging that he did not feel well enough to be present. There was nothing to say but to beg him to take care of himself, for he was certainly looking very ill, and to drive off.

Ma'amselle Ulrika and the two girls — wealthy farmers' daughters, who had held the babies at the font—drove off with the intendant's wife. "I am very sorry that the curate is ill," said the latter; "but really it is a comfort to know what the matter was. Such a discourse! One would have supposed he was talking to no one but fishermen and sailors, instead of to respectable people who know what a good discourse is. I have always written down something from the christening discourse of every one of my children, and have had great edification in referring to it afterwards; but I could make neither head nor tail of what was said to-day. The curate looked quite wretched from the first. I hope he may not have the fever. This is just the time of year for it, and this seems very like it."

Ma'amselle Ulrika smiled meaningly, and of course the Frau Intendant asked what she meant.

"It's not the fever; no fear of that," she said. "I saw where his eyes were, and his thoughts too. It's the same old story."

The three others were eager that she should explain herself. Ma'amselle at first refused, affecting great reserve; but at last she was persuaded. "What is there to tell, after all," she said, "but the same old story? She casts her net for every man that comes near her, and is always successful. It really looks hardly natural." She had mentioned no name, but the Frau Intendant and the two girls knew perfectly well whom she meant.

"The curate is the fourth," she said.

"The fourth?" asked the younger of the two sisters.

"Yes, the fourth," Ulrika repeated. "It began with our countess's brother, and then it was his highness's turn, and then came his highness's secretary, an excellent, respectable young man, and now she has cast her toils about the poor Herr Curate, who is the last person, one would have thought, to be attracted by such a girl. I only hope he will get off as well as the Herr Baron did, and leave her to wear the willow."

"It is really scandalous," said the Frau Intendant; "and she the child of such good people."

"How she must feel!" said one of the sisters.

"What will become of her when her father dies?" asked the other.

"She never can stay here," said the Frau Intendant; "there has been too much talk about her."

"Oh, we shall see. I am so sorry for the poor Herr Curate, who will very likely lose his place on her account," said Ma'amselle.

And then the subject was dropped, and the four women drove on in self-complacent peace of mind, feeling no remorse for their cowardly attack upon one who could not defend herself; and in the festivities of the day Hulda was forgotten, except when Ulrika said to herself that she hoped now the curate would learn to know which was his true friend,—herself, who felt so deep an interest in his future, or Hulda, who thought only of winning admiration and lovers.

CHAPTER IX.

Good intentions! Who of us has not at some period of life justified a determination to carry out a favorite plan, regardless of the rights and feelings of others, upon the plea of good intentions?

The countess, too, justified herself upon the plea of her good intentions when her estrangement from her brother lasted too long; but he refused to listen to her plea. Apparently he did not miss his former intercourse with his sister; Konradine's letters appeared to indemnify him for its loss.

"How glad I should be never again to hear any talk of 'good intentions,' or 'frank, honest opinions!'—those flimsy pretexts that people always use who wish to trample upon the rights of others and assert their own will," he wrote in one of his letters to his friend, who was still in her retirement. He did not tell her at whom his words pointed, and she took what he said in its universal sense, and then applied it to her own case.

"I cannot tell you," she said, in her reply, "how much I have suffered from the 'good intentions' of my friends. What wisdom have they wasted upon me, proving to me that in their 'honest opinion' nothing had befallen me but what was just and right! Now, scarcely had I recovered from the annoyance and pain thus caused me, when I instantly exercised my own right to an 'honest opinion' in your case. I did not conceal from you that I considered the connection you formerly contemplated as almost an impossibility. And even now I cannot but believe that we all, my mother, the countess, and myself, were better judges of your wishes and needs than you were yourself. Now, if you can forgive me for this presumption, you must extend some pardon to others who have transgressed likewise, and be again content to live among those who are ever ready to commit the same error, as I, for instance, am doing at present."

She then mentioned that the health of the abbess of the order was failing, and that she had lately shared with her many of the cares of government, and that this new field of action interested and occupied her. "My pleasure in it springs, I am convinced," she said, in conclusion, "from the sense of power that it gratifies, the love of rule. Since it has been denied me to be the wife of a dearly-loved husband and of a prince, I find myself contemplating with increasing complacency the possibility of my fulfilling the duties of abbess in this large community. Ambition too often springs from the grave of love."

These letters of Konradine's greatly interested Emanuel. He could not sufficiently admire her frank judgment of her own trials and experiences; and whereas, when he was with her, her want of reserve scarcely accorded with his feminine ideal, her written words always impressed him as evidences of great force of character. He continually told her of the enjoyment that their correspondence afforded him, declaring that in her he had found what he had always longed for, a friend with a man's cool judgment and a woman's heart; a confidante in whom he could place implicit confidence.

Since she so openly displayed all her cards, as he thought, he, in his thorough uprightness, never dreamed that she could retain in her own hand a last decisive card. She could discuss with him her sufferings from the 'good intentions of others;' but she did not think it worth while to inform him that she was in constant correspondence with the sister from whom he had been so long estranged.

The countess had replied with affectionate interest to the letter of thanks that Konradine had addressed to her after leaving her 'castle by the sea' for the hospitality there extended to her. The correspondence thus begun had at first been infrequent and superficial. Not until Konradine had been for some time in retirement did the countess allude in her letters to her brother, deploring the estrangement existing between them, of the cause of which she had heard from the baroness that Konradine was not ignorant. Then first the idea of effecting a reconciliation between the brother and sister entered Konradine's mind, and this was discussed quite openly between herself and the countess. They were both aware that nothing would so conduce to this end as convincing Emanuel that he had estimated Hulda too highly; that he had invested her with a strength of character to which she had no claim. Thus far they were agreed, but anything beyond this reconciliation hardly entered the mind of either.

In pursuance of her benevolent plan, Konradine made frequent mention of the countess in her letters to the baron, who at first paid little heed to such mention; but in time, used as he became to discuss all subjects with his friend, he brought forward all his causes of complaint against his sister. Konradine warmly defended her, at times in her defence artfully accrediting her with faults that she did not possess, when Emanuel's sense of justice would induce him to espouse her cause. This interchange of letters had now been carried on for a year and a half, and Emanuel, during one of the occasional visits of the Baroness von Wildenau to the Lake of Geneva, had begged Konradine to seize this opportunity of once more granting him the pleasure of her society. But at present, as she playfully but truthfully declared, "ambition occupied her soul. Although she believed that she had outlived her anger and love, both were still powerful stimulants in her life. She longed to prove to the prince that his faithlessness had not left her inconsolable, and as abbess of one of the wealthiest orders in Europe, her position would be all that she could desire. Her separation from her mother had proved to her that, with all their affection for each other, they were happier apart; and the cross of her order, if she were to leave her retirement to mingle with the world, would give her all the privileges of a married woman."

Thus six months more passed away. Emanuel's loneliness began to weigh upon him sorely, and he thought with longing regret of his sister and her family, who had so often enlivened his solitude. About this time Konradine's abbess returned from a short journey that she had undertaken for the sake of her health, so much strengthened and refreshed that she once more took the reins of government entirely into her own hands, thus depriving Fräulein von Wildenau of her principal occupation. Two years she had spent in this comparative seclusion, which she now resolved to exchange for a time for the world in which she had been such an ornament. She could be tolerably certain of not encountering the prince either in Germany or in Switzerland, since his young wife's delicate health detained him upon her Italian estates. Emanuel renewed his invitation to her, just as the countess had proposed, as a final step towards the reconciliation she so earnestly desired, to surprise her brother with a visit.

CHAPTER X.

In the mean time, the summer had passed at the parsonage, bringing at first but small comfort to the poor young curate, who, since the revelation that had been made to him of his own heart, had passed many an hour of miserable indecision and self-reproach.

His duties were for some time afterwards performed for the most part but mechanically. In vain did he represent to himself that he was unworthy to occupy his present position,—that all honest effort here was impossible, since he could not win Hulda's affection and recover his own lost peace of mind. Any resolution that he made overnight to leave a place so fatal to his usefulness, was rendered null and void by his first meeting with her in the morning.

As he listened to her quiet "Good-morning," as he saw how thoughtful she was of his comfort as well as of that of all around her, as he heard her expressions of gratitude to him for the attention that he paid to her father, he could not but determine to remain, satisfied for the present with the friendship she was willing to accord him. He called himself unreasonable and impatient for his hopelessness,—he would so gladly serve seven years for her, or even longer. It was his duty to remain with the old man, who looked daily more and more to him for assistance; and how could he desert Hulda, when the bitter hour was so near at hand in which she would more than ever need a true, thoughtful friend to shield her from the envy and uncharitableness of those who could not appreciate her simplicity and truth?

At such times he felt almost happy. His interest in the flock under his care revived,—his love, more and more unselfish as it daily became, broadened and deepened his character: it gained in manliness and self-possession.

It was the time of the rye harvest, when some matter of business called him one afternoon to the bailiff's. The sun was still high in the heavens, though it was towards evening, and the weather was still sultry. The damp sea-breeze, however, cooled the air, and the lulling plash of the waves upon the shore was sweet summer music.

To the curate, born and bred in an old inland town, the ever-changing aspect of the sea was a source of continual delight. He stood now on the threshold of the parsonage-door, gazing out at the sparkling ocean and listening to the rhythmic cadence of its waters. Then he turned towards the garden. There sat Hulda upon a bench beneath the elder-bushes, whence she could overlook her father's study, the window of which was open. The pastor was asleep in his arm-chair. Not a leaf was stirring. There was no sound save the humming of the bees in the old garden.

The curate went up to where Hulda was sitting, that he might not disturb her father by a loud question, to ask whether she had any commissions for the bailiff's. She sent her greetings to her old friend, and added that the walk would be delightful, particularly in returning. "It is just such a day as the song tells of," she said,

"'Hail to thee, sweet summer-time!
Of all the year the golden prime;
In fresh array the earth is dressed;
The lark springs upward from her nest,
And in the radiance of the sky
Pours forth her magic melody,
And flowers, half hidden in the grass,
Look up to greet us as we pass,'

except that the birds have ceased to sing. In spite of the heat, it will be autumnal at sunset, and our autumn sunsets are gorgeous indeed. Do not stay too long at the bailiff's, or you will miss the spectacle."

Nevertheless he lingered beside her. There was no special reason why he should go to-day, he said.

"But you will miss the view on the way back from the castle. It is far finer there than here," she remonstrated.

Was it kindness, or a hint to him to withdraw? He could not tell. She had avoided all tête-à-têtes with him since Easter Sunday; but the genial summer day that called forth the flowers unlocked his heart, too. He longed to hear kindly words from her lips, and, for want of something else to say, he asked whose the verses were that she had just repeated.

"Who can tell?" Hulda replied. "You must ask the sun, the air, and the waves. It is one of our numerous folk-songs."

"The Herr Pastor tells me that he collected and translated quite a number of these songs for the countess's brother; songs that your mother and you used to sing."

"Yes, we used to sing them."

"And do you never sing now?" he asked, in a tone that conveyed his wish to hear her.

"They are almost all very sad," was her reply; "but my father loved them, and so did I, for I learned them from my mother. My father never wishes to hear them now, and I am glad of it."

He was silent, for he divined what memories the songs would awaken. Hulda arose, and reminded him that it was growing late for his walk. She went with him as far as the garden-gate, and, looking abroad over the glory of the sea, she said, breathing in the delicious air with a sensation of delight, "This is a rarely lovely afternoon." The curate thought he had never seen anything so lovely as her face, now that its wonted melancholy had given place for a moment to a look almost of rapture; and longing to retain that expression there, he begged, "Come with me a little way; or rather," he added, hastily recollecting himself, "do you go to walk, and let me stay with your father. I would rather see you look thus than all the sunsets in the world."

His emotion had carried him away, and Hulda was touched. "You are very kind," she said,—"very kind. I wish I could thank you as you deserve."

But when she saw how his face flushed with pleasure she could almost have recalled her words, and turning towards the house, she said she must go to her father, and that it was high time for him, too, to begin his walk. Still, she could not stifle the hope that had sprung to life within him. With a few quick steps he overtook her, and said, in a tone that came from his very heart, as he seized her hand and kissed it, "Ah, you will surely sing your songs again in some future time?" What could she say to him? How could she pain him? She liked him and had learned to value him. But what good did that do either to him or to her?

And he went his way cheerily and encouraged. The world had never seemed to him so glorious a place, or its Creator so near and loving. He reached the castle and the bailiff's before he was aware of it.

CHAPTER XI.

HERE the harvest was going busily on, the heavily-laden wagons were toiling in from the field, the barn-doors stood wide open; and the bailiff, who was taking a hasty supper beneath the lindens, called to the curate as he entered the gate of the court-yard. "Aha, Herr Curate!" he cried, shaking him cordially by the hand; "it is easy to see that you have been breathing our fresh sea-breeze of late. Your step is as light and springy as a hunter's. Wait awhile, and we shall have you on horseback, and make a rare farmer of you at last. Sit down and take some supper. We had a visit yesterday, too; and look," he added, pointing to an approaching wagon, "we are determined not to starve next winter, whatever guests it brings us."

Ma'amselle Ulrika now made her appearance, and also congratulated the curate upon his evidently improved health. After some conversation upon the parish matter that was the cause of the young man's visit, the bailiff asked after the pastor and Hulda.

The curate told him that the old man was evidently failing from day to day, but that his daughter was unwearied in her tender watchfulness of him. Then, as he was continuing to speak in her praise, he suddenly felt the blood mount to his forehead. Ma'amselle fixed her eyes upon his face, and, unluckily, the bailiff was called away for a few moments.

Almost before her brother was out of sight, Ma'amselle began. She was so glad that the place and his position suited him. She could assure him that the parish would gladly welcome him as the pastor's successor. They had thought him

—the curate—looking and seeming quite ill at Easter; but his confirmation discourse and the Whitsuntide services had been edifying indeed.

The curate thanked her for her kindness, but hoped that the good old pastor's life might be prolonged far beyond what they now ventured to hope.

"Oh," cried Ulrika, "there is not a word to be said against the Herr Pastor; I told her ladyship the baroness so yesterday. But the salary is small for a young man like yourself, and our parsonage is not one of the best hereabouts. A few miles farther inland the parsonages are much finer, and the pastors' daughters honest and well brought up."

Here the bailiff returned and took his seat. He had heard only the last words; but the young man's face and Ulrika's sudden silence told him that something had been said of which he should disapprove. He asked what they were talking of. Ulrika replied that they had been saying that the salary of the pastor to this parish was far too small to allow a young man to think of passing his life here.

"Permit me to observe," the curate here interposed, "that it was your sister, not myself, who said that."

Ulrika was irritated. Formerly he would not have ventured to assert himself in this way. Matters must have gone further than she thought. But her brother here took up the word, saying, in his frank, hearty way, "I'm glad to hear it, Herr Curate; and since the countess has increased the salary on your account, and will increase it further, I doubt not, when our good pastor is no more——"

"Yes," cried Ulrika, no longer able to contain her spite, "if Hulda remains in the parsonage. But the Herr Curate does not seem to me like a man who could be bribed to make a girl his wife simply because the people at the castle wish to get her out of the way!"

"Hold your tongue!" shouted the bailiff, bringing his fist down upon the table so that the glasses rang again. "The only woman in the way here——"

The curate, however, did not allow him to finish. "Do not be angry with your sister, Herr Bailiff," he said, calmly; "she is perfectly right. I should be the last to submit to what she describes; but if the countess should ever intrust me with the care of the parish, I should account it my greatest happiness if I could induce so true and good a woman as Fräulein Hulda to become my wife."

Ulrika stood fairly speechless in discomfiture, but the bailiff held out his huge hand to the young man with, "Bravo, my fine fellow! that was a word spoken in season; you have too much good sense, I see, to heed old women's tongues. Come, I must go, and we will walk part of your way home together. We will leave my sister to recover from the shock she has received as best she may." Thereupon he put his hand through the young man's arm,—a sign of great friendship on his part,—and they walked towards the court-yard gate. As they reached it, the boy who brought letters and papers to the castle twice a week, handed the bailiff a letter addressed in the handwriting of the young princess. He broke the seal and read its contents as he walked along; but, after the first few lines, he stopped, and seemed much moved.

"How strangely true the old proverbs are!" he said, as he put it in his pocket after reading it through. "Misfortunes really never seem to come singly; one after another goes from among us. Well, well, when she was young, we thought she gave herself airs, but she was honest and true-hearted. The countess will feel it deeply——"

The curate interrupted him to ask what had happened.

"I forgot," he replied, "that I have not told you. The old Englishwoman, Miss Kenney, has just died at the princess's castle, and Princess Clarissa writes to ask me to let them know of it at the parsonage. She was only ill a few days, and her end was peaceful and happy. This will be sad news for the parsonage, and yet who can tell that it is not the best thing for her?"

The curate asked if he alluded to Hulda, and what he meant.

"I mean that it is well for the girl, and for you too, my dear fellow," the bailiff replied. "Since you have spoken so frankly to us to-day, I have no concealments from you. You probably know that the pastor has asked me to take charge of his daughter when his eyes are closed forever?"

The curate shook his head.

"It was the only thing he could do," the old man continued; "the pastor has no living relatives; and the relatives, if there are any, of the girl's mother are poor people on the countess's distant estates. Now, Miss Kenney, who has been devoted to Hulda ever since that affair with the baron, whom I shall never forget or forgive for behaving as he did, had an idea, I know, of training the girl for a governess,—to go to England and earn her living as Miss Kenney has done here." He paused for a moment, and then continued: "All this has naturally had some effect upon Hulda, and my sister with her eternal gossip, setting the people talking everywhere in the parish, has done the rest. Hulda declared to me a little while ago, that she should certainly not remain here after her father's death; that this was no place for her, she should earn her living elsewhere." Then, seeing that the curate's countenance fell, he clapped him on the shoulder, and cried, "Cheer up! courage! A girl's resolution is not like the laws of the Medes and Persians, and there are two of us now to the fore to induce her to alter it."

In the mean time they had come to where their paths separated. On the right lay the broad harvest-field, where the work was still going merrily on, and on the left the sun was slowly descending into a sea of liquid blue and gold. The bailiff stood still.

"Break the news of poor Miss Kenney's death gently at the parsonage," he said. "The pastor has known her for many years, and eternity is all very well; but just look around you,—with everything so beautiful here, it is cursed luck to have to leave it. Still, when the time comes, it will be all right, I doubt not."

The curate was too much occupied with thoughts of Hulda to administer the reproof that he would have thought right at any other time not to withhold. As he bade his companion farewell and turned away, the bailiff called him back. "Tell them at the parsonage," he said, "that Frau von Wildenau breakfasted with us yesterday."

The curate asked who she was. "They will tell you," replied the bailiff, who was in a hurry. "She was going to Russia upon business, and confirmed what I had heard before, that the countess's eldest brother is in a dying condition. That was grist for Ulrika's mill."

The curate asked what he meant.

"Did she never tell you of the Falkenhorst parchment, and the old superstition connected with it?"

"Never," replied the curate.

"Well, then, it was because she had a wholesome dread of you," said the bailiff; "for she likes nothing better than to tell how the Falkenhorsts have been cursed by the underground folk, and will die out, so that the estates will fall to the family of our countess."

These words made a melancholy impression upon the young man. "Must I contend with such follies here?" he cried. "I never thought of such a task."

"Yes," replied the bailiff, "some of the heads hereabouts are full of such nonsense. I advise you not to allude to it; there'll be more chance of its being forgotten. But if Baron Emanuel does not marry, it is a fact that the Falkenhorsts will soon die out. Our countess, you may be sure, has her own ends to answer in the journey the baroness told us of yesterday, which she is about to make with the young canoness, Fräulein Konradine, to visit Baron Emanuel in Switzerland. Each seemed well enough pleased with the other when they were here in the castle together, and perhaps the beautiful canoness may help you to win Hulda for your wife, Herr Curate."

And he turned into the harvest-field, while the young man walked on towards the quiet village, his mind full of the gravest and most solemn thoughts, illuminated, however, by the bright rays of the hope in which he could not but indulge of a happy issue to his love. How he longed to have Hulda by his side to see her lovely face radiant in the glow of this glorious sunset, which fulfilled all her predictions of its beauty! He wished to reach home, and yet he shrank at the idea of bearing sorrowful tidings to the ears of those who were so dear to him.

The bright sunlight was still gilding the roof of the little church when he entered the gate of the parsonage-garden, where to his joy Hulda was still sitting. The evening was so exquisite that the pastor had had his arm-chair carried out into the open air. As the curate approached, it seemed to him that the delicate, worn features of the old man were paler and more transparent than ever. He called out to the young man, "Now, Herr Curate, you see how magnificent we can be here. In spite of our insignificance, I cannot but feel that a loving Father has made this last year of mine on earth one of special plenty and loveliness in order that I may enjoy it."

The curate and Hulda would have bidden him hope for many more years, but he shook his head, and asked after the result of the curate's business with the bailiff.

The young man's report interested and satisfied him, and he then proceeded to expatiate upon the kindness that had been extended to him during his lifetime, and upon the generosity of his patrons. His successor would enjoy the same patronage. He would probably desire a new parsonage. The count had contemplated building one many years since, but the old place had been too dear to its present master. "It is different with you," he concluded; "you will need a better parsonage; and Hulda has already made a sketch of the old house which she can carry away with her."

The curate felt hot and cold in a breath. "I hope"—he cried, and then suddenly paused. He could not venture to declare what wild hopes were his. In reply to the looks of surprise from both father and daughter at his sudden silence, he said, "I hope you will not be too much distressed by the sad tidings I bring you from the castle. The bailiff has just received a letter from the princess announcing the death of her old friend and governess after a short and painless illness."

Hulda uttered a low cry of distress. Her father was apparently unmoved. "It is harvest-time," he said, "and the grain is ripe. She has passed the dark portal, and it is well with her."

He bowed his head, folded his hands, and seemed lost in reverie. Hulda approached him and put her arm about his neck, as if longing to keep him with her. At last he looked up and asked, "You tell me the princess announced the death? Was not the countess with her old friend at the time?"

"No; the countess is with the Canoness von Wildenau, and they are about to visit Baron Emanuel in Switzerland," was the reply.

"With the Canoness von Wildenau?" Hulda repeated, involuntarily laying her hand upon her heart as her head drooped so that her face was concealed. A sharp pang of burning jealousy shot through her heart. There was no doubt of it, Emanuel would be estranged from her; and yet he had called himself hers and hers only, and had declared with his last words that the ring upon her finger was a pledge that they should meet again. Had he forgotten it? Had he sent for

Konradine? Of course, or she could not go to him. He loved her, then; and what was to become of Hulda? What did the ring on her finger mean?

The pain that she suffered stifled her voice. She would have spoken, but could not. She saw her father looking at her with tender anxiety, and the curate, who could not but observe her agitation, standing before her in embarrassment; something must be said.

"I am glad," she said at last, in low, broken tones, "that the countess is to be with her brother after so long a separation." She tried to add that the baron would enjoy Konradine's society also; but the words would not pass her lips. She hesitated, and then asked, hurriedly, "Where did you learn this?"

The curate told in reply how the Baroness von Wildenau had breakfasted at the bailiff's on her way to Russia.

Hulda shivered. "It is growing cool, father," she cried; "shall we not go in-doors?"

The old man slowly rose, saying, "Yes, my child, the evening is at hand; and when our days on earth are drawing to a close, we dare not enjoy the last moments of the dying day in the open air. But do not come in yet, young friend," he added to the curate. "Stay and luxuriate in the magnificent sunset. At your age, on such an evening I never left this spot until the last streak of gold had faded from the western sky."

Hulda put her father's hand within her arm and led him into the house, and to the old sofa in his study, where he had so often sat by her mother's side, reading aloud to them. As in her childish days, she seated herself upon a low bench at his feet, and, as in those old times, his hand gently stroked her silken hair. Neither spoke; the room was dark and silent.

Suddenly Hulda seized her father's hand, kissed it with fervour, and hurried out of the room. The old man sighed gently; hot tears had fallen from his daughter's eyes upon his hand.

CHAPTER XII.

KONRADINE had already left her retirement, and was on her way to join the countess, that together the two ladies might pursue their journey to Switzerland. Their meeting was in every way agreeable to each, heralded as it had been by a twelvemonth's correspondence, during which time the canoness had become very dear to the countess, who found herself quite alone just now, when Clarissa's new cares and interests absorbed her time and attention, while the young count was absent in England, attached to the German embassy there. To Konradine had been intrusted the delicate task of apprising Emanuel of his sister's meditated visit, and with rare tact she had delayed doing so until they were fairly started upon their way, thus giving the whole affair the aspect of a sudden resolve, which the canoness, in her kindly desire to see the brother and sister once more reconciled, had encouraged by every means in her power, and not of a concerted plot to obtain undue influence over the baron. The friends were hardly surprised by the contents of a letter that the countess received at this time from the bailiff, in reply to one from herself, containing directions as to the legacy of five hundred thalers that Miss Kenney had left to her favourite, the pastor's daughter. After the business part of the letter was concluded, he added that the little capital might shortly be doubly useful to Hulda,—alluding to the pastor's feeble condition,—and expressed a hope that the great lady's patronage might be extended to the curate whom she had provided, who had won the confidence and respect of all, and who would in every way be welcome as the pastor's successor in office, especially as the young man evinced a desire to marry among them. And then he proceeded to refer to the object of his choice in such a manner as to leave no doubt in the mind of either the countess or her companion that it was Hulda of whom he wrote. Every possibility of mistake, however, was precluded by the postscript to the bailiff's communication, written by his sister, ostensibly with the purpose of telling how certain small effects of Miss Kenney's had been disposed of, but in which her hints as to the future pastor's wife were very easy to understand.

This conclusion of poor Hulda's dream seemed to the countess thoroughly fitting and natural. She was greatly relieved by it, and Konradine shared her satisfaction, convinced as she had always been that nothing less decided on the girl's part would soothe the baron's morbid conscientiousness with regard to the object of his "fanciful attachment."

As for Hulda, for whom the two friends had so quietly provided a calm, contented future, she was consumed by a burning jealousy that left her no peace by day or by night. It had burst into a flame when first she had seen Konradine, and had smouldered while she knew her in the retirement of the cloister, only to burst forth again upon hearing that she had left it to meet Emanuel once more. Wherever she went, whatever she was doing, she was pursued by the image of Konradine, in her fresh, brilliant beauty, as she had seen her from her sick-bed on that fatal day from which she dated her misery. Then first had the idea suggested itself to her that Emanuel might love another better than herself, that Konradine was better suited to him; and without this idea, she thought, she never could have resigned him as she had done.

What countless times during the past two years had she recalled every detail of that terrible parting, and the days that had preceded it, and always with the renewed conviction that it had been by no act of Emanuel's that they were severed, that she, and she alone, had been the guilty one! How earnestly had he entreated her to be true to him! He had refused to take back his ring; he had no part in her wretchedness. It was a comfort to bear all the blame herself. She could prop up her failing courage with the reflection that her duty to her father had imperatively demanded that she should act as she had done, and that God had required this sacrifice at her hands.

But now that Konradine suddenly appeared again upon the scene, jealousy destroyed the whole structure of her religious submission and renunciation, and a tempest of wild resolves and projects raged within her. She would write and tell him that she had never ceased to love him, to trust and believe in him, for his ring was still upon her finger, and the turquoise had not lost its hue, as it would have done had its giver proved false. But if her letter should startle instead of delighting him? He had withheld from her in all these years the slightest sign that he still loved her, or even thought of her. Ah, what then? Should she tell him of her love, perhaps at the very moment when he was wooing Konradine? Should she beg him to wait for her until——

No, no; she had nothing to tell him. It was too late; the time had gone by.

"The moving finger writes, and, having writ,
Moves on, nor all your piety and wit
Can lure it back to cancel half a line,
Nor all your tears wash out a word of it."

There was nothing to be done. She must forget; forget everything—forget him. But how could she?

She still wore his ring on her finger. She waked in the night and felt for it, and then arose and lit a candle, that she might see whether the blue of the turquoise was still undimmed. She could not rest; she was in torture. She was like the German emperor with Fastrada's ring. She could not forget Emanuel so long as his ring was upon her finger. And what would become of her if she could not forget?

She could not live on thus; something must be done. One day she drew the ring from her finger and resolved to hurl it into the sea. But when she reached the shore she could not do it: it was beyond her strength. She sat down and wept bitterly.

As she lifted her head, the curate was standing by her side. The plash of the waves on the shore had drowned the sound of his approaching footsteps. When he saw the tears in her eyes and on her cheeks, he did not know what to say. He would have excused himself for disturbing her, but could only exclaim, "You have been weeping!" in a tone that told her how deep was his sympathy.

Hulda had felt so utterly forsaken that the sight of a kindly face, the sound of a human voice, did her good, and, overwhelmed by the grief that was crushing her, she cried, "I wanted to put an end to it all!"

He started in terror. "What words to come from your lips!" he said, scarcely believing his ears.

This recalled her to herself, and, wishing to remove from his mind such a dreadful suspicion as his words indicated, and to give utterance to what was tormenting her, she said, "I did not intend any wrong; I only wanted to put an end to it all forever."

She did not notice that in her bewilderment she had but repeated her previous expression, thus only deepening the impression her first words had produced.

"I do not understand you," he said, "and yet I would not misunderstand or doubt you for the world."

The fervour of his tone did not escape Hulda, even in her present distraction of mind; but in her misery she could think only of herself, and she suddenly said, "No, you shall not doubt me! I will be frank with you if you will promise to help me,—to do what I shall ask of you."

He would have promised her, but his conscientiousness was even stronger than his love, and, withdrawing his half-extended hand, he asked, "What do you ask of me?"

His hesitation displeased her, and with more haste and violence than he had ever known her to show before, she cried, "I must put an end to it all—to my love. I must be rid of the ring that binds me to him! I will send it back to-day, for I am lost if I do not. Take it for me to the post this very hour!"

Her lips trembled as she spoke the words, and her voice sounded rough and harsh, but the curate seized her hands, and, looking into her face with eyes of fondest affection, cried, "Indeed I will! Thank God that he has given you strength for this resolve! Thank God!"

He would gladly have said more, but how could he speak of his hopes now, when she was burying her own?

Without exchanging another word, they walked towards the house. At the door the curate paused. "When do you wish me to go?" he asked.

"Can you not go now?" she said, moved by a doubt lest she should be unable on the morrow to carry out the resolve formed to-day.

He looked at his watch. "Is your letter written?"

"I promised my father never to write," was the reply.

"Then I will wait until you have wrapped up the ring," the curate said, and both entered the house, he to make ready for his walk, and she to seal up the golden circlet that was hei all.

She brought him the packet in a few moments. She had

put the ring in a little box that had been her mother's. The curate could not know how she had wavered, how she had fallen on her knees and wildly pressed the box to her lips for the last time, but in her pale face he read the conflict through which she had passed.

"Do not lose it," said Hulda, with that strange confusion of mind that leads one to say the most commonplace things in moments of deepest wretchedness.

"Rely upon me," he replied, taking her hand and kissing it, and then he walked hastily away.

She scarcely heeded his words or his action. She stood looking after him and trying to refrain from recalling him. The thought that she had now voluntarily decided her destiny, that her hand had severed the last tie that bound her to the man whom she loved, was almost more than she could bear. She could not tell whether she had done well or ill, whether she had sinned against him or against herself; all that she knew was that she was unhappy, that everything was at an end, that the future lay dark before her.

As she went into the house, her father called her. She helped him from his couch to his old arm-chair, and seated herself upon the footstool at his feet. Now that he could no longer occupy himself, her conversation was his chief delight, and her affection, few as were the interests of her life, had always provided matter for his entertainment; but to-night she could not talk; she could not even take up her sewing. She sat holding his hand in hers. Her silence struck him.

"You are very quiet, my child," he said.

Her father's voice seemed to loosen the iron fetters about her heart, and she cried, "I have nothing in this world but you, father! nothing, nothing! I have sent Emanuel's ring back to him."

"Thank God!" ejaculated the old man, taking both her hands in his, and laying her tearful face upon his shoulder, where he stroked it gently, soothing her as one soothes a child. "There, there, my child,—cry. Do not try to keep back the tears; they flowed from the eyes of our dear Lord in his hour of agony, and, as he drank the bitter cup in full confidence in his Father's aid and his own resurrection, we must, so far as in us lies, follow his example. You too, my child, will rise again victorious from this bitter struggle."

"I cannot, father! I cannot!" she moaned upon his bosom.

"Not when your father tells you that you relieve his wearied mind by thus redeeming his promise on your part?"

His gentle admonitions quieted her. He gave her time to recover her composure, and, as she knelt there by his side, her hands firmly clasped in his, her heart gradually beat less wildly, her tears flowed more gently. Then he spoke again. "You have done well, my child, to send back the ring before the baron was obliged to demand it at your hands, which he must else have done at some future time. His brother's approaching death imposes new duties and obligations upon him, and I think, as you do, that his choice is made. The resolve that you have to-day, with God's help, put into execution, disburdens my soul of its last care. I could hardly rest quietly in my grave if I thought that I left my child to be repulsed and forsaken."

He paused. Hulda never stirred. "Summer has passed, the autumn is at hand," he continued, "and its yellow leaves will fall upon my grave, but God has blessed my last days upon earth. Your love, the devotion of our young friend, the bailiff's firm friendship, and the constant kindness of the countess have illumined them. And you will not be forsaken. The bailiff has promised to give you a home with him, and the countess will befriend you. Who can tell that, in the future which God has ordained you, it may not be yours to pass your days in peace upon the spot where your mother and I have been so happy? Take comfort, my child. Although I leave you, your heavenly Father will never forsake you. His eye will watch over you when mine is closed in death."

He laid his hand in blessing upon her head. She wept in silent resignation, conscious but of one wish, that the end of her life were at hand and that she might depart with her father. Where was there any place for her in the world?

Outside, the sun was sinking into the sea. The little room had grown dark, but father and daughter still sat silently together. When the bell in the old tower tolled seven, the old man spoke. "It will be late," he said, "when the curate returns, and he will be tired. Have some refreshment ready for him. Does he know what errand he has undertaken for you?"

"Yes, I told him," she replied, softly, as she left the room.

The usual time for supper passed. Her father partook of his, and, giving her his blessing, retired to rest, after she had read aloud to him a chapter in the Bible, as was her wont every evening. She sat alone, waiting for the curate, who would surely return soon.

It was warm and quiet in the little room. The window-shutters were wide open, as they always were when any of the inmates of the house were from home. The clock, that had been standing in the same place for more than half a century, told off hour after hour, with its peaceful ticking. The light was burning in the antique candlestick, as it had burned for so many generations; and the waves outside had beaten upon the shore with that same dull sound for thousands of years. Everything here was as it always had been. It was death in life,—a living death, into which she too must sink, with all her hopes and aspirations. She must forget all that had lighted up her horizon for awhile, and she, with her burning heart, must die, as all around her died. Was she really living now?

She had taken the candle in her hand, and was going from room to room, attending to various household arrangements. No one saw her, for the maid was busy in the stable. No one heard her, and she heard nothing, not even the sound of her own light footfall. She seemed to herself like one of the little folk that Ma'amselle so liked to talk about,—a dim, shadowy presence, silently completing her allotted daily tasks.

She took her knitting, placed a book upon the table before her, and tried to read. Her hands moved mechanically; she fixed her eyes upon the pages, and from time to time turned the leaves; but she did not know what she was reading, for she was counting the days that must elapse before the ring could reach the baron. She tortured both heart and brain with wondering where and how he would receive it, what he would do with it, whether it would bring him content or make him sad. Her poor thoughts were tossed hither and thither in hopeless confusion, until suddenly she had a distinct vision of Konradine taking the ring from the baron's hand and putting it upon her own finger.

She sprang up. Had omnipotence been hers—could she have launched the elf-king's curse——But she would control herself. This would never do. She gazed into the light of the candle until her eyes brimmed over and there was a large prismatic ring around the little flame. She buried her face in her hands, and, when she looked again, the blackened wick had curled and twisted over the candle, making what the country-people called a winding-sheet, ominous, in their superstition, of a death in the house. In spite of herself, a sensation of dread and horror stole over her. She could bear her solitude no longer, and went hurriedly out to look for the maid, but at the door she was met by the curate.

"Oh, I am so glad you have come!" she exclaimed, and then regretted her words, which had been prompted simply by the relief she felt at being no longer alone; for she saw his face light up as he heard them.

"Your errand is done," he said, as Hulda preceded him, with the light in her hand, through the dim passage. The house-door was open; it had begun to rain, and the damp, warm air swept in from the sea. The young man's clothes and hair were wet. "The night is warm," he said, "and I walked quickly; for I did not want to have the Herr Pastor wait for me. Still, I am too late, I find."

Hulda thanked him, and they entered the room together, where the table was spread for two. When the curate had said grace, an office always hitherto performed by the pastor, and the maid had left the room, they were both suddenly struck with the fact that they were thus alone together for the first time, and each grew constrained and embarrassed.

The curate looked again and again at Hulda's hand, where he had so often, with such pain, seen the golden circlet, and Hulda involuntarily felt for the missing ring. Their thoughts were thus linked together, as it were, and yet far apart. All his hopes and desires were centred in her—now more than ever before; while she was meditating on the time when she must leave all that now constituted home for her; for she knew that this would be no place for her. Then, giving utterance to the conclusion of a long train of thought, she asked the curate if he believed in presentiments.

He asked what she meant by the question.

"My father took leave of me solemnly to-night," she said, briefly, with a kind of quiet intensity which was peculiar to her. "Do you think he was moved to do so by a presentiment of death?"

"I think we are justified in believing that a foreknowledge of their own death is vouchsafed to certain self-contained natures," the curate replied, "but I do not believe that others can share such knowledge with them."

"There you are wrong," said Hulda. "I knew of my mother's death, far from her as I was. I heard her call me twice—three times—so that I sprang up to answer her. To-night my father fell asleep peacefully as I watched him, and yet, while I was alone, my mind was filled with the saddest forebodings. Now that you are come, I cannot believe that he will soon leave me. I shall surely keep him some time longer. Do you not think so?"

She arose from the table, and for a few moments stood listening at the door of her father's room, then softly opened it, and went up to the bed where he lay. She could hear nothing. Her heart seemed to stand still with a sudden and deadly terror. She stooped, and laid her cheek upon his, then, with a piteous cry, fell fainting upon the floor.

The pastor was dead. His death had been as gentle as his life.

CHAPTER XIV.

EMANUEL had been expecting his friend's arrival several days, when he received a letter from her announcing her meeting with the countess, who was on her way to surprise him with a visit. The idea of a concerted plan between the two ladies never entered his mind; and he thought it but natural that, under the circumstances, they should have discussed together his estrangement from his sister, whose desire to be reconciled with him certainly was not to be wondered at. No one could tell how short the time might be before they should meet at the death-bed of their elder brother, who had entreated Emanuel, on his last visit to him, to let there be entire peace between them, since they must so soon be the last direct descendants of their noble race, and had urged upon his younger brother the necessity of marrying, and marrying among his equals, that the name which had been so illustrious, and was the representative of such noble estates, might not die from off the face of the earth.

There was much in his admonitions that would formerly have found an echo in Emanuel's mind; but Hulda's love for him had so surprised and enraptured him that all such considerations had been for the time obliterated. Now, after his long separation from her, they asserted themselves with a force which he had scarcely believed possible, although he could not bring himself to imagine any one save Hulda in the place of the wife so urgently pressed upon him by his brother. In his inmost heart he could not but believe that she still loved him, and that she would respond to his call when filial duty should no longer detain her at her father's side.

Unconsciously he found a charm in the full enjoyment of Konradine's friendship, as a solace for his separation from Hulda, while it did not interfere with the delight he took in his romantic memories of his young love.

This was the condition of mind in which Konradine's letter found him. Its fresh, healthy tone did him good; he was glad, after all, to hear of a sister still so dear to him, and the easy way in which Konradine alluded to the many reasons that existed for his marrying put him in an excellent humour, since it entirely contradicted the morbid self-distrust that had been wont to take possession of him at the thought of aspiring to the favour of women.

"I know everything that you will say," she wrote, "to what I urge upon this subject; but have not the circumstances of your life flatly contradicted all your melancholy convictions and answered all your self-tormenting doubts? Have not both the love and the friendship of women been offered you without the asking? Did you sue for Hulda's love? Did you desire of me my friendship? No; both fell to your lot like ripe fruit into the hand of a careless passer-by. Through your timely sympathy I have been enabled to contemplate my future life with equanimity, to take it calmly as it comes. You can carve out what future you please for yourself—can be, and will be, I trust, happy; and, that no painful regret may burden your conscience, let me again remind you of the difference that exists between early youth and the age to which you and I belong. Enjoyment of existence is the prerogative of the young; they grasp it at all hazards, and the desire for it is a powerful aid in restoring the balance of a mind that has been disturbed by suffering. This restoration, I am glad to tell you, dear friend, has taken place in the girl whose memory you still cherish. Solitude has also had its part in her cure; and a heart that has once tasted of love will not starve so long as it is young."

Emanuel paused in his reading; he suspected what was to follow this introduction, and the hand in which he held the letter trembled slightly as he continued. "The bailiff has written to the countess regarding an increase of the income of the pastor's office after his death, which is evidently near at hand. He alludes at the same time to a small legacy left her young friend by Miss Kenney, which, he says, will be doubly welcome just now, since Hulda's marriage with her father's young curate, of whom the bailiff speaks in the highest terms, will shortly take place. He mentions this as a fortunate circumstance; and indeed, dear friend, I think we must all agree with him, for in a short time the lovely young pastor's wife, and you too, will remember your love for each other as but a pleasant dream, the continuance of which was scarcely desirable."

He had read it. It sounded so reasonable, so natural; and yet he did not, he could not, believe it. His present suffering was all his own fault.

He leaned his head on his hand and reviewed in spirit all the months and days between that fair spring evening when he had first seen his love, and the hour of their last sad farewell. She had always been true to the impulse of her heart, regardless of all consequences, and could he blame her for being so now, when those impulses had been trained and influenced by filial obedience and a sense of duty? He could not wonder that a younger suitor, always at her side, had conquered the memory of the absent lover.

He thought over all this, and yet he could not believe it. There was in his heart a confidence in her affection that annulled all the arguments of reason. He could never believe that Hulda had forgotten him, unless she herself should tell him so.

He sat down to write to her, and then tore up the letter that he began. He thrust Kouradine's letter impatiently aside, and yet he was grateful to her for not allowing him to hear such tidings from his sister. He was agitated and uncertain.

He envied those who could be swayed to sudden action by the force of passion; but still the feeling that bound him to Hulda was so deep—it was surely the truest love. "Hulda, Hulda! it cannot be!" he cried aloud, determined to deliver both her and himself, to see her again, cost what it might. Then he again began to write to her, and all hesitation vanished; he told her all, conjured her to listen to no voice save that of her heart and her love, to think only of her happiness and his own. He appealed to the pastor, again entreated his consent to his love, assuring him that he was upon the point of a reconciliation with the countess, in favour of whose son he would gladly yield all title to the family estates. He was only waiting to see his sister, who was about to visit him, before hastening to Hulda's side. Then, although he knew that the post for the north did not leave until the next evening, he dispatched a servant with his letter.

Again his heart was full of old hopes and aspirations. The meeting with his sister, after so long a separation, and the visit from his friend, to which he had looked forward with such pleasure—he wondered now only how long they would stay, and keep him from Hulda's side. He could not understand his own protracted, dreary inaction; he would atone to both Hulda and himself for all this lost time by redoubled affection for her.

He scarcely admitted that there could be any difficulty in arranging matters with the countess. His own private property was sufficiently large to make the addition to it of the family estate a matter of no importance to him. His sister's son was about to marry,—he would resign all title to the old entailed estate in his favour, and the king would doubtless graciously permit the young man to add to his own name the title of Von Falkenhorst.

Weighing all this in his mind, he paced the terrace to and fro in the gathering twilight. He was interrupted by the return of his servant, who handed him a small packet which had been intrusted to him for the Herr Baron by the postmaster.

Emanuel took it from the man; the reflection from the western sky gave light enough to enable him to recognize the delicate handwriting that he knew so well. The coincidence was startling. At the very moment when he was returning to her with entire devotion, a message from her had arrived. He broke the seal, nothing doubting that the enclosure contained the tidings of her father's death, for which Konradine had prepared him; but there were no written words within,—only a small box, from which, as he opened it, fell the ring he had given her.

He could hardly believe his eyes. He unfolded every scrap of paper in which the box had been wrapped, in hopes of finding some written word of explanation of what was surely not inexplicable, but was none the less hard to believe. He could not blame her; he alone was to blame. He alone had destroyed his chance for a happiness which had never seemed so great to him as at this moment when it was lost to him forever. He could but repeat to himself the sad "Too late!" that is uttered at some time of our lives by almost all of us.

He stood upon the terrace, and looked out into the gloom. He knew every part of the landscape by heart, and yet he hardly seemed to recognize it. Thus it was with his knowledge of Hulda. Her soul had lain before him like an open book, but now he failed to understand her. He would have staked his life upon her fidelity. He had not believed that she could forget. He had trusted her implicitly, and in his over-confidence had sinned against her and against himself. And now that she had decided for herself, and was probably happy in her love for a man who was her equal in age and rank,—happier than she could ever have been with him,—ought he to approach her with a renewal of his suit? Had she not, by her own silence, pointed out the path in which she wished him to tread?

He called his servant, and told him to go to the post and recall the letter he had sent there a few hours before; but this had no effect upon the turmoil of his thoughts. He could not understand why she had written him no single word. Why had she not told him that she had been mistaken in her feeling for him,—that she loved another? She knew better than any one else how he mistrusted his own power of awakening affection, and she knew, too, how dear she had been to him—how he had surrounded her with his care before he had ever dreamed that she could love him, that she could be his.

He looked at the clouds as they rose heavily and slowly from the opposite shore, obliterating a star here and there, until they veiled the entire horizon, and the night lay sultry and dark above lake and shore. He watched for the reappearance of a star, but in vain; no twinkling light broke through the gloom.

All seemed over for him in this world. "May happier stars shine o'er her head!" he murmured, as he put her little ring upon his finger.

He would wear it in memory of her whom he had loved, and whom he mourned as one mourns for his lost youth, which never can return. And the night was passed by him in weary watching, tormented by the bitterest of all regrets,—that which is caused by the consciousness of having destroyed one's own happiness.

CHAPTER XV.

THE arrival of his sister and his friend was now most welcome to Emanuel. Nothing else could have so desirably interrupted the solitude of his life.

The countess, whose love of rule, even in trifles, had sometimes, in their former constant intercourse, been a source of annoyance to her brother, was now conscious that from his point of view he had much on her part to forgive, and therefore put a constant guard upon herself. She asked no questions except those which he himself provoked, while at the same time she gave him her unreserved confidence with regard to all her own affairs,—talked continually of Clarissa's happiness as a wife and mother, and spoke of her hopes with regard to her son's marriage. When Emanuel, in this connection, declared his desire to resign, in the young man's favour, all right to the family inheritance, she refused to listen to any such idea. All arbitrary arrangements for the future were distasteful to her, she said, reminding her brother how well fitted he was to minister to the wants and welfare of a large tenantry, and insisting upon the wisdom of the proverb common among the peasants, "Never take off your boots until you are ready to lie down."

She spoke with a gayety which was unusual in her, and which impressed her brother agreeably; and what she said did not fail of its effect. He admitted to himself that there was no longer the reason for his renunciation that had existed upon Hulda's account some days previously. The countess never alluded by the slightest word to the pastor or the pastor's daughter, and Emanuel maintained the same silence with regard to them towards his sister, and also to Konradine, who well knew how to understand and respect it.

For this Emanuel thanked her in his heart. She did not stay beneath his roof, but had taken lodgings in a retired cottage near the lake; and all that he saw of her heightened the charm which he had first discovered in her in his sister's castle. She had attained a noble self-possession and an equability of mood that were very attractive to him. The simplicity of her dress, the small value that she attached to outside trifles upon which the weal or woe of most women is so apt to depend, the confidence with which she asserted her right to judge and act for herself, sometimes made Emanuel forget, in his intercourse with her, that she was still young and beautiful; while these very qualities of youth and beauty heightened sensibly the pleasure he found in her society.

His sister's habits of life, too, promoted his constant intercourse with the fair canoness. During her long residence in Italy, the countess had become averse to all kinds of physical exertion. She knew no appreciation of nature save that which could be enjoyed from the terrace of a garden or the seat of a carriage; she spent more than half the night in the pleasures of society, while the morning hours were passed in repose.

Emanuel, on the other hand, was an ardent lover of nature. All through the trials of his early years, when his own regret at the loss of health and beauty had been heightened by the constant lamentations of an injudicious although loving mother, nature had been to him a refuge and a solace. To ride, to walk,—amid solitudes where the beauty around him never seemed to mock his own loss of it, but to caress and woo him back to a sense of enjoyment, had been for years the greatest delight of his life; and nothing had since interrupted the habit then formed of constant communion with nature.

He understood and loved it, and had learned through it to comprehend mankind. It was a great pleasure to him at present that Konradine shared his love of nature and was physically fitted to accompany him in his rides and walks. However early the hour appointed for a gallop through those lovely scenes, Emanuel always found her awaiting him, and in her health and freshness looking like an embodiment of the morning. She seemed at home everywhere. When they stopped to breakfast at some roadside inn, when they encountered strangers on their expeditions, even in the interchange of friendly greetings with the peasants whom they passed, Konradine developed a rare faculty for assimilating with her surroundings,—a faculty that induced confidence from all around her, and that made it possible for her sometimes to be of practical assistance to those beneath her in rank.

Emanuel once expressed to her his admiration of this peculiar gift, and she admitted that she was conscious of possessing it, but added, with a laugh, "It is due to no merit of mine, however, but to the fact of the existence of the opposite tendencies in my mother. I learned, when a very little child, to help myself,—to create a kind of home, for we lived then almost in the wilderness. Before I could read or write, my mother condemned herself and me to the kind of wandering life she has pursued ever since, and I felt the necessity of arranging and adjusting our various surroundings. This quality has been still further developed in my late retirement, where its practical results were certainly a great satisfaction to me."

"But even without any such results," said Emanuel, "this creative faculty seems to me delightful in itself. We all try to exert it from our earliest years. The child makes a garden for himself in the midst of a garden. The boy makes a collection of extracts from books that belong to him. The youth composes his own love-songs, although those already made are far more beautiful. The man who inherits large estates erects new buildings, or makes alterations, by which he asserts his own individuality. A great part of the attraction that so many find in getting and gaining lies, I believe, in this desire to create."

Konradine agreed with him, but asked how it was exemplified in his own case.

Emanuel grew thoughtful. "That is a question," he said, "which cannot be answered without a long retrospect,—a retrospect that is by no means consoling; for it reveals little to be admired in me."

"You do yourself injustice," said Konradine, "for ever since I first knew you,—and we are old acquaintances," she added, with a charming smile, "you have always been occupied—occupied with——"

"With myself and my own enjoyments," he interrupted her. "My mother's doting affection, the intense desire of all my family for the preservation of our name, the constant care bestowed upon me as an invalid, all combined to inspire me with a belief that my life was of great importance, when the fact is, that no life is of much importance which does not find expression in action."

"But I think I have heard," said Konradine, "that you took great pains to pursue various studies that might fit you for the management of your estates and conduce to the welfare of your tenantry."

"True," he replied; "but I never undertook the management of my property, because I preferred to live in a more southern climate, and because there were none to come after me to make it desirable that my estates should be improved, or that the income from them should be increased. I have more than enough for my own wants."

He paused, and Konradine remained silent. It was the first time that Emanuel had spoken thus of himself, and she knew how beneficial it is to pour into sympathetic ears what has long been pent up within the breast. At last she spoke, hoping to lead him to continue in the same vein. "I am afraid that your long solitude in your villa here has not been good for you; you have been self-occupied, and there is danger for conscientious men in self-occupation. They grow too hard and impatient with their weaknesses. Every one is something of a monster when looked at through a microscope. Surely the good God will have to show mercy instead of justice, if we are ever to see heaven."

"You jest, Konradine, and it becomes you well," he replied. "I am glad that you can do so once more. But, even at the risk of saddening your mood, I cannot jest with you to-day. I think it is good for all of us to be alone at times and take counsel with ourselves. I had occasion to do so several days before your arrival; and as I then came to an understanding with myself upon several points, I trust I shall now be able to shape my life to more purpose than heretofore."

"And what gave you occasion for such self-communion?" she asked.

"The tidings that you first communicated to me, and which were afterwards verified," he said; adding, after a pause, "Something, too, that my sister said, led me to considerations that may have an effect upon my future life. I have always supposed myself to be unselfish, because I placed no great value upon money, and had no desire to grasp the inheritance which must, unfortunately, soon fall to my lot. I have failed to see that my love of selfish ease has been the mainspring of all my apparent disinterestedness. I ought to bear in mind that our possessions are to be regarded not as a means of self-aggrandizement, but of promoting the welfare and happiness of others. I have resolved not to resign my title to the family estate so soon, unfortunately, to be my own, but to make my home there and do what I can among my people, to be of some use in my day and generation."

Konradine asked if he thought himself able to endure the severity of a northern winter.

"You have seen," he replied, "how well I bore it so long as care for another made me forgetful of myself. I will try so to forget myself in care for my tenantry, and perhaps I may be able to win from them a more lasting regard than has been mine from youth and beauty. We all have sacrifices to make; you have shown me how nobly they can be borne. I have true friends; their esteem and affection are surely enough to make life worth the living."

As he spoke, he held out his hand to Konradine, who grasped it warmly, thinking, as she did so, that the inherent beauty of his face had never been so evident as now, illumined by a melancholy smile.

No further allusion was made by him to Hulda, and his sister and friend avoided all mention of her; but they both noticed that he wore a ring on his finger similar, except in the colour of the stone, to the old family relic, and they suspected what ring it was.

CHAPTER XVI.

The pastor had been laid in the grave, and the villagers had all left the church-yard, talking, as they sought their various homes, of their good old friend, their teacher and consoler through long years and in many an hour of trial. It was a comfort that he had died in his bed, and had had a decent funeral, they said, instead of perishing miserably, as his poor wife had done. And now the pastor's Hulda was all alone.

The windows of the parsonage were open, and the little room, the passage, and the path to the church-yard were strewed with twigs of evergreen. In the sitting-room the bailiff was talking in a low tone to the curate, who was still in his gown. Mademoiselle Ulrika had come to the house as soon as the tidings of the pastor's death had reached her; and she was still here, arranging the rooms, with the help of the sexton's wife, but very impatient to be at home again after her three days' absence.

Hulda did not hear what the bailiff and the curate were speaking of, or notice that Ulrika was in the room. She was standing at the window, looking towards her father's grave. At the same window she had been standing with her father and mother when the news of the count's death had arrived; upon that day, for the first time, she had foreseen the possibility of a time like the present. How well she remembered her father's words, and how her mother had clasped her in her arms! She had then feared to be left alone with her mother to seek a new home. With her mother! Now she was utterly alone—forsaken indeed!

"If he only knew!" exclaimed a voice within her, and, sinking upon the window-seat, she buried her face in her hands, sobbing bitterly.

To see and hear her thus was too much for the bailiff's equanimity. He was very tender-hearted, and, besides, the black coat that he wore to-day—which was never brought out except upon great occasions—was much too small for him, and made him very uncomfortable.

"Cheer up, my child," he said to her. "Come here; you cannot go down into the grave with him; it is a sin to wish it. Don't look out there; come here! The Herr Curate and I are here, and will do all that we can for you, poor child!"

"I know it, uncle dear, and I thank you for all your kindness,—and you too," she said, turning to the curate and holding out her hand to him. "I thank you for the tears you shed upon my father's grave; I shall not forget them."

"Was he not a father to me also? Were we not united in our love and care of him?" said the curate. "Ah, it will be very lonely and sad for me here when you are gone!"

His eyes said more than his words, and as she looked at him she timidly withdrew her hand, just as Ulrika, who had been absent for a moment, re-entered the room.

"We will take care of all that, Herr Curate," she said, looking about to see if there was anything she had left undone; "but the chief thing at present is to take Hulda away from here, and for me to get home, where there will be enough to be set to rights, I'll warrant. And when she is established in her old room with us, we can come to and fro and see what is to be done in the future."

Hulda had packed up her small belongings in the way of dress upon the previous evening. The bailiff's vehicle stood before the door, and the horses were growing impatient. Ma'amselle Ulrika put on the black shawl which she always wore at funerals, and Christian strapped Hulda's little trunk at the back of the carriage. The curate stood at Hulda's side, following with his eyes her melancholy farewell gaze at all the familiar objects around her. He knew so well the thoughts that filled her mind.

"You will never forget it," he said, at last.

"How could I?" she replied.

"And do not forget me," he entreated. "Think of me sometimes; I will take care of everything here."

"You will sometimes come to the bailiff's?" she said, and he thought from her tone that she hoped for his coming. He had shared her care of her father, and he alone knew how she had suffered in sending back the ring. They pressed each other's hands. Ulrika was already seated in the carriage, and the bailiff stood holding the door open. The curate conducted Hulda from the house and assisted her to take her seat by

Ulrika's side, for the poor child's eyes were brimming with tears.

Christian, on the box, gave his whip the well-known crack, and they drove off. As they passed through the village the people came to their doors, and waved mute, melancholy farewells to Hulda. The curate could not look after them; he retired to his little room up-stairs, in which he had never seen Hulda, and where nothing spoke of her to him. He was very unhappy, and wished to be alone.

The room that Hulda had occupied at the bailiff's before she had gone to Miss Kenney was all ready for her, and she was soon established in it. Her unhappiness was so great that she cared little for her outward comfort, and gladly assisted Ma'amselle in her daily household tasks, since all labour was welcome to her; it helped the weary hours to pass more quickly.

Ulrika, however, while she admitted that Hulda no longer needed teaching to do what was required of her, was by no means pleased with the silence in which the girl enshrouded herself, as it were. Why should she go about the house never opening her lips? Every one knew, to be sure, that she was sad about her father's death, but then it was an event that she had anticipated for some time, and it was a great mercy that he had gone before his eyesight entirely failed him. She could not be pining for the baron, for he had forgotten her and was about to marry a wife in every way suited to him. And if she had set her hopes upon the curate, she had no one to blame but herself. He could not possibly marry a girl who had been the talk of the place for so long. Every one must see that, Ma'amselle Ulrika thought. And as she prided herself upon her honest expression of opinion, scarcely a day passed in which all this was not reiterated to Hulda. They were never alone together that Ma'amselle did not impress upon the poor girl that she had grieved enough, and that there was no use in thinking of what could not be altered. She, for her part, could not endure the sight of a sad face all the time; it was contrary to her nature to have such a silent girl about her. "Take courage, and press on," was what all ought to say to themselves.

"Press on!" These words rang in Hulda's ears; she repeated them to herself continually. She felt the impossibility of remaining long beneath the same roof with Ulrika, and her heart and her conscience alike forbade her to dream of a marriage with the curate, if he should offer her his hand. But what should she do? where should she go in a world that seemed so dreary and empty to her?

Many a night, as she lay awake, she thought over all her acquirements and accomplishments, and remembered how her father and Miss Kenney had both often told her that she was well qualified to occupy a position as governess. But such a position was not easy to find, and here in her native place a prejudice existed against her that she dreaded to encounter. She had been the object of much unkind remark, and, although her conscience was clear, she had suffered much during the last few years from the meaning smiles and impertinent remarks of the young girls who had formerly been her companions. But whither could she go? Where should she seek the advice and assistance that she so greatly needed?

She knew how often the countess had assured her father that she would always befriend his child, and just before his death the great lady had written to the bailiff, renewing her offers of protection, and promising to do all that she could for Hulda in case she should, as seemed fitting, desire to procure a situation as governess in some other country. But all her offers were as gall to the poor girl, who shrank from the thought of accepting the slightest favour from her father's patroness.

She knew what the countess meant by suggesting her removal to another country. Did they think her possessed of so little sense of honour as not to avoid a man who no longer felt any interest in her? Had she not, unasked, returned to him the token of his betrothal to her?

Sometimes she hardly recognized herself in the Hulda who had grown so timid and shy, now that she no longer shared the shelter of a father's roof, no longer could rely upon his love and care. She was a stranger amid the scenes and the people that had been familiar to her from infancy. She must flee hence,—seek some other abiding-place, where, even if she might be more lonely, she could at least find distraction for her mind, now always occupied with the same subjects. But whither?

As she pondered upon her life, all the petty insults that she had endured during the past two years arose vividly in her memory, and a kind of dread took possession of her. She began to be ashamed of her love, and of the hopes she had founded upon it. She wished to withdraw from every eye; she could not bear to meet the curate again, grateful though she was to him, for she knew that she could not grant him the reward he desired.

Thus the weeks passed, and all went on as usual at the bailiff's after the bountiful harvest. Guests came and went; the bailiff assisted at the hunts that were planned by the gentry in the neighbourhood, and Hulda was obliged to seize an opportunity, when they were alone, to ask him to go with her once more to the parsonage, where she had not been since her father's death.

"Can't you wait until the end of the week?" he asked, good-humouredly. "The curate was here on Sunday. But I'll not keep you." And he arose, to order the carriage. Hulda laid her hand on his arm.

"Uncle," she said, in some confusion, "that, you know, was not what I meant. I care nothing for the curate. But so many of my possessions are still at the parsonage; I must get what I shall need for the cold weather, and some books, and my mother's work-table, if I may have it."

She spoke seriously, to put a stop to his jesting tone, which she did not like. The jest, however, merely concealed his fatherly interest in her; and, patting her shoulder, he added, "Get your books and your clothes, by all means, my dear child; but leave all else that belongs to you where it is. You have left it all to come here, and I am glad there is some one there who has learned to love the old house, and who will take you back to it again to pass your life there, where your father and mother passed theirs."

He went to the window, to order the carriage to be brought; but the arrival in the court-yard of one of his old friends from the neighbourhood put a stop to the drive for that day.

Hulda was not sorry. The bailiff's words had fallen upon her ears with a dull, deadening sound. All the long, weary days, all the tedious hours that she had spent during the last two years in the parsonage, oppressed her, in memory, with a weight like that of a heavy stone closing a tomb; and was it to shut down upon her again? The prospect of sitting her whole life long at the little window where she had sat from earliest childhood, seeing only the church and church-yard, hearing only the plash and murmur of the waves, or the screams of the sea-birds, was terrible to her. It crushed her very heart. Spring and summer seemed to have vanished from her life. The aimless longing with which, when a child, she had looked after the swallows winging their flight to other climes, possessed her again. Was she to resign every hope for some bright gleam in the future? Oh, no! youth and love of life stirred within her as never before in protest against such a fate.

"Am I now young and fair," she thought, and her cheeks burned at this admission, even to herself, "only to mourn away my days here in hopeless solitude? and in order to secure even this dreary future must I perjure myself by feigning love, by deceiving a true heart? Never!"

Without thinking what she did, she turned towards the mirror, and from its depths there looked out at her a lovely youthful face, crowned with braids of shining gold. "An ideal Käthchen!" was what the manager whom she had seen at Gabrielle's had said.

She did not know why these words should recur to her just at this moment, but they rang in her ears as distinctly as if they had been spoken aloud at her side, and all the events of the morning when she had seen the man came back vividly to her memory.

She saw Gabrielle upon the stage in all her majestic beauty, receiving the admiring homage of the public; she sat with her in the pretty little room filled with lovely flowers. She saw her letters arriving, and the manager coming to implore her to play for him. The gorgeous costume which the maid had carried through the room, the elegant trifles that lay scattered upon the tables,—every detail of the scene was clear in her mind. Even then, as she heard the manager and the artiste alluding to the various places where the latter had appeared, the journeys she was about to make, her heart had throbbed in sympathy with such pleasure; and as she remembered it now, the bailiff's words, "pass your life there," seemed to her the most cruel curse that ever angry fairy devised to transform a living being to senseless stone.

Could anything force her to such a doom? She had obeyed

her father, hard as the task had been—had quietly sacrificed to him her youth, her love, and her hopes for happiness. She had for his sake endured years of pain, every hour bringing with it a dull misery of which only she had known. Now her father and mother were both dead, and she had resigned all hope of reunion with her lover. She was alone in the world, there was no one to whom she owed a single duty. And should she voluntarily accept a fate that was to her a living death? Never!

Gabrielle was the only one to whom she had spoken freely of her love. She had not forgotten one word that the great artiste had said to her in kindly consolation. Everything had happened as she had foreseen. Hulda now had her own way to make in the world, and her thoughts turned to her illustrious friend, as the traveller when astray fixes his eyes upon the friendly glimmer of some distant light.

Gabrielle had expressly desired her to come to her if she should ever be left alone and in need of friendly counsel and guidance. The more she pondered upon all the great artiste had said, the clearer did her meaning become to her, the surer was she of what counsel she should receive from her.

To go upon the stage! To become an actress! The idea dazzled and terrified the pastor's daughter, and yet it was not new to her. After seeing Gabrielle, after that morning passed in her room, it had occupied her mind for a time day and night, and she had often recalled the manager's words, "All roads lead to the stage as well as to Rome."

When she retired to her room after supper, she sat down at her little table and wrote until midnight was long past, and then slipped her letter into the leather pouch which hung in the sitting-room, and which held the letters to be taken to the post the next morning by the man going to the weekly market in the nearest town.

As she then lay down to rest, the moon had sunk below the horizon, and the stars, whose gentle light had so often consoled her, were obscured, but she said to herself, "He holds the stars in their courses. He will direct my steps. If the answer that I expect really comes, I will take it for a sign that I am in the right path, and will pursue it in God's name."

CHAPTER XVII.

THE countess found great enjoyment in her present visit to her brother. She had reached an age when general society no longer possessed its former charm for her. Her daughter had gone to a home of her own, and her son was about to form an alliance in every way desirable. Her maternal love and pride were gratified, and all that was wanting to her entire content was that the younger brother, whom she so loved, should fulfil her hopes for him by contracting a suitable marriage. Who was so fitted to make him forget all the trials of his past life as Konradine, the friend whose society evidently became dearer to him every day? The union of these two was now the great interest of her life; and as it seemed probable or the reverse, her spirits rose or fell.

In view of this consummation, the bailiff's intelligence with regard to Hulda had been very agreeable to her, and she decided immediately to present the curate with the living made vacant by the pastor's death. But her worldly wisdom induced her to delay somewhat in the announcement of her intentions to those most interested.

She held that a favour too quickly conferred is scarcely ever sufficiently prized. The curate had already engaged to fulfil the duties of pastor until the close of the year, and, as she jestingly expressed it in a letter to the young count, her son, she did not wish to shorten the "hoping and fearing of love's sweet pain" too much for the young people by making their marriage immediately possible, since with those in their condition all the poetry of existence was at an end as soon as their married life began.

When with Konradine or the baron, she avoided allusion to these matters. If by any chance her last visit to the castle was mentioned, she led the conversation to other subjects. Every one of the three friends had lived long enough to know that as we grow older we must cast off from time to time some memory which, if allowed to retain its hold upon us, would distort and cramp our development. The countess went further, and maintained that it was a sign of narrow-mindedness, of an incapacity for development, to cling to an unfortunate love or to retain too closely the impressions and associations of youth. To boast of an unaltered mind, of an unchanged opinion, was little else than to flaunt one's poverty of nature in the face of the world.

In answer to some declaration of this kind that she made one day when the three friends were together, Emanuel remarked that, in spite of what she said, she would be the first to be surprised at any open advantage taken of the freedom to change that she advocated.

"At the risk, my dear Adelheid," he said, "of appearing to you 'incapable of development,' I must confess that the constant change that characterizes everything mortal has always oppressed me, and I can only steel myself against the melancholy that it produces by calling to mind the results it sometimes brings about. I remember the gloomy impression made upon me as a boy by Schiller's 'Everything circles in eternal change,' and, later in life, by Goethe's 'On the same stream we never float again.' I long so in my inmost soul for the continuance of all that I have liked or loved, that I dread to see again scenes where I have been very happy, and which my memory invests with an ideal light, or people whom I thought especially lovely, and from whom I have long been separated, lest I should be painfully impressed by the constant change in all things, which brings me nothing but distress, except by admonishing me to make some genuine use of moments forever fleeting."

"You always will be an amiable enthusiast," said the countess, "to whom fate, if it were just, would assign the boon of eternal youth."

"Ah," cried Konradine, with a warmth that gratified Emanuel, "in his power to appreciate and sympathize does he not possess a youth that is lost to us? Is it not a pleasure in the midst of this work-day world to find any one still clinging to the faith and the ideals of youth? I wish I could share the baron's temper of mind. I assure you, my friend," she said, turning to Emanuel, "I am often ashamed, when I am with you, at finding how much younger you are than I in the confidence and hope that are the prerogatives of youth."

Emanuel thanked her, and the countess did not contradict

her, because such an expression of admiration for the baron on Konradine's part gratified her; but she could not refrain from throwing out a suggestion that a continual recurrence and adherence to the memories and ideals of youth were calculated to unfit one for correctly appreciating the present.

"It would certainly be great folly," replied Emanuel, "to allow the past to rob us of enjoyment of the present or of hope for the future. But I think we can give all due weight to what is commonplace and usual, without resigning the sacredness of our ideals. One may be very well content to live and labour in the valley that is his home, even although he has breathed the air of mountain-tops, whence he has looked abroad upon the glory of the world. There is a difference between an idealist and an idle dreamer."

"Of course, of course," said the countess, with a shade of impatience. She never could listen to general observations without giving them a particular application, a personal significance. Therefore she instantly added to her assent to what Emanuel had said, that idealism always seemed to her especially dangerous in any connection with matrimony. "For how could a husband who persisted in clinging to his youthful ideals tolerate, much less affectionately contemplate, the change that years must effect in his wife, in her beauty, her freshness, the youthful flow of her spirits? How could any wife endure that her husband's first love should continually hover before his mental vision in eternal youth and beauty? And what a shock for such an idealist to encounter by chance, in after-years, this early-beloved ideal transformed into a very commonplace mother of a family!"

She had intended this for an easy conclusion to the conversation, but her mind had been full of her brother's past love-affair, and in what she had said she had made it but too evident that such was the case. She repented her words instantly, for the baron, to her surprise, showed that he had so understood her, by replying, with all his native gentleness, "I have sometimes asked myself whether, after all that has occurred, I should like to see Hulda again, and have decided in the negative; not for fear that she should be unlike herself, but because I am not yet sufficiently resigned, and because I am still far from easy upon the score of the wrong that we did her, and its consequences."

"The wrong that we did her!" exclaimed the countess. "I am conscious of no wrong with regard to her."

"I am surprised at that, Adelheid," Emanuel replied, without heeding the impatience of her manner. "I, for my part, remember very distinctly the stormy evening shortly after our arrival at the castle, when we discussed for the first time the pastor's family, and the daughter in particular. I remember how you then refused to listen to my warning when you told me of your plans, and how you persisted in usurping the place of her parents with regard to her."

This irritated the countess. "You forget," she replied, "that you then told me expressly that the girl's presence in the castle would give you pleasure; and certainly Hulda improved greatly under Miss Kenney's care. Her future is provided for, and for her father's sake everything shall be done for her that lies in my power. My conscience is perfectly easy."

"I wish I could say the same," said Emanuel.

The countess shrugged her shoulders impatiently, and, to put a stop to the conversation, which was embarrassing to her in Konradine's presence, said, "Your remorseful anxiety confirms me in my view of the danger that lies in idealism. The girl is now betrothed to a man of her own rank in life. What better fate could she have?" Then, rising and turning to Konradine with a smile, she added, "How strange that a man otherwise free from vanity should not be able to conceive that a girl can forget him and be happy with another, perhaps even happier than with him!"

To these words Emanuel replied, with an earnestness that by contrast was almost solemn, "Give me the certainty of that, Adelheid, and you will relieve me of a great anxiety; for you are right,—I stand convicted of unpardonable vanity, although not in the sense you indicate. All my life I had longed for just such love as Hulda freely and frankly gave me. Instead of cherishing it and guarding it tenderly, I required from her a proof of it that was beyond her strength. I left her to an influence that exerted its time-honored, sacred right to sway her,—left her, in my vanity, because I thought her love insufficient, and trusted to separation to teach her how to value my affection and to lead her to me again. It was only when she silently sent me back my ring that I appreciated what I had lost, while doubt whether she can forget me and be really happy still assails me."

"Then put the question frankly to her," said the countess, who thought only of how he could be satisfied of what she was sure was true.

"Ought he to hazard the chance of producing fresh discord in her soul by such a question?" asked Konradine, who had listened with profound sympathy to the conversation. "It might be dangerous, when her young heart has turned to another love, to conjure up old dreams. It would, at all events, be startling and confusing, like the reappearance of one whom she had believed dead."

"Yes, yes, that alone prevents me from putting the question to her," said Emanuel, much moved. "I have thrown away my right to her. I will not bring discord into her present life. But the day, if it should ever come in the far future, when I see her really happy with another, will relieve me of what must else be an enduring feeling of remorse, and, whatever time may take from her or change in her, for me—I am not ashamed to say—she will always live in memory as I first saw her, as the fair daughter of Ceres, an ideal of youthful grace and purity, and I shall never cease to be grateful to her for once loving me."

He arose, and left the room in some agitation. Tears stood in Konradine's eyes. She had never admired him so much or prized him so highly as at this moment.

"How few there are like him!" she exclaimed to the countess, who forgot her brother's words of reproach to herself in her joy at what she could not but see was a reassuring expression of regard for him on Konradine's part.

That evening the countess wrote a letter to the curate, conferring upon him the vacant living, with an increase of salary, and another to the bailiff, expressing her satisfaction at Hulda's betrothal, and her desire that the marriage should take place shortly, to which end she sent a generous gift in money as her contribution towards the establishment of the young couple.

CHAPTER XVIII.

EMANUEL'S frank explanation had entirely effaced all vestige of restraint and reserve between his sister and himself, and Konradine became dearer to the countess every day, as she saw how her interest in the baron increased. It was a great pleasure to the sister to find that the fair canoness, whom she could not but look upon as the baron's future wife, knew how to appreciate and value even those qualities which the countess herself had been but too prone to regard as the weaknesses of his character.

Every day of this delightful autumn drew closer the bonds of intimacy and cordial sympathy between the baron and his friend, and each was thinking with regret of her approaching departure, when the few days of pleasant intercourse that yet remained were cut short by a letter from the physician attached to the household of the baron's elder brother, who was at present in the south. It besought the brother and sister not to delay coming to the invalid, who earnestly desired to see them once more before his death, which was close at hand.

This intelligence had been daily expected for some time, and yet when it arrived the countess was deeply moved and agitated; for when is death anything but a shock to the living, however they may have looked for its coming? The three friends were together when the letter was received, and the countess shortly left the room to give orders for the departure of herself and her brother, which was arranged for noon of the next day. Konradine arose, and went out upon the terrace. Emanuel followed her.

The sun was high in the heavens, the air as warm as in summer, and the roses were blooming everywhere, hanging in huge clusters from the boughs of the laurels and fig-trees, around the trunks of which they were twined. Konradine gazed around her, and across the gleaming surface of the lake to the snow-crowned mountains on the other side, and said, "How strange it is to think that to-morrow we shall see it all no longer, that this beauty will not exist for us! One can hardly believe it."

"We owe you much for the delightful days we have passed together here," replied Emanuel, "and I do not like to think that they are over. We are so apt to resign ourselves like children to a belief that the pleasant existence we enjoy in the present will be lasting, until suddenly some rude shock arouses us from our fancied security and reminds us how far we are from the goal we had hoped for."

"What you say is especially applicable to my own case just now," said Konradine. "This morning I received a letter from our abbess which will probably put an end to all my plans and expectations for the future."

Emanuel asked what she meant.

"You know," she replied, "that a few weeks ago a place was left vacant among us by the betrothal of one of our associates. The abbess tells me to-day that this place has been accorded to Prince Frederick's eldest sister, the Princess Marianne, and that she will come among us this autumn."

"And you do not wish to meet her?"

"I have not the slightest objection merely to meet her; but the idea of long-continued intercourse with her is very distasteful to me. And there can be no doubt that this place has been given to her, and accepted by her, with the distinct understanding that she is to be the future abbess of the order. She is much too proud and arrogant to have condescended else to place herself for a time upon an equality with the rest of us. This, of course, renders of no avail all that has hitherto been done in my behalf, and makes of no effect the promises that have been made me. The princess would, doubtless, like to retain me by her side to relieve her of the cares of office so far as is possible; but, under the circumstances, the task would not be an agreeable one to me."

"Did you really, then, contemplate devoting your future life to the service of your order, of that organization of women?" inquired Emanuel.

"Why not?" she asked. "I found there a home, and constant occupation, two things unknown before, and which I never can know upon our Esthland estates so long—and I hope it may be very long—as my mother lives, for she intrusts them entirely to her agent, in whom she places entire confidence. I liked my retreat, and looked upon a final return to it as certain."

She ceased, and Emanuel was silent for some time, until he gently laid his hand upon hers, as if to attract her attention. As she looked up at him, something in his expression struck her, and she asked what moved him.

"I am wondering whether I may venture to ask you a question that lies very near me at this moment," was his reply; then he paused, and it seemed to him that the beating of his heart was audible as he went on. "I am not fitted, Konradine, to speak of love to such a woman as yourself; my late experience would tell me this, if I had any doubt upon the subject. And you have loved a man with whose brilliant attractions I could in no wise compete. But I can offer you a home worthy of you, and a field of action upon the estate that I inherit, the responsibility of which I shall assume more readily if you will share it with me, if the conviction that you can give life fresh value to a man who knows your worth and regards you with devoted and affectionate admiration can indemnify you for the absence of those qualities in which I am lacking."

These were the last words that Konradine had expected to hear, but his serious composure impressed her deeply; and, burying her face in her hands, she cried, "Oh, why do you say this to me now,—to-day?"

He turned away, startled, but, controlling himself, replied, "Forgive me, if I have troubled you. Think my words unsaid. Forget, as I will forget, that I asked more than you can give."

"Must I owe to your compassion," she said, "what you would else never have offered me?"

"What can you mean, when I ask you for so much and can bestow so little?" said Emanuel; his old mistrust of himself awaking within him. "I will not urge you, I will not retort upon you what you have just said. Only this I must declare and you must believe: your companionship is my greatest blessing. To win your esteem, to contribute to your happiness, would make me happy indeed——"

Konradine did not let him complete his sentence. "No more," she cried. "I must and will believe you. You must see how dear you are to me,—our aims are the same. I trust you implicitly, and am yours." She held out both hands to him; he pressed them to his lips, tenderly calling her his own; and with hearts touched and softened, inspired by mutual regard, and full of faith in the future, they walked arm in arm to the house, to announce their betrothal to the countess.

Seldom had she experienced such joy as at this moment. She called Konradine her sister, her daughter, and rejoiced that her dying brother's last moments would be made happy by such cheering intelligence. In her delight she would have had Konradine go with them to receive his dying blessing, but this Emanuel would not hear of. He would spare his future wife the distress that awaited his sister and himself, and then, too, he shrank from intruding his own bright hopes for the future upon the last moments of a brother about to leave this world forever.

He therefore readily agreed to Konradine's proposal, that their betrothal should not be made public until her mother had been informed of it and her formal consent obtained. Konradine also desired to return to her retirement at the appointed time, and to be present there when the princess arrived.

The brother and sister started for the south the next morning, and twenty-four hours later, Konradine, in one of Emanuel's carriages, and attended by his confidential valet, whom he had left behind for the purpose, set out for her retreat.

CHAPTER XIX.

While the friends in the southern villa were rejoicing in warmth and sunshine, the winds were sweeping from the sea in icy blasts around the castle and the little parsonage in the north. The autumn tasks out-of-doors were at an end, and even the bailiff scarcely liked to stir from the warm room with its cheerful fire, whither, to his great satisfaction, the curate often came to help him to while away the long evenings with talk upon parish matters, or a game of chess. He was only too glad to provide a conveyance to take him home again through the stormy nights, if he might thus buy the pleasure of his society, for the bailiff had reached the age when, for a man of his standing, to talk is much more interesting than to read. He could no longer pore over the newspapers for a whole evening; they were full of the rights of the people, and freedom, and progress—matters that seemed to him to have nothing to do with true order and government, and of which no one used to hear a word. He grew sleepy over them, and that vexed him, for his sister, who never seemed to know what weariness was, was sure to laugh at him if he lost himself for a moment and nodded.

When the bustling day was ended, Mademoiselle Ulrika was never tired of playing Patience, as Monsieur Michael had taught her. She foretold all sorts of future events from her cards, and believed in them implicitly.

The curate was present one evening as she was laying her cards upon the table where Hulda sat at work, and although he was arranging the chess-board for a game with the bailiff, his attention was chiefly given to what Mademoiselle was saying to the girl. That he might have some share in their conversation, he asked who Monsieur Michael was of whom he had heard her speak, and who had taught her Patience.

"Did I never tell you about him? A charming young man, private secretary to Prince Severin."

"A fine private secretary!" the bailiff exclaimed. "He was the prince's servant, a vain, pretentious, worthless fellow, whom the prince had to dismiss. He found his vocation, however; he is a play-actor now."

"Who told you so?" cried Ulrika, who, with her contempt for everything relating to the theatre, could not listen quietly to such an aspersion upon her favourite.

"Who told me? Why, the postmaster's son, who used to see him here, wrote it to his father. He has seen him play."

"It is a dangerous calling," said the curate.

"I don't believe it! It is not true that he has gone upon the stage," said Ulrika.

"Other people have gone before him," said the bailiff.

"None worth anything," Ma'amselle declared, and her brother made no reply, for the curate had just said "check" to his king, and he had no time to listen to his sister's fancies. Her cards gave her small satisfaction, it would seem, this evening, for she soon put them away and left the room. The bailiff, when his game was finished, went into his office to get some papers that the curate was to take to the schoolmaster, and so Hulda was left alone with the young man. She sat at the table, sewing; the allusion to Michael had distressed her. The curate saw that she was depressed, and seated himself near her.

"It must sometimes be hard for you to bear Ma'amselle Ulrika's sharp speeches," he said; "you have grown so reserved and silent."

Hulda replied that she had become accustomed, as her mother had done, to Ulrika's ways.

"I cannot tell you," he went on, "how constantly I think of you in your old home, when I use your piano, or look around upon all that you have left behind, and remember that you do not enjoy here even the peace that we all so need. Sometimes it seems to me that you must be conscious that I am wishing for you, and that you must long for your old home as a young bird does for the nest——"

His earnestness and warmth of manner troubled her, and, suddenly interrupting him, she said, without looking up from her work, "It is easy to see you were not born in the country. No full-fledged bird ever returns to the nest which the parent birds have left."

"Fräulein Hulda!" he said, evidently much hurt. The bailiff's return prevented his saying more then; but when he rose to go, he held out his hand to her, and said, almost in a whisper, "I hope you were not thinking of yourself in what you said of the bird and the nest?"

The bailiff called out that the carriage was waiting, so that Hulda was spared the necessity of a reply; and the curate, a prey to hopes and fears, drove away into the night.

CHAPTER XX.

THE next morning, as they all sat at breakfast, the boy brought in the post-bag. The bailiff unlocked it immediately, saying, as he looked into it, "It is long since we have had so large a mail."

"Is there anything for the parsonage?" inquired Ma'amselle.

"Yes; a letter, and a packet of papers beside."

"I thought so; the cards were right last night, after all," cried Ulrika. "The living has come, I am sure; and there is a letter for Hulda!" Her brother, however, took it from her and handed it to Hulda, asking, "From whom is it?"

"From Emilie and her mother," she replied, turning away, that he might not see her blush.

"That friendship still exists, then," the bailiff remarked, knowing that when Hulda had stayed in town she had formed an acquaintance with the wife and daughter of the countess's intendant, and that they had corresponded with her after her return. "What do they say?"

Hulda had taken her letter to the window, and contrived, unperceived, to slip into her pocket a smaller letter, enclosed within the one from her friends. The latter she read hastily, and answered, "They wish me to visit them."

"With the roads in such a state? There can be no hurry about it, however," said the bailiff; and he arose, and went with his papers to his desk in the corner.

Hulda longed to escape from the room and read her other letter, but Ulrika asked her to hold a huge knot of yarn for her to wind,—she wanted it for her knitting.

The poor girl counted the seconds as they were ticked off by the tall clock in the corner. Her cheeks burned with impatience. But it was of no use; the skein was tangled, and seemed to increase rather than diminish in volume. She had enclosed her own letter to Gabrielle in one to her friend in the town, begging her to see that it was sent, and to forward to her the answer, should any arrive; and now this answer, deciding her fate, was in her pocket. Surely there was no end to this terrible yarn. A couple of skeins were still unwound, when carriage-wheels were heard in the courtyard.

Ulrika arose and went to the window, with the ball in her hand. "I said so," she cried; "he has not driven over for nothing; he has got the living!" And opening the window, she called out, "Good-morning, Herr Pastor!"

The young man hastily got out of the carriage, and came into the house. The bailiff would have gone to welcome him, but he had no time. The new pastor advanced, in the best of spirits. "Forgive me," he said, gaily, "for coming so soon again; but I could not stay away. The living is mine!"

"I congratulate you, Herr Pastor," cried the bailiff. "I am heartily glad to keep you with us; and others are glad, too," he added, glancing with a sly smile towards Hulda, who, however, did not see him, for since the young man's entrance she had stood with downcast eyes,—an attitude which the bailiff thought extremely natural and becoming under the circumstances. "Sister, let us have a bottle of wine, to celebrate the good news." When it was brought, he filled four glasses, and, beckoning to his sister and Hulda, said, "Come, both of you, drink to the health of our new pastor. And you, Herr Pastor, I congratulate with all my heart. All can now be as you wish; and I must tell you that I have a little something more for you, and not for you alone, to begin housekeeping with." Then, as the young pastor looked confused, and Ma'amselle inquiringly, he went on: "I have had a letter, too, from the Frau Countess, and you and I," turning to his guest, "can clink glasses upon the intelligence it contains; Fräulein Konradine and Baron Emanuel are betrothed, and——"

"Did not I tell you so," Ulrika interrupted him, "when they were here together?"

The bailiff had made this announcement with a purpose; he had hoped it would influence Hulda with regard to the young pastor; but when he saw the girl rise from her seat and go to the door, at the same time growing deathly pale, he shook his head impatiently, and called out, "Hulda, Hulda, what are you about?"

Before the words had left his lips, however, the pastor was

at Hulda's side. His anxiety on her account conquered his jealousy.

"You are not well, Fräulein Hulda," he said, and begged her to allow him to accompany her. Knowing that she could not escape the interview he sought, she acquiesced. Ulrika would have followed them, but her brother peremptorily ordered her to sit still, and she contented herself with saying, scornfully, "What a fuss every one makes about the girl!"

The bailiff grew impatient, but did not betray it in words. He walked to and fro in the room, knocked the ashes from his pipe, filled it and lighted it again. He looked over his papers, but was too restless for business. He sincerely hoped that the girl, whom he really loved, would now put a stop to all the talk there had been about her by consenting to become the wife of a worthy man; but they were taking a great deal of time for what ought to have been settled in a couple of moments. He arose and tapped the side of the barometer.

"Do you think," asked Ulrika, "that it will tell you the princess's mind?"

Before he could reply, steps were heard in the passage, and brother and sister turned towards the door as the pastor entered.

"Alone, Herr Pastor?" the bailiff asked, in evident surprise, while a smile of malicious triumph curled Ulrika's lips.

The young man's grave face told them what his words confirmed. "It is not to be," he said; "such happiness is not for me."

"Is the girl beside herself?" exclaimed the bailiff, going hastily to the door.

The pastor detained him. "Do not say one word to her. She is not to blame; God guides her and knows what is best for her and for me. My own desires misled me. It was not her fault."

"Fault or no fault," cried the bailiff, "a girl ought to be married, and she should thank God when she has the chance of such a husband as you would make. I will put a stop to all this nonsense." He made a sign to Ulrika to call Hulda; but Ulrika did not stir from her seat, and the pastor took his hat and bade farewell. The bailiff could not detain him; he longed to be alone; his simulated composure was costing him dear. In a few moments the carriage in which he had arrived bore him out of the court-yard, and the bailiff returned with anger in his looks. He pulled the bell which was to summon Hulda so violently that the cord was left in his hand, and then seated himself in the huge chair in which he always took his place if offenders were to be called to account, while Ulrika quietly began to count the stitches in her knitting.

"What occurred just now between you?" the bailiff growled out to Hulda as she appeared before him, pale, and her eyes red with weeping.

She could scarcely speak; but, raising her clasped hands, she turned to him a face beautiful in its distress, and entreated, "Do not force me to tell you what was so hard to bear."

"Hard?" sneered Ulrika. "I should suppose it would be easy for you by this time to turn the heads of respectable men."

"Be quiet!" ordered the bailiff, who had already begun to pity Hulda, so completely alone in the world, and so young, to be exposed to his sister's sharp tongue. "Don't stand there and cry like a child,—that will do no good,—but speak, and say what you propose to do now."

She knew not what to reply, and he grew angry again. "The countess has just sent me money for you, and has increased the salary of the living that she has bestowed upon the curate; he is an excellent man, whom you might be proud to call your husband, and you have sent him away for nothing. You will again be the talk of the village, and there has been enough of that. My house is no place for such a girl."

"You know you really have no claim upon us," said Ulrika, who could no longer contain herself.

"I know I ought to go away," said Hulda; and then she added, in a lower tone, "and I wish very much to go."

The bailiff stared at her. "You want to go away? Whither? And what do you propose to do?"

For weeks Hulda had been preparing herself for the moment when this question should be asked her, and she had determined boldly to declare her intentions. But now her courage failed her. After the way in which the bailiff had expressed himself on the previous day with regard to play-actors, she could not confess her plans, at least not until she knew what Gabrielle advised,—and she had just opened her letter when she had been summoned to appear before her angry friend. Therefore she only said that she wanted to try to earn her living.

"And what do you mean to do?" scornfully inquired the bailiff, who held firmly to the belief that no woman of cultivation could support herself.

"I have been brought up in the conviction that I should have to help myself," she replied, with more firmness. Her dignity was wounded by the sneering tone of her former protector. "My poor dear father and Miss Kenney always told me so, and——"

"Then you are going to be a teacher, like Miss Kenney, and an old maid!" the bailiff interrupted her; he detested unmarried women of a certain age, and governesses. "But who will take you about here, where there has been so much gossip, especially when this last affair gets abroad, as you may be sure it will?" And he cast a significant glance towards his sister.

"For that reason I beg you to give me a little of the money that Miss Kenney left me, and send me to town, where I am certain of a welcome at the Herr Intendant's until a suitable situation is found for me," she replied, her courage rising against the injustice with which she felt she was treated.

"This is your plan, then! all charmingly devised and arranged! And the curate encouraged and then jilted!" Ulrika said, contemptuously; and the bailiff did not reprove her, but, falling into her mood, added, bitterly, "And all because of that miserable love-affair with the baron, who will live happily in his castle with his wife, and never for one moment trouble his head about whether you go to ruin or not."

This was more than she could bear. She stood boldly erect, and, although her temples throbbed and her lips quivered, she said, firmly, "I shall not go to ruin, Herr Bailiff, even although none trouble themselves about me. And God is my witness that I have never encouraged any one; never aroused, either by word or look, a false hope in the pastor's mind. This he will tell you himself. I have long known that I could not stay here, and I beseech you to be kind, and send me away as quickly as possible. I should go to ruin if I stayed here."

The bailiff very nearly muttered an oath; the vein in his forehead swelled, and he looked steadily in the girl's face for a minute, entirely at a loss what to say or how to act. She looked like innocence and gentleness themselves. He could hardly bear it. He had neither wife nor child, and his sister was no comfort to him. Hulda he loved as if she were his own daughter, and it vexed him that she should wish to go out into the world. He thought her all wrong, and yet he could not refuse her; she was evidently in earnest. She should have her will, and if she failed his house should still be open to her, and she could return to it, tamed, he trusted.

His mind was made up, and he instantly recovered his equanimity. He clasped his hands behind him, as was his wont when he had arrived at a decision, and said, slowly, "And so you would like to go to-morrow?"

She replied that she should be glad to go then if she could. He went to the almanac, consulted it, and, returning, said, "There is nothing to prevent; you may go. I will let you have the money that you need, and will attend to anything that you wish at the parsonage. You can start to-morrow at eight o'clock."

She gently thanked him, but he repulsed her, which grieved her, for she had always been fond of him, and knew that he meant well by her. He took his cap, but refused to allow her to bring him his stick, saying that he could get it for himself. Then he went out into the court-yard.

Ulrika told her to see to the packing of her trunk, and that she had no need of any further service from her to-day, and she retired to her room to read Gabrielle's letter.

CHAPTER XXI.

So much had been lived through in so short a time that as Hulda sat with the open letter before her she felt half stunned, as if in a dream, from which she must shortly awaken to find herself still uncertain as to where she should turn in her loneliness and perplexity. But the mere sight of the actress's clear, decided handwriting consoled her. The letter was all she could desire. "I understand perfectly, my poor child," so it ran, "all you would say to me. We all desire either some especial happiness in life, or some absorbing pursuit, and if we cannot attain the first we do what we can to make the second our own. But let me remind you that an actress's life is one of toil and trial; even if she reach the goal of her hopes, there are sharp thorns among her laurels. It remains to be proved, also, whether your talent is sufficient to insure your success You only can decide whether you possess the courage, the determination, and the confidence in yourself that are indispensable to a theatrical career. Weigh this question well, and if you decide in the affirmative, apply to the manager whom you saw that morning at my room. I have written to him, telling him of your intention, and have recommended you to his especial favour. If you meet with opposition from those around you, you must carry out your determination in spite of it, and remember that in this case the dangerous words are true, that the end justifies the means."

She added that she had great confidence in Hulda's capacity, and that her astonishing resemblance to herself would probably be of service to her. The whole letter was written in a simple, business-like way, and the writer ended by declaring that if Hulda was willing to take her advice she herself must of course be allowed to supply the means to make such action possible. She enclosed a check for travelling-expenses to X——, where the manager resided, and there would be found a deposit at the banker's sufficient to meet the young girl's necessities until the manager had decided upon her capacity. When that time arrived she begged that Hulda would write to her again, and until then she wished her courage, patience, and God-speed.

Hulda gave a great sigh of relief when she had finished reading this letter, which brought her consolation and sympathy as well as encouragement. As Gabrielle had said, happiness was denied her, and she turned to the pursuit of an absorbing occupation. The labour of her life began from this hour.

"Childhood, home, and love are gone!" she said to herself. "I must leave those things which are behind, and press forward to those which are before."

Her preparations for departure were soon completed, for her possessions were small, and the day was still before her. When the bell rang for dinner she went to the table, but to-day was unlike all other days. The bailiff talked to his sister and his people, but they said nothing to Hulda, and the servants looked at her curiously. They already knew that Fräulein Hulda had refused to marry the pastor, and that the bailiff would not keep her with him any longer.

The afternoon dragged on slowly enough. Ulrika would not accept her assistance in any household task. "No," she said, "such work is not fit for governesses or fine ladies. They must take care of their hands."

When night fell, she went to the window and looked out. How often she had stood there, looking across to his windows in the castle, and listening to the soft notes of his piano as he improvised and played! All was now silent and dark. She had no place even in his thoughts; his happiness was complete without her. He knew himself beloved; he had been delivered. Delivered by her! But the curse had recoiled upon her own head. She was forgotten, forsaken, unloved, and now she was about to begin life homeless and alone.

She was still standing in the same place when the bailiff entered her room. He brought her the money she had asked for, and advised her to sew it into her dress.

"I will try to arrange with the pastor about your furniture and your father's books," he said. "He can make use of those things, and it is scarcely worth while to remove them. I will put away for you whatever he gives me for them."

She replied that she cared very little about it, and he said no more, but left the room.

Late in the night, when all had gone to rest, she thought with sorrow of the young pastor, and wrote him a few lines, begging him to forget that he had asked of her what she could not grant, thanking him again for all the kindness he had shown both her father and herself, and requesting him to accept, in token of her gratitude and sisterly affection, the piano with which he had cheered so many of her father's sad moments.

The next morning she gave this letter unsealed to the bailiff, who, at her request, read it, and approved it with a quiver of the lip very unusual with him. He embraced her tenderly as she got into the carriage, and she kissed him and Ulrika, and thanked them for all their kindness.

"Don't speak of it," said Ulrika, who could not say good-bye, as she hurried into the house.

When the carriage had driven off, the bailiff found his sister sitting crying on the bench by the stove.

"This is just what you wanted," he said, passing her to go into his office.

"It was all her doing," she replied, rising, and going to the window.

The carriage was already out among the fields. There was the spot—Hulda remembered it well—where she had first seen Emanuel.

PART III.

CHAPTER I.

GABRIELLE'S letter to her old acquaintance, manager Holm, informing him that the lovely young girl whom he had met in her rooms, on a winter's morning, a year before, desired to go upon the stage, was duly received. He remembered the girl perfectly, and he smiled at the meagre account of her antecedents which was all the great actress saw fit to give him.

He had sustained the heroic parts, when a young man, in the theatre of which he was now manager, and had found acceptance with the public, and especially among ladies, as he still perfectly well remembered. He prided himself upon his knowledge of the world, and of women in especial, and thought he knew when it was discreet to understand and be silent in default of exact information. He immediately assured Gabrielle of his entire readiness to serve her.

The theatre was one of the principal social interests of the large old commercial town, and Holm was very popular as a manager. He had assisted in the development of several gifted actors and actresses; to such the social characteristics of the place were remarkably favourable. The nobility of the surrounding provinces, who passed the winters in town, as well as the wealthy merchants and foreign consuls of the place, all owned boxes at the theatre, while the officers of its garrison, the young officials of the government, and the members of its university made a very appreciative public. They formed strong attachments for certain artists, and were not easily satisfied when they were obliged to lose any one of their favourites, as was at present the case.

The actress sustaining the principal parts was on the point of leaving the stage forever. She had been a great favourite for several years, and had been secretly betrothed for some time to a wealthy merchant's son, who, now that his parents were dead, was about to marry her. Her contract would come to an end just at the time when the lengthening days and lovely weather deprived the theatre of some of its chief supporters. The manager had been contriving for months how to sustain the interest of the public during this trying time, and he was delighted to hear from Gabrielle of this young aspirant for dramatic honours, who was described as full of talent, very like herself, and very beautiful.

He wrote to Hulda as soon as he received Gabrielle's letter, to tell her to come to him as soon as possible, since, in consequence of the great artiste's representations, he was determined to put her capacity to the test immediately, and, in case he should find it sufficient, to do all in his power to educate and form her for her new vocation. He also told her that lodgings in the city should await her arrival, and gave her all needed information concerning her journey. Then, as her name was rather commonplace, he advised the adoption of another as her dramatic title.

At that afternoon's rehearsal he was in an uncommonly good humour. He jested with the retiring favourite, in whom he already saw the wealthy merchant's wife, begging her to use her time well, and imprint her image upon the memories of her adorers, lest it should be effaced by the successor whom he designed for her. He did not, however, reveal to Feodora the name of the *débutante*, or tell her more concerning her, and, because he maintained this air of secrecy with regard to her, it was soon spread abroad in theatrical circles that the manager was about to bring out a new actress, around whom was thrown a certain veil of mystery.

The next day Holm encountered, in the coffee-house where he read his paper daily, two of Feodora's most ardent admirers,—one a wealthy nobleman from the country, and the other a physician of excellent standing, both of them men whose verdict would go far to make or mar a theatrical reputation.

Scarcely had he exchanged greetings with them, when Herr von Hochbrecht asked what the report meant which Feodora had mentioned to him at the rehearsal. "It really was not necessary," he said, "as a spur to Feodora's ambition, which was never more aspiring than at present."

"Certainly," added the doctor, with a sarcastic smile; "she is very desirous that her husband may be reminded frequently in future years of the brilliant triumphs she resigned for his sake."

The manager assured them that there was no trick in the report they alluded to. He had, of course, been looking about for some time for some one to replace Feodora in the public favour, and, as he despaired of finding any established actress who could compete with her in the natural grace of her manner and bearing, he had resolved to educate and bring forward a very young girl who might in time fill all the parts of the favourite.

"And have you found this young girl?" asked Hochbrecht.

"I can hardly say that I found her," the manager replied. "She came to me without any seeking on my part, like a bird flying in at my window."

Then he went on to tell how he had first seen her in Gabrielle's room a year before, and how even then there had been some talk of a stage career for her. She had grown up in a country parsonage.

"And is she a pretty girl?" asked Hochbrecht.

"A beauty!" the manager declared; while, to give effect to his words, he kissed the tips of his fingers and threw the imaginary salute into the air. "A beauty of the first order, born for the stage. Tall, with a proud carriage, a beautiful bust, light-brown hair, and very large eyes—the mother over again."

"You knew her parents, then?" asked Hochbrecht.

"No; the girl is an orphan."

"But you have just mentioned the resemblance of the daughter to the mother," the doctor reminded him.

"Not at all," cried the manager. "I never saw her parents." And when the friends, whose curiosity was aroused, pressed him further, he took the tone of a man who had unguardedly allowed words to escape him that should not have been spoken, asserting that he had no knowledge of the girl except that which he had obtained from Gabrielle, whose *protégée* she was.

"Whom does she resemble, then?" asked Hochbrecht, who was not easily deterred from pursuing a subject that interested him.

"Gabrielle!" replied the manager, quite as if he had already said so.

The friends exchanged meaning smiles. The manager declared that there was nothing to smile at; he had not the least idea how Gabrielle first became acquainted with the girl,—probably she had been attracted by the striking resemblance to herself, for she had been the first to call his attention to it.

"You are prudence itself," said the doctor, lightly tapping him upon the shoulder. "No one could more gracefully swallow his own words to conceal an indiscretion. Don't be annoyed. You have said nothing, we have heard nothing, and shall see in your young *débutante* only an innocent child from a country parsonage."

Then all three talked upon other subjects, and not until they were about to separate was the manager asked the name of the expected beauty.

This reminded him of the change he had advised, and, without waiting to think whether Hulda would consent to lay aside her own honest name, he unhesitatingly gave that of a well-known family, several of whose members had gone upon the stage, and to which Gabrielle's mother had belonged. It was not a very uncommon name, and sounded especially well in connection with Hulda. The manager, therefore, had small doubt of being able to persuade the girl that it would be a mark of gratitude to her protectress thus to take shelter behind the ægis of her maternal title.

Herr Holm never bestowed a thought upon the conclusions that the world might draw from this name in connection with Hulda's resemblance to Gabrielle. Of course he begged his friends to be silent regarding all he had told them, since it was impossible to tell yet what the girl might turn out to be. They promised; but in the dearth of political interest at that time in Germany, the theatre furnished the staple of conversation, and before two days had gone by the appearance of a beautiful young *débutante* was discussed everywhere in the town, and reports as to her antecedents were circulated which were very soon related and believed as facts.

CHAPTER II.

HULDA found her plan far less difficult of execution than she had feared. The intendant's family, to whom she confided her intention, had relatives upon the stage, and did all that they could to smooth matters for her by undertaking to apprise the bailiff of the welfare of his ward, for so he considered her, without as yet shocking his prejudices by informing him of the nature of the employment she had procured.

It was quite late in the evening when she was received at the post-station of the old commercial city that was to be her home for the present by the respectable elderly matron with whom the manager had arranged that she should lodge.

Frau Rosen, the widow of a clerk, had, after her husband's death early in life, maintained herself and her children by letting lodgings in the small house which was her all, and in the garret rooms of which she resided. Its vicinity to the theatre had been a great advantage to her. She had found lodgers among the actors and actresses, and gradually her care and attention had given her house a reputation among them. Her children were now grown up, and had left her, with the exception of the youngest daughter, who was her mother's assistant in household matters, while she added to their small gains by her skill as a milliner and dressmaker.

As economy was Hulda's chief consideration, only a small room had been assigned her, but it was neat and comfortable, and well warmed, while its two dormer-windows permitted a good sweep of sky to be seen from within. The kindly welcome, also, that she received, from both the mother and the daughter, did much to cheer the poor child's failing spirits. Everything that was most formidable to her in her new life was quite familiar and commonplace to the two women. They knew every one officially connected with the theatre, from the manager himself down to the barber and tailor, and were never tired of telling of all the histrionic celebrities whom they had at various times sheltered beneath their roof. Among these was the admired Feodora, now about to leave the stage, and, upon one occasion, while she was their lodger, she had received a visit from the famous Gabrielle, of whose beauty and majestic bearing Frau Rosen spoke with enthusiasm.

Scarcely had the mother alluded to Gabrielle, when her daughter Beata called attention to Hulda's resemblance to the great actress, and mother and daughter congratulated her upon a circumstance that would go far to prepossess the public in her favour. All that they said tended to reassure and encourage Hulda, and when she was left alone in her little room she looked around her with a degree of content to which she had long been a stranger. She was glad to be out of the reach of Ulrika's sharp tongue, and to know that there was no danger of encountering the young pastor, whose suit had so distressed her. She would—she must—forget all that had passed away never to return; and it was a relief to feel that no one knew where she was, that she had vanished from the knowledge of Emanuel, who had been faithless and had forsaken her. There was nothing here to speak to her of the past, except the stars, which shone with the same mild light as on the sea-shore far away, and to which she had first confided her love and sorrow. They were still looking down upon her, telling her of her childhood and of her father and mother, and to them she now vowed that she would always be true to herself and to the faith in God which had been taught her in her once dear home.

But as soon as sleep descended upon her weary eyelids the scene changed. Once more she stood in the spacious hall of the castle, where she had first seen Emanuel's picture, and the golden sunshine, reflected from the sea, flooded all the place so brilliantly that the polished floor looked like flame, and she saw from its depths the elf-king issue, followed by all his train of "little folk." On costly salvers and in gleaming caskets they carried all sorts of beautiful things, gay garments, sparkling crowns, and green laurel-wreaths. The little king laid all this splendour at Hulda's feet, and she saw that it was all destined for her. She rejoiced to possess it, and would have placed upon her brow a brilliant diadem. But as she took it in her hand, and stepped up to the mirror that hung between the windows, she saw in its depths Emanuel's handsome head, and his eyes were regarding her with so melancholy an expression that she started in terror, and the diadem fell to the floor and crashed into a thousand pieces. The sparkling bits flew hither and thither, so that the eye could scarcely follow them, and, when their last gleam had faded away, Hulda looked around her, and found herself alone. The king, with his train and all the magnificence they had brought with them, had vanished. They had left her but one small ring with a blue stone. She stooped to pick it up, and as she was putting it on her finger she saw that it was the same that she had sent back to Emanuël, and those words,—never to be forgotten,—"Thee and me shall no one sever," glittered upon its golden surface.

She waked, with a low cry of joy, and felt for the ring upon her hand. It was not there. Had she not sent it back herself? She could not at first tell where she was, but the gray light of morning was already stealing in at her windows, and quickly brought her to herself.

At eight o'clock Frau Rosen knocked at her door, and received her modest orders; and, when the hour came that the manager had appointed for her interview with him, she betook herself to his house, in the vicinity of the theatre, anxious but hopeful.

The rehearsal for the day was over, and the manager was in the best of humours. He met her in the street as he was coming from the theatre, and, instantly recognizing her, kindly bade her welcome. "Was I not right," he asked, "in telling you that all roads lead to the stage as well as to Rome? I saw, even before your protectress presented you to me, that you were one of us; I knew I should sooner or later find you on the stage."

He then introduced her to his stage-director as the expected pupil. The actors meanwhile, who were leaving the theatre, passed the group, with a bow to the manager, and a curious glance at Hulda; and by evening every one connected with the theatre knew that Gabrielle's daughter had come, and that she was certainly beautiful, and very like her mother, but that she looked timid and frightened enough to have just fallen from the skies.

Strange indeed was the world in which Hulda now found herself. There was nothing in it to remind her of the teachings of home. The manager took her into his study, and invited the director to accompany them, that they might judge of her capacity. First he asked her to repeat any poem that she knew by heart; then he gave her a scene to read in a play which she had never seen, and in which the director read the second part; and when, in answer to his questions, she admitted that she knew something of music, he opened the piano and requested her to sing to him. He asked her if she had ever attempted anything in the way of dramatic representation; and although the manner in which the two men stared at her embarrassed and distressed her, she did her best to do what was required of her. In spite of the timidity and confusion of mind that at times threatened to overwhelm her, she was conscious of a kind of defiant delight in knowing that at last she had taken her life into her own hands,—that she was doing what every one hitherto interested in her, with the sole exception of Gabrielle, would have disapproved, and Emanuel probably more than all.

Her bearing and expression gained by this mood; she held herself more erect, and her voice sounded full and free. She saw that her judges were pleased with her, and their exclamations of approval from time to time cheered her.

When the trial of her powers was at an end, the manager told her, with an air of condescending kindness, that he had decided to make the attempt to fit her for the stage. All advantage in the matter was hers. It would require months of instruction and careful study before she could appear before the public, who were, after all, capricious, and might not be pleased with her,—in which case he should have lost time and trouble, while she would have gained in education and culture. Still, for Gabrielle's sake, he was willing to make the attempt, and she could go to work immediately.

She listened to him as to the voice of destiny. Everything was going much more smoothly than she had anticipated. She would have thanked him, but in her emotion she could find no words in which to express herself. He dismissed her with a shake of the hand, and, as she was putting on her hood and jacket, advised her, since she was now at all events about to tread those boards which are called the world, to adopt a style of dress more in keeping with the present fashion and her future prospects. Ma'amselle Beata's ready fingers would soon make all right for her.

"You must begin with your hair," he said. "Those beautiful thick braids wound around your head would, as I told you a year ago, if you would let them hang down your back, be very becoming to Käthchen von Heilbronn; but in real life they have a very countrified air. A Grecian knot, with long English curls, would suit you very well. Take counsel of our barber, if you cannot devise something for yourself. We must look as lovely as possible,—it is your duty, mademoiselle,—a duty, I think, that you will perform extremely well."

He meant to have gratified her by this little compliment; but to his surprise he saw that he had failed to do so, and that she gravely listened to his advice and silently took her leave. He could not understand it, for he knew nothing of her. He did not know that the suggestion with regard to her hair carried her far away from all that he was hoping would allure and interest her.

Must she no longer wear her braids smoothly wound about her head? And Emanuel had so liked her way of wearing her hair!

She was frightened at finding that the manager's words served only to call up this memory. There was a spell upon her. Everything that she thought or did served but to lead her back to him. She wished she could hate herself, and hate him; for she could not forget him, although he had so entirely forgotten her.

CHAPTER III.

THE two men looked after Hulda with satisfied smiles as she walked across the square before the theatre to her lodgings.

"A queenly bearing! What natural dignity of carriage, in spite of those old-fashioned clothes!" exclaimed the manager. "I have given up the idea of subjecting her to any long course of training, and allowing her to appear gradually in subordinate parts, now that I have tested her powers. Her talent is undeniable. She is very beautiful, and can easily learn several parts. We shall thus oblige Gabrielle, and perhaps induce her to play for us, that she may see how we have polished the rough diamond intrusted to our care."

Some discussion ensued as to what further should be done for Hulda; and the manager requested his director to see, if he could, that she was well treated.

"I mean," he added, "by the women,—she will soon win over the men. But Fräulein Delmar grows spiteful as she grows older, and I am not perfectly sure of Feodora in this case. Women are almost always petty, and entirely unreliable when their vanity comes into play. The Rosens, where I have taken Hulda's lodgings, will, I know, treat her kindly, and we must try to effect in a few weeks what sometimes needs a couple of years, for the girl is admirably educated, has a knowledge of the classics, and is of imposing presence. All of which will make our miracle comparatively easy."

And in fact everything, now that the great step had been taken, seemed like a miracle to Hulda. Frau Rosen and her daughter, too, wondered greatly at the interest shown by the manager in their young lodger.

True, she was very beautiful and very different from all other beginners whom they had ever known. She was simpler and more dignified, more reserved and much gentler. But there must be some additional reason for all this interest, and they were sure of discovering it by-and-by. Meanwhile they did what in them lay to bring about as quickly as possible the desired metamorphosis in Hulda's appearance, and the girl's cheeks flushed, her eyes sparkled, and she could not suppress a self-satisfied smile when she looked at herself in the mirror after the change had taken place.

"If he could but see me thus!" she thought, and for a moment she exulted in the consciousness that she was beautiful, far more beautiful than Konradine, so beautiful that she should like to be seen, that she might enjoy the effect she was certain of producing. And with the affectation which is born of awakened vanity, she asked Beata if she did not think her ugly in her new dress.

It was the first wilful prevarication she had ever uttered, the first time she had pretended to what she did not feel. But, as if her nature were transformed with her dress, she found a satisfaction in the deceit, and listened with a new delight to the assurances of the mother and daughter that she was charming.

She could scarcely wait for the time when she was to go to

the theatre, to be present at rehearsal. She went from her mirror to the window, and back again to the mirror, to convince herself that it was her own face which she saw there. Was this the girl whom Ulrika had so despised, who had looked forward to a life spent in a lonely parsonage, listening to the dreary beat of the ocean upon the shore, and watching with longing eyes the flight of the sea-birds?

She did not know how bewitching she looked, as she clapped her hands like a child at the sound of the music of the band that accompanied a detachment of soldiers from the garrison to the parade-ground. Everything pleased her to-day, the passing equipages, the crowds in the street, yes, even the old cake-woman at the corner, whose chief interest in life was to watch the lodgers at the Rosens', and who knew more about them than some of them would have cared to tell. She had been on the watch all day long, and had her own thoughts when she saw the beautiful girl come to the window for the third or fourth time and look out into the street.

Hulda laughed to see the old woman regard her so attentively, but she no longer shrank back, as she would have done on the previous day, when a passer-by looked up at her. She would have to be looked at; she must lay aside her country-girl shyness and timidity with her old-fashioned costume. She must learn to bear herself with freedom and confidence, like Gabrielle, like the princess and Konradine. How could she ever appear upon the stage if she were confused by the gaze of a passer-by? She must, at all hazards, assert herself; how else could she justify the step she had taken?

The weather was dry and mild, the sky slightly cloudy; but the sun still shone with a light that well became the fine old houses, the pointed gables, and the huge towers of the Rathhaus, as she walked across the square—with a self-possession that would have been impossible a few days before—and entered the vestibule of the theatre. Several men were standing together there; they must have known who she was, for one of them, a young, handsome man, approached her, and, addressing her by the new name that the manager had given her, offered to conduct her to the stage.

She followed him through narrow passages, up steps, and along corridors lighted only by a glimmer of lamplight, that made fantastic work of the shadows, until they reached the dimly-illumined stage, before which stretched the dark, mysterious depths of the auditorium. Hulda looked about her, dismayed by the disorder everywhere. Walls were being pushed aside on one hand, and on the other a marble balustrade was tottering to its fall. In the background men were spreading out a canvas that fluttered in the draught of air, and that looked like anything rather than the blue sky it was intended to represent. On the right two statues were being adjusted beneath some shabby trees, and on the left a faded grassy bank was pushed into the foreground. Ropes hung down here and there; some boards were lying on the ground; and among it all the actors and actresses were grouped about, laughing and talking, while workmen in dirty shirt-sleeves ran to and fro.

The play in rehearsal was "Tasso," which all the actors had played over and over again. No one showed any interest in it, no one said a word about the evening's performance. No one dreamed what a significance there was for Hulda in the fact that "Tasso" was to be played on this particular evening. Surely it was a good omen, for it was in "Tasso" that she had first seen Gabrielle.

The director was already upon the stage, and came forward to meet Hulda and her escort as he saw them advance from the background.

"Aha!" he cried, "you have already found your future associate, and I am glad to see that even you are not too tall for our Lelio. Yes, my dear Lelio, you need shun no comparison," he said, gaily, holding out his hand to the young man, and adding that he was anxious to have mademoiselle soon undertake some of Feodora's youthful parts. He thought that if Lelio would help her a little, mademoiselle might try her fortune in a few months; and if she succeeded, they would not grudge Fräulein Delmar the twenty-nine years which she had for two lustres at least declared to be her age.

"Oh, she will be raging!" Lelio replied; "but let us hope that she may be induced to give up the idea of undertaking any of Feodora's youthful parts. The mere thought of playing with her has oppressed me like a nightmare; a nightmare from which mademoiselle's presence delivers me," he added, with a gallant bow to Hulda.

He suddenly ceased speaking, however, for a black-haired

lady, rather under middle size, approached, and was greeted as Mademoiselle Delmar. She scanned Hulda from top to toe, contracted her eyebrows as if not able to see her quite distinctly, and finally put up her eye-glass and asked, "Mademoiselle Hulda, I presume, the manager's new *protégée*?"

Then, without waiting for an answer, she turned away, and Hulda distinctly heard her remark that it was very easy to see from her clumsy figure that the young person came from the country. There was nothing to be done on the stage with such a figure.

At this moment the manager entered, and with him came a lady still young and very handsome. She wore a velvet jacket trimmed with costly fur, and as she took off her hat Hulda saw that there was a jewelled comb in her hair.

After what Frau Rosen and Beata had said, this could be none other than Feodora. She entered with an air of command that pleased Hulda, for it reminded her of Gabrielle. The new-comer held out her hand to Lelio, and passed Fräulein Delmar by with a slight inclination. The signal was given, the lookers-on withdrew among the side-scenes, the workmen vanished, the rehearsal began, and there stole over Hulda the same sensation of awed expectation which she had experienced on the evening when she had seen Gabrielle for the first time.

The charm of the wondrous poetry again asserted its power over her. She no longer saw the tawdry trappings of the stage; the laths and scaffolding vanished; the dead canvas and painted wood disappeared; majestic trees stretched their evergreen boughs towards heaven, and roses bloomed beneath an Italian sky. Her delight, her enthusiasm, grew with every scene. The play was well cast. Feodora was a lovely princess, and Lelio, with his tall, slender figure and distinguished air, his delicate profile and wealth of chestnut curls, was everything that could be desired for a Tasso. All seemed well pleased with themselves, and, as far as was possible, with one another.

In the pause between the first and second acts, the manager, who sustained the part of the duke, perceived Hulda, and addressed a few words to her. Meanwhile Lelio said to Feodora, with whom he was upon the best of terms, "Have you seen her? There she is,—Gabrielle's daughter."

"Is she really as like her as they say?"

"Very like, only much more beautiful than the mother ever could have been. She will make an exquisite Juliet. The Delmar was in a fury when she saw her."

"And fury certainly does not become her, or make her look m :ch younger," said Feodora, with a laugh, as, accompanied by Lelio, she walked directly across the stage towards Hulda.

It was so unlike her to treat an unknown stranger thus that the manager could not but admire the gracious way in which she addressed the astonished girl. "Did I not tell you the other day," he said to the director, "that there was no reliance to be placed upon Feodora?"

"A passing whim,—nothing but curiosity," the confidant replied. But Feodora was animated by no whim in what she did. She knew perfectly well what she wished and what she intended her amiability should effect.

She admired Gabrielle, imitated her as far as she could, and loved her after her fashion. Sharing in the universal belief that Hulda was Gabrielle's child, she determined to act the part of a friend to the beautiful girl, especially as she knew that by so doing she should irritate Fräulein Delmar, whom she cordially disliked. She was still young enough not to dread a comparison with youth and beauty, and the time was at hand when, as one of the wealthiest women in the city, she should have it in her power to extend patronage instead of craving it.

With the most amiable condescension, she asked Hulda when she had last heard from her protectress, adding that it was surely the best earnest of future success to be befriended by a Gabrielle. Then she observed how happy she should be to be of service to her so far as her duties at the theatre and her engagements with her future bridegroom would at present permit, while in the future she trusted to be of real assistance to her.

She uttered the last words loud enough to be overheard by Fräulein Delmar, who remarked, with a scornful smile, to the actor by her side, "Feodora is queening it again to-day upon the strength of the Van Vlies money."

"And yet she will sometimes long to be back again," he replied.

"Sometimes?" cried the lady. "She will die of ennui in her

gilded cage, which you may be sure she would never enter if she did not feel that her time had gone by, and that Van Vlies would soon tire of bribing the claqueurs. She cannot live away from the stage or without a public to coquette with."

"Oh," said Lelio, "I believe she will like very well to sit comfortably in her proscenium-box and look down upon us all, applauding you and me now and then as she may see fit."

The lady turned away in disgust, and the rehearsal went on to its close; after which the manager took Hulda into his study to give her the parts he wished her to commit to memory, and the girl went cheerfully home, without a suspicion that already, without any action on her part, there was a clique in her favour, and that she was regarded with hostility in certain quarters.

With the artlessness of a child, she related what had occurred to Frau Rosen and Beata, and they, to her great surprise, had reasons ready for all that had amazed or pleased her. They spoke of Feodora's liaison with the man she was about to marry, and of Fräulein Delmar's passion for the handsome Lelio, who was proof against her wiles, since he was in love with a woman of rank, who would not listen to his suit. And they repeated much more gossip of the same kind in connection with the other actors and actresses attached to the theatre; their words, innuendoes, and terms of expression all sounded easy and natural, as if what they conveyed were not too often directly opposed to morals and decorum, and as if the license which seemed to reign in these circles were the rule of the world. As she listened, a disagreeable memory was awakened in Hulda's pure mind.

Only once before in her life had she heard such words. And yet to-day she did not shrink from all that these women said, as she had done from Michael in the forest. The beautiful Feodora, the handsome Lelio, the wealthy merchant, and Fräulein Delmar's jealousy interested her. The conversation occupied her, and she was at once attracted and repelled by it. But she had no answer for the question that she could not but put to herself: "What would your good old father, your pious mother, the curate, and the bailiff, what would Emanuel think, could they be by your side at this moment and listen to what these people are telling you?"

Emanuel? Whose fault was it but his that she was here?

He had always compared her to the fair daughter of Ceres. Now she had tasted the ill-omened fruit of the pomegranate, and belonged to the world where it grew; henceforth that world must be hers; she could and would not leave it.

She set herself at work to study the parts that had been given her. It was a pleasure to commit them to memory, and she ceased only when the time came to go in the evening to the theatre, where the excellent representation of "Tasso" completed the spell thrown around her.

Early the next morning she carried to the post a letter to the bailiff, announcing her firm determination to go upon the stage.

CHAPTER IV.

After his brother's death, Emanuel instantly began his journey to his ancestral castle, only allowing himself a few days to visit Konradine in her retreat. The betrothed pair resolved that, out of respect to the memory of the elder brother, their betrothal should not be publicly announced until the new year, and that the marriage should take place some time in the spring. Meanwhile, the countess was to spend the winter in the capital at her own house, where she had invited Frau von Wildenau and her daughter to visit her, and where it would be easy for Emanuel to see his betrothed from time to time. At present he pursued his journey towards his Lithuanian home, at ease in his mind, finding unwonted satisfaction in the consciousness that, for the first time in his life, a task was actually allotted him.

His betrothal with Konradine, the death of his only brother, and his consequent inheritance of the family estates, all occurring in quick succession, formed a new epoch in his life. Until now he had enjoyed the fullest freedom of action, and had been governed as to his pursuits by his own inclinations alone. Now there was a duty in life for him to perform, that would materially interfere with the liberty he had so prized. But, to his surprise, it cost him very little to resign this liberty;

and as he drew near to his northern home he found himself looking forward with eagerness to his arrival there, although he knew that only desolate apartments and mournful reminiscences awaited him.

At the last post-station his own horses were in readiness. The coachman and outriders were all strangers to him. It was years since he had seen his home, and it was long since his brother had made any stay there. The farms had been leased, and the leases were running out. It was necessary that he should look after his inheritance.

The sun was setting when he reached the bank of the river that bounded his estate on the hither side. The boat that was to carry him across was awaiting him, and the tones of a melancholy song, with which the boatmen were beguiling the time, fell upon his ear even before he could see the water. He had known the song from boyhood, but he had heard it not long ago. How well he remembered the day and the hour, and how it had moved him, when Hulda had first sung it to him!

The boatmen pressed forward to offer their services to their lord. The old man at their head had been boatman here all his life long. He had rowed Emanuel across when he was a child in his mother's arms. He could speak very little German, but he persisted, in spite of all that Emanuel could do, in kissing his master's coat and hands. Although the new lord understood the Lithuanian tongue but imperfectly, he could comprehend enough of what these people said to know that they were congratulating themselves and one another upon the better times that were to follow their master's return to his own home, to live there as his forefathers had done.

In the darkening night, over the broad road already hardening with the frost, his four horses bore him through the forest of huge old pines, until the village on its borders was passed, and he drove into his court-yard, where the flickering light of pine torches gave glimpses of the massive walls of his ancestral home.

The castellan had done all that he could. He had served under Emanuel's father, and knew the customs of the house. The room that the baron had formerly occupied was ready for him now, and everything had been arranged as comfortably as possible. But the halls were so spacious and empty, every footstep echoed so drearily from the marble floors, the light from the heavy lanterns hanging from the ceiling threw such a pale gleam upon the iron balustrades of the galleries, that Emanuel thought with involuntary regret of his beautiful home by the Lake of Geneva, and could not suppress a shudder as he remembered that he was the last of the direct line of his ancient race. The castle was as desolate and gloomy as a burial-vault, and the forced cheerfulness of the tenants, the tears of his brother's people when they saw him, were not calculated to increase his comfort. But what of that? He was not here for the sake of his own ease, but to fulfil his duty as the lord of the land, to found a new home for Konradine, his future wife, a Falkenhorst that should rival all that it had ever been in past ages; and he felt his courage rise for the work that lay before him.

There certainly was work enough to be done, as he became fully aware on his first glance from his windows, his first ride through the village, his first talk with his agent and the pastor.

The invalid condition of the former lord of the castle had for many years prevented his taking any interest in his estates, and abuses had crept into their management which it distressed Emanuel to contemplate. After talking with his agent and the pastor, he mounted his horse and rode around among his tenantry, where everything confirmed the melancholy accounts he had just heard.

He could not bear to tell Konradine of the want and ignorance among his people until he had devised some means for bettering their condition, and therefore, in a few days, he rode over to visit his neighbour, one of the wealthiest and most thrifty land-owners and landlords in all the country round, sure that from him he should obtain valuable counsel and advice.

His welcome from old Herr von Barnefeld was cordial in the extreme. He had been an intimate friend of Emanuel's father, and was delighted to know that the son of his old neighbour intended to make his home upon his paternal estate.

His own children were all married and established in homes of their own, with the exception of the youngest son, who, with his family, lived in his father's house, which, by the consent of his brothers and sisters, was to fall to him at his father's death, since none of the Barnefeld property was entailed.

The old man was rejoiced to do all that he could to assist Emanuel with his knowledge and experience in the improvement of his property, and in a short time affairs began to wear a far more cheering aspect. There was also much to be done in and around the castle in order to make it a fitting home for his bride. The hours of each day vanished he could scarcely tell how. He enjoyed even the fatigue that evening brought. Every week made his work more interesting to him, and his letters to Konradine were full of an interest in practical matters and affairs of the world around him, of which, when she had first known him, she would hardly have believed him capable. As he developed new energy and devotion to his work, she was inspired by a faith in him, a reliance upon him, unknown to her before. Much of this apparently new capacity for labour was, of course, due to the improvement in his health, which seemed to be thoroughly re-established. The prophecies of the physicians were verified in the entire disappearance of all the ominous symptoms that had distressed his sister and his friends.

The countess had, immediately after her son's marriage, established herself in her town-house, in the capital of her native province, whither Frau von Wildenau shortly followed her; and towards the close of the year Konradine took her final departure from the cloister and joined her mother at her friend's house.

The late count's relatives and her large circle of friends welcomed the countess with joy, but as she was in mourning for her brother, and as Konradine, as a future member of the family, also wore mourning, the house could not be thrown open as in former times. Still, there was a joyful event in prospect—Emanuel's marriage. Neither the countess nor Frau von Wildenau was addicted to retirement, and the presence in the house of a future bride gave occasion for constant society, which grew more brilliant as the season advanced.

Although the countess and Konradine abstained from taking part in any large entertainments, confining themselves entirely to receiving guests at home, there was nothing to prevent Frau von Wildenau from enjoying society to the full; and night after night she would return from brilliant balls and *fêtes* to enliven the comparative retirement of her friend and daughter with her account of the evening.

On one such occasion the future sisters-in-law, whose affection for each other had greatly increased from their present community of interests, were still sitting together over the tea-table, when Frau von Wildenau returned, much earlier than was her wont, from a ball given by the wife of the general in command. Fearing that some sudden illness was the cause of her return, Konradine went hastily to meet her, but her mother assured her that she was perfectly well, and had only been agitated by some news which had been brought by a courier to the general just before the ball, and which his wife's imprudence had allowed to transpire.

"There will be an end to all festivities for a time, since the court is going into mourning for three weeks," she said, and then paused, in so meaning a way that the others felt sure that the news she was about to impart bore some reference to them.

"Is any one of the reigning family dead, then?" asked the countess.

"Unfortunately, yes," replied Frau von Wildenau. "And, if one were not conscientiously opposed to saying or thinking anything of the kind, one would say it was a vengeance of Fate. I, at least, although I still admit the force of the reasons which influenced his family and induced Prince Frederick himself to treat Konradine as he did, cannot forbear the thought that this is a Nemesis."

"The prince is not dead?" cried Konradine, with a terror that she could not conceal.

"No, not the prince; but the princess has just died in her confinement, and the child is dead also," replied her mother. "The general's wife, who was much attached to her, was terribly shocked. She could not appear at the ball, and of course there was a gloom cast over the assembly. I was much moved, for it seemed to me a Nemesis."

Konradine, during her mother's remarks, had regained her composure. The colour had returned to her cheeks, and, with a haughty curl of her lip, she said, "I see no Nemesis in the matter. The prince has attained the honour he looked for from a marriage with the niece of a sovereign. The loss of an insignificant, unloved wife will distress him as little as the loss of his child. He is, and always will be, the nephew of a king, a fact of which he seems to me the very man to take every advantage in the future."

She took up her embroidery with apparent equanimity. The countess, whose kindred character enabled her to understand what was passing within her, admired the resolute bearing, the instant self-control, of her brother's betrothed. She came to her assistance with a question as to whether Frau von Wildenau had a suitable dress for the occasion,—had she brought a mourning toilette with her? and perfectly succeeded in diverting the conversation from its former subject.

CHAPTER V.

When Hulda wrote to the bailiff of her determination, she timidly wondered how he would receive the intelligence, and whether he would do anything, or what he would do, to induce her to desist from what she knew well enough would outrage his ideas of respectability, decorum, and even morals. She was hardly surprised that he made no reply whatever to her communication; but, instead of a letter from him, there arrived one from the young pastor, to whom the bailiff had evidently gone for advice and sympathy in his surprise and distress. The warnings and entreaties, however, of which the young man's letter consisted, inspired though they were by the tenderest care for her spiritual welfare, only grieved Hulda, without making any decided impression upon her. She had said it all to herself, before the charm of her new life had taken her captive. Now that she had succumbed to it, she could no longer look back or think of retracing her steps. She must pass on to the goal that seemed nearer and nearer to her desiring eyes.

The director had spoken of Feodora's amiable welcome to Hulda as the result of a "passing whim;" but, to the astonishment of every one, the whim did not pass. Before long she had induced the manager to intrust to her alone Hulda's training for her first appearance, and to allow her to select the part in which that appearance should be made. He willingly granted her these requests, for he felt confident that her prudence as well as her vanity would guard her against any mistake that could imperil the position she had so long held in the favour of the public.

Feodora was perfectly aware that praise too lavishly bestowed excites human expectation to a pitch that even the finest and best will fail to satisfy, and she also knew how powerful a stimulus is unsatisfied curiosity. Therefore she advised her new pupil, who, however, hardly needed the advice, to confine herself closely to her work, to avoid intercourse with her associates for the present, and to go but seldom to the theatre. Even Feodora's future husband and her most intimate friends scarcely ever saw Hulda, and they expressed themselves very guardedly concerning her. The desired end was attained. People grew curious about Hulda; they asked what Feodora meant by her mysterious conduct, and finally came to the conclusion that she was contriving how to produce a great effect when she should bid farewell to the stage. They were not mistaken.

Feodora was heart and soul an actress. To act was a necessity of her nature. She would sometimes give an artistic presentation of herself, with all her whims and moods, as if it had been some part written for the stage; indeed, her friend the doctor was right when he said that she really felt nothing except what she pretended to feel, and that she was in earnest only when she was jesting.

Her contract expired at the close of the year, and she was to bid farewell to the stage as "Thekla," in "Wallenstein's Death," the part in which, years before, she had first appeared before her present public.

The day of this last appearance had arrived; every seat was taken, and the manager had decided that a short farewell address must be made upon the stage to the heroine of the evening. The morning rehearsal had already begun, when a whisper went around the theatrical company that Feodora contemplated a great surprise for the public in the evening. At first it was laughed at, for all knew of the little scene that was arranged for the close of the tragedy, when Lelio was to recite the poem that the doctor had written, and to present to Feodora a laurel-wreath from her associates in art, and no time had been allowed for any unexpected display upon Feodora's part. But when it became known that the manager, Lelio, and the director had been continually with Feodora within the last few days, and had supped with her on the previous evening, in company with Herr Van der Vlies, Herr Hochbrecht, and the doctor, and that Hulda had read for them to their great satisfaction, there was a wide-spread curiosity, and also some uneasiness, with regard to Feodora's intentions. One of the actors supposed, with a sneer, that Feodora was to appear as Melpomene, another said that a ship belonging to Van der Vlies & Co. was to be represented, sailing towards her, offering her symbolically the treasures of Potosi, and bearing her away as the future queen of Golconda. There was no end of jests and surmises upon the subject; but when Lelio was questioned, it appeared that Hulda was not to make her *début* as "Käthchen von Heilbronn," as had been the manager's original intention, but first as "Emilia Galotti," and afterwards as "Luise Miller" and "Thekla."

"Why have I not been told this before, since I shall have to play with her?" cried Fräulein Delmar, with whom Orsina and Lady Melfort were favorite rôles; and, turning to the manager, she declared, with much temper, that she was not inclined to assist in a surprise for the public that was likely to prove a wretched failure. She should lend herself to no representation that would inevitably be ruined by the awkwardness of a beginner.

"Well, then, I must do my best to find some one who will play the parts," said the manager, with a calmness and even indifference that startled her and made her uncertain what to do. She would have questioned Feodora, but would not give her the satisfaction of seeing that she was disturbed.

Meanwhile the rehearsal went on, and the two women conducted themselves as usual towards each other. Fräulein Delmar said nothing to Feodora that could betray her irritation until just as she was about to leave the theatre, when she encountered the favourite with Lelio in the vestibule. Then she addressed them with great lack of courtesy, saying, "The next time that you devise schemes without consulting me, I must beg you not to depend upon me for aid in their fulfilment. I am not inclined to sacrifice myself to this new goddess whom you wish to introduce to the public. I refuse to play in such a farce."

"Indeed?" Feodora replied, as if disagreeably surprised by what had been said. "I am sorry to hear it. What is to be done? You know how much I am interested in the dear child for the sake of Gabrielle, who sent her to us." She paused for a moment, and then added, as if prompted by a sudden idea, "Well, if the worst comes to the worst, I must play with Hulda."

"You?" Fräulein Delmar cried, scornfully. "My parts? After solemnly taking leave of the stage? As Madame Van der Vlies, perhaps?"

Feodora replied, with the air of languid distinction that she so well knew how to assume, "You seem to think it so impossible that you tempt me to try. You know I am ambitious and vain, and originality and novelty possess great charms for me." And with a graceful inclination she left the theatre with Lelio.

In the evening the house was crammed. All were anxious to do homage to the universal favourite. Every calumnious whisper with regard to her previous life was forgotten, and Herr Van der Vlies was envied the possession of a bride so gifted and so lovely.

The curtain rose again after the close of the tragedy, disclosing a scene representing a garden where were assembled the entire company. Lelio's reading of the farewell poem and Feodora's graceful acceptance of the laurel-wreath enchanted the public. But in the midst of the applause, while the costliest flowers were raining upon her, and a chorus of "bravas" was filling the theatre, the favourite advanced to the foot-lights, and by a gesture entreated silence. In an instant a profound quiet reigned in the crowded house, and Feodora, after saying a few words by way of thanks for the kindness and encouragement that had always been extended to her, added, that to bid adieu to all present was very painful to her, and that she longed in some way to testify her gratitude; wherefore she had asked and received permission from the manager to appear as a guest upon that stage in three more representations. She should take that opportunity of presenting to them her pupil, who she hoped would be her successor in their favour; and she entreated them to extend to the young *débutante* the same forbearance that had made her own theatrical career in the city which was to be her future home a constant enjoyment to her.

A storm of applause followed her little address, with its welcome announcement, and the curtain fell.

As the audience left the house, they read on huge placards in the vestibule that, before the close of the present month, Feodora would appear, as a guest, in the parts of Orsina, Lady Melfort, and the Countess Terzky; and that Mademoiselle Hulda Vollmer would make her *début* with her, as Emilia, Louisa, and Thekla.

CHAPTER VI.

THE rehearsals for these three performances began the next day, and great was the demand for seats. The manager was charmed with Feodora's sagacity, for every one was talking of her, and of her lovely pupil, who was seen in the morning driving to the theatre with her. The first rehearsal far surpassed the manager's expectations, and made a great impression upon the other actors.

Fräulein Delmar shut herself up, and said that she was ill, and the manager was not disposed at present to grudge her the repose that her real or imaginary indisposition required.

Feodora was the heroine of the day. Every one and all things conspired to do her homage. Those of the company who were to sustain subordinate parts on the three evenings were determined to do their best to support worthily their former associate, who on the eve of retiring to a life of ease and luxury had shown such an enthusiasm for her profession. No one thought of Fräulein Delmar, except to laugh at her ill temper.

The evening at last arrived upon which Hulda was to appear for the first time before the public as Emilia, that being the part selected for her on this occasion by Feodora. The first act and the first five scenes of the second act of Lessing's great drama had gone smoothly and well—Claudia

Galotti had just uttered her doubts with regard to her husband—when the door in the background was hurriedly thrown open, and with hasty steps, "in great distress," as the poet describes her, Emilia comes upon the scene.

Her first words, "Thank God! thank God! Here I am in safety. Or has he followed me?" burst from Hulda's lips with wonderful effect, startled and terrified as she was by her first sight of the crowded auditorium, where her own voice was the only sound to be heard. The timidity, the confusion, which even the most gifted beginner cannot at first overcome, the faltering step, the uncertain glance, and the slight tremor in the voice, all served to heighten the display of Emilia's passionate distress. The public were astounded by such a natural rendering of the part by a *débutante;* and when Emilia, hastily throwing aside the veil that had hidden her face, disclosed features of exquisite beauty, a murmur of delight ran through the house, causing Hulda's heart to throb with a wild sense of triumph.

Feodora had chosen well. No other part could have shown to such advantage Hulda's culture, talent, and beauty. Her gradual advance in freedom and ease of expression after the beginning of the scene belonged entirely to the character that she represented; the audience were carried along with her; and when Feodora appeared as Orsina, more attractive than ever, interpreting her part so cleverly that one seemed to understand for the first time what a finished artist she was, the applause was overwhelming.

Teacher and pupil were called before the curtain again and again at the close of the piece. Both audience and manager felt that Hulda was all that was needed to supply Feodora's place. Of course, Fräulein Delmar would do what she could to surpass the favourite's brilliant performance. Everything looked smiling and bright; and when Hulda threw herself, in the dressing-room, at Feodora's feet in a passion of gratitude, the retiring favourite clasped her in her arms with a maternal tenderness that became her so well that she could not help regretting that this scene also had not been played upon the stage.

The other performances followed the first in quick succession, and the two heroines reaped the laurels in "Wallenstein" and "Cabal and Love" that their first appearance together had justified all in expecting. These three extra performances of Feodora's had been permitted by her bridegroom, Herr Van der Vlies, only upon condition that their marriage should take place on the day succeeding the last of them. It was to be extremely private, and immediately afterwards the newly-married pair were to start upon the grand tour, not to return for a year; such absence from the scene of Feodora's triumphs and from all her former associates being judged best for her by Herr Van der Vlies.

Feodora had acquiesced in this arrangement; indeed, she could hardly desire that any great parade should be made of her marriage with a man with whom her relations had been more than equivocal for some years. She had stipulated, however, for permission to give a supper after her last appearance on the stage, to mark the boundary between the life of freedom she had hitherto enjoyed and the quiet existence she was to lead in future.

For this supper she had, with the lavish generosity which Van der Vlies had long supplied her with the means of displaying, presented Hulda with an evening-dress of the richest materials, and immediately after the close of the evening's performance Hulda drove with her to her house, where Feodora's maid was at their service to array them for the little réunion.

The manager, the director, Lelio, and several other of Feodora's most intimate male friends were already in her brilliantly-lighted drawing-room when the mistress of the house with her young companion joined them, Feodora magnificently dressed, and Hulda in a pink silk, with bare neck and arms, and with roses in her hair,—a riddle and a wonder to herself in her novel splendour.

The doors of the adjoining dining-room were then thrown open, disclosing the supper-table, glittering with plate and glass and adorned with costly flowers and fruit. Feodora took the manager's proffered arm and requested her betrothed to conduct Hulda to the table, where Hochbrecht sat on the girl's other hand, and Lelio opposite.

That very morning she had signed a contract with conditions greatly in her favour, by which the manager engaged her for the next two years as a member of his company. She was now an actress, free and independent. This was the first *fête* she had ever seen where she was upon an equality with the other guests,—the first in which she had freely received the attentions and homage of the other sex. She knew she was beautiful; this evening she was told so repeatedly. Every one present seemed to possess a kind of right and title in her; and when the words of praise addressed to her, the looks directed towards her, made her temples throb and her cheeks glow, she did not dare to cast down her eyes. She must learn to rule this circle with her glance, as did Feodora, whose place here she was to fill, and who had told her that she must do all she could to secure the friendship of the doctor and of Hochbrecht; they could be of service to her in the future. And she must also win over Lelio and secure the good will of the manager and the director. She must be amiable and obliging, that she might attain her aims.

There had always been something offensive to her sense of truth and delicacy in these counsels of Feodora's, but the desire to test their efficacy to insure herself friends and supporters when Feodora should have departed was strong within her. The influence of the moment was also powerful, and when the manager, who was an admirable mimic, told his best stories and incited even Feodora's grave lover to merriment, how could Hulda resist the contagion?

The few drops of wine that she tasted, the talking and laughing around her, the compliments to her beauty, even her own face as she saw it reflected, crowned with flowers, from an opposite mirror, helped to intoxicate her, as it were. She sat amid the gay gods of Olympus; the old life by the dreary sea, where she had been too grave for some, too frivolous for others, had vanished forever. Friends and admirers surrounded her, the future laughed before her, and she felt that she was born to enjoy the present.

She sat quite silent for a time, for she had no brilliant tales to tell, and she had not yet learned the art of laughing cleverly at others for the entertainment of their friends. It vexed her, for she longed to be as animated and witty as Feodora, whose eyes rivalled the diamonds in her ears and on her neck.

Feodora also would have had her pupil less silent, for in a gay assemblage it is not pleasant to feel one's self the object of the calm observation which always seems to lurk behind silence on the part of some one present, and it happened fortunately, therefore, that one of the guests, Herr Philibert, a young and wealthy friend of Van der Vlies, told of some little adventure that had befallen him in Esthland, and brought into his narrative two or three words in the Esthland dialect. Feodora asked what they meant, and turned for an explanation of them to Hulda, who replied that she was entirely ignorant of the Esthland tongue, although she understood, as Feodora was aware, something of Lithuanian. Then, as a matter of course, Feodora asked her to sing for her friends a couple of Lithuanian songs that she had already sung for her.

Hulda readily complied, and seated herself at the piano. But, as she was running her beautiful hands over the keys by way of prelude, she reflected that the melancholy melodies which she had been accustomed to sing would be out of place in this gay scene, and yet she hardly liked to sing the few dancing-songs which she knew from having copied them for Emanuel's collection, but which she had never sung. However, there was no choice left her, and she sang with great brilliancy and freedom of expression the verse:

"Leave sighing and sorrow;
Why think on the morrow?
Let us dance and be merry to-day,
With stockings and shoes,
Or without if you choose;
What's the odds? let us dance while we may."

She sang it first in Lithuanian and afterwards in German; then, incited by the applause and admiration with which it was greeted, she sang another that she had never sung before; and, as every one was in the mood to find whatever she did charming, there was no bounds to the enthusiasm of her auditors. She was induced to sing German and French songs; and Feodora's two old friends, Hochbrecht and the doctor, declared that they now swore allegiance to her standard, since Feodora had forsaken them; while Feodora laughingly released them from their vow of allegiance to her, bidding them to be constant and true to her successor.

Lelio proposed a toast: "*La reine s'en va! Vive la reine!*" And at last, long past midnight, Philibert, who was captivated by Hulda's beauty and loveliness, drove the young *débutante* home in his carriage, and as he helped her to descend from it imprinted a kiss upon her bare arm, from which she shrank in a kind of terror.

She could not sleep for a long while, for a sense of triumph, mingled with many agitating reminiscences and fantastic images, filled the chambers of her brain.

Everything swam before her eyes in a flood of golden light such as streamed into the hall on the afternoon when she had first seen Emanuel's picture. She was fairly dazzled by the brilliancy around her, in which no outline was distinct; this very indistinctness, however, charmed and fascinated her. Lelio's beauty, Philibert's gallantry, the extravagant homage of Feodora's friends, all delighted her. If only Philibert had not escorted her home! if only she had not sung those songs! She heard the melodies in her dreams, but it was not she who sang them. They echoed through the silence of a summer night above the quiet shrubbery and lawn of the castle park, floating from the windows of his room where the light had long been extinguished.

CHAPTER VII.

THE year was within a few hours of its close, and all was so quiet in the countess's house that the ticking of the clocks could be heard, and even the footsteps of the servants in the carpeted corridors were distinctly audible.

Frau von Wildenau was reclining on a lounge, watching the quivering flame of the fire on the hearth, while in the next room, the door of which was open, Konradine was sitting at her writing-table. Suddenly her mother arose, and, stretching her arms above her head, gave utterance to a sigh so profound that it was almost a cry, and her daughter started up in terror and came into the room, asking what was the matter.

"Nothing, nothing," was the reply. "Go on with your letter; don't let me disturb you."

"But you cried out, dearest mother," said Konradine.

"I was only seeing whether I really am alive," her mother made answer, with a laugh; "whether I really am myself, and in the full possession of my senses; for the superhuman order and regularity of this household fairly paralyze me. I forget how to move or even to think. As I lay there and watched you write, and thought, 'Now she is going to seal that letter and put it on the corner of the chimney-piece, where the countess leaves her letters, and to-morrow, just at nine o'clock, the servant will march in to take the letters and ask for orders, I was seized with such a weariness of this measured existence that I was tempted to snatch all those letters and throw them into the fire, that there might be some interruption to the wooden regularity that prevails here. Indeed, I am counting the hours until your marriage; for both of us are rapidly growing old under this influence."

"And yet order is a great saving of time, and in a certain sense lengthens life," remarked her daughter.

"There! that very observation is a sign that you are growing old," said her mother, hastily. "You would never have made it before you entered that order and spent so much time with the countess. When did youth ever take heed of time, except to wish it away, that some hoped-for enjoyment might draw near? Age hoards time because so little is left to it."

She walked quickly to and fro in the room; but Konradine did not reply. She knew that it was best not to remonstrate with her mother in such moods; but she had scarcely seated herself by the fire when Frau von Wildenau began again.

"While you were writing, I could not help remembering that New Year's eve when we were overturned in the snow and took shelter in the countess's castle. What a cordial welcome Emanuel gave us then! And to-night?"

"You forget the loss the countess has sustained this year," said Konradine.

Her mother would not admit that to be any excuse. "I am often accused of selfishness," she said; "and yet I have never intruded my own sorrows or trials upon others, and I cannot see that any one has a right to do so. The countess's elder brother is dead, it is true, but Emanuel is still alive, and it seems to me that it is his duty to enliven your New Year's eve for you."

"He is very busy, and the season is inclement," Konradine replied, as if in excuse of Emanuel's absence.

Her mother laid her hand upon her shoulder. "How grave

and self-sacrificing that sounds! Your voice had quite a different ring in it on that New Year's eve when you stood before the mirror in the castle, knotting up your hair that had fallen over your shoulders. You were gayer then than now."

"Gayer, perhaps, but not in such harmony with myself,—not so secure of the future as at present."

Frau von Wildenau left her daughter's side, and stood gazing into the fire; but after a pause she said, looking Konradine full in the face, "You say you are in harmony with yourself. That might do very well for the canoness with the cross of her order on her breast. But in the world we require more, and you are not perfectly happy!"

Konradine shrank at these words, but replied, hastily, "Who that knows what life is can expect to be perfectly happy?"

"We do not expect it, and yet we all desire it," answered her mother. "This is what troubles me. Will you be content all your life long with the friendship and esteem that exist between Emanuel and yourself? I was glad when you wrote me of your betrothal; but now that I am with you, now that I remember that my blood flows in your veins, I must ask you, as your mother, while there is still time, Do you love Emanuel? Shall you be happy with him? Shall you always bless the evening that carried us to that castle in the north?"

At that moment a post-boy's horn broke the stillness. The two ladies hurried to the window. There was a loud ringing at the garden-gate. The castellan hastened to open it, and by the glare of the carriage-lamps they recognized Emanuel's light vehicle as it drew up before the door.

Konradine hurried down-stairs and threw herself into his arms. She thanked Heaven that he had come, lavished terms of endearment upon him, and conducted him up-stairs in triumph.

The whole house was infused with new life. The countess was delighted to see her brother looking so strong and well, and the surprise had the effect of instantly reconciling Frau von Wildenau to her future son-in-law. She herself related amusingly how cross and melancholy it had made her to spend the last hours of the year without any pleasant occurrence to enliven them, and how she had even gone the length of addressing a solemn exhortation to Konradine, begging her to reflect while it was yet time whether she really could endure a quiet life on Emanuel's northern estates.

She was charming as she thus ridiculed herself, and Konradine looked very happy, and seemed never to tire of thanking her betrothed for the pleasant New Year's eve he had prepared for her.

CHAPTER VIII.

"YOUR brother really looks like a different man," Frau von Wildenau remarked to the countess, a few days afterwards, as the two ladies stood at the window, watching the betrothed pair drive off to make some visits in the town. "Even Konradine, who professes to be above such considerations, asked me yesterday if I did not think Emanuel much finer-looking than formerly."

The countess made no reply. She herself thought Emanuel very much changed for the better, but this frank allusion to such a change on the part of the baroness displeased her, and the idea that Konradine had spoken of it to her mother, who would very likely repeat what she had said to Emanuel himself, was still more annoying. Had not Konradine been content hitherto with Emanuel's exterior? Had she not found enough to satisfy her in his expressive eyes and in the nobility of his features? Or had it been impossible for her to forget the manly beauty of the prince?

The countess had a very high opinion of Emanuel's betrothed, but for a moment she could not forbear the thought that in this case the simple child of nature, the pastor's daughter, Hulda, had been her superior. Hulda had loved Emanuel unconditionally, with no thought of exterior advantages or disadvantages.

It was long since she had thought of Hulda, but, now that she was suddenly reminded of her, she wondered that she had heard nothing of her marriage,—that the young pastor had said nothing of it in the letter of thanks she had received from him; and she determined to question the bailiff, who was coming up to town shortly, concerning the young girl.

Emanuel's visit was protracted longer than had at first been intended by him, and the time for his marriage was arranged for an early date in spring. A few days before his departure, as he was sitting after supper with the countess and her guests, the servant brought in the evening paper and a weekly journal partly devoted to dramatic criticism and intelligence. Emanuel took up the paper, while Frau von Wildenau turned over the leaves of the journal.

"Here is an article," she said to the others, "that really gives us some hope for the future with regard to our German stage. I think it is Hochbrecht's, for I recognize several remarks that he made to me when I met him in B—— last year, when he had just learned that Feodora was really about to resign her profession. It appears from this that a week after she had left the stage she reappeared upon it three times for the purpose of introducing to the public a pupil of her own and of Gabrielle's, a Mademoiselle Hulda Vollmer. This girl played Emilia, Thekla, and Louisa Miller with extraordinary dramatic power, and this article extols not only her talent, but also her great beauty." She then read aloud: "A tall, majestic form, a head and colouring reminding us of Titian's pictures, and a mobility of feature which, combined with the expressive glance of large blue eyes, is capable of portraying a wide range of emotion, make Mademoiselle Vollmer a rarely attractive actress. With the exception of the incomparable Gabrielle, we do not remember to have ever seen such an Emilia upon the stage."

Konradine made some jesting remark upon the excitability of theatrical critics, and mourned that the hopes they raised were so often doomed to disappointment, and a lively discussion as to various actresses ensued on the part of the three ladies, in the course of which Emanuel was appealed to by Konradine for his opinion.

To her astonishment, she found that he had not been attending to the conversation, for he passed his hand once or twice through his thick curls, as was his habit when striving to collect his thoughts, and asked, "My opinion? What about? What was my sister saying?"

When the baroness and her daughter had bidden good-night, and retired to their rooms, he lingered with his sister, who was gathering together a few scattered trifles in her work-basket, and suddenly asked her whether she had lately heard anything of Hulda.

The countess was not surprised at this question; in fact, she had rather wondered that he had not made any inquiries of this kind before, for she knew how true he was to the memory of all whom he had ever loved; but she hardly liked to confess that she knew nothing about the girl, and therefore replied to his question by another, inquiring what had put it into his mind to ask about Hulda just at that moment.

"I should think you would know," he answered,—"the name of the young actress of whom we have just heard, and the striking resemblance of the description of her to Hulda. She often, too, reminded me vividly of Gabrielle. But how is Hulda? Do you know anything about her? Is she happy in her marriage? I have naturally said nothing about her lately, but I am greatly interested in her fate. I trust she is content. I must always think of her with the deepest sympathy."

"I confess, to my shame," replied his sister, "that it is long since I have asked or received any tidings of her. But to-morrow I can atone for my neglect, as I have requested the bailiff to come up to town to see me upon business matters. He is to arrive to-night, and to-morrow we can learn from him all that we wish to know. I am convinced, however, that everything is as it should be, else he would have instantly informed me."

Emanuel said no more, but requested a servant to bring him word as soon as the bailiff should arrive, and the next morning he sought him in his sister's room.

The countess was sitting at her embroidery-frame, and the bailiff at a writing-table, with his books and papers before him. Immediately upon her brother's entrance the countess exclaimed, "Imagine what the bailiff has just told me! I ought to have been informed of it before! The marriage between Hulda and the pastor never took place!"

"Never took place?" asked Emanuel, and his colour changed rapidly. "Why not? What happened?"

"Why not, indeed, Herr Baron?" replied the bailiff. "That is just it; and, as I have told madame the countess, I should not have failed to tell her, if it had not been just that. But how can one tell such a thing of a girl who has lived with us, and whose father and mother we loved?"

The bailiff's reply heightened Emanuel's impatience, and he repeated his question eagerly, upon which the good man related, after his own fashion, how Hulda had refused to marry the excellent young pastor, and had left his house, ostensibly to seek a situation as governess, but that she had really "joined the play-actors."

"Impossible!" cried Emanuel, cut to the soul by the intelligence, and, turning to the bailiff with an authoritative air, from which those accustomed from their youth to command are rarely free, however kindly their nature, he said, in a tone of harsh reproof, "And you allowed this? You did not immediately inform the countess of it? You did nothing to dissuade the girl from such a decisive step?"

"Pardon me, Herr Baron!" replied the bailiff, proudly. "I had nothing to do with allowing it, for when she left us I had no idea of her intention. She never told me of it until the step was taken, and I could not receive her in my house after she had once trodden the boards. Nevertheless, our young pastor, at my request, wrote her a letter remonstrating with her."

"And what did she reply?" Emanuel asked, eagerly.

"What could she reply?" asked the bailiff. "She wrote a long letter full of such phrases as one finds in romances, about lofty calling, irresistible impulse, and all such nonsense." He paused for a moment, and then added, "All that was done for Hulda at the castle was done with the kindest motives, and she learned much from Miss Kenney that might help her to earn her living, but it would have been better for her had she stayed quietly at home. Then I should not have been standing here justifying myself for what really is no affair of mine. I did my best for her, as her father's friend; my conscience is clear. Why should I have told the Frau Countess of what Hulda herself was so ashamed to do that she first laid aside her father's honest name? And you, Herr Baron? I never suspected that you even remembered the girl. At all events, she must do as she pleases now; but I thought better of her, I confess."

The baron could not endure to hear Hulda slightingly spoken of, for he thought he could now understand all that had hitherto been incomprehensible in her conduct. She had been over-persuaded to send back his ring, had been forced into a betrothal with the young pastor, but, in her despair at the prospect of marrying a man whom she did not love, had taken her future into her own hands, and embraced a profession for which, as was evident, she was rarely gifted, and in which her beauty would doubtless be a great aid to her success. He wished to hear nothing further from the bailiff, and the countess was quite weary of the conversation, both on her brother's account, and because she considered as presumptuous the bailiff's hint at the wrong that had been done to Hulda in taking her from her home. She therefore looked at the clock, remarked that they were losing time, and took up her embroidery. Emanuel had other matters awaiting his time and attention, and left the room,—his thoughts at first busied with Hulda alone. But as the day wore on, they were of necessity occupied by other interests, and as he grew calm and cool, he began to regard her whole conduct since his separation from her as the consequence of the inevitable development of her peculiar temperament; and he could even join composedly in the conversation concerning her theatrical career, carried on by the three ladies in the evening.

CHAPTER IX.

THE winter was taking its departure; only in sheltered corners of narrow streets was there any snow left. The children began to play once more in the open air, and the old cake-woman, who had her table at the corner of the square opposite Hulda's lodgings, put up her linen awning, that the mid-day sun might not spoil her wares. The awning, however, did not interfere with her observation of her neighbours, and on this particular morning there was more than usual to interest her going on at the Widow Rosen's.

"That is the fourth rose-bush that has been taken in there to-day," she said to a girl who was buying a basketful of cakes. "Four rose-bushes and a great orange-tree full of blossoms fit for a queen, not counting the bouquets that the gentlemen have carried in themselves. And that is only the least of it. Early this morning, as I was setting up my table, there came a toilet-table, with everything on it of pure silver. It came from that rich young Philibert; my son is his servant, and that is how I know. And two other great boxes have gone in besides; and all is for Fräulein Vollmer; it is her birthday. Look! There she is at the window."

She pointed to one of the windows of the second story, at which Hulda appeared for an instant and as quickly vanished.

"She is beautiful," said the girl; "every one admires her; they talk a great deal about her at our house."

"It seems wonderful," said the old woman, "when I think that she only came five months ago. I can see her now, just as she arrived from the station with the Rosens, in her short petticoat. She had the garret-room then, and used to feed the sparrows with part of her breakfast every morning. They were not half so grand as the parrot that Herr Philibert sent her by my son the other day."

The cakes were paid for, and as the girl put the change into her pocket she looked up at the windows filled with flowers, and sighed. The old woman asked what ailed her.

"Oh, nothing," she replied; "but it is hard for us when we see what some people can do with their good looks."

"No one can say any harm of Fräulein Vollmer," the old woman said, in a tone of warning.

The young girl coquettishly tossed her pretty head in its cap with gay-coloured ribbons, and curled her red lip. "No harm? Oh, we all know what men are,—nothing is given for nothing! Those theatre-people are all alike!" And she walked quickly away, conscious that she had stood gossiping too long.

"Those theatre-people are all alike!" The girl only repeated the substance of what she had often heard from her mistress's guests. Hulda herself was made conscious, she could hardly have told how, of the small respect in which actresses were held among the wealthy citizens' wives who constituted the chief society of the commercial town; and yet, since the first hour of her arrival there, fortune had befriended her.

No other young actress had ever succeeded in so short a

time in achieving the position which Hulda had now attained. She sometimes asked herself how it had all happened, but without finding any answer to the question.

She, too, had been constantly thinking on this her birthday of that first gray November evening when she had arrived at Frau Rosen's, with all her possessions in her one little trunk. The garret-room had, by Feodora's advice, been given up on the day when she had signed the contract of her two years' engagement, when her future had first seemed secure to her. She was perfectly conscious now of her talent and of her beauty. It was impossible that she should fail to improve in her art if she continued to study. The path upon which Gabrielle and Feodora had plucked their laurels and reaped all kinds of conquest and delight lay open before her, as once before them. To-day, in spite of the early season, roses were blooming upon her table and in her window, as she had once seen them in Gabrielle's room. She was young, and she felt it a great happiness to be an artist, to devote herself to the personification of the creations of great poets. Her father had been the first to inspire her young mind with admiration for these great geniuses, when during the long winter months the lonely parsonage was half buried in snow and ice, or when the long summer twilight hung above the little garden.

Still, no true artist is ever content with his work. All share the pain that it is to find performance fall so far short of what they have hoped to achieve; and this pain is especially the portion of the dramatic artist, whose performance depends so largely upon the aid of others, upon their capacity and their good will, and who cannot correct the failure of one moment in the next.

After Feodora's departure, Hulda had been made painfully aware of the importance to an actress of the good will of her fellows; for Fräulein Delmar, enraged at being thrown into the shade by Feodora's performance of her favourite parts, and unable to visit her displeasure upon Feodora herself, wreaked it upon poor Hulda, whom she annoyed as far as she could without damaging her own performance.

The manager, the director, and Lelio understood this perfectly well, and saw why Hulda failed to make many points where she had succeeded when playing with Feodora. They did all they could to come to her assistance; but all the actresses who had had secret hopes of succeeding Feodora in the public favour resented this usurpation of their rights by a stranger, and sided with Fräulein Delmar. Thus, without any fault of her own, Hulda inherited behind the scenes the hostility of Feodora's enemies, as she had before the curtain inherited the favour of her friends.

She had hardly been a month upon the stage before all the women attached to the theatre were convinced that Hulda was far vainer, more ill-tempered, and more calculating than Feodora had ever been; that when she acted with other women she thought only of herself and of the impression she was making upon the public, and that only when there were men upon the scene did she become all fire and flame, seeming actually inspired.

The manager and the other men attempted to justify Hulda's conduct when she was attacked in their presence; but this only made matters worse, for it irritated Fräulein Delmar still more, and excited the envy of the other women, whom it convinced that, with all her air of dignified repose, Hulda was secretly bent upon exciting the admiration of every man who approached her. When the poor girl tried to keep upon a kindly footing with the younger actresses, Fräulein Delmar accused her of attempting to estrange from her her nearest friends. She had always intrigued in vain against Feodora, and had been embittered by her want of success. Now Hulda was obliged to feel the effects of her failure.

There was no end of petty scandal-mongering; and gradually Hulda became conscious that she was regarded behind the scenes with a kind of suspicion, faint and shadowy, but akin to the ill will that had arisen against her in her old home. There was nothing for her but to turn for an explanation of this to those who had always befriended her.

The doctor smiled when Hulda lamented that her fellow-actresses were not kindly disposed towards her. "Did you suppose," he asked, "that commonplace people would amiably acknowledge superiority? Or did you think that ugly women would take delight in the beauty of one of their sex? Mistrust mediocrity among women; it will always be hostile to you." And Lelio said very much the same thing.

"No one, unless, like yourself, bred in the solitude of a country life," said he, "would ever dream of finding the embodiment of his ideals upon the stage." The experienced artist valued and admired Hulda because she was, beyond all others, the one with whom he was best able to play well, and because out of his own purity and nobility of mind he was able to appreciate the genuine worth of her character. "Remember," he once said to her, "that morning when for the first time you passed through those dark passages to the stage. There is no daylight upon those paths. If you do not carry your sun within you, if you are not clad in an armour that will enable you to defy the assaults of envy, if you have not a world within yourself where you are both law-giver and judge, return immediately to your village."

His counsels were consoling, for they awakened in Hulda a consciousness of strength to resist, and, besides, he prophesied for her, if she did not relax in her efforts, a future to which her present success was only the introduction. A proud sense of triumph stirred within her at this thought. What did she care for the petty jealousy of her rivals? Feodora had often told her how she had been annoyed by the envy and ill nature of her associates, how commonplace respectability had slandered her when she had attracted the admiration and homage of its husbands and sons, how she had suffered from the narrow-minded prejudices of the family of Herr Van der Vlies. Had not Gabrielle gone through the same before she had lately been secretly united with the prince in a morganatic marriage? The histrionic artist, in whose performances other women delighted, crowding to see her, inviting her to their drawing-rooms as a celebrity, but refusing to admit her to a social equality with themselves, had no other resource than to take advantage of being thus thrust forth from the social pale. Let her rejoice in the freedom to which a strict morality, too often simulated, condemned her. She could not live as others did, chained to the threshold of home, could not learn to use her wings in such a cage. Could she restrict her admirers to a respectful bow when she had just been torn from the arms of a Max Piccolomini, or had in trembling agony proved all the depths of human misery in Gretchen's cell?

No; Hulda saw more clearly every day that whoever would portray and understand mighty passions, whoever would explore the heights and the depths of existence, drawing thence the manifold emotions which it is the actress's task to embody, must be allowed a certain freedom inconsistent with conventional social rules. She must be a law to herself,—must for herself set up the 'Thus far shalt thou go, and no farther,' of her daily life. The manager, Lelio, Feodora, were right. She must put away the pastor's daughter if she would be an actress. And why should she not? She certainly would neither think nor do what was wrong.

CHAPTER X.

All the morning of her birthday was spent by Hulda in receiving visits from those men whom she numbered among her friends. She was no longer timid or shy in their society; to be at ease with those of the other sex was part of her vocation.

She could not certainly refuse to receive her critics, upon whose good will so much depended, or the actors, whose support was so welcome to her. It would have been folly to deny herself to the two elderly friends of the drama who had transferred to her the allegiance they had formerly given to Feodora, or to refuse to see Lelio, for whom she felt a sincere friendship, which was frankly and honestly reciprocated on his part.

Scarcely a day passed on which Lelio did not visit her. He was of an excellent family, and had gone upon the stage in opposition to the wishes of his friends; his whole education and early surroundings enabled him to recognize and appreciate Hulda's genuine excellence. Her magnanimity of mind, her pure moral sense, were highly prized by him, and the neatness and order that reigned in her apartments gave them an air of home that he greatly enjoyed. As she was almost always his associate upon the stage, he read with her the parts which she was obliged to commit to memory, and with which he had long been familiar, and his advice and knowledge of the stage were of the greatest assistance to her. He befriended her wherever he could; and there were not wanting those who declared that Lelio would soon forget his distant love for the sake of his new associate But the fact was that it was

Lelio's love for another that made his pleasant intercourse with Hulda possible. He was the only one of all the men around her who never approached her with the kind of gallantry against which she had learned to be upon her guard. He alone knew how she had come to leave her home and appear in public, and to him alone could she tell how sometimes a sharp pang of home-sickness would assail her, a longing for the artless inexperience of earlier days.

She had just been telling him how her father's and mother's tender affection, in spite of their poverty, had always prepared for her some little surprise upon her birthday,—how beautiful she had thought the homely dress or the new book that was her birthday-gift,—and he had left her, with the tears of loving remembrance scarcely dry upon her cheeks, when Herr Philibert made his appearance.

He was handsome and young, his mother's Spanish blood showing clearly in the pale olive of his complexion, his dark eyes, and his fiery temperament. His demeanour was that of the wealthy patrician, with something of the frivolity of the pleasure-seeking man of the world. On the evening, however, when he had escorted Hulda to her home from Feodora's supper, his conduct had so startled and shocked her that she had since avoided him as far as possible.

He had made this avoidance matter of complaint in a letter to his friend Feodora, and she had gaily remonstrated with Hulda upon the subject. He had then visited her in company with Hochbrecht or the doctor, and was constantly behind the scenes at the theatre. Gradually Hulda had come to expect to see him, whenever she played, in his box near the stage, where he was always eager in his applause and never failed to throw costly flowers at her feet whenever there was any occasion for so doing. Lately she had admitted him when he had called upon her at her lodgings, and his visits had grown more frequent. She had not thought it worth while to refuse to accept from him two or three trifles of small value, but this morning she had been very much annoyed that he had ventured to send her a magnificent gift, which, with her landlady's and her maid's connivance, had been placed in her room before she entered it for her breakfast.

She therefore awaited with no pleasurable sensations the visit that she was convinced he would pay her.

"I am late," he cried, before she had time to say a word to him, "because I did not want to share you with any one to-day. I knew you were not going to rehearsal, so I waited until the others had gone to the theatre, and here I am, to repeat the same old song——"

"Which I know so well," she interrupted him, with a smile.

"And which I shall continue to sing to you," he continued, without heeding her interruption, "until you are convinced that I can never cease to adore you, and you consent to believe that in me you have a friend whom you may always command."

"That has not been my experience to-day," she replied.

He asked what she meant.

Hulda felt that she must come to some explanation with him, and it annoyed her. She conquered her embarrassment, however, as well as she could, and, quietly addressing him in a tone of entreaty, she said, "There is something ungenerous in refusing to accept an offered kindness. But if, as you say, I may command you, why have you refused to accede to the request that I once made you?"

She paused for a moment, and as she noticed how his face flushed with suppressed impatience, she walked to the table upon which stood the rose-bush that he had sent her, and then continued, "I was as pleased as a child with these lovely roses. Such flowers were a rare pleasure in my old home. Why diminish this innocent enjoyment of mine by sending me a gift the magnificence of which frightens and oppresses me?"

"A very trifle!" he cried. "Not worth a word. The dim mirror here in your room has long been an eyesore to me. It seemed to me a sin that you alone should not see how beautiful you are. Yet what mirror can show you this, since at the back of it there must be only a dead metal, instead of the heart that lurks behind the eye?"

She received the compliment with a conventional smile, but, without being diverted from her intention, continued, "And what if I should make an appeal to your heart? Would you heed it?"

"I will do anything that you desire," replied Philibert, who thought the girl in her present serious mood more attractive than she had ever seemed to him behind the foot-lights.

Nevertheless, she hesitated, and seemed hardly able to proceed. At last she said, in a constrained voice, "I am all alone; there is no one to care for me but myself, and there is nothing that I can call my own save a clear conscience and my untarnished reputation." She paused again, and tried to smile, but it was too hard a task. "I wish," she continued, "that you would not sneer, as so many do, at the actress who wishes to play the pastor's daughter. I could do nothing, and be nothing, all my efforts would be vain, if I thought I had given any one the right to despise me, if my conscience were not pure."

"Have I offended you? Have I presumed? Or what have I done?" cried Philibert, to whom such a scene with a lovely young actress was an entirely novel experience, full of charm. "I owe so much enjoyment to you and to your talent, is it wrong to try to repay you in some faint measure?"

"I do not play for you alone. I play for every one,—it is my calling,—I am paid for it," she replied, firmly.

"You receive a salary for what you do for the crowd," Philibert rejoined, eagerly. "But if your acting—if the delight of seeing you—is worth more to me than it can possibly be to the crowd, may I not attempt to testify my gratitude to you? May I not offer you, in return for the pleasure you give me, some little gratification?"

She shook her head. "Your applause pleases and encourages me," she replied; "but, I entreat you," and her voice trembled as she spoke, "do not make me presents that might compromise me. Do not give me cause to blush, by allowing others to see in my possession articles of luxury that I cannot have earned. Give me no cause to irritate you by sending your presents back to you."

"Incomprehensible girl!" said Philibert, quite at a loss what to say. She observed this, and it gave her courage.

"I know," she cried, "that you meant kindly by me. But you did not see Hochbrecht's puzzled look when he saw that toilet-table, fit for a princess, in my room; you did not feel, as I did, the doctor's smile as he examined the various articles upon it; and you did not hear my friend Lelio's question, 'How comes Herr Philibert to make you such a present?' I had to tell him that I took no pleasure in your gift, and that I had given no one permission to place me under such an obligation. And he believed me."

Whilst she spoke, she had entirely recovered her self-possession, and her beautiful features were flushed with emotion, as she looked Philibert proudly in the face. He listened to her, he watched her, with the same pleasure that she gave him upon the stage. Her youthful dignity, her gentle gravity, the deep emotion with which she spoke, touched and moved him as he had been moved by her acting.

But his estimate of women, as well as his knowledge of human nature, had been formed in a miserable school. He had never known such an actress as Hulda, had never witnessed such a scene as this in an actress's apartment. He would have doubted his own convictions if he had not believed that behind this appearance of stern virtue lurked a spirit of calculation, and that Hulda had laid to heart Susanna's words in "Figaro," "Lightly won is lightly prized." But this view of her did not diminish his admiration for her. He merely determined to adopt the rôle that she prescribed for him, until the time arrived when he could safely take that tone with her that his passion prompted.

He therefore promised what she asked. He seemed to be touched by her purity; he praised her prudence, and the care she took to avoid all appearance of evil, blaming himself for not having been more thoughtful. But he begged her not to be too exact.

"An actress is not a simple country girl," he said. "She occupies a position similar to that of some sacred picture, and must be content to receive offerings laid upon her shrine, not for the sake of gratifying her so much as to relieve the feelings of the devotees. And," he continued, "you alluded to Lelio just now, as if he were an immaculate Knight of the Round Table. Do you really believe that he will always be content to play the first scene of Romeo and Juliet with you, and hear from that beautiful mouth the assurance, 'Ay, pilgrim, lips that they must use in prayer'?"

"You know," replied Hulda, "that Lelio is in love." And then she blushed, conscious that her remark would seem ridiculous to this man.

He laughed aloud. "A moral song," he said, with a sneer, quoting Mephisto. But he rose to take his leave, saying, "I see you mistrust me, because I do not conceal from you my sentiments towards you. Ask Feodora, ask your mother——"

"My mother?" Hulda interrupted him.

"I mean Gabrielle," said Philibert, without heeding her surprise. "Ask Gabrielle, or any one in whom you have confidence, whether you are not far safer with a frank, ingenuous man like myself, than with your older acquaintances, or even with a Lelio, for your friend and adviser. I have promised to obey you, to avoid everything that could compromise you in the eyes of the world. You know how passionate is my admiration for you, and you are upon your guard with me. What have you to fear while I obey you implicitly? There is no danger where all is frank and open dealing, and I have no fancy for favours won by fraud. You can rely upon me as far as you can rely upon yourself, for you rule me as you rule yourself."

He kissed her hand in taking leave of her. Then, as he stood at the door, he said, "That poor mirror—you will let it stay here, will you not? You will not shame me by sending it away? And, believe me, Hamlet's words are fearfully true, 'Be thou as chaste as ice, as pure as snow, thou shalt not escape calumny.'"

He kissed her hand again, shook it cordially, and was gone.

For a moment she stood motionless where he left her. Hamlet's words sounded like a curse from his lips. She shuddered at his frankness, and yet what he had said was true. She had nothing to fear while she could rule herself.

Gabrielle had bidden her remember that the path she thought of choosing was not thornless, but smooth and full of danger. She had chosen it in full reliance upon herself. She could not reproach herself as yet. But in her father's house she had known nothing of the perils that beset her here.

She passed her hand across her brow, as if to brush away the memories that crowded upon her. As she turned round, her gaze fell upon Philibert's gift. The mirror was very beautiful. She saw herself reflected in it as never before, and yet she would have given much if the toilet-table had not been there, to give rise to all she had just said and heard, and to future gossip, upon which she would not dwell.

CHAPTER XI.

A FEW days after Emanuel's departure from his sister's house, intelligence was circulated in the city that the general in command there had been transferred to a post in the vicinity of the court.

At first the report was scarcely credited, the general had retained his command in this province for so many years, and, as he had been very reserved upon the subject, the name of his successor was not known. Curiosity and genuine sorrow at his departure assembled an unusually large number of friends at his weekly reception.

The countess, who was a relative of the general's, felt that on this occasion she must emerge from her seclusion, to express to him and to his wife her sorrow at losing them from a society to which their constant hospitality had added such a charm for so many years. Of course her two guests accompanied her.

The suite of reception-rooms was already quite full when the countess and her companions appeared in them. It was easy to see that an unusual degree of interest and expectation animated the assemblage. People stood conversing eagerly in knots, and, as they talked, all eyes were turned towards the centre room, where the explanation of the universal interest was evidently to be found; and Frau von Wildenau was about to ask a friend what it all meant, when Konradine suddenly seized her mother's arm, as if in terror.

She turned hastily towards her daughter, who had entirely lost her composure. "The prince!" she gasped, in a whisper, as she leaned against the pillar of a doorway, unable for a moment to stand without support.

In the centre of the room, so that he could instantly be seen from the door, stood Prince Frederick, by the side of the general, in earnest conversation with some of the provincial civil dignitaries.

The baroness was startled at seeing him there, and still more startled by her daughter's condition. "You are very ill," she said; "will you not retire?"

"I retire?" her daughter repeated, as the blood rushed again to her colourless cheeks. "Retire? Wherefore? Retreat, with the countess looking on? Never!"

She uttered the words softly and in broken tones, but she had in a minute recovered her self-control. For when the countess, who was also greatly surprised at sight of the prince, approached her, she advanced towards her and said, "That, then, is the general's successor. I wonder why we were not informed before?"

"I have just been asking myself the same question. I wish we had known it, for your sake," replied the countess. "Such meetings are always agitating."

"Certainly; but I knew it must come at some future time, and I am glad it is over," Konradine replied, with a composure that rejoiced her friend.

Meanwhile they had entered the room, and the general advanced towards them, thereby attracting to them the attention of the prince. He seemed hardly to believe his eyes; then, with an ease that was all his own, he extricated himself from the group of people about him and hurried towards the countess.

"You here, madame!" he cried, as he offered her his hand. "I thought you were in the north. And you, too," he added, in a lower tone, with a bow, to Konradine and her mother. "What a surprise this is! We have passed through much since we were last together."

"Your highness has sustained a severe loss," said the countess, wishing to come to the assistance of her friends. She knew what a shock this unexpected meeting must be to both Konradine and the prince, and she did well to remind them by her words of all that had separated them, also giving the prince a cue as to how these first embarrassing moments might be bridged over. He instantly availed himself of it.

"Yes," he said, "I have had a great sorrow, have suffered a terrible loss. It is hard to see youth and beauty slowly fade and die. I am grateful to his majesty for transferring me to this post, far from the scene of my anxiety and suffering."

The tone in which these words were spoken showed that they came from his heart, and Konradine, who knew every expression of his countenance, saw that his brow, usually so smooth, was clouded by an unwonted gravity, and his whole figure seemed to have gained in manliness and majesty. It was insufferable to her to hear him thus lament his departed wife. She clenched her teeth to suppress an exclamation of angry pain, and she remained behind when the prince, still engaged in conversation, escorted her mother and the countess to the other end of the apartment.

Her power of self-control was severely tested this evening. She could not tell, of course, how many of those present knew of her previous relation to the prince, but she could see that she was observed with stealthy curiosity, and she felt that she owed it to herself and to Emanuel to preserve a perfectly indifferent air, as well as to make manifest to the prince that she had forgotten, as he had done,—that she had found in a calm and true affection a compensation for the loss of the passionate devotion that had once united them.

Perhaps the prince was animated by a like desire when, in the course of the evening, he approached the woman he had loved and forsaken. His adjutant, who was sitting beside Konradine, arose as he drew near, and the prince seated himself in the vacant chair.

"I regard it as a good omen for the future," he said, "that I have met you on this first evening of my residence here. I made sure of seeing you here at some time when I was sent hither, since your future home is in this province. I had something to say to you, and I was desirous of saying it as soon as possible."

"Your highness is very kind," she replied, as in full sight of every one she curtsied, with a smile; "but," she added, in a lower tone, "I cannot understand this desire on your part, nor see what satisfaction its gratification can give you."

The prince received this rebuke with great composure. "You repulse me," he said; "and, although you are justified in doing so, I am disappointed." He paused for a moment, and then added, "Just before coming here, I passed a day in the cloister with my sister. I must tell you how it rejoiced me when I heard some time ago that you had left it and were confidently anticipating a happy future."

"Yes, confidently," Konradine repeated, in a tone of voice which, in spite of herself, had something of defiance in it. The prince, however, quietly replied that he was delighted to hear this assurance from herself. "I know you well enough," he said, "to be sure that you will obey the true impulse of your heart, and," he added, very gently, "even where this is not the case a genuine regard is possible. There is an affection, a persistence in tenderness which one must be entirely wanting in sensibility not to appreciate, and which it would be impossible not to miss painfully. It is strange how little we really understand ourselves, and how often we are more surprised by ourselves than by others. But," he added, as he rose, "we will speak of this at some other time. Where are you? I forgot to ask."

Konradine replied that she, with her mother, was the guest of the countess.

"So much the better. Then I shall see you shortly. I have a message for you, the delivery of which lies very near my heart."

"For me?" asked Konradine. "And from whom?"

"I will tell you that to-morrow," he replied, as he turned away to a group of ladies.

In the carriage on the way home, Konradine was left entirely to her own reflections. The two elder ladies conversed concerning the departure of the general and the arrival of the prince, and the social changes that would ensue. Neither addressed a question to her: indeed, they both instinctively avoided all remark that might hint at any especial interest that these events could have for Konradine, and, instead of the usual quarter of an hour spent in the drawing-room to discuss the evening, all bade one another good-night as soon as they reached home.

The sigh with which Konradine entered her own room and snatched the wreath from her throbbing temples sounded almost like a cry. Restlessly pacing to and fro, she took off the bracelets from her arms and the pearls from her neck and tossed them here and there, wearied with their weight. Everything was a burden to her,—everything; she knew not what she was doing or what she wanted to do.

"Assailed by a tempest in what I fancied was a safe harbour," she groaned, "and driven out to sea again!" The tears refused to flow. She threw herself upon a lounge and lay there for a time. No sound was audible in the room save her own long-drawn sighs. She could not bear to hear them; it was terrible to be so unhappy.

Rest, rest—she craved rest. She rang for her maid, and was undressed. Then she lay down, and tried to sleep. Impossible! One moment she bitterly regretted that she had ever seen Prince Frederick; the next she exulted in his manly grace and beauty. She heard the sound of his voice, as he had spoken to her, and tried to forget it, when she remembered what he had said. She would write to him that she could not see him again; and then she despised herself for the cowardice that would have prompted such a confession of weakness. What was this message that he had spoken of? What did he mean? What could he ask of her? he who evidently was cherishing the memory of a dead wife!

Questions and doubts of all kinds assailed her. She was in torture; she rose from her couch, and her glance encountered Emanuel's portrait. She turned to those earnest eyes as the storm-tossed mariner turns to the harbour lights.

"May his slumbers be more peaceful!" she thought, and hot tears streaming from her eyes relieved her overcharged heart.

CHAPTER XII.

Frau von Wildenau and the countess saw plainly the next morning at breakfast that Konradine had not slept, but neither questioned her upon the subject. At noon the countess received a visit from the prince.

He told her how sudden and unexpected had been his appointment to his present post, and then referred to her brother's betrothal, expressing the greatest respect and esteem for him. "I need not tell you," he added, "what an interest I take in Fräulein von Wildenau's future."

His frankness caused a like candour upon the part of the countess, who declared that she confidently looked forward to the happiest results from the union of her brother with Konradine, since their marriage would be founded upon mutual esteem and respect.

"And will Frau von Wildenau take up her abode with her daughter?" the prince asked.

The countess replied by a simple negative. The prince then glanced at the clock upon the chimney-piece, and, remarking that he had but a quarter of an hour more at his disposal, asked if Fräulein von Wildenau would kindly grant him the interview which he had requested upon the previous evening.

Although the countess had not expected this request, it did not surprise her. She had always regarded Konradine's former engagement to the prince as a most unsuitable arrangement, for which Frau von Wildenau alone was to blame. She had entirely sympathized with the prince's subsequent conduct, in which she was sure Konradine had fully acquiesced. Doubtless the unexpected meeting of the previous evening had been somewhat embarrassing, and it was natural that the prince should desire to see his former betrothed, that he might remove any possible embarrassment for the future. That he requested this interview through the sister of Konradine's future husband was a proof of his high-mindedness.

Therefore she left the room, that Konradine might be sent for. The prince arose, and when she appeared advanced to meet her, thanking her for her kindness in acceding to his request.

"I am come," he said, "to fulfil a commission which I regard as sacred, and to leave with you a token which I promised, if it were possible, to place in your hands myself."

His gentle and almost solemn manner as he spoke these words was so different from what Konradine had expected, that she could hardly command herself. She inclined her head, without speaking.

"The message that I told you of," he went on, "comes from my dead wife. At the time of our marriage I was in a miserable state of mind, a prey to constant mental warfare. Her love humiliated me, for I did not deserve it. We were very unhappy. Instead of condemning me, however, her affection was strong enough to pity me, and you also, so truly, with so genuine a compassion, that the contemplation of such loveliness of character, such forbearing gentleness, won me to her, and I now have the consoling assurance that some happiness was hers, disturbed only by the consciousness that it was founded upon the ruin of another's hopes. In spite of her knowledge that you were anticipating a bright future, this consciousness disturbed the last days of her life, when her gentle spirit would else have been perfectly at peace with the world she was about to leave. 'I have been the unconscious cause of sorrow,' she said, 'to one whom I shall never see.'" The prince produced a small jewel-case, touched the spring by which it opened, and handed it to Konradine. Within lay a simple little ring. "This ring," he said, "the princess always wore. In that last hour she drew it from her finger. 'Give it to Konradine,' she said, 'if you ever see her again, and tell her to forgive me for having been so happy with you at her expense.'"

He bit his lip, and walked to the window, where he stood looking out at the garden buried in snow. Konradine had covered her face with her hands, and her tears were flowing fast.

In a few minutes the prince had regained his composure. As he returned to where Konradine was sitting, she held out her hand to him. He grasped it warmly, and for a few moments they did not speak. Surely, when they had parted neither could have foreseen such a meeting as this.

Konradine put the ring upon her finger; the prince kissed her hand. "My errand is done," he said; "forgive me for making you sad."

"You cannot mean such words," she replied.

She accompanied him to the door of the antechamber, where he turned to her once more, and asked, "Will you remember me to the baron, and permit me to see you again?"

"I answer, 'with pleasure,' to each request," she replied, cordially.

"*Au revoir*, then!" he said; and, shaking her once more by the hand, he was gone.

She went to the window, and looked after him. How many times she had done the same thing but a few years before! He was the same, and yet changed. Never before had he been capable of such depth of feeling. Had she dreamed it all? Her heart was calm and still. She looked down at her hand; there was the ring. The prince had really been here; she had spoken with him, and he had left her at peace with herself and with him. She had sympathized with him in his sorrow for the loss of a wife whom he had loved. Upon her finger she wore a token sent her by the princess who had once stepped between her and the fulfilment of her hopes. Her heart was full of compassion for the man whom she had first loved and then hated; and she sat down, calmly and quietly, to write to Emanuel.

She informed him that she had met the prince, on the previous evening, at the house of the general, and of everything that had since occurred. She withheld nothing from him; she told him of her restless misery during the night, and of the peace that had now descended upon her soul, declaring that she had never so thoroughly belonged to him as now, when there was no room in her heart for anything but gentle pity for the man she had once loved and then hated.

She repeated many times how much she longed to tell him all this, face to face; and then went on to say that since she had been so touched by the princess's remembrance of her, she had accused herself of harshness in her entire forgetfulness of Hulda. "I did all that I could," she wrote, "to banish the thought of her from your mind; and yet perhaps she has been greatly in need of a helping hand in the path she has chosen to pursue. Ought we not to think of her, now that we are happy? I would so like to share with every one the peace that I at present enjoy. May the same calm brood over your spirit when you receive this from your Konradine!"

As she wore the little ring, she was obliged to repeat to her mother and to the countess more of her conversation with the prince than she would otherwise have done. Her mother asked to be allowed to examine the ring. It was formed of several artistically contrived circlets that fitted together and were held in place by an enamelled shield, bearing the words, "Aimez-moi toujours." Its value lay in the workmanship alone.

The baroness examined it with the eye of a connoisseur, and while she was fitting together the circlets, she said, "It is an exquisite work of art, and the whole matter is very touching. But do you know that, to me, the idea of the prince's dying wife committing to her husband's care a ring with this inscription upon it, which he was to give to you with his own hands, is very extraordinary? It is so very—high-strung,—ideal,—if you can use the word thus."

"The dying woman could hardly have thought it could be

thus construed, nor could I," said Konradine, an angry blush suffusing her cheek.

"Yes, but the question here is not of your idea of the matter, nor of the princess's," said the baroness. "We do not live in a world where to the pure all things are pure. And since I think it odd that the princess should have requested her husband to present you with this entreaty for an eternity of affection, I am afraid others may share my commonplace view of the matter. I would not wear the ring, if I were you."

"I shall always wear the ring, and it shall be buried with me!" said Konradine, emphatically.

"I think the prince might else have cause for offence," said the countess, hastening to divert all possibility of further difference between mother and daughter, although she did not disagree with the baroness. "There is no need to tell the history of all our rings, and this one is so simple that it could hardly excite curiosity. It is perfectly true, however," she said, under her breath, to the baroness, when Konradine had gone to the other end of the apartment, "that these royally-born people are so accustomed to make each thought and feeling of theirs an affair of state, that they cannot allow even death and sorrow for the dead to pass as they do with us. Others must be dragged into sympathy with them." She broke off suddenly, annoyed that she had been led to speak to the baroness in any but the highest terms of the reigning family, in respect for whom she had always been bred, and to whom she was bound by a loyal affection.

But the baroness, from this very circumstance, formed a correct estimate of the countess's distaste for the whole affair between Konradine and the prince.

CHAPTER XIII.

Emanuel had so arranged his daily affairs that the arrival of the post twice a week always found him at leisure to read his letters slowly, with a due enjoyment of every word of Konradine's, and to reply to them immediately.

On this particular day he was charmed to receive an enclosure from her twice as bulky as usual, and he sat down to read in a most enviable frame of mind.

But before he had nearly finished he sprang up, half-minded to order his travelling-carriage instantly. He could be by her side in twenty-four hours. Their marriage might take place at an earlier date than had been appointed, and he could bring her hither where no danger could threaten their peace. But she did not expect him, had not asked him to come. Could he confess what urged him immediately to seek her? He was ashamed to admit to himself that it was a sudden outburst of jealousy. For what had happened? What had Konradine written to him that could justify him in mistrusting for one instant a woman whom he had always found so frank and true?

All that she said was so natural, her ingenuous avowal to her betrothed of what she thought and felt, the confidence with which she leaned upon his supporting affection,—all this was so reassuring that, as he read the letter for the second time, his doubts were soothed and almost put to rest. The effect, too, that the conduct of the princess had had upon Konradine with regard to Hulda was very grateful to him. Emanuel had always been pained by the depreciating tone that his betrothed as well as his sister had used in speaking of the poor girl, who had suffered so much from the want of sympathy in those around her. But dear as her memory was to him, grateful as he was for Konradine's offer, he could not bring himself to regard any intercourse with her at present as advisable, or even possible.

He spent so much time in reading and re-reading the letter from his betrothed, that it was late when he opened the one from his sister. It informed him, of course, of the meeting with the prince, and of his subsequent interview with Konradine, circumstances regarded by both the baroness and the writer as unfortunate, to say the least. In view of antecedent events, everything that could give rise to gossip was to be avoided, and she suggested that her brother's marriage should take place earlier than had been intended, and that his betrothed should spend the intervening time in visiting some friends at some distance from the capital.

Emanuel knew his sister, and had foreseen the contents of her letter; but nevertheless it annoyed him. That she should regard vulgar gossip as of sufficient weight to influence his future plans was contrary to his sense of honour and refinement. He therefore replied to her that he saw nothing in the arrival of the prince that should have the slightest effect upon their future plans; and as the tone that he took in writing was extremely calm, it had a very desirable influence upon his own state of mind. He grew composed as he wrote, and when he began his answer to his betrothed he had regained all his former sense of ease and security.

He reciprocated, he wrote, the prince's courteous remembrances, and begged her, upon a fitting occasion, to assure him of his sympathy in his sorrow. Then he thanked her for her kindly mention of Hulda, but added that he could not think it best to intrude upon her present life with any memories of the past. "I have never forgotten her," he went on, "and I do not conceal from you that I never shall forget her. I should no more try to forget her than a beautiful spring morning the air of which had refreshed my very soul. My feeling for her has nothing in common with that which binds me so firmly to you. And yet I should hesitate wilfully to introduce her presence, like a new element, into our existence. But should the time ever come when Hulda is brought near us, as the prince has lately been to you, and should she then be willing to grasp in friendship the hand once offered to her in love, it would be my pride to extend it to her, and to know that your arms would be open to receive her."

Then he expatiated upon the unusual forwardness of the season, and, strive as he might, could not forbear, at the close of his letter, preferring a request that, since every arrangement for her reception in his home would be completed much earlier than he had anticipated, she would permit him to bear her thither sooner than had been at first proposed.

He was in excellent spirits when he had finished the letter; but after he had sent it to the post, a strange disquiet took possession of him. He could not help picturing to himself the prince as a member of the little circle in his sister's house, enjoying a pleasure from which he himself was debarred. The lonely evening never before had seemed so long. He could neither read nor write, and he welcomed the hour for retiring for the night. But his dreams were so disturbed that he arose and dressed, and tried again to fix his mind upon his books. In vain. Why had he abjured his early determination never to marry? And when, almost unsought, the truest affection had fallen to his share like a ripe golden fruit, he had not even closed his hand upon it; he had allowed it to slip from his grasp, to be trodden under foot.

Hulda had loved him! And he had never so loved another! This conviction, which had been soothed into slumber in his soul, had been awakened to new life by what Konradine had proposed in her letter. Had not Konradine, as well as he himself, often acknowledged that the bond between them was one woven only of cordial confidence and esteem? Their marriage was an arrangement for their mutual advantage, by which he secured a noble mistress for his ancient house, and intellectual companionship, and she a protector, an honoured name, and great possessions. Did she perhaps look to these last to indemnify her for those personal advantages which had been denied him?

He could not but confess in his heart, offensive as it was to his sense of honour, that want of confidence in himself made him distrustful of the woman who was so soon to bear his name; that the jealousy which had been first aroused by the intelligence of the prince's arrival left him no rest. Would marriage suffice to silence it? Was it ever silenced when once aroused?

Even the morning brought him no repose; the light of day produced no answering gleam in his mind. He was at odds with himself, and anything but happy.

CHAPTER XIV.

Meanwhile, all was going on smoothly in the countess's home. Konradine half regretted her entire frankness with Emanuel when she fancied that she saw some of his old mistrust of himself in his request for an earlier marriage than had been agreed upon; but, since she felt herself to blame in arousing it, she yielded to his wish without demur. She mentioned that the prince had several times repeated his visit to the countess, and that she had also met him elsewhere.

Soon after this letter had been despatched, the prince made his appearance at the countess's tea-table, and Konradine, in the presence of her mother and her friend, informed him of the early day in spring which had now been appointed for her marriage. He expressed himself warmly in favour of a short period of betrothal, especially when those intending marriage were of ripe years, as in this case.

Frau von Wildenau, who was always ready to discuss matrimony, since such discussion gave her an opportunity for reviling the marriage state, remarked that she thought that the length of the period of betrothal was of very little consequence.

"Matrimony," she said, "is an experiment, based upon mere hypothesis, the fortunate result of which must always be matter for amazement and congratulation. We are very pleasantly surprised when we find a glove or a shoe which was not made for us fit us exactly; and yet all, for the most part, enter upon matrimony in the firm faith that they have found a human being who will fit them, in every respect, far better than is possible for any glove or shoe."

The prince had formerly been amused with such remarks from the baroness, but they were no longer to his liking, and he thought he perceived that they were distasteful also to Konradine and the countess. Other guests arriving at the moment fortunately interrupted the conversation; and as they arose from table, the prince, for the first time availing himself of his former ease with Konradine, withdrew with her to a window-recess, and said, in a more confidential tone than he had hitherto permitted himself, "It is very remarkable how entirely unchanged Frau von Wildenau is; time has really no effect upon her. She looks as fresh and young as during the winter when I first made her acquaintance, and is the same, I perceive, in mind and sentiment."

"Your highness is aware," Konradine replied, warding off any implied censure of Frau von Wildenau, "that my mother was not happy in her marriage."

"I know that, I know that," said the prince; "but one should not generalize from one's individual experience."

"And yet it is your own experience that causes you to disagree with my mother," Konradine rejoined, gently.

"True! true!" cried the prince. "We are subjective in all these things. Still, we must rid ourselves of disagreeable memories, unpleasant experiences. How else can we endure a life that is so full of them? The baroness used to agree with me here; she used to think it wisdom to forget all that dis tressed us."

"And she is of the same opinion still. Nevertheless, there are things which we cannot away with, which we can never forgive or forget."

As she said these words, Konradine thought only of her mother and what she had suffered, but no sooner had they passed her lips than her cheeks flushed crimson, for she saw the significance that they might have for the prince coming from her, and her sudden blush really made him think that she had uttered her own personal conviction, and that her observation was aimed at him. For just so, her cheek, neck, and brow flushed with sudden crimson, had she stood before him on that far-away morning when they had separated. He had suffered more than she had believed; and she was now as proudly beautiful as then.

She did not dare to look at him. He could not at first find one word to say. They were both confused, and both silent. The prince felt that he had received from her a reproof which, after their late reconciliation, she was not justified in making, and his life had not taught him to suffer injustice silently. He would have replied bitterly, but his sense of honour prevented him; and, as he looked at Konradine, he saw how she was struggling with emotion, an emotion which he instantly felt to be contagious.

"I have nothing to say to you in self-justification," he said, perfectly conscious as he spoke that this declaration, or rather confession, was in no wise called for by what Konradine had said.

"I was not thinking of myself—believe me! Forgive me!" she replied, with a gentle tremor in her voice; and, as if her words were not enough, she held out her hand to him.

He took it in his own. "Most gladly do I believe you!" he cried. "Your friendship is so dear to me, your sympathy so precious! Only, never misunderstand me again."

"Never!" she replied.

"I only meant," he continued, "that we should banish from our minds the memory of all that might depress and embitter us. How could we wish to forget what we have once loved? How become indifferent to what has been lovely and dear in our eyes? We could not so rob ourselves!"

He said it all in agitated haste, which did not dissipate either her confusion or his own; and, in a final effort to overcome it, he added, "Never utter so harsh a word again, for I am defenceless in your presence!" He raised her hand to his lips, and their eyes met in the old, unforgotten glance. Each felt that it was so.

CHAPTER XV.

THE circumstance just related, slight as it was in outward seeming, served to put the prince and Konradine upon their guard. The prince was conscious that he had paid too frequent visits at the countess's house, and he allowed the duties of his position to occupy him more entirely.

For this forbearance Konradine was grateful. The countess made no remark upon the prince's withdrawal from his previous frequent intercourse with herself and her guests, but congratulated herself upon the smooth course that affairs were taking. The fire, however, was but smouldering. To avoid and to abstain were powerless to extinguish it.

Konradine was always comparatively at peace with herself while she was writing to Emanuel. She confessed to him that she too longed for the time when she should accompany him to his ancestral home, when she should have an aim in life and the constant and present assurance of his love and sympathy. Now that the season was nearly at an end, the evenings spent in the theatre were more frequent than formerly; she admitted to Emanuel that she found there a distraction of mind that served for a time to still the restlessness that was apt to take possession of her during the day.

The prince also, in default of other entertainments, was almost every evening to be found in his box in the theatre, opposite to that of the countess, where he would sometimes make his appearance, driven by his desire to speak with Konradine if only for a fleeting moment.

At such times the conversation was exceedingly superficial. The prince never forgot to ask after Baron Emanuel, now and then jestingly inquiring of Konradine how long the baron would allow him the pleasure of paying his respects to her here.

How long? A question which Konradine asked herself every evening, when she counted the days that were to elapse before the coming of her bridegroom, before her marriage. She wrote to the baron now daily. There was a warmth in her expressions that cheered and soothed him; she constantly addressed him as her only friend, her support and defence.

But the corresponding warmth in Emanuel's letters had no power to allay her daily-increasing restlessness, the growing feverishness of her mind and heart. Formerly she had hailed the advent of his written words with delight, and spoken of them to her mother and her friend; but by degrees they had lost all their influence. She was never more agitated than immediately after their arrival. She complained that she could not sleep; she began to lose her blooming colour, and started at any sudden noise. Even her music failed to interest her; she could no longer, she declared, either sing or play; she ceased, too, attending the theatre.

It was evident that her nerves were greatly affected, and the countess grew quite anxious upon her account; but the baroness was in no wise alarmed.

"To be as gay and bright as a morning in spring upon the eve of marriage," she said, "requires the thoughtless spirits of sixteen. You must remember that Konradine has been in society for fifteen years, and she may well spend many an agitating and anxious moment in inquiring of herself, Will friendship prove more enduring than I have found love to be? Will a marriage based upon respect and esteem indemnify me for the fading of my youthful visions and guard me from the assaults upon my peace which the future may have in store for me? Her nervousness seems very natural to me."

"But she is ill," the countess insisted.

"So much the better for the baron," laughed the mother. "The care of a wife suffering from slight nervous attacks will keep him busy, and prevent him from being self-occupied."

The countess was silenced, but hardly satisfied. Nevertheless, if, as she feared, it was the meeting with the prince that had agitated Konradine, it was surely best to leave her to herself and her own firmness of character.

The year of mourning for the baron's brother was not yet ended. It had therefore been decided that the circle of those present at the marriage should be but small, and since the arrival of the prince it had been contracted still further, that his presence might be avoided.

Every preparation for the wedding was concluded. Emanuel had promised to arrive a couple of days previous to that upon which the ceremony was to take place, and he was expected the next evening.

The day was fine, the countess had driven out, and the baroness was making farewell visits, for when the bride and bridegroom departed she was to visit her distant estates.

Konradine had been all the morning in her apartments, after a sleepless night. She had lost the courage even to be frank with herself, and mortification at her condition certainly did not improve it. Sometimes she was possessed by anger against the prince. "Was it not enough to ruin my former hopes? Must he, after finding happiness himself, come to destroy mine?" she said to herself.

Such moods did not last long; reason came to her aid in conquering them; but she was very wretched, and even the right to be wretched would be hers but for a few days longer, a few hours longer, for the struggle must be over, her weakness vanquished, before Emanuel's earnest eyes should meet her own to read there the very depths of her soul.

But how was it to be done? Disguise it from herself as she might, now, a few days before her marriage, a few hours before the arrival of her future husband, her heart longed for the prince's love, and he was devoted to the memory of a departed wife.

There was no help for it; her mind perpetually recurred to these thoughts, and Emanuel was to come on the morrow.

She left the house, to try what physical exercise would effect in reducing her mental restlessness. In her short Esthland jacket, with its fur trimming close around her throat, and a purple silk kerchief twisted about her head after the provincial fashion, she went into the garden and began to pace to and fro in one of the broad alleys.

It was noon, and the gardeners had gone to their dinner, leaving the doors of the green-house open. Konradine passed by it once or twice, casting an absent glance at the flowers which had been placed at the open windows and doors to catch the air of spring. Suddenly it occurred to her to look for the myrtle-bush from which her marriage-wreath was to be cut. Its closely-folded buds had begun to be faintly tinged with pink on their outside leaves; the sun of the last few days had been grateful to them,—they would soon open. She looked at them with melancholy in her heart. "It is time he were here!" she said. "I wish he were here!" she added, as the sound of approaching wheels was heard; and with that faith in the power of a wish, which every one has felt in some highly-strung condition of mind, she hurried along the principal avenue of the garden to the court-yard, in the full expectation of seeing there Emanuel's carriage.

But before she had gone far she became aware of her error. It was not the carriage of the baron, but that of the prince. His servant had gone into the house to announce his arrival, and the prince, perceiving Konradine from the window, alighted without awaiting his return, and came towards her.

At the entrance of the garden there was an extensive bit of lawn, with here and there some weather-stained stone statues, and here they met. The prince held out both hands to her.

"How long it is since I last saw you!" he cried; "and how fortunate I am to find you here! I was afraid you were ill, from never seeing you even in the theatre. And indeed you do not look so well as you did." His gaze rested upon her for one moment, but it was clear and untroubled.

She thanked him for his sympathy, and offered to conduct him to the house. He asked if she found it too cool, and when she replied in the negative, he said, "Then let us stay out here, the air is so delightful, and we can talk as we walk."

"As your highness pleases," she replied, courteously.

"Your words are gracious, but your manner says, 'I should be better pleased if you would leave me,'" said the prince. "Nevertheless, I so seldom have the good fortune to find you alone, that I will not be frightened away, and you must not grudge me so rare a pleasure. Besides, you are to leave us in a few days."

She replied that she expected Emanuel the next evening.

"So I heard from the countess, whom I saw a few days ago," the prince rejoined; and they walked on together for a few steps in silence. "In fact," he suddenly began, as if in conclusion to a long train of thought,—"in fact, we all live under the influence of ideas begotten of our desires and our fancy, and we are subject to painful disappointments, because we forget that others, upon whose aid in the fulfilment of our hopes we have involuntarily reckoned, do not share them with us. We are, and shall always be, as Goethe says, 'children, and hopeful fools.'"

Konradine asked what he meant.

He hesitated for one moment, and then, his fine eyes glowing with the proud frankness that had once captivated her, he said, "I confess to you that I had imagined a different meeting for us. The time is past when I feared to think of you or to meet you. If we are not what we once were, we are certainly not less capable than formerly of understanding and appreciating each other. You were the constant theme of our conversation——"

"I?" Konradine interrupted him, looking at him with astonishment.

"If you can doubt it, we never understood each other, and I am a very dreamer," he said.

Meanwhile, they had reached the end of the walk, and, instead of turning to the right to enter a side-path, Konradine retraced her steps towards the house. The prince followed her lead, but after they had walked on a little farther he stood still. He had grown thoughtful, and with a gravity in strong contrast to the cheerfulness he had hitherto displayed, he said, "In a few minutes we shall part, perhaps forever! It might be better to suppress what you seem to have no desire to hear, better not to offer you a hand whose reconciling grasp you are not inclined to return. But there is an honour of the heart that craves satisfaction, and I should like to justify myself to you to-day before I leave you. Konradine, will you hear me?"

She inclined her head in mute assent.

"Then walk with me once more through the garden," he asked; and she turned with him.

"You doubted being the frequent subject of our conversation," he began; "and yet the confidence established between the princess and myself during the first melancholy months of our married life was based upon her knowledge of the passionate affection that I had entertained for you, and of the enduring pain that the loss of you caused me. You accused me of coldness and selfishness. I seemed harsh and rough——"

She would have interrupted him, but he would not suffer her to speak. "No," he said; "do not try to soften what I say. I have never forgotten that day or that hour, as I have never forgotten you. You never appreciated how unanswerable were the arguments of reason that forced me to act as I did and resign you; and you never knew how all those arguments were powerless in assisting me to endure the sacrifice that I made. You did not see how I was obliged to arm myself against myself with the weapons of harshness and cruelty, with which I could have destroyed myself, but with which I did nothing but wound you. Believe me, Konradine, I did not deserve the scorn with which your outraged love turned from me. You were not more unhappy than I, and——"

"No more! no more! I cannot bear it!" Konradine fairly gasped, as she leaned against a stone pedestal, and covered her face with her hands, that the prince might not perceive the passionate emotion that had mastered her.

The prince started at these words. Never since they had seen each other again had he heard such a tone in her voice The sound awakened an echo within his own breast.

He laid his hands upon her shoulders. "Speak," he cried; "say one word, Konradine! I am free—and so are you. There is yet time. I love you, Konradine; and you have forgotten and forgiven. Speak, I conjure you, and say you are mine!"

"No!" she said, firmly, as she retreated from him; "no!"

He looked at her; the force that she put upon herself made her features rigid and cold. She went slowly towards the house, and he walked silently beside her.

"Twenty-four hours," he said, "still belong to you and to me!"

"No," she repeated, as if incapable of any other word.

Thus walking beside each other they reached the entrance of the garden. Neither looked at the other. Their eyes were downcast. At last the prince raised his head. "When I saw you again," he said, "I did not mean to ask you for what I now implore you. You were betrothed. You told me of your peace and happiness; you deceived me, and you deceived yourself. Will you persist in thus deceiving yourself and the baron? Can you offer him only friendship, when he asks for a wife's affection? Pause, Konradine! What are you about to do?"

"To keep the promise which I freely made to a man whom I esteem," she replied, firmly.

"And to swear a vow in which your heart has no part."

"To swear such a vow as you swore to the princess with a bleeding heart, to keep it, to conquer myself as you have done, and to confer happiness in entire self-forgetfulness. Farewell!"

"Farewell!" he repeated, dejectedly. They pressed each other's hands. At the door of the house she parted from him mute and tearless.

CHAPTER XVI.

THE next evening Emanuel arrived. Konradine threw herself into his arms and welcomed him with an eagerness that enchanted him. Then she stooped, as Hulda had once done, and kissed his hand.

"Dearest love," he cried, "what are you doing? What do you mean?" But she did not reply, and he was too happy to question her action further.

All the evening she was charming. Never before had she seemed to her betrothed so young, so maidenly; and there was a gentle tenderness in her manner to him that became her well. When the family separated for the night, the countess detained her brother in the drawing-room for awhile, that she might enjoy a few moments alone with him. "We shall see but little of each other," said she, "when you are established for the rest of your life at Falkenhorst."

He hoped, he told her, that she would spend some weeks at least of every year in her ancestral home, and expatiated upon the kindness that had been shown him by his neighbours the Von Barnefelds.

"What you say of these neighbours of yours pleases me much," said his sister. "The solitude will not be so great for Konradine and yourself as I had feared. A life of complete retirement is a terrible test, I think, to which to put a newly-married couple."

Even this general observation startled Emanuel. He had Konradine's happiness so strongly at heart that the least hint that the life he found full of interest might not be all-satisfying to her was sufficient to rouse the ever-lurking demon of self-mistrust within him. He could not conceal this from his sister's keen eye.

"Do not misunderstand me," she said. "I should be sorry to think that I had raised a single doubt in your mind as to Konradine's future content. Remember, she is no longer a young girl; she has loved and suffered, has had experiences that she cannot forget, and, although she has borne herself nobly, her late intercourse with the prince has had its effect upon her. The leave that he took of her yesterday accounts for the exhaustion on her part that I noticed when I returned from my drive, and she must be treated with great forbearance and tenderness."

Emanuel was pacing the room to and fro as his sister spoke. She was not certain that he was listening. Suddenly he paused before her.

"I wish," he said, "that you had let bygones be bygones. I know you mean kindly by me, but you have done me no good." And he bade her good-night and left her without giving her his hand as usual.

That night was sleepless for both Emanuel and Konradine. The next morning when they met each felt that some reconciliation was necessary, and yet there had been no quarrel. Emanuel was more silent than upon the previous evening, and Konradine was as gentle and careful as a child who wishes to avoid reproof.

During breakfast, a note was handed to the countess. "From his highness the prince," the servant said.

"He writes me," said the countess, as the others looked inquiringly at her, "that some tidings which he received yesterday morning decided him to start upon his tour of inspection to-day. He sends his remembrances to you and to your mother, my dear Konradine, and begs me to present to you his wishes for your future happiness."

Konradine inclined her head, and when she, with her mother, had left the room, Emanuel asked his sister whether she would permit him to see the prince's note. She silently handed it to him. It contained the intelligence of his departure, and concluded with, "Pray present me cordially to the baroness and Fräulein von Wildenau, and express to the latter my wishes for her future welfare. May she enjoy that happiness which I now know never can be mine!"

The words were no more than the prince was perfectly justified in using, but they planted a thorn in Emanuel's breast. He gave the letter back to his sister without a word. That day and the next passed calmly, but a dull weight burdened Emanuel's spirits, and the confidence that his first moments with his betrothed had inspired was entirely gone.

He was melancholy, and would not ask himself why, because he dreaded the answer to the question. The attention Konradine paid to his slightest wish, the pains she evidently took to please him, only distressed him the more, and his disquiet increased with the approach of the wedding-day.

Each seemed to regard the other as an invalid in especial need of forbearance and care. All her dutiful observance of the rules she had laid down for herself did not save Konradine from despair; all his trust in her did not relieve Emanuel's suffering. They were both wretched.

Every day convinced Emanuel that Konradine's late intercourse with the prince had revived her old love for him, and the prince's letter to the countess strengthened this conviction. Without a word on Konradine's part, he guessed what had happened: that there had been some revelation between her former lover and herself, and that she had dismissed him and resolved to be true to her word to her betrothed. The agitation of the struggle, and joy at the victory she fancied she had achieved, explained the meek and tender affection with which she had first received him. The revulsion, the reaction followed, and now she was pondering and weighing it all in her mind. What if the result should be regret for what she had done?

Thus they lived on until the day before that appointed for the marriage, when, according to the custom of the country, Konradine was to receive all her female friends who wished to bid her farewell and to bestow upon her some token of their affectionate remembrance.

Although the countess was anxious that in her mourning any appearance of unusual festivity should be avoided, the rooms were hung with wreaths and filled with flowers. The ladies came and went, and sat talking in groups, while servants handed about ices and refreshments. The countess was charmed that all was going so smoothly, and felt that her brother's future was at last secure.

Many of the visitors had left; Konradine's bridesmaids were still with her, and a couple of elderly ladies were bidding farewell to Frau von Wildenau, when a carriage drove rapidly up before the door, and immediately afterwards a young cousin of the countess entered the drawing-room, evidently in a state of unusual agitation. She was very sorry, she declared, to come so late, but she had received a terrible shock. Just as she was getting into the carriage, her husband, the general of a regiment of cuirassiers, had received tidings calling him instantly from home, and she had awaited his return.

Frau von Wildenau asked if anything serious were the matter.

"Ah," replied the general's young wife, "I had determined not to say one word about it to cloud such a day as to-day, but you will be sure to hear of it, and you had better learn it from me than from the papers. Yesterday, at the review at B——, Prince Frederick's horse suddenly shied; its rider undertook to discipline it, it reared, fell over backwards, and the prince was taken up senseless,—fatally injured, they fear, by a blow upon his head."

The last words had scarcely left her lips when, with a low, agonized cry, Konradine clasped her hands above her head, and fell fainting on the floor, before any one could go to her support.

There was general dismay and confusion. Frau von Wildenau and Emanuel lifted the senseless form from the floor and laid it on a lounge, and the countess dismissed the guests, accounting for Fräulein von Wildenau's sudden indisposition as best she might. They departed, expressing their sympathy, discussing the prince's accident, and trusting that there would be no reason for postponing the marriage. The countess was perfectly calm and self-possessed; but she felt it a relief indeed when the last visitor had gone and she was free to inquire after Konradine and her brother.

Frau von Wildenau met her in the antechamber to Konradine's apartment. She informed her that her daughter had shortly recovered her senses, and had refused even to lay aside her dress. Emanuel was with her, and they had requested to be left to themselves.

The countess remarked that it was much better so; the baroness was silent. The ladies then separated; the settlement of the affair did not depend upon them.

CHAPTER XVII.

KONRADINE was leaning back wearily in an arm-chair. Emanuel was seated beside her. The burden of the hour lay heavily upon both.

"Forgive me, Emanuel!" she began, at last, for she could no longer bear the silence. "Forgive me! Do not turn away from me. I was not my own mistress. It was stronger than I!"

"I know it," he replied; "I saw it. What is there to excuse or forgive? Let it go; it is past." He controlled himself by an effort that lent a stern rigidity to his features, bringing out strongly the native nobility of his fine head.

"I cannot see you thus," she began again. "Do not condemn me before you have heard me. I was yours, and meant to remain so. On the day before your arrival the prince first spoke to me in the tone of a lover. I repulsed him firmly. Until then no word of his had reminded me of the past, and I was determined to keep my promise to you unbroken——"

"It is well for me and for you that you were unable to do so," Emanuel interrupted her; "that fate prevented you from so degrading yourself and me."

Again there reigned a gloomy silence between them, until Konradine laid her hand upon his, and said, with tears in her eyes, "I cared so much for you, I was sure of leading a happy, peaceful life by your side; my trust in you and my reliance upon you are so unbounded——"

"And I will not fail you!" he again interrupted her. "I do not accuse you; I alone am to blame for the error that was made. There can be no true marriage founded upon friendship when one is formed, as you are, to awaken and to receive love. I should not have been so misled as to suppose I could ever gain and retain the love of youth and beauty. I should have been content with the friendship that you accorded me; been content to live a lonely life, and die, the last of my race, in fulfilment of the ancient curse."

"Emanuel!" she cried, "I pray you do not speak thus! What are you talking of?"

"Dreams," he replied. "But what is dream, and what reality? A dream has made me happy all this time. It is dissolved, and I am awake. Can you or I change what is past? And if we could, do we wish that we had gone on and contracted the closest union, I full of unfounded faith, and you with your heart full of a love in comparison with which the compassionate tenderness——"

"Emanuel!" exclaimed Konradine, in a tone of entreaty.

But he repeated the expression, "in comparison with which the compassionate tenderness and friendly esteem that you felt for me were cold and faint. We should be thankful to fate, and obey its decree willingly."

As he arose and walked to the window, there was a knock at the door; a servant wished to know if the countess might see Fräulein Konradine. Emanuel replied, in her stead, that they would be glad to see her, and the countess entered.

She was quiet and sympathetic, treating the whole affair as a by no means alarming attack of sudden indisposition. Then, as if the only matter for anxiety were the accident to the prince, she said she was glad to be the bearer of cheerful tidings. The prince's wound, at first thought fatal, was, although severe, not at all dangerous. They hoped to have him brought home in a few days, and that he would shortly be perfectly restored.

Emanuel listened calmly. When the countess had finished, he turned to Konradine. "You see," he said, "the first accounts are always exaggerated. You need not be anxious, and I can depart immediately."

"Depart?" the others cried, in a breath. "Are you going away?" the countess asked.

"Konradine has need of rest, and it will be good for me also," replied Emanuel.

The countess looked from her brother to Konradine, and then at her brother again, utterly at a loss, for the first time in her life. Anger at her friend, pain on her brother's account, wounded family pride, and her distaste for the publicity and the social gossip that the rupture of her brother's engagement at this last moment, as it were, would produce, all assailed her at once. "Do not decide immediately," she entreated her brother. "You must not let him go," she said to Konra dine. But Emanuel paid her no heed; and, as if he wished witness to his farewell to his betrothed, he hastily held out his hand to Konradine, and said, "Farewell!"

Konradine threw herself at his feet, and cried, "Do not leave me thus, Emanuel! You know how dear you are to me, —how it breaks my heart to give you pain. Tell me——

He gently raised her from the ground, and, taking her hand, said, "You will forget what you now suffer, in the love that awaits you!"

"And you? and you?" she cried.

"I shall endure what I must as best I may. Farewell!"

She threw her arms around him, weeping. He gently extricated himself once more, and, pressing her hand, said, almost in a whisper, "Be happy!" and was gone.

Before nightfall he was upon his way. The servants went softly whispering about the corridors and antechambers of the countess's house.

The countess had a long and confidential interview with her family physician, to whom she poured out all the woe her wounded pride was forced to endure. He also saw Frau von Wildenau and her daughter; and Konradine was induced to keep her room for some days—a rest of which she certainly was in great need—while the countess despatched notes to all who had been bidden to the marriage, informing them that the ceremony had been postponed on account of the sudden illness of Fräulein von Wildenau.

Three days later the countess departed from the city, to pay her long-contemplated visit to her daughter. The baroness and Konradine left before the end of the week. The prince had not yet returned to his palace; but the news from him were favourable, and no doubts of his speedy recovery were entertained.

The countess had been long with her daughter, Frau von Wildenau and Konradine had passed the summer at a watering-place, and the prince had entirely recovered from the effects of his fall, before the breaking of Baron Emanuel's engagement had ceased to be the theme of rural gossip upon the countess's estates or among the tenantry at Falkenhorst.

CHAPTER XVIII.

In the world in which Hulda lived, a year or more passed away, after the breaking of Emanuel's engagement, without bringing to her ears a single whisper regarding him or any one in any way connected with him. Then it happened one day that the doctor, who was paying her a visit, mentioned that the king had shortly before raised to the rank of countess a Fräulein von Wildenau, a former canoness, that she might more suitably contract a marriage with Prince Frederick, the widower of his deceased niece.

"Whom?" asked Hulda, scarcely believing her ears. "Whom has the king made a countess?"

"A canoness,—Konradine von Wildenau," the doctor replied, carelessly.

"Impossible!" cried Hulda. "Konradine von Wildenau is the wife of the Freiherr von Falkenhorst."

The doctor bethought himself for a moment. "It seems to me," he said, "that I heard something about that—something about a broken engagement, I cannot exactly remember what. But I am sure of one thing,—that Baron Emanuel von Falkenhorst, the possessor of Falkenhorst, is unmarried. Some one dining with me lately mentioned that he was the last male representative of his name, and that the estates would lapse to the female line if he, who is about forty years old at present, did not marry. But what do you know of the future Princess Frederick?" he added.

Hulda made some indifferent reply, and the doctor was quite satisfied; but she could not forget what she had heard, nor could she tell whether she had been pained or pleased by it. One thing seemed certain,—whatever experiences Emanuel had passed through, he no longer remembered her.

In the course of two years she had become entirely accustomed to her position. The public for whom she played were always charmed with her, the manager and director had come to be fully aware of what a treasure they possessed in her, and since of late she had received most favourable proposals from other towns, they were ready to do all they could to retain her in her present position. There had even been some talk of her appearance at the royal theatre, in the capital of the kingdom, since one of the principal actors there had fulfilled a starring engagement with the Holm management, where he had seen and appreciated Hulda.

Her understanding was developed, her strength of character increased, and she continued eagerly to pursue all the means of self-culture of which she could avail herself. The honest attention that she had learned to pay to duty during her youth, beneath her father's roof, stood her in good stead now; she neglected no opportunity of that careful study the want of which no genius can supply. Her ambition was always awake, her pride in her art was pure and genuine.

Her friends were all ready to admit that hers was a rare nature. Even Philibert, whose selfish passion was at first always prone to overstep the barrier which she interposed between herself and her admirers, at last learned to ask no more favour from her than she could gracefully dispense to all. Certainly Hulda could ask for nothing more in her present position, so far as regarded her art and the public. But the applause that greeted her before the curtain contrasted strongly with the ill will that she encountered behind the scenes.

Fräulein Delmar had not forgotten or forgiven the circumstances of Hulda's first appearance. She was never weary of showing her petty spite towards the innocent cause of her former defeat; and all the subordinate actresses, who had founded hopes of fame upon Feodora's retirement, espoused the cause of Hulda's enemy. In a thousand ways they annoyed Hulda. There was nothing that did not afford them a pretence for slighting or insulting her. They cast meaning glances over their shoulders at her when new costumes were ordered for her, sneering at the director's sudden extravagance and lavish generosity. They whispered together when Lelio appointed times for reading her parts with her, and many a malicious word, which she could not help overhearing, cut Hulda to the heart, which had just throbbed with exultation at the public applause.

While she hoped to influence her enemies to lay aside their prejudice against her, she had spoken to her friends of her sorrow at finding it so strong. The doctor took her to task for allowing it to annoy her. "A kind fairy gifted you in your cradle with great beauty and rare artistic talent," he said. "We men are all ready to pay you homage, and you are miserable because inferior women will not admire you too. Fie! you must not be so grasping, my child."

Hochbrecht and Philibert took another tone. "You portray love and passion," they said, "so perfectly that you touch all hearts, and you expect women with not a ray of talent to believe in it as a result of your imagination and not of your experience. To do that they must possess your own gift of fancy. We are the only ones to be pitied, for they believe us far happier than we are."

But nothing that the doctor or her friends could say ever reconciled Hulda to the pettiness and jealousy, the small deceit and mean curiosity, that she encountered in her present life behind the scenes. She was grateful that in her inmost heart she could preserve memories which had nothing in common with the present, and to which she could flee when it oppressed her too heavily.

Often, when she opened the windows of her room early on Sunday morning, and the wind was lightly stirring the branches of the trees in the square, the birds were singing, and the sound of the church-bells floated on the air, she was seized by a longing that both refreshed and pained her.

Her thoughts would wander back to the home of her early childhood. She heard the sand upon the floors crackle beneath her tread as she waited to walk to church with her father and mother, dressed in the simple costume of the country, her hair wound in smooth braids about her head. Again she sat by her mother's side in church, and felt the cool sea-breeze sweep in through the curtain at the door. She saw around her the honest faces, furrowed by toil and weather-beaten by storms, the red-cheeked, white-headed boys and girls, who all knew her and liked her because she was the pastor's Hulda. She longed for those old days as for the salt breath of the sea and the beauty of nature.

At the beginning of her dramatic career she had been regular in her attendance at church; but the sense of loneliness that so often oppressed her increased when she sat among all those strange faces; she could not follow the preacher's words, for old memories of her father, and gradually she had given up the habit of church-going. Sometimes she was afraid that she was losing even the power to pray. She would fold her hands and—the train that she was to try on the morrow would come into her mind. She would try to examine the thoughts that had passed through her mind during the day; but she could not bear to recall its many little annoyances, and if the words of prayer passed her lips mechanically, she shrank from such a mockery of worship. It seemed to her as if she were kneeling like Gretchen before the altar, and that she could hear the whisper of the fiend:

"How otherwise was it, Margaret,
When thou, still innocent,
Here to the altar cam'st,
And from the worn and fingered book
Thy prayers didst prattle,—
Half sport of childhood,
Half God within thee!"

Then she would clasp her hands firmly, and fervently thank God that her heart was still pure and her conscience free from stain; then she thought with profound affection of her father slumbering in the little church-yard far away, of her tender mother buried in the depths of the sea, and her whole soul would arise in the burning supplication, "Lead me not into temptation, but deliver me from evil."

What else could she desire before God? Not for His ear were the dreams of pride or ambition, and for whom beside herself should she pray?

Her parents were dead; her guardian had repudiated her—he sent her without a word the yearly interest of the small sum left her by Miss Kenney. She knew nothing of the pastor or of the family at the castle. The only one of whom she always thought, the man upon whose head she would have invoked Heaven's choicest blessings in spite of the misery he had caused her, Emanuel, did not need her prayers, for he was happy,—happy without a thought of her; and yet in thought she was always with him.

Every intonation of happy love—all the tones of woe with which she touched the hearts of her audience—she owed to him, and to him alone.

She thought of him when trying to avoid all contact with

what was false or impure; her memory of his faith in her purity, his grave disapproval of all that was false, kept guard over her always. Should she ever see him again? If that time should ever come, he should find that she was worthy of the love he had once given her and withdrawn from her. His image followed her everywhere, earnest and grave as the voice within, warning and exhorting like another conscience.

CHAPTER XIX.

HULDA had been three years upon the stage, when the newspapers announced that one of the brilliant stars in the theatrical world, Michael Lippow, would shortly arrive in town, his services having been secured by the Holm management for six performances. The news was received with delight, and the tickets for each evening's entertainment were quickly exhausted.

Very little was known concerning the antecedents of this artist. It was maintained that he was of excellent family, that he had not always been devoted to a theatrical career, but that no less a person than the incomparable Louis Devrient had been his teacher and his model. He was little over thirty years old, an excellent linguist, finished in appearance and manner, and renowned for his wonderful power of metamorphosing his exterior according to the part he was to play.

He was first to appear as Marinelli, in "Emilia Galotti," and on the last night of his short engagement would play Mephistopheles, in "Faust," Lelio and Hulda sustaining severally the parts of Faust and Gretchen for the first time.

This was a great gratification for these ambitious young artists. They had been studying Goethe's great work for months past, and that they should first appear in it with the famous Lippow was considered to be great good fortune. What might not be the good results from his visit? Lelio's contract with Holm expired late in the fall, and Hulda's engagement was to end with the winter. Lippow was to go to Vienna the next year, and if the performance with him succeeded they might be called thither.

The summer was at its height on the morning when the actors began to assemble for the rehearsal at which the great man was to make his first appearance. Fräulein Delmar, dressed, in spite of the morning hour, in green silk, with a bird of Paradise in her Leghorn bonnet, had thrown herself into a chair, and was engaged in polishing with her lace handkerchief her gold eye-glass.

The director rallied her for thus making ready for a good view of the celebrity.

"Of Lippow?" she cried. "Do you think I am polishing my glass for him? Not at all. He is a trained artist; there is nothing new to be seen in him. I am looking for our divinity, our Venus Anadyomene, as Hochbrecht styles her in his measured verse. I wish to see what attitude she will take towards Lippow."

Scarcely had she spoken the words when the manager appeared upon the stage with Lippow, and Hulda came slowly forward from the side-scenes. She looked like summer itself, in her fresh white muslin and round straw hat wreathed with cornflowers, and holding in her hand a lovely branch of moss-roses, which Philibert had handed to her as she entered the theatre.

Involuntarily every man turned to look at her as the manager indicated her by a motion of his hand. But scarcely had Lippow and Hulda looked at each other when they paused and started in unfeigned surprise. A name, an exclamation, hovered upon Hulda's lips; but a look, a warning look, from Lippow stayed its utterance.

Fräulein Delmar, the manager, and the director, all noticed the strange incident. They looked at one another, but found no clue to the riddle.

Lippow, however, regained his self-possession in an instant. He hurried towards Hulda, and, with an air of finished courtesy, said, offering her both hands, "Is it possible! Can I believe my eyes? Is it you, Fräulein Hulda? Who would have thought that we should meet here, after our sudden separation in the castle by the sea? We certainly have cause to be thankful for such good fortune."

He intentionally prolonged his greeting to give Hulda time to recover herself; but her answer sounded cold and formal after such warmth on his part. An abyss seemed to open before her. The idea of daily intercourse with this man, with Michael, of playing with him every evening, of enduring his touch, of acting Gretchen with him, inspired her with actual horror.

The rehearsal of Emilia was half over before she had in any degree recovered from the terror which this meeting had caused her. Why had she never thought that Michael Lippow, of whom she had often heard, must be one and the same with Prince Severin's servant, who in his time had exercised so decisive an influence upon her fate? She had heard the bailiff say that Michael had joined the play-actors, but she had never known his last name, and she had not dreamed that the praises she heard lavished upon the finished artist had reference to the man who lived in her memory as the personification of all that was vile. She had recognized him at the first glance, although he was greatly altered, and in carriage and bearing bore but small resemblance to the supple, obsequious valet whom she had seen in former years. In spite of her dislike of him, as he stood before her now she could not withhold her admiration from the artist.

Still, although his rendering of his part was admirable, and he was loud in his praises of Hulda's talent and improvement, she was thankful when the rehearsal was over, and she could collect her thoughts and banish sad memories of the past to the depths whence they had been summoned by Michael's appearance.

At the breakfast given by the manager to Lippow when the rehearsal was concluded, men only were present, and all were charmed by the versatility and talent of their guest. He had seen more of the world than was at all usual in those days, knew the great capitals of Europe well, and had studied Talma in Paris and Kemble in London. He was brilliant and easy in conversation, and, to all appearance, most unpretending for a man of his reputation. He provoked confidence without ever giving any in return, and before the festivity of the morning was at an end he knew all there was to be learned about Hulda, had listened with surprise to the universally believed report as to her parentage, to Lelio's account of his disinterested friendship for her, and to the expression of Philibert's hope of winning her sooner or later for his own, without having for an instant betrayed any particular of his own former acquaintance with the young actress.

The evening's performance on this first day of Lippow's sojourn in town was confined to a couple of farces, performed by subordinate members of the company. The great man was to appear on the following night.

Hulda's windows were open, and she was alone. Six o'clock had long struck, and the approach of evening was already cooling the air. Its gentle breath stirred the leaves of a myrtle-bush upon the table before her, and the room was filled with the fragrance of the roses which Philibert had given her that morning. She was dreamily watching the light clouds floating hitherward from the east, seeming to bring her upon the breeze a greeting from her old home by the sea.

She was longing, like a prisoner, for freer air and a fuller enjoyment of nature. Her father and mother had surrounded her with love in that far-away home on the sea-shore, and she had, with childish curiosity and eagerness, thirsted for a city life among stone walls and crowded streets—for gay dresses, ornaments, and the applause of the many. All these were now hers; nay, she could confidently expect them to be hers in future in even fuller measure; but did not she long now for the dear old life of the past, just as she had then longed for an unknown future? Was she happier now than she had been then?

She was lost in sad reverie, when Frau Rosen knocked at her door, and, as if she were announcing a great piece of good fortune, informed her that the hero of the day, Herr Lippow, wished to pay his respects to her. Her first thought was that she would refuse to receive him, but she reflected that this would be of no use, since she must be thrown with him daily for awhile, so she sent to request him to come in, and ordered candles to be brought.

Beata, who was anxious to see the famous actor, took the candles from her mother, and preceded the guest into the room. She wondered that Hulda should receive with such an air of reserve the handsome man of whom every one was talking, and who so courteously and respectfully addressed her, congratulating himself upon meeting her again after so long a separation.

Scarcely, however, was the door closed behind the girl, when Michael threw himself down upon the lounge beside Hulda, and, seizing her hand, held it firmly between both his own, while, leaning towards her, he said, in a tone of easy familiarity, "'Pon my honour, my lovely friend, your grace and dignity enchanted me to-day. Do you know, Hulda, that you have become an excellent actress?"

Although she could not instantly withdraw her hand from his clasp, she recoiled from him, and, with the same grave reserve with which she had received him, replied that she was obliged to him for his encouragement, and was glad that he thought well of her representation of "Emilia."

Michael laughed aloud. "Enough! enough of this!" he cried. "What do we care about 'Emilia,'—about the farce with which we must amuse the rabble, because we need their money? No, what enchanted me was your bearing in the rehearsal to-day. Countess Clarissa herself could not queen it more royally than you do at this moment. Absolutely perfect! but *basta, Signora, basta adesso!*"

"I did not know," said Hulda, oppressed by his familiarity, "that I should find in you——"

"I know; oh, I saw that," he interrupted her, "and you must have seen, fair lady, that I know how to understand, to obey, and to be silent."

He bowed with mock reverence, but, as Hulda's face still continued very grave, he also changed his tone and his expression. He let go her hand, folded his arms, and, leaning back in the corner of the lounge, said, "You choose to take the matter seriously? Well, then, as you please. It is an affair of but a few words. You, gracious lady, will please to forget that you ever saw me in the castle by the sea, in Prince Severin's society, not absolutely master of myself or my own actions. I, in return, will forget the little liberties and amusements that you then, under the guardianship of the all-virtuous Miss Kenney, permitted yourself with the enthusiastic baron and the susceptible prince. Our lives begin from yesterday. I am of distinguished parentage, an actor from choice, in opposition to the wishes of my relatives. You? You will have the kindness to instruct me as to what part you choose to play. Only, dearest girl, no farce when we are *tête-à-tête*. For, in truth, I find you far lovelier than ever,—maddeningly lovely!"

He attempted to approach her again, but she arose and stood before him glowing with shame and anger, scarcely able to find words to express what she felt.

"I had forgotten you!" she cried. "You have nothing to fear from me. Your name has never passed my lips, shall never pass my lips, if I can avoid it. Do and say what you choose. I have nothing to shun, nothing to conceal."

"Nothing?" Michael asked, with a sneer. "In all innocence, then, you saw fit to lay aside your father's name and provide yourself with an illustrious mother?"

"I?" cried Hulda, who did not in the least understand his last words.

"Oh," he quickly went on, "I do not blame you. On the contrary, I admire your wisdom. Every one who wishes to be seen must have a pedestal to stand upon, and since Gabrielle has in her princely retirement forgotten at her husband's side all former follies, she need not grudge you the reflection of her former glory, especially since you do credit to her name. Only before me, my fair friend, who admired you when you were taking the linen from the line in the parsonage garden, and enjoyed the delight of your society—precious memory!—at Ma'amselle Ulrika's, pray descend from your pedestal, and let us understand each other."

"This is incredible!" cried Hulda, who began to understand the ambiguous way in which during these years so many people had spoken to her of Gabrielle. "This is incredible! A disgraceful invention! Whose is it?"

"How should I know, my fairest? Not mine, at all events!" Michael replied, with cool indifference. "But never let it turn one of those golden hairs gray. A daughter like yourself, what mother would not be proud to own? what man not enchanted to father?"

Hulda had sunk upon a seat at the other end of the room, and was crying bitterly. To know the memory of her pious father, her gentle mother, and Gabrielle's fair fame thus insulted, and to discover that she was accused of spreading such a report, of branding her own existence with infamy, was more than she could bear. And yet this report must have been in circulation ever since she first trod the stage. Michael surely had not invented it. She alone, in her artless security, had been ignorant of it; in her innocence she had aided to spread it abroad. Who had originated it? What had given rise to it. These thoughts overcame her, and she was filled with disgust for the society and the world in which she lived.

Michael still sat upon the lounge, watching her. Suddenly she remembered that he was a witness of her tears. She arose, and hastily dried her eyes.

"Admirable!" cried Michael. "Every motion is perfect. You must let Gretchen lie just in that posture in church before the altar. It could not be finer, and the shape of your head is exquisite."

"Odious!" exclaimed Hulda, turning from him. But he was not one whit abashed; he seemed rather to enjoy the dislike of him which she manifested.

"You must be indulged," he said. "For the next fourteen days you are mine; and as you apparently belong to those realistic artists who must absolutely feel what they represent, only continue to increase your detestation of me during that time, and we shall produce a perfect furor in Faust."

He had arisen and was standing as he spoke. To Hulda his words, "for the next fourteen days you are mine," sounded like a curse.

"Yes," she cried, scarcely knowing what she said, "fourteen days! but never again!"

Michael smiled. "Sweet innocence," he said, "do you not remember how you protested on that rainy evening in the forest that you would never look upon my face again? And yet here we are together, a stage hero and heroine, the admiration of a little world. You seem to me to have wonderfully retained your youth. Have you really never asked yourself how we shall regard each other at the end of fourteen days, when we shall have learned—and the lesson will be worth the learning, believe me—each other's value, and that we can together command theatre, public, and manager, if we please?"

"I do not desire such command," Hulda said, coldly. "All that I ask——"

"At last!" cried Michael. "I can then have the pleasure of doing something for you!"

"Yes!" replied Hulda." "And I demand it as my right." She paused, for her lips trembled, and when she spoke it was in a dull monotone. "Tell every one, every one who knows anything of me, that you have seen me beneath my parents' honest roof; that you knew me when I was in Ma'amselle Ulrika's service,"—she selected the strongest word she could think of, to give emphasis to what she wished to say,—"tell them that I am the child of worthy people, and that there is no other tie between Gabrielle and myself than that of gratitude on my part for her kindness."

She thought thus to give him his dismissal, and that he would leave her. But he still stood gazing at her, for she seemed to him more and more beautiful every moment. His gaze distressed her. He saw that it did so, and he enjoyed her annoyance as the beginning of his triumph. He bowed assentingly, and said, as if they were upon the best of terms with each other, "My lovely friend, you shall be obeyed, rely upon it. When we next meet here, my charming fair, I trust you will not prove so entirely inaccessible as you now are to this poor mortal, whom you affect to despise because he admits that he is a child of earth, and no seraph."

He seized her hand, kissed it passionately, and hastily left the room with an "*A rivederci!*"

Hulda heard his steps descending the stairs, and the house-door close after him. Then she breathed freely, and, ringing the bell, gave orders that if Herr Lippow ever came again he should not be admitted. Neither Frau Rosen nor Beata could understand such an order. "What can she mean to do?" said Beata. "She has some plan in her head."

"Of course she has," said her mother, "and a very fine plan. She will catch Philibert; for she is just as prudent and cold as Feodora."

CHAPTER XX.

EVERY evening that Lippow appeared, the theatre was crowded. There had been no such receipts since Feodora's last three nights; and even Hulda, repugnant as Michael's presence upon the stage always was to her, could not but admit that he was a great artist.

The manager, the director, Lelio, and all the *habitués* of the theatre, with Philibert at their head, were loud in their admiration of him. In private as well as in public he contrived to make himself quite the hero of the day.

He had attempted several times to see Hulda again at her lodgings, but had never been admitted. He was unused to such repulses, and by no means inclined to submit to them in this case. His vanity was piqued, and his admiration of her beauty increased daily.

He tried to treat her refusal to admit him as a jest, and to conquer her coldness and reserve by an air of easy friendliness. He reproached her one evening, behind the scenes, in the presence of Fräulein Delmar, for such treatment of an old acquaintance and companion.

Hulda pleaded, in excuse, excessive fatigue, and the necessity that she felt of giving all the time that she could to the study of her new part.

Fräulein Delmar observed that Hulda had always boasted of her excellent memory.

"And yet she forgets her friends!" Michael said, "and has no remembrance of the corridors and antechambers in the old castle, where we young people used to laugh and talk so merrily that the joyous echoes rang again. But, *tempi passati!* the pastor's pretty Hulda has become a great actress, and forgets her whilom associates in the count's castle."

The flippant tone in which these words were uttered irritated Hulda, and the thought that Fräulein Delmar was present caused her to forget all prudence.

"I have forgotten nothing," she said, "nothing! I remember perfectly distinctly every event at the castle. But the memory of them awakens no pleasure within me; and I wonder that you can refer to them."

Her cue was given, and she went upon the stage. Lippow smiled. "The same enchanting caprice, the same charming soubrette,—provoking in her coquetry!"

Fräulein Delmar opened wide her eyes. "Soubrette?" she repeated.

"Soubrette, or—companion to a superannuated governess," he said, carelessly. "Call it what you will. Her mother had been a servant in the castle; she was born a serf on one of the countess's estates, and, being very pretty, she found favour with her superiors, as did her daughter. She was afterwards married to the pastor on the estate, and her daughter was quite a pet at the castle."

"But what about Gabrielle? What has this to do with

her? How did she come across Gabrielle?" Fräulein Delmar asked, eagerly.

"Gabrielle? Perhaps she was her maid."

"Maid? They said she was Gabrielle's daughter," said Fräulein Delmar, more and more interested.

"What an idea! Who said so?" exclaimed Michael, with well-feigned indignation. "What a groundless slander!"

Fräulein Delmar assured him that the report was everywhere credited. Hulda herself had never denied it when it had been hinted at in her presence. She had rather boasted of Gabrielle's protection.

"And she was a waiting-maid?" she exclaimed, with exultation. "You knew her as such?" she said, indignantly. "A waiting-maid, and giving herself such airs! It is disgusting!"

Michael laid his hand upon her arm. "Softly, gracious lady; do not be unjust. A pretty waiting-maid belongs in the nature of things to every distinguished household, and is by no means to be despised, especially when there is the making in her of such an artist as our lovely Hulda. I certainly have nothing to say against her, and yet, Heaven knows, I have small cause to defend her, for it was owing to her that I had a most unpleasant encounter with Prince Severin and Baron Emanuel, the son-in-law and the brother of the countess. The affair caused me in the end to take to the stage, and sent Mademoiselle Hulda back to her father's house. Well, I am not sorry, and the fair Hulda probably owes her present position to the protection of her two cavaliers."

The second act of the play was at an end, and the actors retired to their dressing-rooms while the scenes were changing. All went on smoothly to its close, and the public were delighted.

Hulda had grown more composed during the progress of the play; but she would gladly have recalled her words to Michael, for she had learned to dread his smile. She was troubled at the thought of his hostility, and her loneliness oppressed her.

If there had only been some one whom she could ask, "What do you think he will do? What have I to fear?" It would have been a relief to pour out her heart on paper to some one. But whither should she turn? Not to Gabrielle;

she had told her of the thorns which beset the path of an actress, and to her she must be mute when these thorns wounded her. And Feodora was away with her husband,—and there was no one else beside.

No one! for she had cut herself loose from the friends of her childhood's home, and, even if she had not, their counsel would have availed her little in the world in which she now dwelt, and from which the young pastor would fain have lured her back to the old parsonage. She thought of it with emotion. How many still lived unknown and content in such a little home! Such a fate had once been hers, but she had rejected the love of him who would have bound her to it always. Was it her fault that her love for Emanuel had sprung to life within her when she was little more than a child?

Michael's presence had called up all the past, and again she was conscious, with bitter pain, of her unhappy, rejected love. What was all the applause of the crowd in comparison with the look of pleasure with which Emanuel had once listened to a song from her? How happy she had been at his side! What blissful hopes hovered above her sick-bed when he had placed the ring upon her finger! And now? Where was the happiness that his love had brought her? What could she hope for now but the admiration, the homage, that gratified her ambition but never satisfied her heart? Was this what she had so longed for in life?

She dared not pursue these thoughts; they were vain, and did but cripple her power. She sat down to her piano, and tried to lose herself in playing and singing the melodies of her childhood and her home.

CHAPTER XXI.

The following evening "Faust" was to be played. Lelio had promised to come in the morning to read with her; but he did not appear; instead came Philibert, "to rest himself in her society," as he said.

The expression seemed to her rather familiar; but he was so full of the delights of an entertainment he had given to Lippow the preceding evening, at his villa, and had so much to say, that Hulda scarcely had time to reply. There was, however, something odd in his conduct towards her; it was greatly changed. He seemed to be trying to emulate Michael's flippant manner, and to bear himself as if he had established a kind of claim upon Hulda. She said nothing, but she endeavoured to show him, by her grave air of reserve, how distasteful such behaviour was to her.

Philibert laughed at her serious face. "In the name of all that is sacred, fairest Hulda," he cried, "are you never going to resign your rôle? Why make us all miserable for nothing? Must one positively be either a prince or a baron to find favour with you?"

Hulda uttered a cry of absolute terror; for now she knew the cause of Philibert's changed demeanour; but he interpreted her cry according to his own ideas.

"You cannot complain of me," he said. "I have never tried to learn anything with regard to you that you wished to conceal, and I certainly should never adore you the less because in times past, before I knew you, you were perhaps scarcely so strict in your watch over your heart as at present. The only thing——"

Hulda could no longer contain herself, and with glowing cheeks she interrupted him, while her eyes filled with angry tears. "The only thing that I have to say to you is, that I think it most insulting that you should believe the words of a strange man, who was dismissed from the service of Prince Severin because he conducted himself improperly towards me, sooner than mine, although you know me well, and although no one can with truth reproach me with my conduct at any period of my life."

She arose and went into the next room. He was about to follow her, but paused, reflecting that he certainly had made a false step in acting upon information which might not after all be correct. Still, he was not prepared to admit that he had insulted Hulda. He was always true to his character of selfish egotism, and was ready now to ascribe her indignation to his own folly in having spoiled her by the great respect and forbearance that he had always shown her. He thought he knew how to tame her without allowing this day's interview to be productive of unpleasant consequences.

He took out a card from his letter-case, wrote upon it Faust's words,—

> "How short and sharp of speech was she!
> Why, 'twas a real ecstasy,"

added an "unchangeably yours" above his name, and, after placing it where it must meet Hulda's eye immediately upon her return, left the house.

She entered the room as soon as he left it, saw the card, read it, and tore it into pieces.

This was the pain she could not away with; this it was that made the position which she occupied at times unendurable to her. Although her soul and her life were both pure, men regarded this purity as only a matter of whim, and to be laid aside at some time of her career. An actress was looked upon as game, sooner or later to fall a prey to the successful huntsman, and men permitted themselves to think and speak of her in a way that would be an insult to other women.

What to her were the applause and admiration of an audience, although the expression of them made her heart throb exultingly, if in the retirement of her home she was not safe from insult to her moral sense and maidenly dignity? What pleasure could she take in the flowers thrown to her by women as a return for the delight her acting had afforded them, while she felt herself shut out like a pariah from social intercourse with them? The admiration that was yielded to the artist was no consolation for the want of the respect that should be paid to the woman. She could not endure the consciousness that she was continually in danger of attack; it humiliated her in her own eyes to be obliged to exculpate, to defend herself. And this very afternoon, when she had hoped to be absorbed by her art, when "Faust" was to be played, the burden of her existence seemed heavier than ever.

The weather was charming as she drove to the theatre, where the spacious vestibule was already thronged with people. As she passed, Hulda was recognized by many; she was pointed at and stared at, so that she was glad to enter the long corridor that led behind the scenes. On her way to her dressing-room she met Michael and Lelio, both already dressed. She had hitherto seen Lelio only in youthful costumes; in the dress of Faust, for the first act, he seemed like a stranger, and as such he now conducted himself towards her. He did not offer her his hand, he refrained from his usual friendly greeting. She could not understand his behaviour, and, since he had not kept his appointment with her in the morning, she asked, "Are you not well, Lelio? Has anything happened?"

He replied in the affirmative. She begged him to tell her what had befallen him. He made an evasive reply, and she thought she saw an unpleasant smile upon Michael's face. She could not tell, however, whether it was the effect of her question or of the paint which, in the most masterly manner, he had employed for Mephistopheles. He soon solved her doubt.

"You see now, fair lady," he said, as Lelio walked away, "that every one is not so patient as your humble servant; not every one will bear with your caprices as does your old friend, who forgot everything as soon as he saw you. Everything, Hulda! everything! To-night we shall enjoy together a fine revenge. To-night you will sing '*Io trionfo!*' with me."

"I do not understand you," said Hulda, the terror that she always felt in this man's presence stealing over her.

"Have patience, and you will see!" he said, bowing with the sneer that suited his rôle, and limping away. She went to dress. The overture was nearly finished, and after it the first act passed brilliantly.

The magnificent rendering of Mephisto, never exaggerated, always sustained, not only held the audience entranced, but also delighted the other actors. Hulda's fancy was as it were spellbound by it. She seemed to see Michael for the first time in his own character, as if until now he had always been disguised, and the shudder with which she should dramatically have regarded him was genuine.

At last the curtain rose for the second act, and Gretchen issued from the church on the right of the stage, and advanced to cross the scene, her head bent, her prayer-book in her hand. Lelio, as Faust, hastily approached; she raised her eyes at his address, and saw just above her, in the proscenium-box, Clarissa and Prince Severin.

This, then, was what Michael had meant.

A tremor ran through her limbs, a burning blush suffused her neck and cheeks; she could hardly lift her eyes; the few words that she had to utter were spoken with the shrinking timidity of a child, and she did not recover herself until she had left the stage and no longer felt the eyes of the prince and Clarissa's glass directed towards her.

The audience found the first encounter of Gretchen and Faust admirable; it was the unanimous opinion that maidenly terror had never been so naturally expressed before. It augured well for Hulda's success in her new rôle.

How did she play it? She could not tell, for her heart was full to breaking. She could scarcely recover herself amid the memories that came surging over her. Intense longing to see Emanuel only once more, to hear him speak one word, overpowered her as she saw Clarissa; and she had loved Clarissa herself so dearly. Clarissa had been as kind as a sister to her. What must she think when she saw her here with Michael? How could she comprehend that Hulda had left her home to become an actress?

There was no need to feign the longing and the woe in the song at the spinning-wheel. She could hardly sufficiently restrain the emotion that filled her eyes with tears, and never had she felt so painfully, so intensely, how she had belonged to Emanuel alone, how he had been all the world to her, and how passionately she still loved him and him only, as when, in the recklessness of despair, throwing aside all maiden shame, she sang the last two verses from her very soul:

"My bosom yearns
  For him alone;
Ah, dared I clasp him
  And hold and own,

And kiss his mouth
  To heart's desire,
And on his kisses
  At last expire."*

A storm of enthusiasm greeted her at the close. The prince leaned far over the front of the box and applauded vigorously. He evidently wished to attract Hulda's attention. Clarissa dried her tears, and as Hulda looked up at her she thought she saw in the fine eyes—eyes that were so like Emanuel's—a glance of kindly recognition.

Hulda clasped her hands upon her breast as she curtsied to the audience when she was called before the curtain; but she thought only of Clarissa. She would have given all the fame in the world to have thrown herself only once into the princess's arms as the pastor's Hulda.

The tremendous force of the poem took complete possession of her during the rest of the play. She forgot herself utterly. Only when the fiend whispered in her ear as she knelt praying before the altar did her own longing stir within her, but to be overborne by the mighty stream of poetry that carried her through the drama upon its waves.

When the curtain fell at the close of the evening, the actors in the principal parts were loudly called for; and when Hulda appeared, conducted by Michael and Lelio, the prince's "Brava! brava!" repeated so often and with such enthusiasm gave the cue to the audience, who overwhelmed her with applause, creating her, as it were, the heroine of the evening.

Michael could scarcely contain his rage. For years he had looked forward to the day when he should verify his own words and cause his former master—the man who had so maltreated him—to regard him with admiration. To-day this gratification would, he thought, have been his, for Mephistopheles was the part in which he had won the most enthusiastic applause; but his hopes had been in vain. The growing enthusiasm of the mass had followed him from scene to scene; but the prince and Clarissa had been entirely unmoved, and at the last decisive moment the prince's dislike had snatched from him the triumph of which he felt certain, to bestow it upon a pretty face. He hated Hulda with a bitter hatred. He would

* Bayard Taylor's translation.

have liked to crush her under foot, and, scarcely moving his thin lips, he whispered, loud enough to be heard both by Hulda and Lelio, "What a faithful Celadon! He has not forgotten the good old times, or what the future may have in store for him."

"Odious!" exclaimed Hulda, as she withdrew behind the curtain. Her pleasure in the applause she had received was gone. Insulted, melancholy, at odds with herself, and wearied in mind and body, she turned from the scene of her triumph to the solitude of her rooms, to ponder sadly upon the days when she had helped the Countess Clarissa with her *tableaux vivants* and longed so childishly for the world in which she now lived. Ah, it was no paradise! There was neither rest nor peace to be found in it.

CHAPTER XXII.

THE princess had been so delighted by Hulda's beauty and talent that she would gladly have sought her out that very evening after the close of the performance. She reminded her husband how she had always maintained that Hulda was a most remarkable person. "If only," said she, "that disagreeable Michael had not been upon the same stage, I should have enjoyed this evening's entertainment more than any acting I have ever seen before. But it must be very difficult for the poor girl to have to play with Michael and be in constant intercourse with him."

The prince shrugged his shoulders. "You forget that Hulda is no longer the pastor's daughter who was for awhile beneath your mother's roof. She has been two years upon the stage, and the boards of a theatre are slippery ground for a woman's feet."

Clarissa indignantly repelled any idea that Hulda could be less lovely and true than she had known her.

"It may be," rejoined her husband, "that your confidence does not mislead you, but let us be cautious. It would be very unfortunate both for her and ourselves to excite hopes by advances on our part which we might afterwards regret."

His wife insisted, however, that no caution was necessary; she hoped she should see her the next day. Then she wondered whether Baron Emanuel had ever seen her upon the stage, what he had thought of her, and whether her art had consoled her for her lost love. "For," said she, "Hulda's love for our uncle was pure and fervent."

"Emanuel, too, loved her,—loved her very dearly; he made no concealment of it," the prince added, with the air of one alluding to what is long past and done with.

"It was all the more inexcusable on his part to give her up," cried Clarissa.

"You are romantic enough for a country pastor's daughter yourself, dear," said her husband, as supper was announced.

The landlord of the hotel waited upon them at supper, and trusted, with a profound bow, that their highnesses had enjoyed the performance at the theatre; adding that Herr Lippow was staying in the house, and that the great actor had mentioned that he had formerly been acquainted with his highness.

The prince, at these words, looked at his wife with a meaning smile that did not escape the host's observation, although the princess immediately questioned him as to whether he knew anything of Fräulein Vollmer.

"No more, your highness," the man replied, "than what is generally known about our actresses. She lives very retired, and is very prudent——"

The prince interrupted him. "Then no one knows anything to her disadvantage?"

"Nothing at all, your highness, since she came here," replied the host, with an evident emphasis upon the last words.

The prince noticed it. "What do you mean?" he asked.

The man looked from the prince to the princess. "No one knows exactly," he replied, "how the young lady came to go upon the stage, or where she comes from. There are all sorts of stories about that. Herr Lippow seems to have known her very well."

This was too much for the prince's sense of justice. "Herr Lippow," he said, very decidedly, "certainly knew Mademoiselle no better than did the princess and myself. We take a more than common interest in the young artist, because she is the daughter of a clergyman upon the princess's family estate and once belonged to her mother's household. Remind Herr

Lippow of this, and tell him plainly you heard it from me. Pray do not forget to do so."

With this an end was put to the conversation. Clarissa was grieved and annoyed. Her husband was all the more anxious to gratify her desire to see Hulda, and the next morning he left the hotel some time before his wife's hour for rising. In the hall, as he went out, he asked of the host where Hulda lodged. The man would have sent a servant to show him the way, but this service the prince declined; and Lelio, who happened to be just entering the hotel to keep an early appointment with Michael, saw the prince take his way to Frau Rosen's.

Immediately after Michael's first performance with Lelio and Hulda, he had proposed that they should together give a test performance in the royal capital, where he was at present engaged, and had written to make arrangements to that effect. Only upon the previous morning he had spoken of the great advantage that both Lelio and Hulda would enjoy in thus paving the way for a departure from the provincial town where they had been fettered for so long. But to-day he seemed to have changed his mind. He pretended to have found a letter awaiting his return from "Faust," in which the manager of the royal theatre refused to give Hulda an opening there, since he had once seen her play, and had been by no means impressed. "And, indeed," said Michael, "she is far too vain to be really effective with others. She is too much occupied with herself."

Lelio, who had played with her now for more than two years, and had never thought her vain or self-occupied upon the stage, stated his opinion of her; but Michael maintained that she played to the audience, and was always ready to coquette with the men in the proscenium-box.

"Why, you yourself must have seen last night how palpable her coquetry was with one of her earliest friends and patrons. Her eyes were so riveted upon Prince Severin that in the love-scenes you were almost ridiculous, making love to her ear and chin, while she was regarding the prince. And you and I were no more than her train-bearers when the prince saw fit to single her out for his special admiration, even in the presence of his wife, who long ago learned to put the best face upon his vagaries."

Lelio's nature was honest and true, and he was not naturally inclined to believe evil of others; but his vanity as an actor was his weak point, and he could not endure the idea of having stood like Hulda's train-bearer, while the prince lavished his applause upon her alone. He did not understand why he had not immediately seen through all Hulda's manœuvres to attract the prince's attention; and, more annoyed than he cared to show, he said, as if to himself, "He has just gone to see her."

"Who?" asked Michael.

"The prince, to see Hulda," Lelio explained. "He was asking the host where she lived as I passed the office."

"In order to make it seem as if he did not know," said Michael. "Or perhaps you really believe the prince's arrival an accident, just on the day when Hulda was to play Gretchen for the first time, and when he might be of use to her? Oh, she is a sly one! She always knew how to take precious good care of herself. We must be on our guard."

He said no more; but Lelio felt bitterly aggrieved and mortified.

He had thought well of Hulda, and had helped her when he could, but she had deceived him in every respect. He had been a tool in her hands, to be used for her own ends. This was more than the vanity of a man, and especially of an actor, could forgive. He had done with Hulda; he despised her.

Meanwhile, the prince had not found Hulda at home; but Beata had shown him to her room, where he had written a couple of lines to her, which he sealed and left upon her table.

When he returned to his hotel, the princess was awaiting him at the breakfast-table. He bade her guess where he had been so early, a riddle that she easily solved, thanking him for leaving Hulda an invitation to come to her during the course of the day.

"How did her rooms look?" Clarissa asked.

"So pleasant and so exquisitely neat that I kept looking round for Miss Kenney," replied the prince.

Clarissa declared that this was a very good sign, and he did not contradict her. "Nevertheless," he said, "one or two things betokened an unusual degree of luxury. Her writing-table was beautifully furnished, and in the adjoining room, the door of which stood open, there was such a toilet-table as never could have been procured with the salary paid by a provincial manager, while of course the prescribed parrot was not wanting, and I suppose the inevitable poodle had gone to walk with its mistress."

Clarissa laughingly scolded him for his suspicious nature; and, as they were not to proceed on their journey until late in the afternoon, he left her to visit one or two military friends in the town.

He had not been long gone when her servant brought her a wreath of cornflowers, saying that the lady who had brought them begged that her highness would allow her to see her.

"It is Hulda!" cried the princess, and instantly ordered that she should be admitted. As she entered, Clarissa, touched by the remembrance of former days, went to meet her, with both hands extended. Hulda stooped, as of old, to kiss her hand, but the princess prevented her, and pressed her lips upon her brow.

Then, as she saw how elegantly Hulda was dressed, and remembered what Severin had said about the luxury in her rooms, she grew embarrassed, and Hulda noticed it.

"I must entreat your highness's pardon for my intrusion," she said; "but when I saw you in the box last night I was so overcome by home-sickness that it left me no rest. Therefore I came out early this morning, and thought the cornflowers might plead for me."

"There was no need of that," cried the princess; "believe me, I had not forgotten you. We were delighted last evening to see what an artist you have become; and the prince went to your house this morning to ask you to come to me."

Hulda did not know this,—she had come of her own accord; and now that she felt the uncertainty in Clarissa's manner, she wondered how she had found courage to do so; for in Clarissa's presence the fidelity and devotion with which she still clung to the man who had forgotten her, oppressed her like some heavy weight. She could not conceal from herself that it was the hope of hearing something of Emanuel that had lured her hither, and this consciousness robbed her demeanour of that easy grace that had gradually become natural to her. She wished she had not come.

Her embarrassment infected Clarissa. They sat in silence for a few moments, and then the princess said, "You really enchanted us last evening; there is a great future before you. I trust you are happy in the profession you have chosen?"

Hulda easily read the thoughts of her noble questioner. "Yes," she replied, "I am proud of my profession, and the applause that you and the prince, your husband, accorded me last evening made me very happy for the time."

"For the time? Then you are not so always?" the princess asked.

"Who could say that she was always happy?" Hulda replied, with evident reserve.

"True, true," the princess assented, with a conventional sigh. "But," she added, prompted by a certainly pardonable curiosity, "how came you to leave your home, to break off your engagement with the pastor and go upon the stage?"

Hulda was chilled and saddened. She had hoped that Clarissa had really been fond of her, and she was not even informed as to the most superficial facts of her life. But she quietly replied, "Your highness is in error upon one point. I never was engaged to the pastor."

"No? I thought I heard that he wished to marry you, and that you were betrothed to him."

"He wished to marry me."

"And you refused him? Why? My mother has a great respect for him; she praises him highly."

"He deserves it all, and I myself esteem him greatly; but——"

"But?" the princess repeated.

"I had no heart to give him!" Hulda replied, firmly and gravely.

The tone in which she spoke these words, the blush that overspread her cheek, revealed to the princess the thoughtlessness and injustice of which she had been guilty with regard to her. Hulda now prepared to depart, feeling sadly that this meeting had not answered her expectations. A similar thought probably occurred to Clarissa.

"Are you going," she cried, "already?" And the affection that she really felt for Hulda asserted itself in spite of all other considerations. "Have you no more time for me? I so rejoiced at the idea of seeing you again, of thanking you for the pleasure you gave me last evening; and, more than all," she added, "I hoped to hear from you that you were happy. But it seems to me that you are not so content as my interest in you would have you. You do not look happy. Is there anything that distresses you? Tell me what it is, dear Hulda."

As she spoke, she took Hulda's hand and drew her down again upon the lounge beside her. The tone of her voice touched Hulda; she did not wish to appear ungrateful, and, collecting herself, she said, "I cannot explain to your highness how I came to go upon the stage; it would take more time than you have to give me, and I assure you I take delight in my art. But the world in which I am forced to live is very different from the one in which I grew up. I am a stranger in it, and I trust I shall always remain so. One may be a great artist, greater than I can ever hope to become, and yet be very lonely."

She paused, wondering how she could have said so much. Clarissa shook her pretty head thoughtfully. "The prince was right," she said, "when he told me that the path of a famous actress is not so brilliant as I had supposed it, but beset by dangers—and——" She did not finish her sentence, but added, hastily, "Now I am doubly glad to have seen you!"

Again she paused, and then, clasping Hulda's hand in both her own, said, "One need only look into your eyes, Hulda, to know that you have remained true to yourself. But will it always be so? It would give me great pain, should I ever see you again, to find that you had not been able to withstand the dazzling temptations that must inevitably assail you. I always thought well of you; I loved you, and hoped one day to have you with me."

She paused once more, for she remembered what had put a stop to these intentions and plans, and she was also struck by the contrast between Hulda's present position and the lot she had meant to provide for her. But fear lest Hulda should, as the princess phrased it in her own mind, go astray, conquered her confusion. "Do not think me intrusive, but did they not try to dissuade you from going upon the stage?"

"What good would it have done?" replied the artist. "All must follow the dictates of their own judgment in planning their own future."

"And have you never regretted the step that you took? Suppose you had deceived yourself as to your powers?"

"Then," said Hulda, and her glorious eyes looked full and clear into those of the princess, "no earthly consideration would have tempted me to remain upon the stage. 'A house divided against itself must fall.' I have relied upon myself and the powers with which God gifted me, and I shall never be——"

She interrupted herself suddenly, for she had almost uttered the words, "I shall never be unworthy of Emanuel's love," and arose again to take her departure.

Clarissa also arose. She felt Hulda's superiority, and it humiliated her; but her affection for Hulda and her good heart helped her to conquer the weakness that rebelled against such humiliation. She asked if Hulda would not await the prince's return.

Hulda took out her watch, and replied that she must go to take her part in the rehearsal of a comedy.

"A comedy, after our conversation? That must be very hard!" cried Clarissa.

"One becomes accustomed to forget one's self in one's work," Hulda rejoined, with a patient and gentle expression that made her, Clarissa thought, quite irresistible.

She took the light mantle from the lounge, where Hulda had laid it upon her entrance, and said, as she put it around her shoulders, "My mother will be rejoiced to hear from you; she, and all the rest of us, had such a warm friendship for your family."

Hulda asked after the countess. Clarissa replied that she was with the young count, who had had a son born to him, and that she hoped to see her when the prince and herself should return in the autumn from the visit they were about to make. She then accompanied her to the door, but upon its threshold she was suddenly overcome by an emotion of sympathy for the young artist; she had, as it were, a revelation of all that Hulda had suffered and endured, and, turning to her, she threw her arms around her and clasped her to her heart.

"Dear Hulda!" she cried, "farewell, and, whatever may happen to you, remember how I have learned to-day to love and value you, and that in me you have a faithful friend. Think of me often!"

They were both greatly moved, and embraced and kissed each other. Then Hulda went to her work, and the princess stood at the window, looking after her.

"What a wife she would have been for Emanuel!" she thought, and the prince, when he returned, found her quite carried away by her enthusiasm for the young artist.

CHAPTER XXIII.

THE prince and Clarissa had never before visited Castle Falkenhorst, whither they were now bound; nor had they seen Baron Emanuel since the news of the severe illness of the prince's father had occasioned their sudden departure from the countess's castle.

Years had passed since then, but from the time of his rupture with Konradine Emanuel had never left his ancestral home, except to attend to business matters in the provincial capital.

He had resisted all efforts upon the part of his relatives to lure him thence, and had found in the labour and duties of his position a peace of mind which was evident in his letters, and which went far to reconcile those who loved him to the solitude of his life.

Since the birth of the young count's first son the countess had become completely absorbed in him, and the idea of uniting two names and two inheritances in his small person was fast taking possession of her. She no longer troubled herself with regard to her brother's future. She lived almost entirely in her son's family, and even her correspondence with Emanuel and with her daughter and son-in-law was greatly interrupted by the care and attention she bestowed upon her young grandson.

Emanuel had driven to the river-bank to receive his guests; he was delighted to show to the prince, who was much interested in the management and improvement of his own estates, the manifold alterations and improvements that had been made at Falkenhorst since he had inherited it.

Roads, bridges, hedges, and the cottages of the labourers, as well as the labourers themselves, had all undergone great changes. Clarissa declared that she never should have recognized the castle or the surrounding grounds from the pictures of it which she had seen, and which, greatly to her mother's displeasure, she had found extremely gloomy and unattractive. "Indeed, it is a blessing, my dear uncle," she said, "that you have been able to make the old place look so cheerful and home-like."

Emanuel was in the best of spirits, and the old confidential intercourse was soon established between the uncle and niece. One morning at breakfast the conversation turned upon the many privations that necessarily resulted from a life in the country. The two men in their walk afterwards pursued the same theme, and shortly came to speak of the day and night that the prince and Clarissa had passed in the old commercial town which was Hulda's present home.

The prince asked whether his wife had told her uncle of their late theatrical experience, and when Emanuel replied in the negative, went on to say, "Do you remember my valet, the man whom I sent off from my mother-in-law's castle? He has become an actor, and has grown quite famous. He was born for the stage. You must have seen his name, Lippow, in the papers. I really could hardly help laughing when our host informed us, upon our arrival at his hotel, that we should have an opportunity of seeing the celebrated Lippow that evening as Mephisto. Of course we availed ourselves of it."

"And what did you think of him?" asked Emanuel.

"Admirable! an admirable actor!" replied the prince. "I asked myself continually how such a scoundrel could ever become so finished an artist."

He said nothing more, and Emanuel walked on undecided for awhile; then suddenly, with an effort, he said, "I suppose you must have seen Hulda also? She is greatly praised. Is she a good actress?"

"More than that!" replied the prince. "Some of her tones and gestures are absolutely irresistible. Clarissa was so touched by her acting that she insisted upon seeing her in private and talking with her. I wonder that she has not told you of it. She always had a great affection for Hulda,—as we all had.

She sent her a little remembrance when we left. Let her tell you about it herself."

A servant here approached to announce the arrival of Herr von Barnefeld, not, however, before Emanuel had been made aware how impossible it was that he should speak of Hulda himself, or hear her spoken of, with indifference, and how precious, he might almost say sacred, her memory was to him.

CHAPTER XXIV.

THE most delightful weather prevailed at Falkenhorst during the visit of Emanuel's guests; the days passed quickly in the enjoyment of a companionship from which the baron had been so long debarred; and when the last afternoon of the prince's stay arrived, it found the guests as unwilling to depart as the host was to speed the parting. Severin rode over to pay a farewell visit to the Von Barnefelds, whose society he had greatly enjoyed during his stay, and Clarissa and Emanuel betook themselves to the shelter of the castle, and the embrasure of one of its windows, to avoid a passing shower, that had interfered with their drive. As they sat looking over the wide expanse of field and fell, Clarissa suddenly laid her hand upon Emanuel's and said, "As I look abroad from this window, and then around me in this grand old castle, and reflect that you are alone here in your woods and fields, alone in this huge home,—even in winter,—this immense estate seems to me more like a burden than a pleasure to you."

Emanuel looked at her with a smile. "You are the first," he said, "who has ever suspected that such a large estate might not be a pleasure to me, and therefore I do not hesitate to confess to you that I looked forward with no satisfaction to its possession. At the time of my brother's death, however, when I hoped to found a happy home here for Konradine and myself, I became interested in the place; and," he added, quietly, after a short pause, "when that expectation was not fulfilled, the work I found to do here was a great consolation. There was full occupation for my time and thoughts in the improvement of the condition of those about me, who looked to me as their lord and master."

"And you are contented, then?" asked the young princess, looking affectionately up into his face, and noticing as she looked the few white threads among his dark curls. "You are still young, Emanuel, younger than Severin. Do you never think now of marrying?"

"The experiences that I have had," he replied, "are not encouraging."

"Oh," cried Clarissa, "I do not mean to urge you, my dear uncle, as my mother used to do. You and Konradine were not suited to each other. You never loved her——"

"And when I did love," he interrupted her, "loved with intensity, and was loved in return with a rare affection, I was fettered by this entailed estate, and resigned for its sake a happiness that can never be mine again, invoking upon myself, in my deluded folly, the old curse, from which love would have delivered me."

He stood up. Clarissa was grieved; she had not meant to pain her uncle by awakening such memories within him. She arose also, and took his arm.

"Forgive me!" she said, gently.

"What is there to forgive?" he replied; then, pressing her hand, he added, "We will not speak of that! But I hear from the prince that you saw Hulda upon the stage, and in your rooms. Tell me all about it, my child, and just how it happened. I shall so like to hear you admire her. How did you find her? and is she happy? Is she still as lovely and as gentle as in those dear old days?"

He sat down, and drew Clarissa beside him. She nestled close to his side, and in the darkening twilight told him of her whom he loved, told him all that he wished to hear.

She kept nothing from him; neither the surprise that it had been to her to see Hulda upon the stage, nor the delight she had taken in the artist. She told him how the prince had warned her against seeking Hulda out, how he had jested about the arrangement of her rooms, and that what he said had caused a certain mistrust of her in her own mind. Then came the account of the interview, and the love and respect it had awakened for Hulda, from whom she had parted affectionately and sadly.

As she spoke, she warmed with her theme. Emanuel did not once interrupt her. Sometimes she thought that the hand she held clasped in hers trembled, but it had grown too dark for her to see his features distinctly. When she had finished, he arose.

"And I imagined her entirely absorbed in her profession, which had a charm for her in her earliest years. I thought of her as surrounded by admiration and intoxicated with applause. I wished to think her happy," he said.

Clarissa said she thought her happy, so far as her profession was concerned.

"If she is not entirely at peace with herself, she cannot be happy," said Emanuel.

"When she had gone from me," said Clarissa, "I thought I had not shown her plainly enough how I prized her, and, because I could do nothing for her and had nothing of any value with me, I sent her a couple of lines and a little crucifix that I had worn from childhood and that she used to admire greatly when she was with us in the castle."

"The little gold crucifix with the cherubs' heads?" asked Emanuel.

"Yes," said Clarissa, in some embarrassment; "the crucifix of the Baroness Erdmuth. I ought not, perhaps, to have given it away, and I should be sorry to have my mother know it. But I really had nothing else at hand just then; and as, according to the family legend, it preserves its wearer from danger, I thought Hulda might need it more than I. I am sure she was pleased with it. Do not be vexed about it; it was a sudden impulse."

"I?" cried Emanuel. "I shall always be grateful to you, Clarissa, for sending it." He kissed her hand and said no more.

The servants soon after brought in lights, and, after some talk upon other matters, Clarissa said, "When we were speaking just now of the little crucifix, I remembered that all the old silver, and many memorials of our ancestors, of which my mother has often spoken, are here in the castle. Will you not show them to me before I leave Falkenhorst?"

Emanuel was quite ready to do so. He sent for the castellan, who had had the care of these relics now for two generations, and before long the old man, with a solemnity that would have befitted some grand state ceremony, arranged in due order upon the table before the young princess heavy old silver tankards, artistically wrought silver urns, silver table-furniture, mighty silver candlesticks, and a variety of small boxes decorated with silver nails.

The silver plate was magnificent, but the contents of the boxes were comparatively worthless,—consisting of antique ornaments of no intrinsic value; to each of them, however, some family legend or tale was attached, with all of which Emanuel was familiar, to Clarissa's great delight, who listened eagerly to what he had to tell her of her ancient family. She was just replacing the articles in their several caskets, when the old castellan brought from a cabinet near by a small wallet of faded red velvet tied about with a golden cord.

"Never mind that," said Emanuel, when he saw it; but his exclamation aroused Clarissa's curiosity. She asked what the little bag contained, and was told that it was the old manuscript concerning the elf-king and the curse which he had called down upon the House of Falkenhorst.

The princess wanted to see it, and her uncle untied the golden cord, carefully opened the old wallet, and took thence a leather cover containing a few leaves of yellow parchment, upon which the legend, with every detail, was written, in a cramped, stiff handwriting.

Clarissa found it quite impossible to decipher the antique characters, and, as she expressed a wish to hear it, Emanuel undertook to read it to her. As he slowly and distinctly pronounced at its close the elf-king's terrible curse, which had so strangely rested upon the Falkenhorsts for centuries, until in Emanuel's person the race was nigh to extinction, Clarissa could not suppress a shudder.

The old castle, the old castellan, the old relics, even her uncle and her own presence in this castle, seemed phantom-like and weird to her, and, stretching out her hand for the parchment, she cried, "But that is terrible! How could so evil a document be preserved for centuries?" And, as she thought of her own two lovely boys, she added, "If there were any such legend concerning the fate of our house, I would destroy it, that its dark predictions might never cast a gloom over my children's life."

Emanuel smiled. "You would destroy," he said, "what lives from parent to child in the mouths of the people? Even were it possible, it would not, I think, be desirable. Is not the idea of being delivered from a curse by youth and love beautiful and poetical?"

"Uncle," she asked, suddenly, "did Hulda know of this old legend?"

"Yes," he replied, "she knew it." And he arose to put the red wallet back in its cabinet. Clarissa went with him. In the corner of the shelf there was a little box, of comparatively modern form. Without asking permission, she opened it; within lay a golden ring with a blue stone, and on the inner side she read, "Thee and me shall no one sever."

She looked at Emanuel, but did not venture to ask who had worn the ring, which was silently laid in the box again and put back in its corner. Just then the prince came in from his ride.

He examined the articles upon the table, expatiated upon the beautiful model of the silver, and, taking up and weighing in his hand one of the huge tankards, said, "What magnificent use the Von Barnefelds would make of the value of this!"

Clarissa laughed. "Never let my mother hear you say such a thing!" she cried. "When I am with you and Emanuel I feel that I am in red republican society; nothing is sacred in your eyes."

"But we would never destroy any written documents or family records," said Emanuel. "Your mother, however, need not be afraid. When your brother comes into possession of Falkenhorst he shall find all the old family relics safe and sound, and in their place——"

Clarissa and the prince would not listen to such words, and Emanuel was silenced.

Meanwhile the castellan was putting away all the antique magnificence. When he came to close the little cabinet in which was the ring with the blue stone and the inscription, Clarissa noticed that Emanuel took it from its box and put it upon his finger.

CHAPTER XXV.

After Lippow's departure there was a lull in theatrical activity for awhile. Both actors and public felt the reaction from the unwonted enthusiasm that had prevailed. To Hulda this period of comparative repose was unspeakably refreshing. To a certain degree she was mistress of her time, and could ponder to her heart's content upon her interview with the young princess, and the warmth and tenderness that Clarissa had shown her at its close. The whole day, after seeing her friend, had seemed transfigured; and in the evening, when she returned to her rooms from the theatre, she had found a little packet awaiting her, which Beata said had been left for her, without any message, by a servant of Prince Severin's.

Hulda instantly recognized the handwriting on the cover; within she found a little crucifix, and two written lines·

> "Be to yourself forever true;
> Know, for the rest, God cares for you!"

The writer had signed these lines with her Christian name, and Hulda read them with tears in her eyes, as she pressed the crucifix to her lips. She had seen it that very morning upon Clarissa's neck. She had recognized it then, and remembered how in other times, she had known that it was regarded as a kind of amulet, never leaving the neck of its possessor day or night, and she understood the tenderness that had suggested sending her this token, so prized as a family relic.

She was no longer alone; she could turn in memory to the friend whom she had so loved, and when she longed for sympathy could recall the name of a pure and spotless woman, whose life had never been touched by the taint of calumny that had spared neither Feodora nor Gabrielle.

What were the triumphs won by those women, compared with the peace Hulda saw in Clarissa's eyes? And was not the princess's confidence in her, her affection for her, worth more than all the applause she had ever received upon the path which, before she knew how full of thorns it was, she had chosen to tread?

After this short lull of leisure, thorns there were in abundance. Hochbrecht questioned her one day as to her relations with Gabrielle; and when Hulda told him the truth, with an indignant repudiation of any complicity in the false reports that had been circulated, the critic smiled contemptuously, while he gave her to understand that such unconsciousness as she pretended to was quite incredible, and that her indignation seemed to him the result of the detection of her very clever ruse.

She felt the insult in his looks and tones, and in her outraged dignity told him that her doors would be closed against him in future. Such treatment from an actress, and from one, too, for whom he had done such good service, was new in his experience. He jested with Philibert about this fall from Hulda's favour only because he had credited her with a clever ruse, and Philibert listened willingly, after his own repulse and Hulda's consequent refusal to receive his visits.

"We have spoiled her for the sake of her beauty," said he. "We have all been imposed upon by her air of innocence. The coy divinity must be brought to her senses, and there are ways and means to do so. Had it not been for the enthusiasm of Prince Severin at the representation of 'Faust,' she would have found, although she certainly did play admirably, that friends who are not appreciated may grow cold."

Hochbrecht was quite of his opinion. "A couple of scenes from the 'Taming of the Shrew' might be of service to this Kate," he said, with a laugh; and the friends consulted upon the "ways and means" that Philibert had alluded to.

But Hulda was troubled and anxious with regard to the alteration in Lelio's manner towards her. She had grown much attached to him, and every day made his estrangement from her more evident and painful. At last she asked him to appoint a time to visit her, for she had much to tell him. He coldly replied that it would be impossible for him to do so during the next few days, and she knew that he was shortly to leave town.

This took place one morning at rehearsal, and, as she pondered it at home, she could not bear the thought of losing the friendship of the man whom during more than two years she had found so honest and true.

She sat down at her writing-table. "What have I done to

you, my friend," she wrote, "that you turn from me? Wherein have I deserved that you should entertain an unfavourable opinion of me? And you evidently do so without giving me a chance to repel any slander which may have reached your ears. We all have a right to know of what we are accused. I cannot let the day pass without doing what I can to retain a friend whom I thought so loyal. I depend upon your coming to me."

She had hoped this would bring him to her instantly; but it was late in the afternoon before he made his appearance.

"I hesitated to come to you," he said, "because I would have spared both you and myself a conversation which cannot but be distressing. You know, Hulda, how much I prized you, how I delighted in the relation between us, which was that of the purest friendship, and how I relied upon your truth and honour, more even than upon my own——"

"And what has altered all this?" Hulda interrupted him. "Do you trust me no longer? What have I done to put an end to your faith in me?"

He had seated himself upon the lounge; he leaned his head thoughtfully upon his hand and made her no direct reply. "I do not blame you," he began, after a few moments. "I am no moralist; I have seen much of the world and of every form of passion, and I know well how easy it is for the wealthy and the noble in rank to entangle in their snares youth and inexperience."

"But what has this to do with it?" interrupted Hulda. "Why do you say this to me? What does this preface mean?"

He paused, and looked her sternly in the face. "But what," he continued, "I cannot forgive, what makes me turn from you with disgust, is your daring deceit, your hypocritical display of purity and innocence; this seems to me so——"

"Lelio," she cried, "what do you mean? Whom have I deceived? Who dares to accuse me of hypocrisy? If Lippow has done this, it is he who is the deceiver and hypocrite. You have done me a terrible injustice if you have listened to the words of that man."

"I say nothing," he went on, "of your allowing me to believe that Gabrielle was your mother——"

"What? Have I not repeatedly told you of my parents and of my poor mother's terrible fate?"

"You have; but you never contradicted the report that has been in circulation ever since you came here——"

"Because I never knew of it; because even now I cannot understand how it originated."

"And yet it might do Gabrielle even now a great deal of harm," said Lelio. "But this is not all. Why did you tell me of your stay in the countess's castle, of your relation to Baron Emanuel and to Prince Severin, if you could not tell me the truth with regard to them? It is this delight that you have taken in deceit, this determination to pursue the devious ways of falsehood, because you thought there was no one who could contradict you,—this playing with the danger of leading us all astray,—that has destroyed all my confidence in you; not that those men took advantage of your youth and inexperience. Heaven knows we are none of us angels. Gabrielle was no saint, nor was Feodora, but they were frank and open."

Hulda had risen; her agitation had given place to an absolute composure. "You have gone too far, Lelio," she said, firmly. "There are accusations which a friend cannot utter without making further friendship with him impossible, and against which it would be a disgrace to defend one's self. You have listened to Michael Lippow, and believed him and not me. I can do nothing but be silent and regret that I sought this interview."

Lelio had also arisen, and his sensations were by no means to be envied. He had been much attached to Hulda; he had ranked her far higher than any other woman whom he had ever known upon the stage, and her present virtuous indignation, her composure, the pure and womanly expression of her whole bearing, touched his conscience. He began to see that he had gone too far, that he had done wrong in heeding the slander that a stranger had poured into his ears. But he was not magnanimous enough to confess the wrong that he had done, without an effort to make her at least his involuntary accomplice. He said, gloomily, "If you had but mentioned to me at any time that you knew Lippow!"

"How was I to know that this Lippow was the prince's valet? He circulated all sorts of fables with regard to his antecedents, and the newspapers were full of them. And what was there to induce me to speak to you of a man whom I trusted I should be able to forget?"

To this Lelio replied only by silence; he felt that he was dismissed, but could not make up his mind to go. He saw the weariness in her looks, and it touched him more than her words.

"I cannot leave you thus!" he at last exclaimed. She did not answer. He then began to reveal the web of slander that Michael had woven around her, and, distasteful as it was to her to do so, she involuntarily defended herself.

Thus they gradually came nearer to each other again, and at last felt that they were reconciled. Lelio proposed to accompany her in a walk, and she accepted his escort. They walked along as usual to all outward seeming; but Hulda had a sense of aloofness from him. The old relationship was gone.

Upon their return, at Hulda's door Lelio held out his hand. "Blot these last days and hours from your memory," he begged, "and do not think ill of me. We men are not worth much; but it is the fault of you women if we do not think highly enough of you."

"It may well be so upon the stage," said Hulda.

"The world is pretty much the same everywhere," he replied. "It is no Paradise."

"But there are spheres where one breathes 'a purer ether, a sublimer air,'" she insisted.

"You are thinking of the lovely princess and of the crucifix," he made answer; "but you do not know all that goes on in those higher regions."

They made arrangements for the next rehearsal, and parted. They were to play together only twice more, and then Lelio was to take a six weeks' vacation, during which he was to play for a few nights in the capital. Neither was sorry that the time of separation was so near.

CHAPTER XXVI.

A NEW play-house, bidding fair to rival the royal theatre, had been lately opened by private subscription in the capital of the kingdom, and during his stay there, Lelio, anxious to do all in his power to atone for his injustice towards Hulda, had so spoken of her to the management as to strengthen them in their desire to secure her services at the close of the year, when her contract with Holm should have expired.

They opened a correspondence with her for this purpose; but suddenly, to her great surprise, the negotiation was broken off. Lelio's letter apprising her of this unwelcome news was in her hand when Beata announced Fräulein Delmar. This was so uncommon an event that Hulda was startled, aware that a visit from Fräulein Delmar boded her no good. Her visitor had not been long with her before she expressed her compassion for Hulda's solitary condition, with no friend at hand to counsel or sympathize with her.

Hulda replied that a faithful friend was undeniably a great blessing; but the ambiguous smile upon Fräulein Delmar's face perplexed and annoyed her. "I have pitied you from my very heart," the lady continued, taking Hulda's hand in hers; "for you have none of Feodora's cold, calculating nature, and Philibert, too, is not like Van der Vlies."

"I do not understand what your remark points at," said Hulda, hastily.

"Why, do you not know," replied Fräulein Delmar, "that it is Philibert who has put a stop to your being engaged at the new theatre?"

Hulda started. She had said nothing to any one concerning her affairs or hopes, and yet others knew more about them than she.

"Philibert," the other continued, "does not deny it; in fact, he tells it to everybody who will listen. The proprietor of the new theatre is, as you know, his intimate friend. He asked Philibert about you, and he said he was obliged to tell him that you did not improve, that you were monotonous, and

Heaven knows what else. He promised to let him know if you really made any progress in your art; he would watch you closely, and would speak to you upon the subject."

Hulda had grown pale with terror and irritation. "He will find it difficult to do that," she said, "as he is no longer admitted when he comes here."

Fräulein Delmar looked at her inquiringly. "You have refused to admit him?" she repeated, as though hardly able to believe her ears.

"Yes, once for all. You need not suppress the fact, but tell it rather to all who will listen," was the reply.

Fräulein Delmar shook her head. "How I pity you! how much I pity you!" she said. "A man who seemed to adore you. But they are all alike."

Then, as no reply was made to her expressions of pity, she arose, and, laying her hand upon Hulda's shoulder, said, "But it will pass over. You must not take it so to heart. You are young. You were inexperienced,—we were all so once,—you were deceived in him."

"No!" cried Hulda. "No! I was never deceived in him, not for one moment, since the first evening that I met him at Feodora's farewell supper. No! he was deceived in me, and that he could be so weighs now upon my conscience as if it were my fault."

"How excitable, how violent you are!" said Fräulein Delmar, as she rose to take her leave. "Believe me, you ought to take things more coolly. Although you have not known it, I have always wished you well, and if I can be of service to you, pray call upon me."

Hulda thanked her, and accompanied her to the door, scarcely able to collect her thoughts. She had long known that the ground beneath her feet was unsafe, and that those around her were not to be relied upon, and were actuated but too often by the meanest motives. But now she could not tell what their hostility contemplated; she was, as it were, feeling her way in the dark. She longed to leave this theatrical world, which had looked so bright in the distance, and began really to repent that she had ever become an actress.

A few nights afterwards she was to play "Emilia." It had always been a favourite part with her; it was the one in which she had made her *début.* She was glad to find so good a house when the curtain rose, and her first entrance and exit were followed by enthusiastic applause, especially from the boxes of the provincial nobility. Suddenly a hiss was heard from the pit; the boxes, irritated, applauded more loudly; the galleries sided with the pit, and a wild confusion arose in the house, which was but slowly reduced to order again. Hulda was utterly disconcerted.

"You may thank Philibert for this," said Fräulein Delmar, with a hypocritical expression of sympathy. Hulda had just said as much to herself.

How she contrived to go through the rest of the drama, how she endured the renewed outbreak of applause and hisses, the boxes and stalls greeting her efforts with the warmest enthusiasm, she could not herself have told as she threw herself exhausted upon her couch, after her return home.

Fortunately, she fell into a profound slumber. It was long since she had slept so soundly and so dreamlessly. The broad sunlight was peeping through her curtains when she opened her eyes and recollected, with a shudder, the occurrences of the previous evening. She wondered, as she looked in her mirror, that shame and terror had not left their traces on her countenance. On her table lay the part of "Marie," in Goethe's "Clavigo." She had always wished to play it, and it was now to be produced here for the first time in many years.

She sat down and read it through, but she could not fix her thoughts upon it; she did not know what she was reading. Suddenly she remembered that the manager had told her on the previous evening that the disturbance had been all owing to herself, and that he must speak with her. What had she done? In what had she failed? What could he wish?

She was still pondering these questions when, at an early hour, the manager made his appearance.

His air was very friendly, and he began immediately. "I was obliged, my dear Fräulein Vollmer, to come myself, as you see, to inquire after you. It was a little lively in the theatre last evening, and I have noticed that your nerves are easily affected. It takes very little to agitate you."

"I should suppose," replied Hulda, "that what occurred last evening would have affected any nerves. I certainly have not yet recovered my composure."

"You take the affair too seriously, my dear child, far too

seriously. Don't you know that that little skirmish will be of the greatest advantage to you? There is a tremendous party in your favour, and upon your next appearance the house will be crowded from pit to gallery."

"I was about to beg you to relieve me from duty for a few days. I must recover my self-possession, I must conquer myself, for I confess to you that I feel entirely unable to face, the day after to-morrow, the public whose hisses still ring in my ears. I must try to forget them."

"What can you be thinking of, my dear Fräulein Vollmer? Why do you listen to the hisses, and not rather to the stentorian bravas of our country nobles, who quite conquered the few hissers, whose motives, of course, you divine? Let me tell you a secret from my experience of the stage, which may be useful off it also: we must listen only to what we wish to hear, and never heed what can hurt us."

"That I shall never learn!" cried Hulda. "What good result can ever ensue from self-deception?"

The manager smiled. "My dear child, the good result is that it deceives others. For example, if you send to-day for little Doctor Berthold, who writes the criticisms for our daily paper and is the theatrical correspondent of several others, and lament over the events of last evening, he will believe that you made a terrible *fiasco;* but if, when he comes, you expatiate upon the delight which the zeal and enthusiasm of your friends afforded you, and their victory over the hired clique which opposed you, he will take his tone entirely from you, and spread your fame abroad."

"I shall do neither!" said Hulda, contemptuously. "I have never requested his visits, and certainly shall not do so now."

"You are wrong, my child, very wrong. Your noble enthusiasts, your rich *dilettanti*, like the doctor and Hochbrecht, will do you no good here. Their judgment is capital, their articles are sure to be read, but they are not for the masses; they will never make a reputation. Little Berthold did more for you than you seem to know anything about, while Philibert sprinkled his writing with golden sand. You will have to do that yourself now, unless indeed you make it up with Philibert. He is a man of great wealth, a man——"

Hulda arose. "Herr Holm," she said, "I must beg you to

say no more. No one has a right to criticise my management of my private affairs; there I must be allowed to judge for myself."

The manager also stood up. He was naturally quick-tempered, and his manner was offensive, although he tried to control himself.

"Oh, I have no idea," he said, "of interfering in your private affairs; only, mademoiselle, you must arrange your private affairs with discretion, so that they shall not interfere with my interests. It is not usual to publish abroad the fact that one is tired of a worthy friend and admirer. It is scarcely the thing to close one's doors upon men of standing and position; and if one has been imprudent enough to do so, it would be best not to inform a good friend of the fact, that she may tell it to whoever will listen. But this is your private affair; it is nothing to me."

She would have interrupted him, for she suddenly understood the whole matter, but he gave her no chance to do so.

"I have done, mademoiselle!" he said. "I thought it my duty to warn you. You think there is no need to heed my warning; you have a right to do as you please. But you must insure me the success of Mirandolena, which you will play on the evening of the day after to-morrow; and I hope you will at least have the prudence to receive courteously the young Von Brinkens, who intend to visit you to-day. With such principles as yours, you ought not to have gone upon the stage. We actors are no saints. The theatre is not a nunnery, and the theatre-going public does not know how to treat nuns."

He said the last words in a jesting tone, for he really would have been sorry to offend Hulda, whose talent he knew how to prize. But this very jest wounded her deeply. It capped the climax of all the degrading experiences with which she had been forced to struggle; it robbed her of words and of her self-possession.

The manager noticed this, and would gladly have recalled his jest. He told her she must not take it too seriously; that he had meant well by his advice, and that she must tell him that she was not angry with him.

"Why should I be?" she rejoined, with a frigid inclination. "You have simply given utterance to your view of the position of an actress before the public; you have a perfect right to do so, since I am in your pay. And perhaps it is best that you should do so."

He expressed his repentance, and said several flattering things to her; but, as she paid him very little heed, he took his leave, observing that he hoped she would soon recover from her little attack of temper.

As the door closed behind him, Hulda sank into a seat and burst into tears. They brought her some relief.

When she began to recover herself, the idea of leaving the stage—an idea that had lately often presented itself to her mind—again occurred to her. But it was not easy to decide to do so, for she loved her profession. She had quaffed, full and free, the delight of awakening by her power an echo of inspiration in the hearts of an audience. She had looked forward hopefully to the future.

And if she left the stage, what other calling was there for her, poor and solitary as she was?

She thought of the princess, and of the aid that she had promised her. She knew that Clarissa would be glad to help her to carry out such a resolution. But Clarissa was Emanuel's niece; and as, when very young, she had revolted from accepting any assistance from the countess, so now she could not bear the idea of applying for aid to any one of the circle to which Emanuel belonged.

The day passed in anxiety and irresolution. Her thoughts wandered restlessly from one possibility to another, from the times of her childhood to that future which had once lured her on by its brilliancy, but from which she was now half resolved to exclude herself forever.

In her mental restlessness, she began to occupy herself with outward objects. She took out from their concealment many an old memorial of her home, brought thence when she thought she never should return thither, and among them she found two notes from her parents, sent from the parsonage to her at the castle, and her father's old Bible.

It was long since she had read in it. She remembered what comfort she had found in its faded leaves; she read over the verses underscored by her father's hand, upon which his dear eyes had so often rested while sight was still left to them. As she was turning over the pages, she found a paper that she herself had laid between them, fixed in its place by a silken thread.

She opened it, and read aloud, scarcely knowing that she did so, written in her father's clear hand, "The motto chosen upon her confirmation-day for my child's guidance through life: 'What shall it profit a man if he shall gain the whole world and lose his own soul? Or what shall a man give in exchange for his soul?'"

As she read these words, she felt suddenly animated by fresh energy. She was but one of the countless hosts whom these sacred words, sounding through the world from divine lips, had strengthened in danger and uncertainty. Her father's eye seemed still upon her, and his hand guiding her and supporting her in her resolution to deliver her soul from the snares that surrounded her.

Meanwhile the day had darkened. Beata brought in candles, and the newspaper from the capital that came by post every evening.

Hulda scarcely glanced at the theatrical intelligence, which usually claimed her chief attention. It possessed little interest for her this evening. But among the advertisements for employment and employés the following instantly caught her eye:

"A family of wealth and standing, spending both summer and winter upon their estates, in a retired part of the province, are anxious to secure for a young girl, fourteen years of age, a governess capable of giving instruction in music, French, and English, and willing to pledge her services for the next three years if all else should be found satisfactory."

The salary which was offered was unusually high, and the name of a post-town to which an answer might be addressed was given. This advertisement seemed to her providential, and she obeyed the impulse that prompted her to take advantage of it. As she had years before, in an hour of doubt and anxiety, turned suddenly to Gabrielle, so she now seated herself at her writing-table to offer her services to these strangers.

She stated clearly what she was capable of teaching, but she suppressed the fact that she had for some years been an actress. She mentioned that she was the daughter of a pastor, determining to tell the rest of her story after she had gained the confidence of her employers; and it was with a throb of relief and pleasure that, for the first time for years, she signed her own name.

As she laid down the pen and read over her letter, she was assailed by a momentary indecision, the contrast seemed so great between her present independent position and the trials she might have to encounter, subject to the caprice of others, on a lonely country estate. But the words again sounded in her ears, "What shall it profit a man if he shall gain the whole world and lose his own soul?" and she sealed the letter and sent it to the post.

When she heard the house-door close behind the servant who carried it thither, she went to the window and followed the girl with her eyes as far as she could see her; then she returned to her table to gather up her papers and put away the dear old Bible.

"Alone, then, and forgotten," she said to herself,—"forgotten and uncared for forever, but pure and true to myself, worthy of my father and mother, and of his love!"

She was at harmony with herself once more. What the future was to bring forth, time alone would show.

CHAPTER XXVII.

To Emanuel, in his lonely castle, this winter seemed longer than any former one of his life. The visit of the prince and princess had served vividly to remind him of the delights of the intercourse and sympathy of a home-circle, and the little ring which he now wore on his hand brought constantly to his remembrance the lovely girl to whom he had once given it in pledge of affection.

Formerly he had endeavoured to banish Hulda from his thoughts; but since his conversation with his niece she had scarcely ever been absent from them. He longed to see her once more.

She had been hardly more than a child when he had won her love. Then her sense of truth, her clear judgment, her entire simplicity, and her susceptibility to beauty and goodness, had been as attractive in his eyes as her beauty. What must these years of study and experience have done for her! and

Clarissa had borne affectionate testimony to the unstained purity and nobility of her nature.

More than once he half determined to write to her; but it would fill a volume if he attempted to tell her what his life had been since he parted from her, or what had induced him to act as he had done. And where was the use of such an explanation? If Hulda had forgotten him and perhaps given her heart to another, it would be ridiculous to explain what had lost all interest for her; and if, as he scarcely dared to hope, she still cherished his memory, if she could forget and forgive, words were useless,—love believes and trusts.

In the evenings, when the rain beat against the window-panes, or the wild wind howled around his old castle, he saw her in his mind's eye, in the fulness of her ripened beauty, richly dressed, receiving the homage of a crowded theatre, pleased with herself, tasting the delights of triumph, and he asked himself, Could she endure to live in retirement? Would she be happy?

It was only too probable that she would refuse to resign for his sake the excitement of her life, the admiration of the many, to sacrifice to him her brilliant theatrical career. There was no equality between them. He was no longer young; he could resign for her sake nothing which, with his present experience of life, could weigh for one instant in the balance against the precious treasure of her love. The gain was all his if she still loved him, for he knew her value and what she would be to him. He was often undecided; but the delay of indecision quickened his passionate longing to put his fate to the touch.

At one moment he determined to see her upon the stage, the next he thought it would be impossible. Blame himself as he might, and strive against it as he could, his old distrust of his capacity to arouse affection stirred again within him.

One morning, as he was standing at his library-window, a horseman galloped into the court-yard. Emanuel recognized him immediately as the old Herr von Barnefeld. Some important matter must have brought him from home thus early.

He was always an honoured guest, and Emanuel went down to the hall to receive him.

"Why are you so early, my dear Barnefeld?" he called out to his friend, who was just alighting from his horse.

"Yes, why am I so early?" Barnefeld replied. "You must ask my wife that question. She sends me hither with a message to you."

Then, as he walked into the house with Emanuel, he continued: "The ladies have sent me over to discuss with you a matter in which you cannot have the slightest personal interest."

"But I hope I can be of some assistance to you," said Emanuel.

"My wife thinks you can, for she wishes me to ask you about a young woman."

"Is one of your boys about to marry?" asked Emanuel.

"Not that I know of," replied Barnefeld; "but then I am generally the last to be consulted upon such matters. But the wife of my eldest son wants a governess for Constance, her girl, and some weeks ago she put an advertisement in the paper to that effect, to which she has received a number of answers. Among them is one from a young person, the daughter of a pastor formerly upon your nephew's estates."

"From Hulda?" cried Emanuel, his face flushing.

"I think that is her name," Barnefeld replied, taking a letter from his pocket and looking for the signature. "But, my dear fellow, you are blushing like a girl. Has that anything to do with this pastor's daughter?"

"Oh, nothing in the world. I knew her parents,—both of them,—her mother came from about here; and I know the young girl also. She spent some time in my sister's house. She is very well educated; very musical, too, and as good as she is beautiful."

Herr von Barnefeld shook his head. "If I did not know you thoroughly," he said, "I should think you were jesting with me." Then he proceeded to ask a series of business-like questions, which Emanuel did his best to answer with becoming exactness and composure. "You think, then," said his guest, at last, "that we may try her. I thought so too; but the women wanted me to see you about her. Her letter is very simple and to the point."

Emanuel asked permission to read it, and it was handed to him, but he had almost over-estimated his self-control. Every word was a reproach to him, and yet filled him with an intoxicating sense of delight. It was wellnigh impossible not to betray to his guest the emotion that agitated him.

As Herr von Barnefeld took his leave, Emanuel said, "I am doubly glad to have seen you, for I am going away shortly for awhile."

Barnefeld asked whither, and Emanuel mentioned the province and the town where Hulda lived.

"It is a pity," said Barnefeld. "If it were some weeks later, you might bring the governess back with you. But she says she cannot come before Easter."

"I can see after her," said Emanuel, a sudden project suggesting itself to him. "Give me her letter as my credentials, or give me only the young person's address and one of your cards, and I will go and see her for you."

This was an excellent plan, Herr von Barnefeld thought. He instantly wrote a few lines upon one of his cards, which he gave Emanuel, and, wishing him a prosperous journey, rode contentedly home.

A few hours later, Emanuel was on his way to Hulda.

He travelled day and night, and arrived at his journey's end late in the afternoon of the second day. The proprietor of his hotel, who knew him well, since he had lodged there upon a previous occasion, came to receive his orders, as the hour for dinner was past, and did not fail to mention that he had had the honour of receiving the Prince and Princess Severin beneath his roof in the autumn. The family always stayed in his house when they visited the town. He brought to the Herr Baron the newspaper and the programme of the theatrical performance for the evening. They were playing "Faust." Hulda was even now upon the stage.

"If the Herr Baron is fond of the theatre," said the host, "there is still time to see a couple of acts. Our first actress, Fräulein Vollmer, is a very beautiful Gretchen. The princess sent for her to come to her when she was here. 'Faust' himself has not been so well played since Lelio left us, and it is more than likely that this is Fräulein Vollmer's last representation of Gretchen."

"Is she about to leave the stage, then?" asked Emanuel, undecided whether or not to go to the theatre.

"Not at all," said the host; "but there is some talk of her

accepting an offer from the management of the royal theatre in the capital; the manager came yesterday to see her." Then he went on, as if by way of explanation: "Fräulein Vollmer has gone through a great deal of trouble and annoyance here. There was positively a clique formed against her. The Herr Baron knows what the stage is. She would have nothing to say to one of our wealthiest men here, Herr Philibert, and he revenged himself rather severely. Then there was some talk of her leaving the stage. But just at that time Herr Philibert had a large estate left him by an uncle in England, and he went there to take possession. He intends to live there now, it is said. That smoothed matters for Fräulein Vollmer; and now that they are so anxious to have her at the royal theatre, our manager is doing everything that he can to keep her here, for the public fairly adore her."

Emanuel listened to every word, saying to himself the while, "Is it possible that this man is speaking of Hulda? Is this the girl to whom you were once betrothed, whom you forsook, and whom you are now hoping to carry away as your wife?"

All his life during these last years seemed incredible to him. But he must see her, and upon the stage, and immediately.

He ordered a carriage, and drove to the theatre. More than half of the play was over. His heart beat violently as the usher opened the door of the orchestra-box, and the hand trembled with which he pulled aside the heavy red curtain to look out upon the stage.

Yes, there she was. He sat down in the farthest corner of the box, where he could not be seen by her. He could scarcely control himself. He was like Faust when Helen's image is shown him in the magic mirror.

Gretchen was seated at her spinning-wheel. She was all unchanged, fair and lovely as when he had first seen her, Ceres' blooming daughter among the golden wheat, the wreath of cornflowers in her hair.

> "Save I have him near,
> The grave is here,
> The world is gall
> And bitterness all,"*

were the first words that he heard from her lips.

---

* Bayard Taylor's translation.

How many times she had perhaps sat thus, hoping, fearing, longing, before she could resolve to send him back his ring,—the ring that now burned upon his hand like a circlet of fire! Her sorrow and his own took living shape before him, and cried out for atonement for all the lost past and its fled happiness.

Happiness! Was not that storm of applause that greeted Hulda at the close of her song, happiness? Was not the enchanting smile with which she appeared when she was called again and again before the curtain, a happy smile? What could call it to her lips in the solitude of his home? Emanuel did not grudge her this delight, this triumph; how could she know what thoughts filled his soul?

Scene after scene impressed him more and more profoundly; the performance seemed endless, and yet he could not tear himself away so long as all those eyes were riveted upon her. He would have snatched his loved one from their gaze, but still Hulda enraptured him by her talent, and he was even proud of the admiration lavished upon her.

An elderly man sat before him in the box. Upon Emanuel's entrance he had moved aside to make room for him, and appeared surprised by the baron's retreat into the background. During the *entr'-acte* he addressed Emanuel, and was evidently a man of culture, and full of appreciation of Hulda's talent. He did not disguise that he was there with a purpose, and Emanuel suspected him to be the manager from the royal theatre. Herr Holm shortly after entered the box.

"Well," he said, addressing the stranger, "do you understand now why I do all that I can to foil you?"

The manager tapped him lightly on the shoulder. "You must resign all hope; I have *carte blanche.* She is perfectly adorable, and quite after the royal taste,—tall, fair, and proud. It is true that she does you and your school infinite credit."

Again the curtain rose; the prison scene began. It was more than Emanuel could bear. That beautiful, beloved face, pale and ghastly in the madness of despair and misery, wrung his very soul. He arose and left the theatre.

The long and weary night was passed by him in serious doubt and trembling hope, and he awoke in the morning from an agonizing dream. The next few hours would decide his fate.

CHAPTER XXVIII.

THE manager of the royal theatre betook himself betimes to Hulda's apartments to offer her the contract which he was empowered to lay before her in case she answered to Lelio's description.

Thus the most brilliant future that an actress could attain awaited her. She could occupy the first position as a tragic actress in the kingdom, and in the capital her social surroundings would be very different from those of the provinces.

The prejudice existing against histrionic artists had long since vanished in the literary and scientific circles of the royal capital. Hulda would there enjoy the society of the most cultivated and gifted minds in Germany, and the salary that was offered her, and the prospect of playing before the most intelligent audience in her native land, were alluring indeed. All that had hovered before her imagination as almost too brilliant for earthly attainment was now within her grasp as it were.

The last few weeks, as his host had informed Emanuel, had glided by smoothly enough for Hulda, without any of those annoyances which had embittered her enjoyment of her art and made her life wretched, and no notice had been taken of her reply to the advertisement. She therefore had no good reason for refusing to listen to the proposals from the management of the royal theatre. But she had not forgotten all that she had suffered, the trials and insults that had made her long for retirement and rest and had determined her, at all hazards, to "deliver her soul." With the pen in her hand, ready to sign the contract before her, she suddenly begged to be allowed until the evening to take the matter into consideration.

The manager from the capital seemed surprised. But he understood the whims of genius, he thought, and courteously accorded her the delay she requested.

At the house-door below he encountered Emanuel, and saw him hand a card to Beata, with the remark that he had a verbal message for Fräulein Vollmer, whereupon he was requested to wait in the small reception-room upon the ground-floor.

"Strange!" cried Hulda, as the girl handed her the card. "Strange that it should come just at this moment!"

Beata could not resist an impulse of curiosity, and read on the card, "Karl von Barnefeld, of Splittbergen," and beneath the words, "The bearer of this, a friend of mine, will have the honour to discuss with you the contents of your letter of ——, and will give you any information upon the subject therein treated of that you may desire."

There was something perplexing to Hulda in the arrival of the answer to her letter just at this time, as if fate were determined that the result of her decision should be due to herself alone, and not to circumstances, and she was half minded to refuse to see the bearer. But she could not reconcile this refusal to her sense of justice, and she accordingly told Beata to admit him.

To Emanuel the few moments since the sending up-stairs of the card seemed an age. At last he stood before her door, the next moment he was in her presence. She suppressed the cry that rose to her lips as he entered, and, retreating from him, leaned, wellnigh fainting, against the high back of her armchair for support.

His heart seemed to stand still. There was not in her countenance one ray of joy, not the smallest sign that Hulda still loved him. How easily his wishes and his unfounded hopes had deceived him! "I should have prepared her. I should not have come thus," he said to himself.

In vain did Hulda summon her self-control. It seemed to her a mockery that Emanuel should come to her upon the errand of another, and with a determined effort to be composed, she said, "I did not expect to see you, Herr Baron."

The force that she put upon herself made her voice sound strained and cold. They stood opposite each other, rigid and silent. Emanuel could not endure this.

"You are right," he cried, in a tone that revealed all his agitation, his fears and hopes. "My presumption to-day is another sin added to all those of which I have been guilty towards you. I should not have come; I will not stay long."

"Herr Baron!" she faltered, interrupting him, and, clasping her hands before her, she gazed gently into his face.

"You have seen Clarissa," he went on, "and Clarissa has been with me. She told me all that passed between you at that interview. She was full of love and admiration for you; but she thought she saw that your life was not all that you could desire. I was distressed, and could not cease to think of what she said."

He paused, scarcely able to control his agitation; his whole soul looked from his eyes.

She sank into a chair; he stood before her.

"A few days ago," he began again, "my old friend and neighbour, Herr von Barnefeld, came to me with a letter of yours in answer to an advertisement in the public paper. He wished to know if I knew you, since you said you came from my nephew's estate. Judge of my sensations!" Again he paused, then added, hastily, "I could not but believe that you wished to leave the stage."

"I had, in fact, determined to do so. I thought it my duty," said Hulda, as much agitated as himself.

"But you have given up the idea,—you have changed your mind!" he exclaimed. "Why should you not? I understand it perfectly. It was foolish to ask you." His forced composure was all gone. He spoke unconnectedly, hurriedly, from the chaos of thought within. "I heard yesterday what proposals have been made to you. How could anything that I have to offer, to entreat of you, attract you for one instant, compared with the brilliant prospect opening before you?"

"You entreat of me?" cried Hulda, and for the first time he heard the unforgotten ring in her voice.

"I saw you, admired you, last evening," he said. "You have become a great artist. You will see the whole world of Germany at your feet——"

"Herr Baron!" she gasped, with trembling lips.

"I," he continued,—"I? What can I offer you? How can I—how dare I ask—when I failed to keep what I once possessed?"

In speechless rapture, not daring to trust her senses, she raised her clasped hands as if in prayer. "Is this real? Can this be?" she said, in a scarcely audible whisper.

"But, oh!" he continued, seizing her hands and pressing them passionately between his own, "if you could forget,—if you could forgive,—if you still loved me!"

In an instant she was in his arms. "What have I done but love you all these long years?" she cried. "What comfort have I had in many an hour of bitter trial save in the thought that you once loved me?"

Then neither spoke. That supreme moment blotted out the memory of years of separation and sorrow.

As they raised their heads and the strong throbbing of their hearts began to subside, a bright ray of sunlight came shining through the window into the room.

"It is so long since I have seen the spring in the country," said Hulda.

They were standing at the window, his arm around her waist.

"It will yield you no laurels in my home," said Emanuel. "But there are cornflowers,—cornflowers in plenty, and you will weave wreaths again."

She gave him an enchanting smile, and again they were silent. Their bliss was so new and strange to them. They were so unchanged to each other, and yet so different from their former selves.

Emanuel looked around him with loving curiosity. This was where she had lived all these years. The contract lay upon the table. He asked what it was. She handed it to him to read; she could not deny herself that small satisfaction.

"You are making an immense sacrifice," he said.

"If you knew the world from which you save me, you would call it a deliverance," she replied. "And I, in my childish fancy, once fondly imagined that I could be your deliverer!"

"And were you not? Are you not my deliverer at this moment?" he said. "Is not your fidelity, your love, which I have not deserved, my deliverance from the sin of which I was guilty towards you, and from the remorse that assailed me whenever I thought of you? And I thought of you always, even when I tried to deceive myself and forget you. The attempt was fruitless; you were always before me."

He took the little ring from his finger. "Will you wear it again, Hulda, the poor little ring that you rejected? Shall it be really true, the beautiful old 'Thee and me shall no one sever'?"

"No one!" she cried, as he placed the little talisman upon her finger. "No one again!"

CHAPTER XXIX.

Beata knocked at the door. "Herr Holm!" she announced, looking in surprise as Hulda disengaged herself from Emanuel's arm. "We are severed already," he said.

"But not for long," she made answer; "and our manager is so fond of dramas with happy conclusions that he shall be the first to learn of my happiness."

"He will be the first to grudge you to me," said Emanuel, as the manager presented himself; and in truth he was not mistaken.

Holm was very unwilling to lose Hulda, and at first would not hear of releasing her from the two months that still remained of her engagement with him.

But Emanuel was lavish in his offers, and the manager knew how to put the best face upon the inevitable. At all events he would rather, he concluded, that she should leave the stage altogether than go to another theatre. He, however, made one condition, which was that she should appear once more upon the stage to bid farewell to her audience; and Hulda herself was not averse to this.

Emanuel consented, but they stipulated that there should be no theatrical farewell scene, as in Feodora's case, and that Hulda should select the character in which to appear. Iphigenia was the part chosen,—the part in which Hulda was most willing to appear before her future husband, and Iphigenia's last words were her own farewell.

The report that Hulda was to leave the stage was in circulation among the actors that very evening, and the papers the next day announced her approaching marriage with Baron Emanuel von Falkenhorst. The few hints that Hulda in her joy had given the manager with regard to her former betrothal to Emanuel were the groundwork for a very pretty romance, which ran from mouth to mouth, and was, after all, not very wide of the truth.

The countess was paying a visit to the prince and Clarissa when Emanuel announced to her his betrothal to Hulda. Clarissa declared herself delighted with the tidings. She called the prince to witness that she had foreseen it during their visit at Falkenhorst, and that she had offered to lay a small wager with regard to it. "And," she said, "that wretched old legend will be fulfilled, the evil spell will be broken, and this fresh young creature's entrance into the family will appease the elf-king's wrath."

"Only the young creature makes no sacrifice!" said the countess.

"A sacrifice there will be, however," said the prince, "and not a small one. Emanuel, by this marriage, yields all right to the entailed estates."

"He expressly mentions that," said the countess, "although it could not be otherwise. The estates, he says, will come at his death to my son or grandson in a very improved condition; and meanwhile, if he should have children of his own, he hopes to found for them a home that will be burdened with no entail. Count Branden and Falkenhorst sounds very well," she said; "and looks very well," she added, writing it in pencil in clear, distinct characters upon the margin of her brother's letter.

The advantages which were to accrue to Emanuel's nephew from his marriage helped considerably to reconcile his sister to the inequality of birth between himself and his bride; and as Hulda expressed a wish to be married in her father's church, and the prince and Clarissa highly approved the plan, the countess invited her to come to the "castle by the sea," and promised, with her daughter and son-in-law, to be present at the marriage.

CHAPTER XXX.

MA'AMSELLE ULRIKA felt as if the skies had fallen when the bailiff one morning brought from the post a letter announcing Baron Emanuel's betrothal to the pastor's daughter. She could not believe it, could not understand it. It came too suddenly,—all at once, as it were,—although she still boasted of always having "her senses about" her.

The castle people had never come to the castle so early in the year, almost before the winter was over; and now here was Hulda coming, and the suite of rooms next to the Countess Clarissa's was to be arranged for her, and there was so much to be done that she really hardly had time to wonder that Simonena's daughter, the pastor's Hulda, was to be a baroness, and sister-in-law to the Frau Countess, and aunt to the Frau Princess. It was inconceivable that her brother should take it all so quietly, only saying that when a man of honour had behaved badly he ought to come to his senses and keep his word. He would not speak at all of Hulda's leaving them to join the play-actors; he only said that if the baron married her it was a sure sign that she was all right; and, besides, he declared that it was not entirely her fault that she had gone away from her native place, "for between ourselves, sister," he added, tapping her good-humouredly upon the shoulder, "a long life with you is no joke; that I can vouch for."

She pretended to be vexed, but she laughed. There would be fine doings at the castle, and she was very curious to know how it had all happened. Hulda had written a long letter about it to the Herr Pastor, and his young wife had brought it up to the bailiff's and read it aloud to them, and it was all very grand and noble. But what Ulrika wanted to know was not in it; she wanted to hear all about the stage and the actors, and how they lived, and that Hulda must tell her herself, if she had not grown too proud and grand.

And when Hulda arrived at the castle with the countess and Clarissa, she won every heart by her gentleness and kindness.

As in a fairy-story one word will transform and create all things anew, so now everything seemed to conspire to do her honour and smooth her path through life. The first day of spring was to be her marriage-day, and the previous evening brought a letter by a courier to Emanuel from Konradine and the prince, containing their congratulations.

"All that was wanting," wrote the Princess Frederick, "to our own happiness was the knowledge of yours. We send you our warmest wishes for the future; let us hope that before long we may renew an intercourse to which we surely owe many happy hours.'

It was a clear, bright morning when the bridal party drove from the castle to the village church. The breeze came fresh from the sea, and the spring sunshine quickened the buds upon the trees and in the fields.

"We have driven along this road together once before," said Hulda, thinking of the stormy night when Emanuel had taken her to her home and her mother had perished.

"And that night heralded the day that now dawns for us," Emanuel replied, wishing to dispel sad memories in her mind. "The love that will illumine our lives was born that night."

The familiar sound of the church-bells, heard from afar, pronounced a blessing upon his words.

No lovelier, happier bride ever stood before the altar. Even the countess could not contradict Clarissa's assertion that her uncle's choice had a most regal presence. She admitted that Hulda was "certainly very presentable."

"And to think that she has been a play-actress!" Ma'amselle whispered to her brother. "Why, she wears that spray of diamonds and enamelled cornflowers on her breast just as if she had always been used to it! If her father and mother could see her now! I can hardly believe my eyes! And will any one tell me that I was not right to teach her to take good care of the 'little folk'? Oh, that brings luck and sunshine on a wedding-day!"

"Nonsense!" muttered the bailiff, as the young baroness extricated herself from the embraces of her new relatives and came towards him. He made her a low bow; but she threw her arms around his neck and kissed him.

"She is a jewel, Herr Baron!" he said, as Emanuel came up to shake his hand. "She is a jewel!" he repeated, his emotion depriving him of other words.

"She is more than that to me!" said Emanuel. "She was and is my deliverer."

THE END.

Seed-Time and Harvest; or, During my Apprenticeship. From the Platt-Deutsch of Fritz Reuter. 8vo Paper cover. $1. Extra cloth. $1.50.

No German author of the present time is more popular in his own country than REUTER. He is pronounced by a competent German critic to be deservedly "the most popular German writer of the last half century."

REUTER is especially noted as the ***rare humorist, the genuine poet and the fascinating delineator*** of the lives of his *Platt-Deutsch* neighbors, and as such is probably more beloved than any other German author of the day. The tale in question is one of his best and most important works, giving its readers, with its other entertainment and profit, a charming acquaintance with the quaint, interesting *Platt-Deutsch* people.

"Fritz Reuter is one of the most popular writers in Germany. . . . The charm of his stories lies in their simplicity and exquisite truth to Nature. He has 'the loving heart' which Carlyle tells us is the secret of writing; and Reuter is not graphic merely, he is photographic. His characters impress one so forcibly with their reality that one need not to be told they are portraits from life. Even the villains must have been old acquaintances. . . . It ('During my Apprenticeship') is one of the best of Reuter's stories, exhibiting his turn for the pathetic as well as for the humorous."—*New York Evening Post.*

"It has a freshness and novelty that are rare in these times."—*Philadelphia Evening Bulletin.*

The Sylvestres; or, The Outcasts. A Novel. By M. DE BETHAM-EDWARDS, author of "Kitty," "Dr. Jacob," etc. Illustrated. 8vo. Paper. 75 cents. Extra cloth. $1.25.

"It is an exceptionally vigorous and healthy as well as happy tale."—*Philadelphia North American.*

"It is one of the author's best."—*New York Home Journal.*

"A capital novel."—*Pittsburg Gazette.*

"The story is well constructed, and the descriptive passages with which the work abounds are worthy of the highest praise. The sketches of scenery are painted with the touch of an artist."—*Philadelphia Ev. Bulletin.*

Myself. A Romance of New England Life. 12mo. Extra cloth. $2.

"This is really a capital story. The characters are drawn with a free and sharp pen, the style is fresh and lively and the plot quite unhackneyed."—*Boston Courier.*

How will it End? A Romance. By J. C. Heywood, author of "Herodias," "Antonius," etc. 12mo. Extra cloth. $1.50.

"It is a fascinating novel, which must exert a good influence, and one that should be widely read."—*Wilkes's Spirit of the Times.*

Doings in Maryland; or, Matilda Douglas. "TRUTH STRANGER THAN FICTION." 12mo. Extra cloth. $1.75.

It is a very perfect story—simple, noble and without that straining for literary effect which constitutes the best attainable definition of the sensational."—*New York Home Journal.*

Dorothy Fox. A novel. By Louisa Parr, author of "How it all Happened," etc. With numerous Illustrations. 8vo. Paper cover. 75 cents. Extra cloth. $1.25.

"The Quaker character, though its quaintness and simplicity may seem easy enough to catch, requires a delicate workman to do it justice. Such an artist is the author of 'Dorothy Fox,' and we must thank her for a charming novel. The story is dramatically interesting, and the characters are drawn with a firm and graceful hand. The style is fresh and natural, vigorous without vulgarity, simple without mawkishness. Dorothy herself is represented as charming all hearts, and she will charm all readers. . . We wish 'Dorothy Fox' many editions."—*London Times.*

"One of the best novels of the season."—*Philadelphia Press.*

"The characters are brought out in life-like style, and cannot fail to attract the closest attention."—*Pittsburg Gazette.*

"It is admirably told, and will establish the reputation of the author among novelists."—*Albany Argus.*

How it all Happened. By Louisa Parr, author of "Dorothy Fox," etc. 12mo. Paper cover. 25 cents.

"It is not often that one finds so much pleasure in reading a love story, charmingly told in a few pages."—*Charleston Courier.*

"Is a well-written little love story, in which a great deal is said in a very few words."—*Philadelphia Evening Telegraph.*

"A remarkably clever story."—*Boston Saturday Evening Gazette.*

*John Thompson, Blockhead, and Companion Por*traits. By LOUISA PARR, author of "Dorothy Fox." 12mo. With Frontispiece. Extra cloth. $1.75.

"Extremely well-told stories, interesting in characters and incidents, and pure and wholesome in sentiment."—*Boston Watchman and Reflector.*

"These are racy sketches, and belong to that delightful class in which the end comes before the reader is ready for it.

"The style throughout is very simple and fresh, abounding in strong, vivid, idiomatic English."—*Home Journal.*

"They are quite brilliant narrative sketches, worthy of the reputation established by the writer."—*Philadelphia Inquirer.*

"Very presentable, very readable."—*New York Times.*

The Quiet Miss Godolphin, by Ruth Garrett; and A CHANCE CHILD, by EDWARD GARRETT, joint authors of "Occupations of a Retired Life" and "White as Snow." With Six Illustrations by Townley Green. 16mo Cloth. 75 cents. Paper cover. 50 cents.

"These stories are characterized by great strength and beauty of thought, with a singularly attractive style. Their influence will not fail to improve and delight."—*Philadelphia Age.*

St. Cecilia. A Modern Tale from Real Life. Part I.—ADVERSITY. 12mo. Extra cloth. $1.50.

"It is carefully and beautifully written."—*Washington Chronicle.*

"A tale that we can cheerfully recommend as fresh, entertaining and well written."—*Louisville Courier Journal.*

Eleonore. A Romance. After the German of E. VON ROTHENFELS, author of "On the Vistula," "Heath-flower," etc. By FRANCES ELIZABETH BENNETT, translator of "Lowly Ways." 12mo. Fine cloth. Ornamented. $1.50.

"A vivid reproduction of German life and character."—*Boston Globe.*

"A bright, readable novel."—*Philadelphia Evening Bulletin.*

"The plot is developed with remarkable skill."—*Boston Saturday Evening Gazette.*

Tom Pippin's Wedding. A Novel. By the Author of "The Fight at Dame Europa's School." 16mo. Extra cloth. $1.25. Paper cover. 75 cents.

"We must confess that its perusal has caused us more genuine amusement than we have derived from any fiction, not professedly comic, for many a long day. . . . Without doubt this is, if not the most remarkable, certainly the most original, novel of the day."—*London Bookseller.*

"It is fresh in characterization, and is as instructive as it is entertaining."—*Boston Evening Traveller.*

Irene. A Tale of Southern Life. Illustrated; and HATHAWAY STRANGE. 8vo. Paper cover. 35 cents.

"They are both cleverly written."—*New Orleans Times.*

"These stories are pleasantly written. They are lively, gossippy and genial."—*Baltimore Gazette.*

Wearithorne; or, In the Light of To-Day. A Novel. By "FADETTE," author of "Ingemisco" and "Randolph Honor." 12mo. Extra cloth. $1.50.

"Written with exceptional dramatic vigor and terseness, and with strong powers of personation."—*Philadelphia North American.*

"It is written with vigor, and the characters are sketched with a marked individuality."—*Literary Gazette.*

"The style is clever and terse, the characters are boldly etched, and with strong individualities."—*New Orleans Times.*

"Simply and tenderly written."—*Washington Chronicle.*

Steps Upward. A Temperance Tale. By Mrs. F. D. GAGE, author of "Elsie Magoon," etc. 12mo. Extra cloth. $1.50.

"'Steps Upward,' by Mrs. Frances Dana Gage, is a temperance story of more than ordinary interest. Diana Dinmont, the heroine, is an earnest, womanly character, and in her own upward progress helps many another to a better life."—*New York Independent.*

"We are sure no reader can but enjoy and profit by it."—*New York Evening Mail.*

Minna Monté. A Novel. By "Stella." 12mo. $1.25.

"A domestic story possessing great spirit and many other attractive features."—*St. Louis Republican.*

"We have in this little volume an agreeable story, pleasantly told."—*Pittsburg Gazette.*

"It is the Fashion." A Novel. From the German of ADELHEID VON AUER. By the translator of "Over Yonder," "Magdalena," "The Old Countess," etc. 12mo. Fine cloth. $1.50.

"It is one of the most charming books of the times, and is admirable for its practical, wise and beautiful morality. A more natural and graceful work of its kind we never before read."—*Richmond Dispatch.*

"This is a charming novel; to be commended not only for the interest of the story, but for the fine healthy tone that pervades it. . . . This work has not the excessive elaboration of many German novels, which make them rather tedious for American readers, but is fresh, sprightly and full of common sense applied to the business of actual life."—*Philadelphia Age.*

"It is a most excellent book, abounding in pure sentiment and beautiful thought, and written in a style at once lucid, graceful and epigrammatic."—*New York Evening Mail.*

*Dead Men's Shoes. A Novel. By J. R. Hader*mann, author of "Forgiven at Last." 12mo. Fine cloth. $2.

"One of the best novels of the season."—*Philadelphia Press.*

"One of the best novels descriptive of life at the South that has yet been published. The plot is well contrived, the characters well contrasted and the dialogue crisp and natural."—*Baltimore Gazette.*

Israel Mort, Overman. A Story of the Mine. By JOHN SAUNDERS, author of "Abel Drake's Wife." Illustrated. 16mo. Fine cloth. $1.25.

"Intensely dramatic. . . . Some of the characters are exquisitely drawn, and show the hand of a master."—*Boston Saturday Evening Gazette.*

"The book takes a strong hold on the reader's attention from the first, and the interest does not flag for a moment."—*Boston Globe.*

"The denouement, moral and artistic, is very fine."—*New York Evening Mail.*

"It treats of a variety of circumstances and characters almost new to the realm of fiction, and has a peculiar interest on this account." — *Boston Advertiser.*

In the Rapids. A Romance. By Gerald Hart. 12mo. Toned paper. Extra cloth. $1.50.

"Full of tragic interest."—*Cincinnati Gazette.*

"It is, on the whole, remarkably well told, and is particularly notable for its resemblance to those older and, in some respects, better models of composition in which the dialogue is subordinated to the narrative, and the effects are wrought out by the analytical powers of the writer."—*Baltimore Gazette.*

The Parasite; or, How to Make One's Fortune. A Comedy in Five Acts. After the French of Picard. 12mo. Paper cover. 75 cents.

A pleasant, sprightly comedy, unexceptionable in its moral and chaste in its language. As our amateur actors are always in pursuit of plays of this character, we should suppose they would find this a valuable addition to their stock."—*Philadelphia Age.*

Fernyhurst Court. An Every-day Story. By the author of "Stone Edge," "Lettice Lisle," etc. With numerous Illustrations. 8vo. Paper cover. 60 cents.

"An excellent novel of English society, with many good engravings."—*Philadelphia Press.*

"An excellent story."—*Boston Journal.*

Cross-Purposes. A Christmas Experience in Seven Stages. By T. C. DE LEON, author of "Four Years in Rebel Capitals," "Pluck, a Comedy," etc. With Illustrations. 16mo. Tinted paper. Extra cloth. $1.25.

"The plot is most skillfully handled, and the style is bright and sparkling." -*New York Commercial Advertiser.*

"The reader will begin the narrative without a desire to finisn it before he has laid it down again."—*New York Times.*

Himself his Worst Enemy; or, Philip, Duke of Wharton's Career. By ALFRED P. BROTHERHEAD. 12mo. Fine cloth. $2.

"The story is very entertaining and very well told."—*Boston Post.*

"The author is entitled to high praise for this creditable work."—*Philadelphia Ledger.*

In Exile. A Novel. Translated from the German of W. VON ST. 12mo. Fine cloth. $2.

"No more interesting work of fiction has been issued for some time."—*St. Louis Democrat.*

"A feast for heart and imagination.'—*Philadelphia Evening Bulletin.*

*The Struggle in Ferrara. A Story of the Reforma*tion in Italy. By WILLIAM GILBERT, author of "De Profundis," etc. Profusely Illustrated. 8vo. Paper cover. $1. Cloth. $1.50.

"Few works of religious fiction compare with this in intensity, reality and value."—*Philadelphia North American.*

"It is a well-told story of the Reformation in Italy."—*Congregational Quarterly.*

Marguerite Kent. A Novel. By Marion W. Wayne. 12mo. Fine cloth. $2.

"'Marguerite Kent,' by Mrs. Marion W. Wayne, is an American novel, original in many of its characters, natural in dialogue, artistical in descriptions of scenery, probable in its incidents and so thoroughly imbued with individuality that the story, which has taken the autobiographical form, has impressed us with a strong feeling of reality and truth."—*Philadelphia Press.*

"Is a novel of thought as well as of action, of the inner as well as of the outer life."—*New York Evening Mail.*

"The plot is novel and ingenious."—*Portland Transcript.*

Episodes in an Obscure Life. Being Experiences in the Tower Hamlets. By a CURATE. With numerous Illustrations. 8vo. Paper cover. 75 cents. Fine cloth. $1.25.

"The scenes are novel to American readers, but they bear unmistakable evidence of truth, and the book, though small, contains much food for thought, much stimulus for action."—*Congregational Quarterly.*

"We recommend the Episodes as a book interesting in itself and full of important suggestions."—*London Saturday Review.*

"We can heartily commend the volume to our readers as a vivid picture of a life concerning which many of them, we are persuaded, know nothing The book is profusely illustrated."—*Our Monthly.*

Student's Hebrew Lexicon. A Compendious and Complete Hebrew and Chaldee Lexicon to the Old Testament: chiefly founded on the works of Gesenius and Fürst, with Improvements from Dietrich and other sources. Edited by BENJAMIN DAVIES, Ph.D., LL.D., translator of Roediger's Gesenius or Student's Hebrew Grammar. 8vo. Cloth. Red edges. $6.

"We predict for it a wide circulation as soon as its merit is known. We cordially recommend it. The Lexicon is printed in an octavo of 701 pages. We have never seen anything so attractive in the form of a Hebrew book. Its execution leaves nothing to be desired." —*Rev. J. Packard, D.D., Prof. of Biblical Learning in the Protestant Episcopal Theological Seminary of Virginia.*

The Text Book of Freemasonry. A Complete Handbook of Instruction to all the Workings in the various Mysteries and Ceremonies of Craft Masonry. Containing the Entered Apprentice, Fellow-Craft and Master Mason's Degrees, together with the whole of the Three Lectures, also the Ceremony of Exaltation in the Supreme Order of the Holy Royal Arch; a Selection of Masonic Songs, etc. Illustrated with Three Engravings of the Tracing Boards. Compiled by a Member of the Craft. 16mo. Tinted paper. Cloth. Red edges. $1.

"It affords a complete handbook of instruction in all the mysteries and ceremonies of the Order."—*Chicago Evening Journal.*

"The compiler of the present Text Book of Freemasonry does not think it necessary to make any apology for presenting it to the notice of the Craft. His only surprise is that no authentic Ritual has hitherto been published. In all quarters the want of such a manual has long been felt, if only for the sake of aiding a uniform working in all Lodges. The enormous influx of new members into the Craft within the last few years, and the increased value of time, has also caused a demand for the Ritual in a printed form for self-instruction. To the younger members who desire to attain a speedy perfection in the knowledge of Craft Masonry, the present volume will be found both useful and acceptable. The Signs, Tokens and Passwords are necessarily omitted."—*The Preface.*

Thrown Together. A Story. By Florence Montgomery, author of "Misunderstood," "A Very Simple Story," etc. 12mo. Fine cloth. $1.50.

"The author of 'Misunderstood' has given us another charming story of child-life. This, however, is not a book for children. Adult readers of Miss Montgomery's book will find much that will lead them to profitable reflection of childish character and many graphically touched terms of childish thought and expression which will come home to their own experience."—*London Athenæum.*

"A delightful story, founded upon the lives of children. There is a thread of gold in it upon which are strung many lovely sentiments. There is a deep and strong current of religious feeling throughout the story, not a prosy, unattractive lecturing upon religious subjects. A good, true and earnest life is depicted, full of hope and longing, and of happy fruition. One cannot read this book without being better for it, or without a more tender charity being stirred up in his heart."—*Washington Daily Chronicle.*

"The characters are drawn with a delicacy that lends a charm to the book."—*Boston Saturday Evening Gazette.*

Why Did He Not Die? or, The Child from the Ebräergang. From the German of AD. VON VOLCKHAUSEN. By Mrs. A. L. WISTER, translator of "Old Mam'selle's Secret," "Gold Elsie," etc. 12mo. Fine cloth. $1.75.

"Mrs. Wister's admirable translations are among the books that everybody reads. She certainly may be said to possess unusual ability in retaining the peculiar weird flavor of a German story, while rendering it with perfect ease and grace into our own language. Few recently published novels have received more general perusal and approval than 'Only a Girl;' and 'Why Did He Not Die?' possesses in at least an equal degree all the elements of popularity. From the beginning to the end the interest never flags, and the characters and scenes are drawn with great warmth and power."—*New York Herald.*

Aytoun. A Romance. By Emily T. Read. 8vo. Paper cover. 40 cents.

"The fabric is thoroughly wrought and truly dramatic."—*Philadelphia North American.*

"There are elements of power in the novel, and some exciting scenes."—*New York Evening Mail.*

Old Song and New. A Volume of Poems. By MARGARET J. PRESTON, author of "Beechenbrook." 12mo. Tinted paper. Extra cloth. $2.

"In point of variety and general grace of diction, 'Old Song and New' is the best volume of poems that has yet been written by an American woman, whether North or South—the best, because on the whole the best sustained and the most thoughtful."—*Baltimore Gazette.*

"In this volume there is workmanship of which none need be ashamed, while much vies with our best living writers. Strength and beauty, scholarship and fine intuition are manifested throughout so as to charm the reader and assure honorable distinction to the writer. Such poetry is in no danger of becoming too abundant."—*Philadelphia North American.*

Margaree. A Poem. By Hampden Masson. 16mo. Extra cloth. 75 cents.

By His Own Might. A Romance. Translated from the German of WILHELMINE VON HILLERN, author of "Only a Girl," etc. 12mo. Fine cloth. $1.75.

"Some of the scenes are powerfully wrought out, and are highly dramatic in their construction."—*Boston Saturday Evening Gazette.*

"The story is well constructed. It is vivacious, intricate and well sustained. . . . It is one of the best of the many excellent novels from the German issued by this house."—*Phila. Evening Bulletin.*

The Daughter of an Egyptian King. An Historical Romance. Translated from the German of GEORGE EBERS by HENRY REED. 12mo. Extra cloth. $1.75.

"It is a wonderful production. There have been ancient novels before now, but none, according to our recollections, so antique as this."—*New York World.*

"The plot is a most interesting one, and in its development we are given an accurate insight into the social and political life of the Egyptians of that time."—*Boston Evening Traveller.*

"It is a valuable contribution to science as well as a highly-wrought novel."—*Cincinnati Gazette.*

Sergeant Atkins. A Tale of Adventure. Founded on Fact. By an Officer of the United States Army. With Illustrations. 12mo. Extra cloth. $1.75.

"It is the best Indian story, because the truest to life, that we have lately seen."—*Boston Post.*

"Apart from its mere literary merits as a graphic, well-told and spirited narrative of border experience and Indian warfare, 'Sergeant Atkins' really gives us all the facts of the Florida war which are necessary to a clear understanding of its origin, progress and character."—*Army and Navy Journal.*

The Warden. A Novel. By Anthony Trollope, author of "The Vicar of Bullhampton," "Orley Farm," etc. 12mo. Fine cloth. $1.

*Barchester Towers. A Novel. By Anthony Trol*lope, author of "Phineas Finn," "He Knew he was Right," etc. 12mo. Fine cloth. $1.25.

"These two novels belong to the admirable Barchester series, in which certain phases of clerical life are developed with much realism and humor."—*N. Y. Tribune.*

*The Scapegoat. A Novel. By Leo. 12mo. Pa*per cover. $1. Cloth. $1.50.

"The book has a good deal of life and spirit in it."—*Philadelphia Age.*

"It is bold and vigorous in delineation, and equally pronounced and effective in its moral."—*St. Louis Times.*

Who Would Have Thought it? A Novel. 12mo. Fine cloth. $1.75.

A bright and attractive romance, with an interesting plot, well sustained throughout.

Tricotrin. The Story of a Waif and Stray. By "OUIDA," author of "Under Two Flags," etc. With Portrait of the Author from an Engraving on Steel. 12mo. Cloth. $1.50.

"The story is full of vivacity and of thrilling interest."—*Pittsburgh Gazette.*

"Tricotrin is a work of absolute power, some truth and deep interest."—*N. Y. Day Book.*

"The book abounds in beautiful sentiment, expressed in a concentrated, compact style which cannot fail to be attractive and will be read with pleasure in every household."—*San Francisco Times.*

Granville de Vigne; or, Held in Bondage. A Tale of the Day. By "OUIDA," author of "Idalia," "Tricotrin," etc. 12mo. Cloth. $1.50.

"This is one of the most powerful and spicy works of fiction which the present century, so prolific in light literature, has produced."

Strathmore; or, Wrought by His Own Hand. A Novel. By "OUIDA," author of "Granville de Vigne," etc. 12mo. Cloth. $1.50.

"It is a romance of the intense school, but it is written with more power, fluency and brilliancy than the works of Miss Braddon and Mrs. Wood, while its scenes and characters are taken from high life."—*Boston Transcript.*

Chandos. A Novel. By "Ouida," author of "Strathmore," "Idalia," etc. 12mo. Cloth. $1.50.

"Those who have read these two last named brilliant works of fiction (Granville de Vigne and Strathmore) will be sure to read *Chandos.* It is characterized by the same gorgeous coloring of style and somewhat exaggerated portraiture of scenes and characters, but it is a story of surprising power and interest."—*Pittsburgh Evening Chronicle.*

Under Two Flags. A Story of the Household and the Desert. By "OUIDA," author of "Tricotrin," "Granville de Vigne," etc. 12mo. Cloth. $1.50.

"No one will be able to resist its fascination who once begins its perusal."—*Phila. Evening Bulletin.*

"This is probably the most popular work of Ouida. It is enough of itself to establish her fame as one of the most eloquent and graphic writers of fiction now living."—*Chicago Journal of Commerce.*

Puck. His Vicissitudes, Adventures, Observations, Conclusions, Friendship and Philosophies. By "OUIDA," author of "Strathmore," "Idalia," "Tricotrin," etc. 12mo. Fine cloth. $1.50.

"Its quaintness will provoke laughter, while the interest in the central character is kept up unabated."—*Albany Journal.*

"It sustains the widely-spread popularity of the author."—*Pittsburgh Gazette.*

Folle-Farine. A Novel. By "Ouida," author of "Idalia," "Under Two Flags," "Strathmore," etc. 12mo Fine cloth. $1.50.

"Ouida's pen is a graphic one, and page after page of gorgeous word-painting flow from it in a smooth, melodious rhythm that often has the perfect measure of blank verse, and needs only to be broken into line. There is in it, too, the eloquence of genius."—*Phila. Eve. Bulletin.*

"This work fully sustains the writer's previous reputation, and may be numbered among the best of her works."—*Troy Times.*

"Full of vivacity."—*Fort Wayne Gazette.*

"The best of her numerous stories."—*Vicksburg Herald.*

Idalia. A Novel. By "Ouida," author of "Strathmore," "Tricotrin," "Under Two Flags," etc. 12mo Cloth. $1.50.

"It is a story of love and hatred, of affection and jealousy, of intrigue and devotion. . . . We think this novel will attain a wide popularity, especially among those whose refined taste enables them to appreciate and enjoy what is truly beautiful in literature."—*Albany Evening Journal.*

A Leaf in the Storm, and other Novelettes. By "OUIDA," author of "Folle-Farine," "Granville de Vigne," etc. Two Illustrations. Fifth Edition. 8vo. Paper cover. 50 cents.

"Those who look upon light literature as an art will read these tales with pleasure and satisfaction."—*Baltimore Gazette.*

"In the longest of these stories, 'A Branch of Lilac,' the simplicity of the narrative—so direct and truthful—produces the highest artistic effect. It required high genius to write such a tale in such a manner."—*Philadelphia Press.*

Cecil Castlemaine's Gage, and other Stories. By "OUIDA," author of "Granville de Vigne," "Chandos," etc. Revised for Publication by the Author. 12mo. Cloth. $1.50.

Randolph Gordon, and other Stories. By "Ouida," author of "Idalia," "Under Two Flags," etc. 12mo. Cloth. $1.50.

Beatrice Boville, and other Stories. By "Ouida," author of "Strathmore," "Cecil Castlemaine's Gage," etc. 12mo. Cloth. $1.50.

"The many works already in print by this versatile authoress have established her reputation as a novelist, and these short stories contribute largely to the stock of pleasing narratives and adventures alive to the memory of all who are given to romance and fiction."—*New Haven Journal.*

The Virginia Tourist. Sketches of the Springs and Mountains of Virginia: containing an Exposition of Fields for the Tourist in Virginia; Natural Beauties and Wonders of the State; also, Accounts of its Mineral Springs, and a Medical Guide to the Use of the Waters, etc., etc. By EDWARD A. POLLARD, author of "The Lost Cause," etc. Illustrated by Engravings from Actual Sketches. 12mo. Extra cloth. $1.75. 16mo. Paper cover. $1.

"On the whole, an indispensable book to the traveler who would enjoy the scenery of the Old Dominion."—*New York Independent.*

"This compact, well-digested little volume supplies a desideratum in the tourist literature of the country. . . . To all such we confidently recommend Mr. Pollard's entertaining and exhaustive guide."—*New York Times.*

"Mr. Pollard's very well-drawn description of it, illustrated by excellent engravings, will find many interested readers."—*Buffalo Express.*

"It is a very attractive book, partly because it deals with portions of Virginia and Virginia life comparatively unknown, and partly because Mr. Pollard is a very sparkling and entertaining writer."—*Chicago Tribune.*

*The Book of Travels of a Doctor of Physic. Con*taining his Observations made in Certain Portions of the Two Continents. 12mo. Extra cloth. Ornamented sides. $2.

"One of the most enjoyable books of travel we have ever read."—*Philadelphia Evening Bulletin.*

"Thoroughly entertaining throughout."—*New York Times.*

Days in North India. By Norman Macleod, D. D., author of "Wee Davie," "Eastward," etc. With numerous Illustrations. 12mo. Toned paper. Extra cloth. Gilt top. $2.

"The narrative leaves nothing to be desired. The style is admirable, the statements are full of interest, the description of cities, scenery and people vivacious and picturesque, and it may be questioned whether any book of the kind hitherto published has so just a claim to popularity as the volume before us."—*Pall Mall Gazette.*

The American Sportsman: Containing Hints to Sportsmen, Notes on Shooting and the Habits of the Game Birds and Wild Fowl of America. By ELISHA J. LEWIS, M. D., Member of the American Philosophical Society, American Editor of "Youatt on the Dog," etc. With numerous Illustrations. 8vo. Extra cloth, gilt. $2.75. Half calf. $4.50.

"Not only charming, but instructive. Dr. Lewis is a scholar, and he has practical knowledge of the subject treated of. His notes on shooting are very full, and his descriptions of the game birds of America and their habits accurate and instructive. His style is pure and graceful. The illustrations to this volume are good, and the work is handsomely gotten up."—*Turf Field and Farm.*

The Old Mam'selle's Secret. From the German of E. Marlitt, author of "Gold Elsie," etc. By Mrs. A. L. WISTER. Sixth edition. 12mo. Cloth. $1.50.

"A more charming story, and one which, having once commenced, it seemed more difficult to leave, we have not met with for many a day."—*The Round Table.*

"Is one of the most intense, concentrated, compact novels of the day. . . . And the work has the minute fidelity of the author of 'The Initials,' the dramatic unity of Reade and the graphic power of George Eliot."—*Columbus (O.) Journal.*

Gold Elsie. From the German of E. Marlitt, author of "The Old Mam'selle's Secret," etc. By Mrs. A. L. WISTER. Fifth edition. 12mo. Cloth. $1.50.

"A charming book. It absorbs your attention from the title-page to the end."—*The Home Circle.*

"A charming story charmingly told."—*Baltimore Gazette.*

Countess Gisela. From the German of E. Marlitt, author of "Gold Elsie," etc. By Mrs. A. L. WISTER. Third edition. 12mo. Cloth. $1.50.

"There is more dramatic power in this than in any of the stories by the same author that we have read."—*N. O Times.*

"It is a story that arouses the interest of the reader from the outset."—*Pittsburgh Gazette.*

"The best work by this author."—*Philadelphia Telegraph.*

Over Yonder. From the German of E. Marlitt, author of "Countess Gisela," etc. Third edition. With a full-page Illustration. 8vo. Paper cover. 30 cents.

"'Over Yonder' is a charming novelette. The admirers of 'Old Mam'selle's Secret' will give it a glad reception, while those who are ignorant of the merits of this author will find in it a pleasant introduction to the works of a gifted writer."—*Daily Sentinel.*

The Little Moorland Princess. From the German of E. Marlitt, author of "The Old Mam'selle's Secret," "Gold Elsie," etc. By Mrs. A. L. WISTER. Fourth edition. 12mo. Fine cloth. $1.75.

"By far the best foreign romance of the season."—*Philadelphia Press.*

"It is a great luxury to give one's self up to its balmy influence."—*Chicago Evening Journal.*

Magdalena. From the German of E. Marlitt, author of "Countess Gisela," etc. And THE LONELY ONES ("The Solitaries"). From the German of Paul Heyse. With two Illustrations. 8vo. Paper cover. 35 cents.

"We know of no way in which a leisure hour may be more pleasantly whiled away than by a perusal of either of these tales."—*Indianapolis Sentinel.*

www.ingramcontent.com/pod-product-compliance
Lightning Source LLC
LaVergne TN
LVHW020105110826
845151LV00001B/61

* 9 7 8 1 4 2 5 5 4 4 4 7 8 *